The Shadow of Cincinnatus

The Decline and Fall of the Galactic Empire

Book 2

Christopher G. Nuttall

Twilight Times Books
Kingsport Tennessee

The Shadow of Cincinnatus

This is a work of fiction. All concepts, characters and events portrayed in this book are used fictitiously and any resemblance to real people or events is purely coincidental.

Paladin Timeless Books, an imprint of
Twilight Times Books
P O Box 3340
Kingsport TN 37664
http://twilighttimesbooks.com/

First Edition, December 2014

Library of Congress Control Number: 2014957680

ISBN: 978-1-60619-320-4

Cover art by Malcolm McClinton

Printed in the United States of America.

Prologue

From: *Meditations on Power: The Terran Federation, The Empire and Marius Drake* (4502 A.D)

What is power?

Some would say that power is the ability to shape events to your pleasing. Some would say that power is the ability to do things denied to other people. And some would say that power is the way to get what you want, when you want it, no matter what others might have to say about it. When asked to choose between sex and power, the cynic will always choose power.

Why? Because power can be used to obtain sex.

But power can also be used to obtain more power. This was certainly true of the Grand Senate of the Terran Federation. An august body, comprised of members who had practically inherited their seats, it reached for more and more power over the Outer Worlds and the Colonies. The Colonies rebelled, of course, but the Senate fought and won the Inheritance Wars, ending the threat of the Federation snapping in two. It should have been the end.

The Grand Senate grew lazy and complacent. It fought a pointless war, purely out of greed, with an alien race that ended up costing more blood and treasure than it had anticipated. It chose to ignore growing problems along the edge of explored space, secure in its power and position. But even the more paranoid members of the Grand Senate failed to realize that it was placing more and more power in the hands of its military leaders. One of them, Admiral Justinian, rebelled against the Federation, intent on claiming power for himself.

It should not have taken long for the Federation to crush the upstart. The Federation Navy outmassed the rebels by over a hundred to one. But other military commanders had rebelled, diverting the Federation's forces, making the Grand Senate take steps to ensure that no future military commander could ever hope to gain enough power to challenge the Senate. And yet, their actions ensured that no quick and decisive war was possible. No Admiral dared take chances when his actions might be taken out of context and used against him. No General dared make plans of his own without fear of being accused of plotting a coup. The Grand Senate was effectively strangling its own ability to make war.

Eventually, Admiral Marius Drake–a hero of the early fighting–came to terms with the Grand Senate. He would marry into their ranks and defeat their enemies. This he did, leading the forces of the Federation to a stunning victory over Admiral Justinian. But the Grand Senate, no longer trusting him, chose to try to kill him. His best friend died saving his life.

And so Admiral Drake led his fleet against Earth, captured the Grand Senate and proclaimed himself Emperor.

Alas for Drake, he was about to discover the limits of power.

Chapter One

Garibaldi, Roman. One of the fastest-rising stars of the Federation Navy and a personal protégé of Admiral (later Emperor) Marius Drake. After his role in the failed peace mission to Admiral Justinian, Garibaldi was assigned to Fifth Fleet as her commanding officer...
-The Federation Navy in Retrospect, 4199

Hobson's Choice, 4098

"You know," Elf said, as she ran a hand through her short blonde hair, "this is the very definition of using a sledgehammer to crush a nut."

Roman Garibaldi gave his friend, lover and ground-forces commander a mischievous look, using one hand to brush the brown hair out of his eyes as he looked up at the gathering fleet. It was smaller, in terms of numbers, than the giant fleets that had fought the Inheritance Wars, but it was an order of magnitude more deadly, the most powerful fleet assembled in the last decade of intermittent warfare. Calling the fleet a sledgehammer sent to crush a nut was a definite understatement.

"More like using a sledgehammer to crush an atom," he said, after a moment. "Or slamming an entire asteroid into a planet to kill a single person. Or..."

Elf snorted, rudely. "Does it bother you?"

Roman shrugged, then shook his head. He'd been on the receiving end of superior firepower–vastly superior firepower–often enough to feel a certain kind of satisfaction at having superior firepower on his side for once. Maybe there were naval officers out there who liked the idea of a fair fight, of matching themselves against an enemy commander with equal strength, but it wasn't a sentiment any sensible officer could allow himself in combat. Besides, the more firepower brought to the party, the smaller the chance of a real fight.

Not that they have much chance anyway, he thought, with a tinge of amusement. *A handful of light cruisers would be more than enough to take the high orbitals of Hobson's Choice.*

He looked up at the running lights of Fifth Fleet. It had only been a month since his most recent promotion and he couldn't resist a thrill of delight at seeing so many ships under his command, although he knew he was far from the only young officer promoted into occupying a dead man's shoes. The war with the rogue Admiral, Justinian, had been good for eliminating much of the dead weight in high-ranking positions, if nothing else. And yet, seeing so much responsibility resting on his shoulders worried him. He'd barely been a Captain long enough to grow accustomed to his ship before he'd been promoted to the flag deck.

"You're thinking again," Elf teased him. "It's a terrible habit right now."

"I know," Roman said, gravely. "But I need to try to plan for everything."

Elf tapped his shoulder. "You should know that isn't possible," she said, sternly. "All you can do is be prepared to adapt to change at a moment's notice."

Roman let out a sigh. "Yes," he said. "But will there be any change here?"

"Probably not," Elf said. "But we have been surprised before."

"Yeah," Roman drawled. "Better to be careful."

He shrugged. Hobson's Choice had been a thorn in the side of the Federation for years, ever since the world had been claimed by an eccentric who had thrown open the doors to anyone who wanted to operate outside the Federation's gaze. Now it served as a clearing house for pirates, smugglers, slavers, rebels and all the others who were more than a little unwelcome on Federation worlds. A vast amount of bribes, paid out to senior officers and sector governors, had ensured that the world remained undisturbed by the Federation Navy. But now everything had changed. Hobson's Choice was about to get a very unwelcome surprise.

His wristcom buzzed. "Admiral," Flag Captain Scott Palter said, "the 143rd has just reported in. They're ready to move."

"Good," Roman said. "Order the fleet to begin cloaking procedures. I'm on my way."

"Good luck," Elf said. She leaned forward and kissed him on the cheek, then headed to the hatch. "Leave some of them for us, will you?"

Roman watched her go, then looked back at the fleet. There was another reason for bringing the entire formation to Hobson's Choice, even if it *was* a staggering level of overkill. Fifth Fleet had been put together in a hurry, from starships that had seen service in the recent war to new-build starships just out of the yards, with crews that had barely graduated from the academy. The mission would, he hoped, iron out any problems long before they ran into anything larger than a pirate ship or two. Even if the warlords were gone, there were plenty of other threats out there.

He smiled, then turned to walk through the hatch and down to CIC himself. It still astonished him that he'd been given command of so many ships, even if it was unlikely he'd ever command a ship personally again. That irked him, more than he cared to admit. He'd never expected to become a Commodore, not with his lack of connections. Starship command had seemed the highest achievable goal. And now he was a Commodore, holding down an Admiral's billet. His family would be proud.

The hatch to the CIC opened up in front of him, revealing a handful of consoles, a large command chair and a giant holographic tank. Lights flickered and flared within the tank, dimming to grey as the ships went into cloak, each one tagged with the starship's name and current status. The temptation to micromanage was almost overpowering, Roman had discovered, finally understanding why so many senior officers had issued so many unnecessary orders. One look was enough to tell him that Fifth Fleet's formation looked a little ragged.

An officer with less experience of actual war-fighting would see that as a problem, he thought, as he took his seat. *But anyone with any sense would know better.*

He looked up at the display, then glanced at Palter. They'd known each other since Roman had commanded *Midway*, where Palter had been his tactical officer. Thankfully, Palter had been available when Roman had been assigned to Fifth Fleet. A month in command hadn't given him the time to get to know most of his officers, particularly as Fifth Fleet was still assembling. The Federation Navy might have expanded rapidly during the war, but it was still badly overstretched. Roman was surprised that so many starships had been assigned to the Rim.

But Admiral–Emperor–Drake fought here before the war, Roman thought. *He felt a duty to do something about the chaos along the Rim.*

He took a breath. "Order the fleet to advance," Roman said. "And prepare to spring our surprise."

ꕥ

"The cargo is secure, sir."

Captain Roger Loewi nodded, impatiently. *Hogshead* had been orbiting Hobson's Choice for weeks, burning precious fuel, while her agents on the surface had been rounding up the cargo and lifting it to orbit. The crew had been growing increasingly unhappy, after discovering that they would neither be allowed to go down to the surface or play their games with the cargo. He'd had to face down two threats of mutiny and one crewman had actually managed to desert, although *he* was no loss. Somehow, slavers rarely attracted the best crews.

The cargo, he thought, sourly. One hundred and fifty women, all young, all healthy enough to bear children for a hidden colony thousands of light years from Earth. The crew was already sniffing round the hold and, if it weren't for the armed mercenaries guarding the hatches, he would have feared for their safety. For some absurd reason, the colonists wanted virgins. God knew it was hard enough to find virgins on Hobson's Choice, let alone girls who had been captured by pirates and traded to slavers on the planet below. He cursed himself under his breath, then dismissed the thought. If he didn't think of the slaves as cargo, he would go mad.

It was a living. *Hogshead* was too old and slow to carry legitimate cargo, even if there hadn't been a hundred warrants out for her arrest on the more civilized worlds of the Federation. And wasn't *that* ironic? Loewi knew for a fact that some of the slaves he'd shipped, properly modified, had been sold to high-ranking Federation officers, who would probably dispose of them before returning to Earth. Who gave a shit about the morality of shipping kidnapped women and children when the alternative was poverty and certain death? Or indenture...

He turned back to the console. "Take us out of here," he ordered. "Now."

"Gotcha, dad," the helmsman said. His son worked the console with a practiced ease. "I hear some of them are..."

An alarm sounded. Red lights appeared on the cramped display.

Loewi's mouth dropped open. For a long moment, his brain refused to accept what he was seeing. There were a hundred and fifty starships decloaking around the planet, spearheaded by five entire *superdreadnaught* squadrons. It had to be a trick of some kind, his brain yammered at him, an illusion created by ECM drones designed to fool far more advanced sensors than *Hogshead's* outdated sensor suite. But the images had a terrifying solidity that drove all doubts out of his head.

"Dad, I'm picking up a message," his son said.

"...Is the Federation Navy," a voice boomed. "Hobson's Choice is now under military control. Cut your drives and prepare to be boarded. Any resistance will result in the destruction of your vessels. There will be no further warning."

Loewi thought fast. The idea of outrunning any of the military ships was thoroughly absurd. They could be given forty-eight hours to run and the military would *still* catch up with them before they crossed the Phase Limit. Not that they'd be given the time, he saw, as new icons flared to life on the display. Hundreds of starfighters were launching from carriers, each one more than capable of blowing *Hogshead* into vapor. They were caught like rats in a trap.

His son looked up at him. "Dad?"

"Cut the drives," Loewi ordered. He knew he was dead. Slaver Captains could be shot without the formality of a trial–and if the bribes no longer protected Hobson's Choice, there was no point in hoping they would protect him. But at least his children and crew would survive. They'd be on a penal planet, but they would be alive. "Cut the drives and tell them we surrender, then lock down the ship. The mercs might have other ideas."

༄༅

"I think we surprised them, sir," Palter said.

Roman nodded. There had been seventy starships orbiting Hobson's Choice when the fleet had decloaked and a third of them had started to try to flee. The others had dropped their drives as per instructions, although there was no way to know if they'd meant to surrender or if they simply hadn't been able to power up their drives in time to escape. Not, he knew, that it really mattered. The fleeing ships didn't have a hope of escaping his fleet and making it out into deep space.

"Good," he said. "Dispatch the Marines. We'll go with Plan Theta."

He forced himself to sit back and watch as his fleet's smaller units moved in to tackle the fleeing ships. A couple cut their drives as soon as the destroyers entered firing range, the remainder kept trying to run until the destroyers opened fire. Roman watched, as dispassionately as he could, as five of the fleeing ships exploded, one by one. They were either pirates or smugglers, he knew, both occupations that earned participants the death penalty. But it was still one hell of a waste.

"The Marines are entering the atmosphere now," Palter informed him. "There's no trace of any resistance."

Roman wasn't surprised. To all intents and purposes, Hobson's Choice was an utterly undefended world. There was no government, let alone a military; there was certainly no one willing to fight and die in the defense of a wretched hive of scum and villainy. By the time someone managed to take control, if anyone did, the Marines would already be occupying the major settlements. Resistance would be utterly futile.

More reports came in as smaller parties of marines boarded the surrendered starships. Most of them were smugglers–few pirates would lurk in orbit when they could be back out in space, hunting for their next prizes–but three of them were slavers. Two of the slavers were empty, having returned to Hobson's Choice for more slaves, while the third was crammed to bursting with young female slaves. They'd been kidnapped, according to the Marines, or sold into slavery by their families. And if the fleet had waited another hour or two before launching the invasion, they would never have had a hope of freedom.

"Move them to the hospital ships," Roman ordered. How could *anyone* sell their children into slavery? He'd grown up on an asteroid and no one had ever threatened him with anything worse than being sent to bed without his supper. But the Rim of explored space was rarely civilized. A family might decide it was better to sell one child, no matter how horrific it was, than lose everyone. "And then transfer their former captors to the brig."

He looked down at the display as more reports came in from the planet's surface. A handful of locals, no doubt expecting the death penalty as soon as they were identified, had tried to put up a fight. The Marines hadn't bothered to try to talk them down, knowing it would be futile. Instead, they'd simply called up heavy firepower from a hovertank and blown the enemy building into flaming debris. The bodies would be found and identified later.

"All the ships have been secured," Palter reported. The display flickered and updated as the Marines took control of the captured ships, showing their status. "Should I dispatch prize crews?"

"See to it," Roman said. It galled him, but Fifth Fleet's logistics were appallingly weak. The Grand Senate had been willing to build thousands of new warships for the Federation Navy, but they'd been reluctant to pay for new freighters. It was a piece of short-sightedness that, he suspected, would come back to haunt them. Fifth Fleet was far too dependent on a small handful of bulk freighters for his comfort. "And prepare them for transit to Athena."

The hours ticked by, slowly. Roman felt growing impatience, even though he knew the invasion was proceeding with astonishing speed. Hitting a more normal colony world, even one without defenses, would take much longer. Hobson's Choice comprised only a handful of minor settlements, after all. They could literally round up everyone on the planet, load them into prison ships, and drop them off at the nearest penal world.

It was nearly nine hours before Elf contacted him, privately. "Roman," she said, once the link was secure. "The planet is under control."

"Good," Roman said. "Any problems?"

"None," Elf said. She sounded perturbed. "But there's an odd shortage of captives."

Roman frowned. A planet was a large place–and someone with the proper training or equipment could remain undiscovered for quite some time, if they tried. And finding them would require more time than he had.

"Did they have a chance to go to ground?"

"I'm not sure, but I don't think so," Elf said. "They only had around twenty minutes of warning before we came down and landed around the settlements. We're interrogating some of the captives now, but it sounds as though a large number of people have been gone for quite some time."

"Someone's been recruiting," Roman said, slowly.

"It looks that way," Elf agreed. "The missing people are all mercenaries or starship pilots, as far as we can tell. And we know we didn't capture many mercenaries when we occupied Admiral Justinian's territory."

Roman considered it. "What about our agents?"

"No sign of them," Elf said. "They weren't planning to stay on Hobson's Choice indefinitely, though."

"True," Roman agreed. The last time he'd visited Hobson's Choice, he'd helped to insert a number of agents from ONI. And no one had heard from the agents since. "Have the prisoners moved to the ships, then earmarked for interrogation," he said. If someone was recruiting...pirates? Smugglers? Or Outsiders? "If we offer someone a chance to escape a hellworld, they might talk."

"I'll see to it," Elf said. Her chuckle echoed down the link. "Easiest invasion I've ever seen, Roman. I didn't lose a single Marine."

"We could do with an easy victory," Roman agreed. The Federation Navy had fought hard in the war, but it had also been badly demoralized. Between the certain knowledge that some senior officers had turned on the Federation, and the Grand Senate's relentless attempts to control the Navy as thoroughly as possible, there were too many officers frightened to do anything without orders–in triplicate. "Good work, Marine."

He took a breath. "Detach a handful of Marines to sweep the surface," he ordered. There was no point in keeping the entire fleet in the backwater system, but they could leave a few surprises behind. "I'll assign a destroyer squadron to the high orbitals. If we're lucky, we should snag a few strays before word gets out and rogues start avoiding the planet."

"Aye, sir," Elf said.

"And then we'll set course for Athena," Roman concluded. He felt a thrill of anticipation at the thought of seeing the Rim. "And see just what's waiting for us there."

He closed the link, then settled back in his chair. All things considered, it had been a cakewalk, almost laughably easy. Thousands of captives had been liberated, hundreds of pirates, slavers and smugglers would face justice and Hobson's Choice would no longer be a thorn in the Federation's side. And the fleet's morale would improve as news of the victory sank in.

Emperor Marius *would* be pleased.

Chapter Two

Drake, Marius. Commanding Officer of the Grand Fleet. Betrayed by the Grand Senate after his victory over Admiral Justinian. Rebelled against their authority and made himself Emperor of Earth.
-The Federation Navy in Retrospect, 4199

Earth, 4098

"I'm not interested in excuses," Marius snarled. "I want to know what happened and why."

General Theodore Ricardo looked unhappy. "We had a riot. On Earth."

"I can see that," Marius snapped. There were times when he thoroughly understood why the Grand Senate had shot so many military officers in the years following the First Battle of Earth. One month of being emperor had convinced him that no one in their right mind would actually want the job. "Why was this one allowed to happen?"

The general hesitated. He was a short balding man, with an air of nervousness that reminded Marius that Ricardo had no real experience on the front lines. The Grand Senate had left him in command of Earth's security forces, apparently believing he posed no real threat to their supremacy. Marius suspected they might have had a point. General Ricardo lacked the ability to take a shit without permission from his superiors, written in triplicate and countersigned by every Grand Senator on Earth. Leaving him in command might have been a mistake.

"The protests swelled beyond our ability to handle them," Ricardo said, finally. "We were rushing troops to the area when it turned into an outright riot. At that point, we lost control of large parts of Atlanta and had to hold back the troops, then advance when we had mustered sufficient manpower. By that point, a considerable amount of damage had been done to the city."

Marius sighed, sitting back in his chair and glowering around the office. It had once belonged to the Federation President and, despite having all of the luxury torn out of it, was still too distracting for his comfort. The president had been a powerless figurehead for nearly a century, ever since the Imperialistic Faction had collapsed following the Blue Star War, but he'd still lived in luxury. And so had the Grand Senate. No wonder they'd been so badly disconnected from their people.

He shook his head, then looked at the display. Troops patrolled the streets of Atlanta and a dozen major cities, while hundreds of rioters–too greedy or too slow to escape capture–were marched off to hastily-erected detention centers. They hadn't expected any form of violent response, he knew. The Grand Senate's policy towards riots among the underclass had been to allow them to burn out in their own time. But then, most of the riots during that period had been staged. *This* one had been real.

"It makes no sense," he muttered. "They want to return to having their wants and needs provided rather than stand up for themselves?"

"It was inevitable," Professor Kratman said. The professor–who had become Marius's Minister of State–seemed unemotional, but Marius could hear an undercurrent of anger in his tone. "The Grand Senate took care of their needs in exchange for their votes. Over the years, it became a formality. And now you've removed their access to the social security network."

Marius gave him a sharp look. "Was it a mistake?"

"No," Kratman said. "The Federation spent far too much money every year just taking care of the population of Earth. But they grew used to sucking at the Federation's teat and now...well, they don't know what to do without it. And then there's the birth control measures..."

"There's no choice," Marius said. "Earth's population is already too high."

He looked down at his hands. On Mars, where he'd been born, it was rare for a family to have more than two or three children, keeping the population relatively stable. The planet simply couldn't afford unrestricted population growth. But on Earth, with food, drink and clothing provided by the government, the population seemed to spend most of its time turning out new children, who would grow to adulthood and start turning out new children of their own. Earth's crime and infant mortality rate was the highest in the known galaxy, yet the population had continued to expand. It was utterly unsustainable.

His solution had been simple enough. The government-provided foodstuffs would be laced with contraceptives. Anyone who ate the food would be unable to have children without medical intervention, at least for a year after swallowing the drug. The idea had been to limit population growth as much as possible, while simultaneously encouraging emigration from Earth to the outer worlds. But the population of Earth had been babied so much that relatively few *wanted* to leave the comfort of humanity's homeworld.

And when there are no real comforts, Marius thought, *that becomes truly pathetic.*

"But we are short of manpower to handle the riots," General Ricardo said. "We should consider making concessions..."

Marius looked up at him, angrily. "Would you suggest we give in to pressure? To threats of violence? To riots that only make life worse for the rioters?"

He sighed. What sort of idiots thought that destroying shops, houses and infrastructure would encourage investment in their areas? Or that it would improve their lives?

"I would suggest that we are moving too fast," Ricardo said. "We should consider slowing down."

"But that would be seen as a sign of weakness," Kratman pointed out, sharply. "We cannot afford to suggest that we would surrender, if pushed hard enough."

Marius tapped the table, sharply. "No, we can't," he said. "The reforms will continue, General, until the time has come when they will no longer be needed."

"Yes, sir," Ricardo said. "And the prisoners?"

"Exile," Marius said, shortly. There was no point in organizing trials. "They can do something useful on a colony world."

He rubbed his temple, feeling a pounding headache building up under his skull. If he'd known just how much stress being emperor would cause him, he might have seriously considered going into exile after the Grand Senate had tried to kill him. Or, perhaps, seizing some of the more productive sectors for himself and leaving the Grand Senate to administer the Core Worlds themselves. But the Grand Senate, for all its honeyed words, had never given a damn about the population. Marius, for all of his harshness, was trying to help.

But no one likes to have medicine forced down their throats, he reminded himself.

"That raises another problem," Ricardo said. "We need more transport."

"The shipyards are turning out more freighters," Marius said. "They will come."

"But slowly," Lawrence Tully said. The Comptroller of Earth sighed. "We have to move carefully to avoid destroying the remains of the economy."

"We need them now," Ricardo snapped. "And not just for transporting prisoners..."

"The problem," Tully snapped back, "is that the entire economy is hanging on a knife-edge. A single false move could completely destroy it, shattering the entire Federation."

Marius gritted his teeth. The headache was growing worse.

"We have to sort out who owns what," Tully continued, as if he hadn't said the same thing over and over again, at every meeting they'd held. "And we have to sort out the legal basis..."

"Enough," Marius said. If the meeting went on, he'd do something he'd later regret. Or, worse, that he *wouldn't* regret. "General, have the prisoners moved to a detention camp and hold them there until they can be transported to a colony world. Keep the troops on the ground and make it clear that any attempt to raise a second riot will result in harsh repression and exile. Find the leaders, if you can, and have them arrested too."

"That will be difficult," Ricardo said. "The old leaders are gone."

Marius sighed. The Grand Senate had once controlled the protest movements on Earth, something that had puzzled him until he'd realized just how effective it was at keeping the lower classes from developing effective ways to make their voices heard. Everything from trade unions to outright anarchist groups had been controlled by the Grand Senate, a web of patronage that had given them staggering levels of control over Earth. But that network was gone now, leaving a new generation free to take its place. God alone knew how it would develop in future.

"Do your best," he said. He raised his voice. "Dismissed."

Professor Kratman hesitated at the door, then left when Marius glowered at him. The others left even quicker, as if they were glad to be out of his presence. Marius watched them go, then sat back in his chair and tried to think. There were too many problems on Earth for any of them to be solved quickly, no matter what he did. And then there were the persistent problems caused by the Grand Senate's mismanagement of the rest of the Federation. A good third of the settled worlds were restless, only held back from trying to declare independence by the certain knowledge that it would draw a harsh response from the Grand Senate. But the Grand Senate was gone.

Life was much simpler on the command deck of a superdreadnaught, he told himself. Even when he'd been trying to keep the political commissioners from interfering in military operations, it had been so much simpler than trying to reform Earth, let alone the remainder of the Core Worlds. *I knew what I was doing there.*

He rose to his feet, guided by an impulse he didn't fully understand, and walked through a sealed hatch that led down into the lower levels of the President's House. It was a larger building than most people realized, although it had been decades since the government had been based out of it. Now some of the old offices had been reactivated, but others had been left alone. Marius had no intention of surrounding himself with a small army of bureaucratic sycophants, not when such inhuman creatures had played a large role in the Grand Senate's decline and fall. But his plans to reform the bureaucracy had floundered on the cold hard fact that he *needed* the bureaucracy to make his reforms effective.

I should have had Tully shot, he thought, as he passed a trio of armed guards. *But he was too effective at his job.*

The secure door hissed open, revealing a detention facility. Quite why there was a detention facility in the basement of the President's House was beyond him, even though he'd spent an hour digging through the archives last month in search of the answer. Maybe he didn't *want* to know the answer. At least one of the Federation's early presidents had been forced to endure a nasty separation from his wife before leaving office. He pressed his finger against another scanner, then opened the hatch. Inside, there was a line of detention cells. Nine out of ten were empty.

He walked to the occupied one and keyed a switch. The forcefield turned transparent, revealing a young man sitting on the bench, looking down at the solid metal floor. He'd once been relatively handsome, Marius recalled, and cut a swath through his superdreadnaught's female crew. Now, dressed in an orange prison uniform, he looked tired and worn, perhaps even on the verge of madness. Marius might have kept him alive, but he hadn't bothered to provide any form of mental simulation. After what the man had done, Marius had decided, he was damned if he was doing anything to make imprisonment any easier to bear.

"Hello, Blake," he said.

Blake Raistlin turned to look at him. His dark skin was pallid and his eyes were sunken, as if he were too tired to sleep. Marius hadn't looked like that since the dreaded final exams at the Academy, back before the Blue Star War. But Blake Raistlin had far more to bear than just the risk of failure, after years of hard work. His failure had cost his family everything, including their lives. Marius had shot some of them personally.

"Admiral," Raistlin said. His voice was almost a whisper. "How nice of you to visit."

Marius studied him for a long cold moment. "You're still a prisoner," he said. "How does it feel?"

"I stopped caring," Raistlin said. "And you're a prisoner too."

"True," Marius agreed. Being emperor was like being in prison. He was all-powerful...but, at the same time, he was limited. And he couldn't go anywhere without a cordon of heavily-armed guards. "But you're the one in the cell."

Raistlin shrugged, expressively. "Why have you kept me alive?"

Marius felt a sudden surge of blind hatred. He'd trusted Raistlin, he'd depended on the young man...and, when the orders had arrived, Raistlin had tried to kill him. And Tobias, his friend, had died saving his life. He should be alive now, Marius knew, perhaps serving as an advisor or even as co-emperor. Instead, he was dead and buried and nothing would ever be the same again.

"Because I can," Marius said. "And because we might need a show trial to distract the masses."

Raistlin laughed. "Being emperor not all it was meant to be?"

"Your people left behind one hell of a mess," Marius said. "Didn't they give a damn about the population of Earth?"

"Of course not," Raistlin said. His voice lightened, slightly. "They were only raised to give a damn about their families."

He paused, dramatically. "Why are you here, Admiral?"

Marius looked through the forcefield, considering his answer. In truth, he wasn't sure himself why he'd come. Raistlin could be left to rot away, eating tasteless prison food and drinking water, until the day his mind finally gave out. Or he could be put on trial. *Or* he could simply be taken out back and have a bullet put through the back of his skull. Marius had killed the senior Grand Senators personally. It would be no challenge to kill Raistlin himself.

But that wouldn't make the young man *suffer*, he knew.

He'd been betrayed. A military organization couldn't survive without trust–and trust was one thing that had been in short supply, after the mutinies and rebels and the imposition of a small army of political commissioners. Raistlin had been trusted, even though Marius had known of his family connections. There had seemed no grounds upon which to reject the talented young man. But, as soon as the orders came, Raistlin had tried to kill his commanding officer. The betrayal could not be allowed to go unpunished.

And you want to make him suffer, he thought. *Shooting is far too good for him.*

"Because I can," Marius said. He paused. "Would you like to know what happened to the rest of your classmates? The ones who served the Federation Navy over their families?"

Raistlin started to giggle. There was more than a hint of insanity in the sound.

"Admiral," he said, "what do you think you've built?"

Marius stared at him, more disturbed than he would have cared to admit. "What do you mean?"

"Riding a tiger is perfectly safe," Raistlin said. He giggled again, then caught himself. "It's when you try to get off that you start having problems. My family rode a tiger for far too long and could never muster the courage to try to get off. Each little compromise, each one a good idea at the time, built up into an overwhelming structure we could never free ourselves from.

"And here you are, *Emperor*," he added. "How long will it be until you become everything you accused *us* of being?"

"You're the last of the Grand Senatorial families," Marius snarled. It was a lie, but close enough to the truth. The lower-level aristocrats had been exiled to a distant world where they would be left alone. It hadn't occurred to him until much later that they might be happy to have left Earth for more reasons than merely being allowed to keep their lives. "And when you're gone, you will be nothing."

Raistlin rose to his feet and walked up to the forcefield, which spat and crackled at him as he stopped. "Look at yourself," he mocked. "What happened to the proud commanding officer who stood unmoved on the bridge as his ship plunged into battle?"

"He found himself having to clean up a mess that should really have been solved hundreds of years ago," Marius said, gathering his temper. "What happened to the young lieutenant who had the entire universe ahead of him?"

"He did his job," Raistlin said. "He followed orders."

He smirked at Marius's scowl. "Tell me, Admiral," he said. "When you were born, on Mars, the planet of war, were you ever exposed to any culture?"

Marius frowned, puzzled. Mars wasn't a barbaric backwater any longer. Hell, it hadn't been anything of the sort since the First Interstellar War. These days, it was as civilized as Earth, perhaps more so. The population hadn't forgotten just how thin the line between life and death could be, even now.

"There's a song," Raistlin said. "From an opera. *Many a king on a first-class throne, if he wants to call his crown his own, must manage somehow to get through, more dirty work that ever I do.*"

Marius gave him a dry look. "I'm no stranger to dirty work," he said.

"But are you prepared, Admiral, for the dirty work you'll have to do as emperor?" Raistlin asked. "You're not the person I knew and respected any longer. The job is changing you beyond recognition. What will you be in ten years, *Emperor*? Will you really give up the job?"

"Yes," Marius said.

He took a moment to gather himself. "You will be put on trial, eventually," he stated, flatly. "And then you will join your family in death."

"See?" Raistlin said. "You're not the person you used to be."

"Neither are you," Marius said.

He hit the switch, darkening the forcefield, then turned and walked away from the cell. It was hard to say which of them had gotten the better of the encounter, even though Raistlin was in a cell and Marius...was in a prison of his own making. He shook his head as he strode past the Marines, too distracted to acknowledge their salutes. No, he knew which of them had come out ahead. Raistlin was right, in so many ways.

But he's still the one in a cell, he reminded himself, as he made his way back to his quarters, where his wife was waiting for him. *And he will die soon.*

Chapter Three

D'Artagnan, Lady Tiffany Eleanor Diana Katherine. Wife of Admiral, later Emperor, Marius Drake. Forced into marriage with him, she rapidly formed a bond with her husband that survived the attempt on his life and remained with him as he took on the position of Emperor...
-The Federation Navy in Retrospect, 4199

Earth, 4098

Marius had never considered himself a marrying man, even though it was an unspoken rule in the Federation Navy that admirals should marry, if only to have a hostess when assigned to command remote bases and fleet deployments. Indeed, he'd assumed he would never be promoted beyond vice admiral after his deployment to the Rim and never really considered looking for a wife. And yet, one had been provided for him by the Grand Senate. It still surprised him, years later, that he'd actually fallen in love with her.

And, perhaps, that she'd become the confidante Tobias had been, before his death.

Lady Tiffany was beautiful, with long red hair and a pale heart-shaped face. She'd once been considered one of the prettiest girls in high society, although she had also been considered largely unmarriageable for reasons that defied Marius's understanding. However it had happened, he was glad she'd come to him, even though her family had intended to use the marriage to control him. He needed at least one person in his life he could trust completely.

She lay on the bed, looking up at him with a thin smile playing over her lips. Marius grinned back at her, grateful that they'd managed to find enough time to make love. He'd never understood how some of the Grand Senators had managed to keep harems, not when he'd found himself working from five in the morning till very late at night. But then, there had been hundreds of Grand Senators and only one emperor. There were too many pieces of paperwork only he, it seemed, could sign.

"I went to see Raistlin today," he said, and outlined their conversation. "Do you think he's right?"

"I think you shouldn't talk to him," Tiffany said, practically. "What do you gain from exchanging words with a murderer?"

"I...I don't know," Marius confessed. He rubbed the side of his head, feeling the last remnants of the headache fading away. "It's like something I have to do."

"It's a bad habit," Tiffany said. "Have him shot, or send him into exile, or do *something*, but don't torment yourself like this. Raistlin will always have the edge on you when it comes to a verbal duel."

"He's cracking up," Marius said.

"And he's trying to make *you* crack up," Tiffany said. "Raistlin was raised in a Grand Senatorial family. Manipulation of your emotions will have been hammered into his head along with his mother's milk. He will be very aware of every crack in your emotional armor and how to open it up for best results. You should not try to talk to him."

She sat upright, then poked him in the chest. "You need to get rid of him and concentrate on the future," she said, firmly. "And there's no shortage of work to do."

"Tell me about it," Marius groaned.

Tiffany crossed her arms under her bare breasts. "Let's see," she said. "There's the economic recovery program, the training program, the colonization program..."

"I didn't mean that literally," Marius snapped. He regretted it instantly. "I'm sorry..."

"You need to find more people you can trust," Tiffany said, ignoring his apology. "There's too much for one person to do."

"But I have a shortage of trustworthy people," Marius muttered. "Where do I get more?"

He sighed, bitterly. Raistlin's betrayal had hurt more than he cared to admit, but it wasn't the only problem. Many of the people he'd picked for his ministers had been people he knew and trusted, but not everyone who fell into that category were able to handle the work of pushing the Federation into reform. Commodore Garibaldi and his generation might be superb fleet commanders–the deaths of so many high-ranking officers had left plenty of room for rapid promotion–but they lacked organizational experience. He couldn't call one of them back and put him in command of economic recovery.

And then there was the problem that untangling the mess the Grand Senate had made of the economy would take centuries, if they were lucky. Marius had thought the fleet command for the ill-fated Operation Retribution had been tangled, but the economy was far–far–worse. Figuring out who actually owned what–and which properties no longer had an owner–would take longer than he had. He'd promised himself ten years as emperor, no more. But the task was already looking to take longer than his entire lifespan.

"You'll need to start looking among the managers," Tiffany said. She gave him a mischievous smile. "Did you really think that we aristocrats did all the work ourselves?"

Marius eyed her, suspiciously. "I *wondered* how you managed to work while hosting endless parties," he said.

Tiffany made a face. "*I* never went to parties," she said. She cleared her throat, loudly. "I believe that most of the High Families had their own crop of managers. They would be loyal to their patrons, of course, but they also have a great deal of practical experience. And, now that their patrons are gone, most of them will be looking for something else to do. You could round them up and put them to work."

"I see," Marius said. "Are they trustworthy?"

"They'll be loyal to their own families, now," Tiffany said. "You could make sure their families remain safe and they'll be loyal."

Or keep them as hostages, Marius thought. Once, it would have revolted him to even *consider* such measures. Now, it struck him as something necessary. Raistlin was right, in a way. He definitely wasn't the person he'd been.

He looked up at his wife. "Do you want the task of finding them?"

"Not if I can avoid it," Tiffany said. She sighed. "But do I assume correctly that I don't have a choice?"

"I'd prefer to leave it in your hands," Marius confirmed. "I don't know how far I trust Tully."

"You can trust him to put his own interests first," Tiffany told him. "But you can also trust him not to think outside the box."

Marius stroked his head. "And then we have the problem of sorting out the rules and regulations," he added. "I've got a meeting this evening to discuss it...boring, boring, boring..."

"But necessary," Tiffany said, firmly. "The Grand Senate screwed up the rules and regulations to ensure they remained on top. Undoing those will be the first step forward towards true economic recovery."

Marius cursed under his breath. He'd never really thought of the Federation as flimsy, not since the Inheritance Wars had ensured that no planet thought it could declare independence and leave the Federation. Even Admiral Justinian and the other warlords hadn't managed to crack the towering edifice. But it was rotten to the core, he knew now, and only sheer luck had kept it intact for so long. If he failed to handle the economic question as delicately as possible, the Federation would collapse into rubble. And then a whole new series of wars would begin.

"Fine," he said, as he rose to his feet. He would have liked to spend the rest of the day in bed with her, but there was far too much to do. They'd had more time together on his flagship! "I'll expect you to sit in on the meeting. And the professor."

"Understood," Tiffany said. She stood as he walked towards the shower. "Do you want company in there?"

ꕥ

Marius was still smiling as he walked into yet another meeting room, this one decorated in blue and green wallpaper. Judging from the handful of portraits on the walls, showing earlier presidents of the Federation, it was meant to reassure rather than intimidate. It made a change from the office he was starting to think of as his throne room.

"Be seated," he said, as he sat down at the head of the table. He'd chosen to shun formality almost as soon as he'd made himself emperor. "What do you have for me?"

"We tried to review all of the rules and regulations that were considered to be in force prior to the Second Battle of Earth," Larimore Hammond said. The portly man had been a legal expert at the Luna Academy before Professor Kratman had recommended him for the task of rewriting the Federation's regulations. "Most of them are starkly contradictory and all of them are impossible to follow, without *baksheesh*. The only purpose they serve is enriching the bureaucrats and keeping the Grand Senate in control of the economy."

Marius sighed. It was a dirty little secret on Earth–and the rest of the Core Worlds–that almost anything could be authorized, if the bribe was large enough. Even in the military, a handful of bribes to the right person could get anything done.

Admiral Justinian, the post-battle analysis had indicated, had bribed heavily to get his operatives into position to do some real damage on Earth. Indeed, if Marius's flight hadn't been delayed by a few minutes, Admiral Justinian might well have won the war in one fell swoop. But even that disaster hadn't convinced the Grand Senate to do something about bribery.

But they didn't have a choice, he thought, bitterly. *They needed the bribes to keep the system running.*

"The codes cannot be revised in anything resembling a satisfactory manner," Hammond continued, firmly. "There are just too many pieces of junk attached to the laws for us to fix them all. Instead, I would like to remove or cancel as many regulations as possible, with our role being restricted to ensuring fair play. This would encourage entrepreneurs to start up new businesses as quickly as possible, eventually absorbing or replacing the old Grand Senate-owned businesses. In the long run, our economy would become a great deal stronger."

"However, it would also weaken Earth relative to the Core Worlds and the outer colonies," Tully put in. The Comptroller of Earth didn't sound happy. His thin lips looked even thinner than usual. "It would have unfortunate long-term effects for the balance of power."

"I don't see why," Marius said, although he had a pretty good idea. "Earth has plenty of industries already."

"It's a problem caused by the educational facilities," Kratman said. "The Grand Senate made some reforms, true, but not enough to take advantage of any economic boom. Earth's population would be left behind."

"Which would give them incentive to learn to work harder," Hammond snapped. "The Grand Senate was strangling the life out of the economy before the coup. Now, we have an unbalanced system that is on the verge of collapse."

"But it will also make it harder for Earth to recover," Tully snapped back. "This solution will cause other problems for us in the long run."

"As opposed to short-term problems," Hammond thundered. "I..."

Marius slapped the table and they fell silent.

"I think we have to admit," Marius said into the silence, "that there are going to be problems–that there is going to be pain–no matter what we do. Is that correct?"

No one disagreed.

"Then we have to strike now, before events slide completely out of control," Marius continued. "We will strike down most of the rules and regulations, leaving the ground as clear as we can for an economic revival."

"But it will cause problems," Tully said. "What if there's an ecological disaster?"

"The regulations as they exist are too strict to allow *any* form of activity," Hammond pointed out. "And when someone slips someone else a bribe, we get the ecological disaster anyway."

His eyes narrowed. "Or are you facing pressure from your subordinates?"

Tully's face darkened. "I..."

"Enough," Marius said, quietly. "Our purpose is to reform the Federation, to allow it to have a chance to breathe, to eventually pass control back to the population. We are not here to assist any special interests."

He sighed, inwardly. The bureaucracy was the largest single employer in the Federation, with literally *billions* of workers. It didn't take much imagination to realize that cutting rules and regulations would mean less work for the bureaucrats, making it impossible for them to justify their employment. The Grand Senate might not have intended to encourage the bureaucracy to grow to unsustainable levels, but it had succeeded beyond belief. It could take years, even decades, to get permission to open a business, if there wasn't a large enough bribe.

But no one used that as the excuse, did they? It was all about protecting the workers from exploitation, or protecting the environment of countless worlds, or even about protecting the owners from themselves. A hundred thousand excuses, each one so calm and reasonable and nonsensical. And each one a mocking nail in the Federation's coffin, because they were useless. Marius knew, all too well, that a bribe in the right place could ensure that anything–absolutely anything–was overlooked.

He tapped his forehead, absently. The headache was back.

"See to cutting the regulations down to the bare minimum," he ordered. He turned to look at Tully. "I trust you have ordered the freeze on recruitment?"

"It's proving hard, very hard," Tully said. "We have a contractual obligation to complete the hiring process for bureaucrats who were applying at the time of the coup."

"There are to be no new bureaucrats hired beyond this point," Marius said. He felt a sudden surge of hatred and had to remind himself, sharply, that he couldn't shoot *everyone* who annoyed him. "We will also be looking for ways to retrain them to do something *useful*."

"Keeping the Federation in order is useful," Tully protested. "I really think that we shouldn't move too quickly..."

"But we have to move now," Marius said. "Or would you sooner watch as Earth collapses into chaos?"

He moved on before Tully could say a word. "See to it, please," he ordered. "Now."

"Yes, sir," Hammond said. "I'll have the revised code on your desk within the week."

Marius watched as Hammond and Tully left, then looked up at Kratman. "What the hell was I thinking?"

"Better to reign in hell than to be dead and buried," Kratman misquoted. "And besides, you have managed to make some improvements already."

"Not enough," Marius said. "Tell me something. Did you ever consider, when you were on the *Matterhorn*, that it wasn't worth it?"

"Never," Kratman said. "But that was before the *real* corruption started to set in."

Marius nodded. The Blue Star War had weakened the Imperialist Faction in Federation politics to the point where it became completely ineffectual. It wouldn't have been so bad if the remaining two factions, for their separate reasons, hadn't worked together to weaken the Federation Navy and bureaucracy. And then Admiral Justinian had tried to overthrow them in one blow. There were days when Marius wondered if the Federation would have done any better if Justinian had succeeded. Someone more interested in power for its own sake might have been better at keeping his subordinates in line.

"I also remember being drenched with work when I reported for duty," Kratman added, dryly. "Don't you?"

"I suppose," Marius said.

He smiled at the memory. Midshipman Drake had bitched about the amount of work he had to do, until he'd been promoted. Lieutenant Drake had been sure he was the hardest-worked officer on the ship, until *he'd* become the XO. *Commander* Drake had cursed his youthful self even as he worked himself to the bone...and then he'd been promoted again. There had been no respite as a Captain, Commodore or Vice Admiral. The splendid cabin and the right to have a staff of his own had come with more paperwork than any one man could do in a lifetime, as well as the risks of commanding a fleet in battle.

"There are too many vested interests for any such change to go unimpeded," Kratman said, after a moment. "We may want to look at selling off shipyards and production nodes to their former managers. Give them a stake in the new order, something to keep them loyal–and productive."

Marius sighed. The Grand Senate, to its credit, had started mass production of everything from missiles to superdreadnaughts and fleet carriers. It wasn't something he wanted to slow down, not when there were countless problems along the Rim that needed handling as quickly and efficiently as possible. The warlords might be gone, but the pirates remained...and there was still a giant question mark over the Outsiders. What were *they* doing? They had to know the Federation's war with its rogue military officers had finally come to an end.

"We will see," he said. He considered, briefly, just taking Tiffany and a starship and heading for somewhere nicely isolated. His sense of duty wouldn't allow it. "How are the new students coming along?"

"Slowly," Kratman said. "The educational base isn't there. But we're working on them."

Marius gritted his teeth. It was absurd that the Federation, with billions of young men and women within the Sol System alone, couldn't produce enough manpower to crew the Federation Navy, but there was no avoiding the problem. Earth's educational system simply didn't produce enough men and women who could read, let alone handle a computer, drive an aircar or anything else *useful*. It would take generations to produce more than a handful of people each year who didn't have to do things by rote.

And we might not be able to trust manpower from the outer worlds, he added, in the privacy of his own mind.

"The sooner we start mass exoduses from Earth, the better," Marius said, finally. "But will it be enough?"

"Not for a decade," Kratman said. "Moving millions of people will take years, even with the contraception drugs. But the sooner we begin, the sooner it will be done."

"If it ever is," Marius said. He shook his head. "I must have been out of my mind."

"It's a dirty job, but someone has to do it," Kratman said. "You're doing fine."

Chapter Four

Chang Li. Former elected Senator from Nova Athena. Sole non-Grand Senate linked Senator in the Federation Senate, thus effectively powerless. Departed Earth following the Grand Senate's imposition of emergency laws and effective state of martial law. Leader of the Outsider Federation...
-The Federation Navy in Retrospect, 4199

Sanctuary, 4098

Very few human eyes–and none from the Federation–had set eyes on the Sanctuary System. It was over a hundred light years from the official edge of explored space, a cold planet circling a cold star. There was nothing to attract the attention of the Federation Survey Service, which concentrated on stars that might have given birth to life-bearing worlds and tended to overlook red giants or white dwarves. Even if a survey ship passed through the system, Chang Li had been assured, there would be little to see. The laboring cadres were hidden deep under the planet's poisonous atmosphere.

She ran her hand through her long dark hair, then sucked in her breath as the shuttlecraft dropped through the atmosphere. Sanctuary was very far from the ideal human world, something that would further disqualify it as a target of interest for the Survey Service. The thought that life might have arisen on its surface wouldn't occur to any of them, she hoped, even though Sanctuary had an intelligent race of its own. But then, even if the Survey Service *had* noticed, it was unlikely they'd care. The planet was completely useless to human settlers.

The shuttle bounced as it passed through the clouds, then broke through and headed towards the base. Li eyed the surface through the shuttle's sensors, feeling her flesh crawl as she saw the creatures moving far below her. The Insects–their real name was utterly unpronounceable to human mouths–looked like giant beetles. Merely looking at them reminded her of the insect phobia shared by so many humans, yet they were an intelligent race in their own right. And, given that they shared a hive mind of sorts, a unique one. There was no other hive mind known to exist in Federation space.

A handful of large buildings–resembling anthills as much as anything else–had been built around the landing pad. She studied them doubtfully for a long moment, then dismissed her worries about concealment. If the Survey Service started sending probes into Sanctuary's atmosphere, they'd discover the Insects in short order, sealing their fate. The Federation would rapidly send forces to convince the Insects to bow down to humanity–or die. There would be no alternative. The Federation had a long memory–and besides, beating down aliens served as its reason for existence. A new alien threat would help to unite it and, just incidentally, keep the Grand Senate in power.

But the Grand Senate is gone, she thought. *And what does that mean for us?*

Another shudder ran through the shuttle as it dropped down and landed neatly in front of one of the giant buildings. Li reached for her mask, pulled it on over her face and walked towards the airlock. Normally, on any alien homeworld, there would be plenty of places suitable for humans, but not here. The Insects had offered to build the human shuttlecraft an airtight walkway, but Li had declined. They were allies, not slaves, even if they *could* breathe human air without problems.

Outside, the chill caught at her despite the heating elements in her suit. She walked across the pad, into the nearest building and through another airlock. Inside, the atmosphere was human-norm, thankfully. She wasn't the only visitor who needed an earth-like atmosphere to live. The entire Outsider Federation leadership had come to attend the meeting.

And if the Federation knew we were consorting with not one, but two alien races, our deaths would be assured, she thought, as she took her seat. *But they'd have to work hard to decide just what they were actually going to shoot us for.*

"Honorable Chang Li," High Lord Slant said. He looked more human than the Insect representative, but nowhere near human enough to fool even a casual sweep. The Marsha resembled green gorillas, although their furry skins were covered by human-designed uniforms. "Welcome."

"I thank you," Li said. The Marsha had been expanding into space when the Outsiders had discovered them and made common cause. She didn't want to think about what would have happened if they'd been discovered by the Federation first. As a starfaring race, they would have been rapidly and cheaply crushed by the Federation Navy. "And I thank all of you."

There was a long pause. "I called this meeting because there have been developments in the Federation," she said. "The Justinian War is over...and Admiral Drake has made himself Emperor of the Federation. We must ask ourselves, now, if we still wish to proceed with our plans."

She waited for the council to review the documents she'd uploaded into the room's processor, thinking hard. Years ago, she'd come to the conclusion that there was no real hope of salvaging anything from the Federation. The Grand Senate held power too strongly for anyone to take it from them legally–and if anyone threatened to get too close to supreme power, they would simply change the rules. Her election had been the last gasp of the colonies, she knew. It had taken years of careful planning to ensure her victory over two candidates backed and funded by the Grand Senate...and yet her victory had turned to ashes as soon as she'd reached Earth. There had been no hope of changing anything.

"Nothing has changed," High Lord Slant proclaimed. "This is the same Admiral who worried us, years ago. We could not expect him to leave us alone."

Li nodded, remembering the first time she'd set eyes on Admiral Drake. He'd been addressing the Grand Senate, begging–pleading, almost–for reinforcements to be sent to the Rim. Drake had even figured out that someone was organizing the Outsiders, the web of semi-legal colonies out beyond the Rim, as well as suspecting the existence of two unknown alien races. He was entirely correct, Li knew, and only the Grand Senate's interest in maintaining its own domains rather than expansion had prevented him from carrying out survey missions of his own. There was no reason to expect him *not* to launch the missions himself, once he was in a secure position on Earth.

"The Federation has also been weakened," General Charlie Stuart said. The short dark-haired commander of the Outsider Strike Fleet looked, as ever, reassuringly competent. "If we'd been in a position to strike three years ago..."

"But we weren't," Li said, a little sharper than she'd intended. If they'd known Admiral Justinian was planning to make a bid for power, they might have tried to take advantage of it for themselves. "There's no point in crying over wasted opportunities."

"There's also the problem that the Federation possesses a vastly greater industrial infrastructure," Director Wilma Ripley pointed out. "Given time, they will out-produce us by a staggering margin."

"Then we move now," Stuart said. He tapped the table, then brought up a chart comparing the Outsider industrial plant with that of the Federation. The Outsiders had a more modern plant with better management, but there were few other advantages. "The longer we delay, the harder it will be to win."

Li winced, inwardly. Forty years of planning, forty years of building up a fleet that could challenge the Federation Navy, forty years...all of which might have been wasted, thanks to Admiral Justinian. The Federation Navy had been top-heavy, with poor training and worse morale, prior to the Battle of Earth. It wasn't anything of the sort now and, if a number of senior officers had been killed, hundreds of talented newcomers had risen up to take their places.

"There is no alternative," Slant said. The humans could make their peace with the Federation–or at least go into exile. The Marsha could only look forward to endless servitude, if the Federation didn't decide they were too dangerous to be allowed to exist. "Your reports make it clear that the Federation is planning a new wave of expansion. This will carry them inevitably towards our space. At that point, we will have no choice, but to fight."

"Striking now gives us the greatest chance of outright victory," Stuart agreed. "A long war would be disastrous for both of us."

"But our industry is not ready," the Insect chirped. It had no name, merely a number. "If our first blow misfired, we would be unable to keep the fleet operational."

Li hesitated, trying to parse out her own thoughts. Caution came naturally to her after a decade on Earth, where the grim awareness that a single slipup would mean her death had kept her mind focused on security. The risks of striking now were immense, she knew; they were, in many ways, unable to match the Federation. And yet, the Federation would never be weaker. A series of hammer blows might topple the structure, allowing them to win by default. Even if they lost the battles, their homeworlds and colonies would remain undiscovered. There would be time to rebuild and try again.

She looked down at the table, thinking hard. There were millions of potential rebels within the Federation, from large insurgent movements on various worlds to rebel groups and discontented citizens on others. Even Earth had its discontents, although the Grand Senate had squashed or co-opted most of *those*. The Outsiders had been making contact with dozens of groups, offering weapons and support in exchange for a coordinated uprising. It was risky—even with the Federation fighting a civil war, they were still keeping an eye on potential threats—but there was no alternative. The more forces they could keep tied down, the better.

But she also knew just how harshly the Federation would respond. It had happened before, after smaller uprisings. Leaders were executed, entire societies were purged or transported or simply buried under crushing piles of debt...and hopes of independence, even of some limited autonomy, firmly crushed. Did she really want that on her conscience?

She shook her head, but she knew it was futile. The Marsha had to go to war, if only to fight for the independence they would lose when the Federation discovered them. And there were too many rebels and insurgents who would fight anyway, once the Federation started tightening its grip. She could do nothing to stop it. All she could do was muster the strength of the Outsider Federation and pray that it would be enough to win the war.

"It seems we have no choice," she said. Victory was the only acceptable outcome. "How quickly can we launch the offensive?"

"We can move our ships to jump-off positions within a month," Stuart said. "But I would prefer to take two months, so we can insert commandos and undercover agents into various fleet bases and other targets. That would give us the greatest chance of capturing as many Federation military installations intact as possible."

"Adding to our fighting power," Li said. She'd watched as the military officers argued their way through the planning stages. "But will it be enough?"

The memory bothered her more than she wanted to admit. There was no escaping the fact that the Federation was *staggeringly* huge. It would take months, even using the Asimov Point network, to move from the Rim to Earth, giving the Federation time to organize its defenses and mount counterattacks. The Outsiders would have the advantage of cohesion and concentration, while the Federation Navy was scattered, but that wouldn't last. And if the Federation managed to parry the blows, it would stand a very good chance of winning the war itself.

"There's no way to avoid going through their bases on the Rim," Stuart said, earnestly. "They would go after our supply lines, given half a chance. We need to take them out before they realize they're at war."

"They will be struck before they realize the blow is on the way," Slant assured them, loudly. The Marsha were a warlike race, one that looked for the next challenge and embraced it eagerly. "And that will be the end."

Li nodded, although she still had her doubts.

They spent the next hour studying the final version of the operational plan. Li watched as Stuart went through every detail, answering questions with a patience she suspected he didn't feel. He'd been involved in the Outsider Federation from the day it had started to take shape, even doing most of the legwork behind assembling the Outsider Navy. She couldn't blame him for wanting to put it to the test, even though it would risk everything. There were only so many simulations they could run, he'd once told her, before they started to lose their edge.

Slant held his tongue until the end, when he started asking questions about assault and occupation troops for Federation worlds. Li had to watch as Stuart explained, carefully, that most of the troops would be human. The Federation was largely xenophobic and, if the locals saw alien troops on the ground, there would be trouble. Memories of the First Interstellar War had yet to fade, even though no one alive remembered humanity's traumatic first encounter with an alien race.

"My people will demand the honor of fighting for glory," Slant said, crossly. It was hard to read the emotions on his face, but the way his fist was twitching was quite indicative. He was annoyed. "We cannot be sidelined."

"There will be assaults on worlds without local populations," Stuart said, sharply. "Your people can assault them, if they wish."

"There is no glory if there are no witnesses," Slant said.

Li concealed her exasperation as the argument raged on. The Marsha didn't have an aristocratic society, not in the sense that the Grand Senate had been composed of aristocrats. As far as she understood it, the Marsha won glory, which translated into breeding and bragging rights. The more successful a person was, starting from nothing, the more honor and power they amassed. Instead of ensuring that their children had the best start in life, their parents actually disadvantaged them. How else could they gain honor? The system made little sense to her, but she had a feeling that human affairs were equally mystifying to the Marsha.

"Glory is immaterial," the Insect said. "All that matters is victory."

"Glory will decide who leads us," Slant said. There was no point in shouting at the Insects. They didn't have emotions, as humans understood the term. "The next generation must have its leaders."

Li held up a hand. "We cannot run the risk of fighting an insurgency in our rear," she said, carefully. "Correcting the opinions many humans have of aliens will take years–and responsible behaviour on our part."

"Human thoughts and feelings are not our concern," Slant said.

"They will be if they make the difference between peaceful surrender and hopeless resistance," Stuart said. "We have no choice but to humor them. Allowing them to grow into the realization that most xenophobic feelings are based on nothing more than propaganda will take years."

On that note, the meeting ended.

☙❧

"So tell me," Li said, when she and Stuart were alone. "What *are* the odds?"

"Fifty-fifty, I would say," Stuart said. "We will have the advantage of surprise, some new technology of our own and a very experienced and motivated set of crews. They will have superior numbers and superior industry, if they manage to get it back up to speed. It will not be an easy task. Their tax base is shot to hell, for a start."

He paused. "Do you still want to make a peace offer? It might be harder to get them to listen after we've started the war."

Li nodded. "It might bring the war to an end," she said. "If we give them a way out..."

She would have preferred to make the offer ahead of the war, but she knew it would give the Federation time to prepare. A hammer blow that shattered the Federation's control over the Rim would shock it, she hoped, enough to convince the emperor to talk peace. The Grand Senate certainly would have considered surrender...

...But would Admiral Drake?

She recalled their one meeting and scowled. Drake hadn't struck her as someone who gave up easily, even after being recalled to Earth to explain his failure. Other admirals might have begged for mercy, or even promised to do more with less, but not Drake. He'd told the Grand Senate, to their faces, that he needed more ships to produce results. And then he'd taken command of the defenses of Earth, saved the planet from a bolt from the blue, and then...

"Emperor Marius Drake will not give up easily," she said. He'd had plenty of opportunities to set up as a warlord in his own right–and, despite herself, she was sure he hadn't *intended* to become emperor. "We will need to ensure the situation is hopeless before he surrenders."

"Then we will have to fight hard," Stuart said. "Two months to get everything in order..."

He shook his head. "It will be chancy, Li," he warned. "But we have no other choice."

"Of course not," Li agreed. "If the Federation ever found out about us, we would be dead. And not just us. Everyone would be dead."

She sat down and stared at the display. It had been years since some of her ancestors had fled the Inheritance Wars. Longer, since they had first left Earth in search of a new home, one where they could live in their own manner. But the Federation had refused to let them go, and their first attempt to make themselves independent had misfired badly. This time, the Federation was weakened and they would never have a better chance at success.

But if it went wrong...

Then we die, she told herself. *But what else can we do?*

Chapter Five

Barany, Governor Richardson. Governor of Athena, Sector Capital. Long-standing client of the Warren Family (Grand Senate). Known for being intensely corrupt. Threatened with recall just prior to the Justinian War.
-The Federation Navy in Retrospect, 4199

Athena, 4098

There was always a sense of...*something*...when one passed through an Asimov Point. It was never easy to describe. Roman had tended to think of it as a kind of anticipation, mixed with fear. Anything, anything at all, could be on the other side of the disruption in space-time that linked two star systems together. And these days, after the Justinian War, it was impossible to be entirely certain of what was on the far side. Even friendly space could turn out to be anything but.

He braced himself as *Valiant* slid through the Asimov Point and materialized in another star system, fifty light years from her departure point. The display flickered, then rapidly started to update, revealing three heavy battlestations protecting the Asimov Point, backed up by a handful of outdated cruisers and destroyers. Athena had been largely uninvolved in the Justinian War and the defenses had never been built up, unlike Earth and a hundred other worlds that happened to be on the front line. Roman had no doubt of his ability to take the system, if necessary. And, no matter how loyal Governor Barany claimed to be, Roman suspected he would be reluctant to cooperate fully. He'd certainly refused to co-operate with Admiral Drake!

"You will have full authority to assess the situation," Emperor Marius had said, before Roman had boarded the shuttle for *Valiant*. It was the last time they'd seen one another, sharing a drink as they discussed the future. "Barany may just be a fool–if so, you can retire him with full honors. If not, remove him from power and send him home."

"Transit complete," Palter reported, interrupting Roman's thoughts. "Moving to assembly point now."

Roman nodded. Fifth Fleet was coming through the Asimov Point in a tight stream of starships, much to the horror of local traffic control. It had been a risk–one mistiming and two starships would collide or find themselves sharing the same space when they materialized–but he'd seen no choice. Quite apart from showing off, it allowed him to muster as much firepower as possible within the system at terrifying speed. If the defenders had wanted to put up a fight, outdated or no, they would have given him a bloody nose. It was the last thing he wanted.

"I don't think anyone would actually *fight* for him," Emperor Marius had said. "Justinian, whatever else could be said about him, had enough charisma to convince his subordinates to go along with him. Barany has none of that, Roman. But he will be desperate if he fears the worst."

And he might well, Roman thought. *By now, he has to know that Admiral Drake is the new Emperor–and Drake complained prominently about him to the Grand Senate. It might be time for him to take his winnings and run before we reach his world.*

He forced himself to watch patiently as Fifth Fleet slowly assembled and shook itself down into formation. The drills had helped, he knew, although there was still a hint of imprecision about the fleet's movements. If they'd still been in the pre-war era, heads would have rolled. A starship out of position by a handful of metres would be considered a major disaster. Now...now it was better to be able to fight than to look good. It would be a long time before the lessons of the war faded away.

"Formation complete," Palter reported. "Local traffic control is requesting permission to switch back to civilian operations. They're claiming to have lost millions in credits over the last thirty minutes."

"Tell them to switch back," Roman said, not bothering to dispute their claims. The military had transit priority, even in peacetime. Besides, using the Asimov Points was so much quicker than making the crossing between stars without them. "And then dispatch the observers to the battlestations."

"Aye, sir," Palter said.

Roman smiled, then glanced at the stream of reports from his ships. There were no major problems, although a couple of ships had barely avoided collisions as they emerged from the Asimov Point. A freak twist in the local gravity field had almost killed four hundred officers and crew, along with destroying two cruisers. Roman muttered a silent prayer of thanks under his breath, then tapped a command into the datanet. The fleet shook itself out and started to glide towards Athena. Governor Barany was waiting for them there.

"Local traffic is surprisingly high," Commodore Sonia Yu said, from her console at the other side of the CIC. The middle-aged woman looked over at Roman, thoughtfully. "There's more freighters in the system than we were led to expect."

"And that means...what?" Roman asked. Athena was a major junction point, with five Asimov Points and a number of colonies within two weeks of FTL travel. "A sign of trouble?"

"Governor Barany's staff didn't declare anything like this level of traffic when they reported back to the Grand Senate last year," Yu said. "He may be skimming taxes from the unreported ships, sir, or he may be up to something more sinister. It isn't a good sign."

"No," Roman agreed. He frowned as more icons popped into existence on the datanet. Athena had only been settled a hundred years ago, the oldest colony world in the sector. It shouldn't have had so much activity, not according to the standard development profiles. "Can you give me a complete breakdown?"

He watched as the analysts went to work. Athena should have had a handful of asteroid colonies, a single cloudscoop and maybe a pair of colonies on the other rocky worlds within the system. Sector Capital or not, there just wasn't the funding available for more rapid development. The outdated fortifications protecting the planet itself had been the single largest investment from the Federation. And yet...

The asteroid belt was brimming with activity, there were no less than four cloudscoops operating in orbit around the gas giant and hundreds of freighters were making their way in and out of the system. It was an incredible leap forward, all the more remarkable because none of it had happened prior to 4092, when the Justinian War had begun. Six years of effective abandonment had led to *this*? Roman couldn't help wondering just what Governor Barany had done to make so much spring up out of nowhere–and it if could be duplicated elsewhere.

"We will enter orbit in five hours," Palter reported. "The governor will have plenty of warning of our approach."

"We're not trying to hide," Roman said. What would the governor do? It was hard to argue with success–and it was clear the governor had been very successful. But he had to know that Emperor Marius had a grudge, not without reason. "Just keep a sharp eye on the planetary defenses."

The hours ticked by slowly. Roman watched grimly as more and more activity came into detection range, suggesting that Athena had jumped two whole development stages within six years. There was a small shipyard in orbit and two more floating in separate orbits around the sun, both civilian-grade but very impressive. The only thing missing was an updated defense grid. There had been no attempt to improve the battlestations protecting the planet from attack.

And that makes no sense, Roman thought, coldly. *If you ruled this system, wouldn't you want to make sure that nothing bad happened to it?*

A thought struck him and he tapped his console, bringing up the system display. It was impossible to be sure, but it looked very much as though there was *no* fear. The freighters made their way in and out of the system without fear of attack, even though there was little hope of support arriving from Athena in time to make a difference, if they ran into trouble. And that made no sense. Everyone knew that pirates and rebels plagued the Rim, looting, raping and killing their way across stage-one and stage-two colonies. Hell, Roman himself had lost his parents to a pirate attack. It made no sense at all.

He keyed his console, linking into the Marine Command Net. "Elf, I'd like you to look at the data," he said. "Tell me what you think."

There was a pause. Roman used it to watch the display, wondering just how many rules and regulations had been flouted. But...Athena had been effectively out of contact with the Grand Senate for six years. What had Governor Barany managed to do without the Grand Senate peeking over his shoulder? And was it really right to punish him for actually taking his system and turning it into a success?

But if he's made deals with pirates, Roman thought, *it isn't something we could allow to go unpunished.*

"Picking up a signal from the planet," Palter said. "Governor Barany sends his regards and invites you to call on him as soon as the fleet enters orbit."

Roman considered it, briefly. He could hardly avoid paying a call on the governor, even if what he suspected was true. And besides, it would give him a chance to take the measure of the governor in person. Emperor Marius *had* given him considerable latitude, after all. But he had a feeling, if the old reports were entirely accurate, that the governor was up to his receding hairline in pirate activity. He'd taken advantage of six years of near-independence to build up a protection racket that was blighting the entire sector.

Roman's earpiece buzzed. "I don't like this," Elf said. "It looks, very much, like the governor has made a deal with someone."

"I know," Roman said. "You have the plans for Operation Swap. Start tailoring them to the current situation."

"Aye, sir," Elf said.

Slowly, Athena herself came into view on the display. She looked like Earth had once been, according to the history books; a blue-green orb hanging against the blackness of interstellar space. But she was surrounded by five heavy–and outdated–battlestations, as well as countless orbital facilities and transhipment nodes. There were far more than the system should be able to support, Roman calculated mentally. The Gross Planetary Product had to be significantly higher than the Grand Senate had been led to believe.

"Link us into System Command," he ordered. "I want us to have complete access to their systems–everything from short-range active sensors to long-range probes and listening platforms. Get the data filtered through to the intelligence analysts and tell them I want a complete breakdown of the system. Specifically, I want to know just what the fuck is going on."

"Aye, sir," Palter said.

Elf's face appeared in the display. "Operation Swap has been updated," she said. "The Marines are on standby, ready for immediate deployment."

"We need evidence, first," Roman said. The emperor might not object if they simply arrested the governor, but if there was to be a trial there had to be evidence. It was just possible that Governor Barany had pulled off a miracle. "Something to prove that the governor is a dirty bastard."

"We already have proof," Elf said. "The system has far more industrial production nodes than it should. Where is the excess production *going*?"

Roman frowned as the analysis popped up in front of him. Athena might have jumped a pair of development stages, but her industries weren't large enough to absorb such a high level of production. Roman could understand wanting to build up a stockpile of spare parts–such a stockpile might have saved the Federation Navy from considerable embarrassment during the early years of the war–but there didn't seem to be *any* such stockpile. And then, sooner or later, the industries would be unable to support themselves, if they were unable to sell their products. No matter how he looked at it, he couldn't escape the impression that he was seeing evidence of heavy corruption right in front of him.

He gritted his teeth. It was absurd! By any reasonable standard, the governor had done an excellent job of ensuring the system remained loyal to the Federation–and survived the economic shockwaves. There were no shortage of horror stories about colonies that had collapsed, while the Grand Senate's attention was elsewhere.

Worlds cut off from supply lines, or raided by pirates, or simply forgotten in the chaos caused by the war. But if the governor had been making deals with *someone*, he had to be stopped. There was no alternative.

"We'll call upon the governor tonight," he said, after a moment's thought. By then, they should have the proof they needed. "And..."

"Admiral," Palter interrupted. "I think you should see this."

Roman swung around as a new icon popped up in the display. "What the hell is that?"

"A starship of unknown design," Palter said. A stream of data ran past the icon as the sensors started to probe the mystery ship. "I think she's alien, sir."

Roman blinked in surprise. Aliens were not allowed starships, full stop. The traumas of the First Interstellar War were still too raw for humanity to ever consider letting its guard down or ever accepting aliens as equals. The policy wasn't something he approved of, not completely, but it couldn't be helped. Allowing an alien starship anywhere near a human world was a clear breach of the law.

And she has to come from the Beyond, Roman thought, sharply. *The governor didn't report her presence to his superiors.*

"Query System Command," he ordered, sharply. "I want a full explanation for her presence."

The answer came quickly. "Apparently, she was salvaged a month ago," Palter said. "They don't know where she came from, sir."

"Really," Roman said. Any contact with a new spacefaring race had to be reported to the Grand Senate at once, whatever the situation. It was laid down in Federation Law. "Have a team prepared to board her, once we've dealt with the governor."

"Aye, sir," Palter said.

Roman forced himself to stand as the fleet entered high orbit. It felt *wrong* to leave the CIC when they were so close to the planetary defenses, no matter how confident his mentor had been that no one would put their lives on the line for Governor Barany. The fleet couldn't keep its shields up without alarming the governor, which meant that the planetary defenses, no matter how outdated, could do real damage before the fleet returned fire. It was a risk, but one he had to take. There was no other way to arrest the governor without risking everything.

"Keep a sharp eye on the defenses," he ordered. "And be ready to snap the shields up without waiting for orders, if necessary."

He strode out of the CIC and down into his cabin, where he donned his dress uniform. So much had been revised since the Justinian War, but dress uniforms had been unaccountably overlooked. The blue and grey uniform that marked him as a commodore–with a very slight service record, marked in gold pips–was hellishly uncomfortable. He'd been told, back at the Academy, that it helped keep the cadets alert, but they'd privately suspected that someone with powerful connections had blackmailed the Federation Navy into accepting their creations. It was the only explanation that made sense.

Shame we don't have time to change it, he thought, as he checked his appearance in the mirror. His brown hair seemed thinner these days, even though he was only twenty-nine and alarmingly young for his rank. The dress uniform made him look older, thankfully. If it wasn't so uncomfortable, he might almost have been pleased. But changing the design was a very low priority at the moment.

His communicator bleeped. "Platoon A is assembled and ready to provide escort," Elf said. "They've all been briefed."

"Good," Roman said. It was almost a shame he couldn't walk into the meeting with Elf by his side, but she had to command the platoon. Besides, it would draw their relationship into the open air, even though he was morbidly convinced everyone already knew anyway. It wasn't in breach of regulations. "I'm on my way."

The Marines, wearing dress uniforms he knew for a fact to be actually *comfortable,* met him at the shuttlebay. They didn't look armed and armored, but Elf had once shown him just how many weapons could be concealed within a dress uniform–or any kind of uniform, for that matter. Watching her remove a whole series of knives, guns and other surprises had been both exciting and terrifying. He'd wondered, once, why prisoners were always stripped naked when they were taken into custody. He knew now.

"Sir," Elf said. On duty, her face showed no trace of any emotions. Like him, she had been promoted rapidly, perhaps too rapidly. But the Marines wouldn't have tolerated her if she'd been dangerously incompetent. "Platoon A is ready to depart. Company Two and Three, as well as WARCAT One, are also ready and waiting in shuttlebay two."

"Thank you," Roman said. It would probably require an entire team of investigators to uncover *all* of Governor Barany's misdeeds, but a WARCAT team could make a start on it and, hopefully, uncover enough evidence to send the governor through the airlock and into hard vacuum. "They can follow us once we've secured the governor."

He smiled, inwardly, as they tramped into the shuttle. He'd never hear the end of it afterwards, once they were alone together. What sort of captain, let alone a commodore, would leave his command deck and put his life on the line, just to snare a corrupt governor? But it was the only way to do it without the governor fleeing for his life...and besides, compared to some of the other stunts he'd done, it wasn't genuinely reckless. The Marines would protect him if the shit hit the fan.

The shuttle rocked, then lifted off the deck and flew out into open space.

Chapter Six

The Federation is divided up into sectors for ease of administration (and also for rigging elections in the Grand Senate's favor). Each of these sectors generally consists of twenty to thirty star systems, with a Governor based at the Sector Capital, which tends to be the star system of greatest tactical/strategic importance. This generally implies the presence of a considerable number of Asimov Points.
-The Federation Navy in Retrospect, 4199

Athena, 4098

The original planners had shown a remarkable–and largely unprecedented–level of imagination when they'd named the planet's capital city, Roman decided, as the shuttle dropped down towards the governor's palace. Athena City might have sounded unimaginative in the extreme, but when nine out of ten capital cities were named something along the lines of 'Landing City' or 'First Landing,' it was definitely an improvement. It was intended, eventually, that the settlers would rename the city they'd founded, but it rarely happened in practice. The bureaucrats objected to having to redo all the paperwork.

Roman had never really liked planetary surfaces. He'd grown up in an asteroid habitat, after all, where the environment could be precisely controlled, without any of the irritating little problems that planet-dwellers faced like tornadoes or unanticipated rainfall. Indeed, he'd been astonished to discover just how vulnerable some planetary settlements were, even without pirates, raiders and terrorists. A single bad harvest could ruin the entire settlement and, if they were unlucky, plunge them all into debt. It made so much more sense, he thought, to move the entire human race into space. Anyone masochistic enough to want to live on a planetary surface deserved everything they got.

But he had to admit, as he stared down at the city, that the planet's settlers had done well for themselves. The endless rows of prefabricated buildings that made up the early settlement had been dismantled, apart from one that sat in the middle of a park and was clearly intended to show the planet's children how far the settlement had come. Instead, there were towering buildings of glass and concrete, far more than he would have expected from such a young colony world. And the people thronged the streets without any sense of care or fear for the future. There was an optimism pervading the city, he thought, that reminded him of the early days at the Academy. It almost felt attractive.

He turned his attention to the governor's palace and groaned, inwardly. The building was massive, far larger than necessary...and a shining testament to the governor's vanity. It was mean to serve as an administrative center as well as his personal residence, but it was too large even for that. Roman shook his head in disbelief as the shuttle landed atop the rear landing pad, wondering just how many credits the governor had wasted on the palace. It wasn't as if the governor was going to stay there indefinitely.

Unless he thinks he is, Roman thought. *Did he think the war would go on forever?*

The shuttle touched down with a bump, the hatch springing open a moment later. Elf motioned for him to stay in his seat as the Marines moved out, then signalled for him to follow them out onto the tarmac. The world smelled faintly of flowers, something that surprised him until he saw the gardens surrounding the palace. Governor Barany liked flowers, Roman saw. It wasn't something he'd expected from Emperor Marius's description of the man.

"Commodore Garibaldi," a young woman said. "Welcome to Government House."

Roman studied her for a long moment. She was tall, wearing a long dress that hinted at her curves rather than revealing them. Long blonde hair hung down to her rear, framing a thin face and highlighting blue eyes and perfect lips. Her skin was so perfect, Roman decided, that it was obvious someone had paid for her cosmetic surgery. It was just too perfect to be real.

"Thank you," Roman said, reminding himself firmly that Elf stood right next to him. "Please escort us to the governor."

The girl looked doubtful. "All of you? We have refreshments and company for your friends..."

"All of us," Roman said, firmly. "Please."

The girl bowed, then led them through the door. Roman had to fight to keep his face impassive as he took in the Governor's House. He'd heard tales of the luxury enjoyed by the rich, powerful and well-connected, but he'd never really seen it before. Giant statues lay everywhere, each one carefully named and dated. Roman had to check his implants to identify a couple of them, all ancestors of the current governor immortalized in gold and silver. It was clear that Governor Barany intended to place his stamp quite firmly on the palace, ensuring his successors knew just who to thank. But Roman found it more than a little gaudy—and completely tasteless.

He kept his thoughts to himself as they entered a long corridor, lined with portraits of strange, almost inhuman people. The governor's artist had a really strange imagination, he concluded, as he saw a topless girl with snakes for hair and a tail where her legs should be. It sent shivers down his spine, although he wasn't sure why. Beyond her, the portrait of a naked girl with pointy ears and fairy wings was almost normal. Someone could have themselves altered to look like her, if they wanted. He just couldn't understand why anyone would bother.

You could have anything you wanted, if you had the resources of the governor, his thoughts mocked him. *How long would it be before you developed a taste for the strange—and the forbidden?*

"Your Excellency," the girl said. "Commodore Garibaldi and guests."

Roman stepped past her and into the governor's office. Somewhat to his surprise, the office was plain and remarkably businesslike. The walls were bare, save for a large map of the planet's surface and another showing the star system itself. But it was the governor himself who dominated the room. He was taller than Roman had expected, and quite remarkably fat, even though there were no shortage of treatments one could use to slim down. It was a message, Roman suspected, even though he wasn't sure he could read it. Perhaps the governor was hinting at his enormous appetites.

"You're young," the governor said. His voice was jovial, yet there was a hard edge that reminded Roman of some of the tutors at the Academy. "How are you in command of an entire fleet of warships? What connections do you have?"

Roman felt an odd flicker of irritation at the man's tone. If he'd been promoted so quickly in peacetime, there *would* have been resentment from his peers and he *would* have had to work hard to prove he could handle it. If, of course, he hadn't been summarily demoted after the Promotions Board reviewed his case. Even the highest level of connections had their limits. But now, in wartime, he'd moved up quickly, like so many others. He was far from unique.

"A great many people died," he said, recalling the hellish hours on *Enterprise*. He'd been...what? *Tenth* in the chain of command? And if there hadn't been a minor error on the ship's blueprints he would have died too, leaving *Enterprise* at Admiral Justinian's mercy. "And I was lucky."

"You must have been very lucky to be assigned a whole fleet," Governor Barany said. He waved a hand towards one of the chairs. "Please. Be seated."

Roman ignored the gesture. "There are a number of questions I need answered, governor," he said. "Starting with the existence of a starship of alien design in orbit, one that was not reported to Earth."

"It was hard to say who it should be reported to," Governor Barany said. "The Federation was in turmoil."

"You should have reported it to the Federation Navy," Roman snapped. "And you have also not reported your own economic successes here. Why not?"

The governor shrugged. "Because the Grand Senate would come and strangle the life out of it," he said. "They always react badly to success that doesn't take place under their mandate."

"The Grand Senate is gone," Roman said. He met the governor's eyes. "I have orders from Emperor Marius to relieve you of your position, pending a full investigation into your conduct. You are under arrest."

He nodded to the Marines, who stepped forward and grabbed hold of the governor. The governor opened his mouth, then squawked loudly as cold hands started to search him thoroughly, removing a pair of data terminals and a device Roman didn't recognize. He watched, as dispassionately as he could, as the governor was pushed down into a chair, then cuffed. The governor didn't seem to be carrying any weapons.

"I suggest you tell your people not to offer any resistance," Roman said. Without the governor, the planetary defenses would likely be too confused to do anything, if they wanted to fight for their former leader. And if they didn't, nothing the governor did would make any difference. "The Marines are on their way."

The governor stared at him. "This is...this is intolerable! I make this world a success and you come to take it from me!"

"You will be investigated," Roman said. "Should you be found innocent, you will be released."

Elf glanced at him. "The shuttles are inbound," she said. "ETA; five minutes."

Roman nodded, feeling his entire body tense. If the locals planned any resistance, the shit would hit the fan just about...now. But nothing happened. He let out a breath as the Marine companies landed, then swarmed out to take control of the palace. None of the governor's servants raised a hand to defend him. Relieved, Roman ordered the next wave of Marines to land and start taking over the planetary defenses, then followed Elf and her platoon as they marched the governor back to his shuttle. To all intents and purposes, they'd taken over the entire planet in a bloodless strike.

But now we have to sort out just what the governor was doing, he mused. *And see just how much of it was treasonous.*

ꙮ

Camille had been lucky. The moment she'd seen the shuttles, she'd known the game was up. She'd ducked into the tunnels as the Marines landed, then put as much distance as she could between herself and the palace before popping up in the governor's safe house. It wouldn't remain secret forever, not when the tunnels were discovered, but it hardly mattered. By the time they found the house, she would be long gone.

She changed her clothes, switching from the dress the governor had designed himself to a simple pair of trousers and a shirt, then hurried out onto the streets of Athena. None of the population seemed to have realized that there had been a shift in the balance of power, although they would–and soon. Far too many of them had worried over what would happen when the Grand Senate turned its attention back to Athena and discovered that the planet's GPP was now staggeringly high. It wouldn't be long before the governor was replaced by a horde of aristocratic locusts from Earth, each intent on draining as much as they could from the local economy. And then...

There would be revolution, she knew. And the locals would have help.

The apartment block was completely unremarkable in every way, identical to the dozens of others scattered around the city. She let herself in through the front door, made her way up to her apartment and closed the door firmly behind her. The tradecraft she'd pushed aside for years to avoid looking suspicious came to the fore and she checked around, making sure that the room was completely untouched. As soon as she was certain, she dug into a pile of datachips and removed one marked SELF-AWARENESS LESSONS, YEAR ONE. It was such a boring subject, she'd been told, that no one would look at it willingly. She took the chip, inserted it into her terminal, then entered the password. Moments later, she was looking at an advanced and thoroughly illegal compression and encryption program.

She sucked in a breath, feeling her heart starting to race as she keyed in her message. Mere possession of an illicit encryption program would guarantee a lifetime in jail, if she wasn't exiled to a colony world. The Grand Senate insisted that all such programs have back doors engineered into them, just to make sure that Federation Intelligence could decrypt the program, if necessary. And they'd discouraged anyone from trying to produce more advanced programs. But *her* program not only had no back door, it was actually more advanced and capable than any military-grade system available to the Federation. The mere presence of such a program would alarm the Federation, if they found out about it.

Carefully, she finished typing her message and hit the encrypt key. Twenty seconds later, the message was firmly zipped up and almost completely undetectable, unless one knew to look for it and had the right equipment. She smiled as she deactivated the chip and returned it to the hiding place, buried under dozens of equally boring chips, then activated the camera on the terminal. A red light flashed on, indicating she was being recorded.

"Oh, Jim, you hunk of burning love," she said, as she removed her shirt and exposed her breasts. The lines were tacky, but no one would pay any attention to them while she was topless and playing with herself. "If you were here just now, do you know what I would do to you?"

She smiled as she finished the recording, then added the compressed file to the video stream. No one would think anything of a girlfriend sending her boyfriend erotic messages; the security officers might enjoy themselves watching her performance, but they would be too distracted to look for anything else. Or so she hoped. Sex had been used to hide misdeeds–other misdeeds–for countless years. And besides, the governor had played a large role in dulling the security forces on Athena. He'd certainly had more than enough reason to make sure they were harmless, as well as incompetent.

Clicking a switch, she sent the message to the upload node, then headed for the shower. It wouldn't be long before someone worked out that she was supposed to be working at the palace, then called to ask her some pointed questions. She didn't want to be discovered naked, not after the rumors about the Grand Senate's latest set of enforcers. The last thing anyone wanted was to draw their attention to Athena.

But she had a feeling, she knew as she stepped into the shower, that it was already too late.

ഌ௸

Mike Higgins had wanted to be an engineer from a very early age. He had been mocked by his extended family, which had served in the Federation Navy since there had *been* a Federation Navy, but he'd always been more fascinated with machines than people. Machines were predicable and understandable, even the ones built by aliens. Indeed, he'd always considered it a shame that there were so few examples of genuine alien technology in the Federation. It was often more interesting than purely human tech.

The alien ship was remarkable, he decided, as his team followed him through the airlock and into the craft. And yet, judging from some of the opened panels, she had been abandoned in a hurry. He peered into one of the panels, then frowned, recognizing some of the circuits. Reaching for his handheld sensor, he swept the panel and felt his frown grow deeper as he examined the results. It was impossible to be sure, but it looked like aliens had captured some Federation technology, then reverse-engineered the systems and put it into production. There were enough oddities about the alien craft to confirm that human minds hadn't built it.

"Curious," he mused. It was a shame he couldn't spend hours exploring the craft, but he wouldn't have the time. The entire craft would have to be disassembled, piece by piece, and for that it would need to be moved to a shipyard. He seriously considered putting in a request for a transfer, even though he knew it might reflect badly on his career. But alien technology was more interesting than even the latest FTL drives from Earth. "Very curious."

He paused, then looked around the cabin. It was clear to his gaze that the aliens were humanoid–and, perhaps, not that different from humans. The consoles were in the right positions for humans, rather than one of the child-sized races humanity had effectively enslaved, while the lighting was quite close to human-norm. Indeed, the whole ship smacked of human-alien *collaboration*. What the hell was it doing here?

"I'm going to try to get a live feed from the ship's data recorders," he said, keying his radio. The Federation insisted on working recorders into every hull, but the aliens might have different ideas. "I want to see where this ship has been."

It only took a few minutes to connect the ship to one of his datacores, not entirely to his surprise. Whoever had designed the ship had wanted it to interact with human technology. It suggested that they weren't dealing with a self-spacefaring race, but one that had managed to get a leg-up from human renegades. Might the Outsiders have given the aliens human technology? And what else might they have built?

The datacore bleeped an alert, then deactivated itself. Mike scowled, and then checked the readings. It was clear, now, that the ship's databases had been completely wiped. Even the most thorough sweep of the datacores would reveal nothing. The ship had been abandoned because it was useless, without its computers. But why hadn't they sought to replace the datacores or simply scuttle her? It was a question he knew he wouldn't be able to answer.

But he knew his duty. "Captain, this ship is a combination of human and alien tech," he reported. "I think that spells trouble."

Chapter Seven

Stuart, Charlie. Descendent of the famous Gregory Stuart, who fled Athens after the end of the Inheritance Wars. Played a crucial role in building up the Outsider Navy for fleet operations in the wake of the Justinian War...
-The Federation Navy in Retrospect, 4199

Base One, 4098

"The report is confirmed?"

"Yes, sir," Lieutenant Juneau said. Her pale face looked worried. "The Federation Navy moved to Athena in force–and arrested the governor."

General Charlie Stuart looked down at the report, thoughtfully. Governor Barany had been a useful idiot, rather than a conspirator, if only because no one with any sense would trust him any further than strictly necessary. His obsession with making money and his willingness to take bribes from all and sundry had made him useful, his complete lack of concern over what happened to products from his system after they left his jurisdiction had made him an idiot.

But, for all of his flaws, he had been predictable.

"Our people have been alerted, I assume?" Stuart asked. "They know to take cover?"

"The cells didn't have any contact with the governor," Juneau said. "He didn't know they existed. And the handful of sources within the governor's office have already burned their bridges. They should be safe."

"Let us hope so," Charlie said.

He shook his head. The timing was suspicious as hell. Did the Federation have an agent or two within the Outsider Federation? Someone who had alerted the new emperor to the threat growing beyond his borders? Or was it a genuine coincidence? Everyone knew that Admiral Drake had wanted to reinforce the borders and hunt down the Outsiders long before the Justinian War had diverted the Federation's attention. It wasn't beyond belief that the bastard had decided to settle scores with Governor Barany and reinforce the borders, now that the warlords had been defeated. He certainly would *want* to do it.

Juneau passed him a second report. "This is everything we were able to find on Commodore Garibaldi," she explained. "The intelligence staff warns that there simply isn't very much, as he's one of the new officers. He didn't even exist ten years ago."

"He would have been a child," Charlie grunted. The Federation had once kept promotion glacially slow, ensuring that their admirals turned rusty before leaving the slots open for younger men. Now, advancement was determined by merit rather than connections. "I doubt he has *that* much experience."

"Admiral Drake does, sir," Juneau reminded him. "And he isn't the only one with a pre-war combat record."

Charlie nodded, then skimmed through the report. Born on an asteroid habitat. Parents killed by raiders when he was a teen. Joined the Federation Navy. Graduated in the wake of the attack on Earth with a First. Assigned to *Enterprise.* Briefly assumed *command* of *Enterprise.* Assigned to another starship, apparently–by then–the protégée of Admiral Drake. Wounded in the final battle of the Justinian War. And then...? Nothing.

"This is just the bare bones," he said. "Can't they find something more useful?"

"No, sir," Juneau said. "I don't think Commodore Garibaldi has had time to rack up anything like Admiral Stevenson's list of sins."

"I suppose not," Charlie said. Any sane navy would have fired Admiral Stevenson decades ago. He was too old and set in his ways to change–and he had a habit of preying on young officers, male and female alike. Chances were that Admiral Drake would dispose of him when reminded that Stevenson was still alive. "He's only twenty-nine."

"Yes, sir," Juneau said. "But he has built up quite a bit of experience."

"Not in fleet operations," Charlie said. "But you're right. We should be careful."

He sighed. Taking out Athena was necessary, if only to secure control of the Asimov Points and use them to funnel his warships deeper into Federation Space. Governor Barany had cooperated, unknowingly, by not funding additional defenses for his planet, no doubt afraid of the Grand Senate's reaction. But the arrival of an entire battle fleet was bad news. Charlie had no doubt that he could secure local superiority, yet it would be costly. And yet, if Commodore Garibaldi managed to retreat, he could harass the Outsiders until reinforcements arrived from the Core. The war might stalemate and eventually be lost.

"Pass the word to the cells," he said. The planetary militia hadn't been a major factor in his planning, if only because it was undermanned, ill-equipped and pervaded with pro-independence sympathies. But the Fleet Marines would be a very different issue. "They're to prepare, as best as possible, for strikes rather than outright takeovers. We don't want to get bogged down."

He looked up at the display, towards where the First Strike Fleet was slowly assembling into formation. He'd planned for two to three more weeks of exercises before they moved–now, the exercises would have to be repeated, with the newcomers included in the enemy ranks. And then he'd have to try to destroy Fifth Fleet, rather than let it get away from the planet and escape into deep space. It was going to be costly.

"And have stealth ships moved to the system," he added. "I want them to shadow the fleet at all times."

Juneau gave him a surprised look. "Stealth ships might still be detected, sir," she said. "And we have a stream of freighters going in and out of the system..."

"We need precise data," Charlie said. "And besides, once Federation Intelligence starts going through the records, they'll shut down most of the shipping lanes. We would be deprived of intelligence when we needed it the most."

He gave her a nod, then turned to his console. There was, as always, paperwork to do. They were rebels and they *still* had to do paperwork. It made him wonder what it would be like if they won, *when* they won. Would they still have to do paperwork then?

Less of it, he told himself, firmly. *And no government servants telling us what to do.*

ᢒᢓ

It had been nearly three years since Uzi and his team of deep-cover agents had set food on Hobson's Choice, posing as a group of mercenaries in need of a job. They'd been snapped up almost as soon as they showed–and verified–their credentials, which proclaimed them to be a band of mercenaries with extensive combat experience. He had thought, at the time, that they would be taken into service with Admiral Justinian and his rebels, where they would have a chance to undermine the bastards from within. Instead, they'd found themselves on a ship heading out past the Rim.

He clicked his cyborg implants unhappily as he surveyed the scene before him. They'd considered, seriously, simply taking over the transport and returning home. Only curiosity had stayed their hand...and they'd discovered, when they reached their destination, the most well-organized rebellion in Federation history. Even the Inheritance Wars, as long and bloody as they'd been, hadn't been as well-organized as the Outsiders. Uzi had almost had a heart attack when he'd discovered that the Outsiders had *superdreadnaughts*!

But it was the aliens who had *really* shocked him. Two different alien races, both working with humans as equals...it was unbelievable. Didn't the Outsiders understand the dangers of treating aliens as anything like equal to humans? But it seemed not, even though one of the alien races was dangerously aggressive and the other was utterly inhuman. The Outsiders were treating them as equals, even arming them with human weapons designed for their use...

He wanted to curse out loud, to scream and shout at them. Aliens could not be trusted! But there was no point. It would have blown his cover for nothing. All he could do was watch, wait, compile his reports and hope there would be a chance to get them back to the Federation. But so far it had proven futile. The Outsiders might not have any qualms about sharing technology with aliens–and some of it was definitely military-grade technology–but they *had* been quite successful at preventing any of the mercenaries from making contact with anyone else. He'd been told that anyone who wanted to resign would be shipped to an isolated world, where they would be held until the war was won.

And it might well be won, he thought, as he started to walk back towards the training simulation. The Outsiders had a *cause.* Worse, they had a unified command system and a network of bases and shipyards that allowed them to pose a significant challenge to the Federation. Worst of all, the Federation was still recovering from the last war. *This could bring down the entire Federation and I can do nothing*!

He gritted his teeth as a line of Insects marched past, limbs twitching in uneasy unison. They weren't human...in his view, insects that large simply shouldn't exist. It was hard to resist the temptation to activate his weapons implants and start blasting away, chopping through them before they had a chance to resist. But would they resist when they had a hive mind? It was impossible to understand them in human terms. They seemed to be both individuals and something greater. And they were armed to the teeth.

You've seen worse, he told himself. *And you've done worse.*

It wasn't reassuring. His career had forced him to train insurgents to commit atrocities, fire on Federation Navy starships, even commit atrocities himself to ensure that his trainees believed that he was on their side. He still had nightmares, sometimes, about the girls he'd burned to death, just to make his credentials very clear. But this was too much. He was assisting aliens in plotting the overthrow of the Federation. The Outsiders might believe that aliens could be trusted, but he knew better. They had their own plans and schemes and none of them included humans, once the war was over.

He stepped into the training ground, pasting a cold smile on his face. It was frustrating as hell to admit, in the privacy of his own mind, that the Outsider recruits would have done well at Boot Camp. They didn't have the problems shared by many insurgents, even the simple inability to rape, pillage and burn in the right order; hell, compared to some of the men he'd trained, they were angels. But his last trainees had served a purpose and these...these could not be allowed to live. He could kill them, easily. It would end the threat they posed to the Federation. And yet it would blow his cover for nothing.

"Attention," he bellowed.

The recruits–no, they were *soldiers* now–lined up in front of him. They'd passed the first stages of training surprisingly well once he'd convinced them to obey orders. The Outsiders prized an independence of mind the Federation preferred not to tolerate. It helped that they had more self-discipline than many Earth-born children. But they'd still needed to be pushed into learning the skills they needed to stay alive.

And where, he asked himself, *are we going? Where will those skills be put to use?*

"Take your suits," he ordered, without bothering with preamble. They'd learned well enough to be given some consideration. "And prepare to enter the simulator."

He'd asked the higher-ups for details of where the Outsiders planned to attack, in the hopes the answer would be revealing. But they'd only noted that the fleet would be hitting a well-developed planet, including Asimov Point fortifications. That only narrowed the list of potential targets down to several hundred, Uzi knew. The only thing that kept Earth off the list was the certain knowledge that it would take years to get the fleet into position to attack Earth without being detected. Admiral Justinian, God damn the man, had taught the Federation Navy to watch its rear.

The soldiers donned their suits, one by one, then lumbered forward into the training simulator. Uzi monitored their progress as the simulation sprang to life, displaying an average planetary capital, complete with a pair of PDCs in position to engage the soldiers as they fell out of orbit. There were a hundred and one ways he could make the simulation unwinnable, or simply immensely costly, but he held his hand. It would only give them skills they could use in battle, when the shit *really* hit the fan.

But where were they going?

He was still mulling over the problem when the simulation came to an end. The soldiers had done well, taking the capital city in exchange for losing a mere forty of their armoured troopers. They looked pleased with themselves, Uzi noted; he didn't bother to tell them that he'd slanted the odds in their favor. There would be time enough for harder lessons when they actually hit an inhabited world.

"Very good," he said, dismissing them. "Catch some sleep. We will debrief properly in five hours."

He watched them go, then stopped as a green figure stepped into the room. Up close, the alien was just human enough to be disconcerting. It was possible, just possible, to imagine a human actually making love...he pushed the thought aside, angrily. What sort of perverted little fucker would want to make love to an *alien*? The Federation had plenty of girls who would do anything, even for a smelly antisocial basement dweller. There was no need to consider fucking an alien...

"Your men are brave," Ground Lord Ma said. "But they are not determined to win."

"They are winners," Uzi said. He'd seen enough of how the Marsha fought to know that the Federation would always have the advantage. Honor in war was all very well, but killing the enemy was much more important. Besides, it wasn't as if they could win alone, without human help. "And they completed the simulation."

"Simulations are not *real*," Ma informed him.

Uzi fought down the temptation to roll his eyes. The Marsha might not understand the gesture, but there was no point in taking chances. They'd probably studied humanity extensively, the sort of study no human would undertake for fear of being accused of having alien sympathies. It could destroy a career if word got out to the wrong person. Besides, what did one really need to know about aliens? They were determined to destroy humanity and that was all. There was no need to know anything else.

"They are the closest we can get to reality, without actually going to war," he said, instead of making sarcastic remarks. Rumor had it that the Marsha used live weapons in their drills. So did the Federation, but no one was actually *trying* to kill trainees. "It helps them learn from their mistakes."

"But there is no glory in it," Ma insisted. "They do not win if they face...*holograms*."

Uzi shrugged. "Some of them were killed in the simulation," he said. "They will survive–of course–and the next time they won't make the same mistake."

"But they will face no true punishment for failure," Ma said.

"They will be laughed at by their comrades," Uzi said, dryly. From what he'd heard, the Marsha made Flagellants look calm and reasonable. A training session didn't give anyone any real lessons until they were bruised and bloody–or dead. He could understand the value of shooting harmless but painful bullets at trainees, but not outright killing them. They would never have a chance to recover from their mistakes. "And they will have to buy the beer."

He sighed inwardly as the Ground Lord marched off. On their own, the Marsha would just run up to humanity's guns and get blasted. They would never have a chance to recover from their mistakes. But allied with the idealistic Outsiders and the cold dispassionate Insects, they would make formidable enemies. And their alliance might prove fatal to the Federation.

It had been part of his work, he mused as he walked back to his cabin, to infiltrate rebel groups and incite them into uprising, so they could be slaughtered by the Federation. And he knew, because of it, just how strongly the Federation was hated along the Rim...or even in the older colonies. The Federation needed time to breathe, time to rethink itself, time even to reform to allow the people some say in their own future. But the Grand Senate hadn't offered anything of the sort. And why not? It would have proven fatal.

It should work if we try to undermine the bastards, he thought. But the Outsiders were far from stupid. Divide and conquer tactics might not work, at least not as well as they had in the past. They knew, beyond a shadow of a doubt, just how badly the Federation would react to them, once they launched their invasion. They'd have to hang together or hang separately. And the aliens would know it too. Exterminating humanity would have to come after the war was over and done with. Until then, they would work together.

He paused outside his cabin, then stepped inside. It was tiny, but he'd had to make do with smaller sleeping spaces in the past. He sat down on the bed, then glanced at his terminal. The first message warned that the fleet would be moving to its target in two to three weeks, something that would be informative if he had the slightest idea of where they actually *were,* relative to the Federation. As it was, he had no idea which worlds were being considered likely targets.

There was a tap on the hatch. He keyed a switch, opening it to reveal Cleo Pearlman. She was young, idealistic and very easy to seduce, much to his amusement. But she also had enough regard for security to keep her mouth shut, at least when it came to operational details. It would have been admirable if it hadn't been so frustrating.

"I heard we're moving," she said. The only benefit of living among the Outsiders was that they didn't pay any attention to intimate affairs. There was no penalty for sleeping with any of them, male or female. "Are you ready?"

"Getting there," Uzi grunted. "But there's still a lot of work to do."

Chapter Eight

Martial Law. The imposition of control by a military force, imposed by authority of the Grand Senate or Federation Emergency Procedures. Military officers replace civilians at all levels, issuing orders; crime and dissent can be harshly punished.
-The Federation Navy in Retrospect, 4199

Athena, 4098

"It looks bad," Investigator Bonaventura said. "This could be the worst case of corruption since Admiral Stevenson was indicted on several *hundred* counts of molesting subordinates, gross incompetence and desertion in the face of the enemy."

Roman looked at the middle-aged woman in surprise. Admiral Stevenson had stayed in his post until Emperor Marius had assumed control of Earth and started to remove officers too loyal to the Grand Senate or too incompetent to be allowed to remain in their posts. Even then, he'd been determined to stay in command of his unit and only the detachment of a squadron of superdreadnaughts had convinced him to surrender his authority. That, and the fact–like Governor Barany–that no one would consider fighting for him. It was a minor miracle that none of his subordinates had considered mutiny before the coup.

"It's that bad?"

"Yes, sir," Bonaventura said. "It's disastrous."

She stood and activated the wall display. "Governor Barany was taking bribes from just about everyone," she said. "The local industries, for example, bribed him to cut their taxes down to the bare minimum, which weren't even paid. This funded their rapid expansion, an expansion that was utterly uneven–and yet they maintained their production rates. We now know that most of their products were purchased by parties *without* the Federation-mandated end user certificates, including weapons, advanced sensor systems and every other form of starship component. The only things he didn't seem to sell are full-sized starships.

"It gets worse. He was apparently running a protection racket as well. Starship crews and corporations that paid up were allowed to run unmolested, while ships and crews that refused to pay–or were simply unable to pay–were targeted by pirates, once they were outside the system. I can't even begin to estimate just how much damage this has done to the sector's overall economy, commodore. There are quite a few planets in real danger of collapse because they're not self-sufficient yet. Indeed, the governor was purposely delaying the shipments that would have allowed them to stand on their own two feet."

"Shit," Roman said. He'd thought he'd seen bad officers–and he'd seen a great many purged, either by the war or Emperor Marius. Now, he understood why some of his former superiors had been so cynical. "And no one gave a damn?"

"I think his patrons in the Grand Senate were receiving their full share of the proceeds," Bonaventura said, darkly. "There was certainly no incentive to remove him, despite Admiral—ah, *Emperor*—Drake's insistence that Barany was in bed with the pirates."

She paused, dramatically. "But there may be something even worse," she warned. "There were recruiting officers operating here, too. Countless spacers and mercenaries have been lured away from the planet and taken...well, we don't know where they went. But the local intelligence officers should have been tracking their movements and, instead, they dropped the ball. They could have gone anywhere."

Roman frowned. A year ago, it would have been assumed that Admiral Justinian or one of the other warlords had been recruiting as many mercenaries as he could. He'd always had a shortage of trained and experienced manpower, at least at first, and he'd been willing to pay through the nose for decent officers and men. But Justinian was dead, along with the rest of the treacherous bastards. Who would be recruiting them now?

He looked up at the display, then back at Bonaventura. "There's enough evidence to indict Barany?"

"Oh, yes," Bonaventura assured him. "There are at least seven separate counts of High Treason we could indict him for, all of which carry the death penalty."

"Have him interrogated, *thoroughly*, then have him sent back to Earth," Roman said. As tempting as it was to have the governor hurled out the nearest airlock, Emperor Drake would want to deal with him personally. "What about the remains of his administration?"

"We've suspended a number of people, but the vast majority may have had no idea of what was going on," Bonaventura said. "However, it will take years to sort out the guilty from the innocent."

The Grand Senate would have killed the whole lot of them, Roman thought. *Either to make it clear that treachery on such a scale would not be tolerated or to bury all tracks that might have led back to Earth.*

He pushed the thought to one side. "Have your people start working their way through the governor's staff," he ordered, instead. "The guilty can be shipped back to Earth too."

"Yes, sir," Bonaventura said.

Roman swung around to face Higgins, who looked uncomfortable in the briefing compartment. Roman didn't blame him. Engineers were rarely invited to high-level staff meetings.

"The alien ship," he said. "What did you find?"

"There's little to add to my original report," Higgins said. He took control of the display and put up an image of the alien vessel. "The ship was designed and built by aliens, but they very definitely used human technology. *Advanced and adapted* human technology. This was not put together by someone following rote instructions, sir. The builders understood what they were doing."

Elf leaned forward. "You're sure it wasn't built by humans to *look* alien?"

"Every human ship, even ones designed more for beauty than for practicality, is built in a similar manner," Higgins said. He seemed more comfortable, now he was talking about something he understood perfectly. "The Federation enforced standardization on every shipyard, even the ones that were sited within the old Colonial Alliance. This ship was not built in a standard human shipyard.

"Besides, there are other odd points," he continued. "The air mix is odd; humans could live there for extended periods, but there would eventually be health problems. Federation specifications insist that life support units be built to extreme standards; the designers of this ship, whoever they were, didn't invest so much effort in maintaining the atmosphere. The internal tubes are badly shaped, by our standards. Anyone larger than a ten-year-old kid would have real problems using them, even in zero-gee. No, the ship was built by alien shipwrights. And that leaves us with a problem."

"I'd say," Captain Heinz Lancelets said. *Valiant's* CO didn't look pleased. "What the hell was she doing here?"

"I checked the records," Bonaventura said. "She was, apparently, salvaged in the Rim and brought in to Athens by a local contractor. They were still bickering over the exact salvage fee when we arrived."

Roman shook his head in disbelief. The Federation Navy had a flat rate it paid for alien technology–and it was far from ungenerous. Any contractor who recovered an entire alien starship would be paid enough to buy a handful of human-built ships for himself, if he wished. And there shouldn't have been any delay over purchase, either. Once the ship was verified as being alien, it would have been purchased at once.

"The governor may have been stalling," Elf said.

"*Someone* certainly was," Bonaventura agreed. "But there's no evidence the governor even knew of the ship's existence. All such matters should have been handled by the local sector officer..."

"Who was never replaced, because of the war," Roman finished. "And whoever was left behind might have had their own reasons to stall."

"Yes, sir," Bonaventura said.

Roman thought, rapidly. There had always been rumors of new alien races lurking beyond the Rim–and the starship's presence proved that at least one undiscovered alien race *definitely* existed. And the simple fact that the starship's existence hadn't been reported to Earth, as far as they could tell, was worrying too. The aliens might already have managed to subvert the planet's government. Perhaps *they* were the ones recruiting human mercenaries for their purposes. Hell, they already knew the aliens had collaborators. The existence of so much human-derived tech proved that beyond a shadow of a doubt.

"This system should be defended," he said, slowly. He didn't aim the question at a specific officer, just tossed it out into the air. "But just how heavily defended is it, really?"

It was Elf who answered. "Poorly," she said. "I had a look at their reports and compared them against our sensor readings. Training and exercise cycles are way down, orbital fortresses are badly undermanned and the sector fleet is spread out over the sector. There was nothing larger than a heavy cruiser in this system until we arrived. The governor was more interested in plowing the sector's funds into his bank accounts than seeing to his defenses."

"Corruption has proved a major problem there too," Bonaventura added. "I have evidence that senior officers within the planetary defenses were involved in selling off pieces of military-grade hardware to civilians. Again, there were no real checks on who was actually *buying* the hardware."

Roman groaned. Pirates always lived on the margins, he knew; it was why their ships were in constant danger of falling apart at the seams. And, perhaps, why they were so brutal to their victims. But they wouldn't have been able to operate at all if they hadn't been supported by vested interests within the Federation itself. The planet that needed equipment without taxes or awkward questions being asked, the officer who wanted funds and was prepared to trade military hardware for money, the governor who wanted to run a protection racket...it was sickening.

Like above, so below, he thought, bitterly. His parents had been killed by pirates, pirates who might have been armed and trained by corrupt officials within the Federation. It had seemed a random attack...but had it really been anything of the sort? Had someone benefited from the near-complete destruction of Isogloss, with Roman the only survivor? If someone could use a pirate attack as an excuse to seize an entire planet, why not an asteroid-mining field?

But he wasn't the scared little boy or junior cadet any longer, he told himself. He could look it up in the records, the records that had been seized before the Grand Senate could destroy them. All it would take was a query to Earth. No one would try to stop him finding the truth...

...And he was woolgathering. Angrily, he forced himself to concentrate on the here and now.

"I'm going to declare martial law over the entire system," he said, firmly. It *was* within his authority, but he'd hoped never to have to use it. He'd seen too many examples of martial law being abused by Federation authorities. "The formal announcement will be made in"–he glanced at the chronometer–"four hours. By then, I want Marines at every vital location within the system and our people in command of the orbital fortresses."

"Our crews will be stretched quite thin," Bonaventura pointed out. "There are over twenty thousand men and women involved in crewing the fortresses alone."

"The Marines can supervise, if necessary," Elf said. "And the fortresses are designed to operate on reduced manpower."

"I wouldn't count on *these* fortresses being designed for anything of the sort," Lancelets said, softly. "The governor wouldn't have been able to keep so many people on the rolls if the stations could be operated with a skeleton crew."

Roman nodded. "Once the system is secure, we will start boosting the defenses as quickly as possible. I want to ensure we have a safe port, if necessary. Our plans to start aggressively patrolling within the sector will need to be put on hold, until we have a secure base. I will be contacting Emperor Marius directly, reporting the situation and requesting reinforcements."

Bonaventura gave him a sharp look. "You expect trouble?"

"Yes," Roman said, flatly. He nodded towards the image of the alien starship. "There's at least one starfaring race out there, linked to human collaborators. What do they want?"

"We could learn a great deal from them," Higgins said. "They had some new approaches to issues..."

Lancelets cut him off with a glower. "Learning from *aliens*? Are you insane?"

The captain turned to face Roman. "Commodore," he said, "I move that statement be struck from the record."

"Do it," Roman said, after a moment. Even a *hint* of alien sympathies could destroy a career, no matter the actual context. The mere presence of an alien starship built with human technology would be alarming enough. "We must assume the worst."

He sighed, inwardly. It hadn't been *that* long since he'd taken shore leave on an alien world, where he'd seen just how badly the aliens had been degraded under humanity's jackboot. They'd rebelled later, he'd heard, and he didn't blame them. The Federation might be hated and feared along the Rim, where Federation membership brought more oppression and exploitation than benefits, but aliens had the worst of it. They were, at best, nothing more than slaves. It was strikingly rare to encounter an alien away from its homeworld, outside a zoo.

And who, a nasty little voice at the back of his mind muttered, *could blame the new aliens for trying to defend themselves*?

"See to your duties," he said, tartly. The voice had to be ignored, right now. There was too much to do, rebuilding the Federation, to worry about alien rights. Something could be done later, he was sure. "Dismissed!"

Elf waited behind until the other officers had left the compartment. "Young Higgins will be in for some trouble," she observed. "That was a very intemperate remark."

"His superiors will not be pleased," Roman agreed. But Higgins was really too good an engineer to lose. "His career will survive."

"Chew him out personally," Elf suggested. "No one else will say a word to him if you chew him out first."

Roman smiled weakly, remembering his first deployment on *Enterprise*. There had been a strict pattern for young officers who happened to screw up by the numbers. They'd be chewed out by their immediate superior, then the next-ranking officer, and *then* all the way up to the XO. But if the XO happened to be the first one to chew the young man out, no one else said a word.

"I'll see to it," he said. "What do *you* make of the whole mess?"

"A mess," Elf said. "Nothing about this makes sense, Roman. That probably means there's more than one party involved, perhaps working at cross-purposes."

"The governor and...the aliens?" Roman asked. "Or insurrectionists? Or...what?"

"We may not find out for a while," Elf said. She rose to her feet, then paced over to sit next to him. "And you were right. We must be prepared for the worst."

Roman sighed. His plan had been simple enough; the superdreadnaughts would remain at Athena, while his smaller units would be assigned to convoy protection. They would aggressively chase every contact they detected, ensuring that the pirates knew there was a new game in town. Any pirates they happened to capture would be interrogated, hopefully allowing ONI to track down their bases, which might lead to rogue colonies beyond the Rim. He'd even been planning to send out new survey missions, once he had a feel for the entire sector. They might have stumbled across an entire world of rebels and started the task of bringing them under the Federation's authority.

But the plan hadn't survived contact with Governor Barany.

"They bought vast amounts of military gear," he mused. "Why would they want so *much* of it?"

It was rare, vanishingly rare, to encounter a pirate ship larger than a light cruiser. The crewing requirements were staggeringly high, beyond the capabilities of any reasonable pirate organization. Besides, the larger the ship, the more complex its operations. Pirate crews were rarely capable of handling such a ship for long, even with automated systems to assist. The pirates seemed to be purchasing material they had no logical use for, save the mere pleasure of ownership. But add in an alien race using human-derived technology and one explanation suggested itself fairly quickly. The *aliens*, not the humans, wanted the technology.

He outlined his thoughts and Elf nodded. "It makes sense," she said. "If they're trying to build up a fleet of their own, they'd need as many weapons and other pieces of hardware as they could get. And we already know they're technologically ingenious."

"Higgins made that clear," Roman said. Actually, his report had suggested the engineer was more than a little impressed with his alien counterparts. The report might have to be edited carefully before it was sent up the chain to Earth. Federation Navy HQ would be unlikely to take a calm view of it. "We definitely have to prepare for the worst."

Elf smiled, then rose to her feet and walked out of the compartment. Roman watched her go, then looked down at the reports on his datapad. There had been so much hardware flowing out of the system that he couldn't help considering it a major threat, if it was gathered together in one place. And Governor Barany hadn't helped. Even if he'd had no idea that aliens–and human collaborators–were active within his system, the sheer lack of oversight had allowed them to get their work done without interference. That would have to stop...

But cutting off their supply lines will tell them we know what they're doing, he mused. *And they might do something stupid–or dangerous...*

He tapped a switch, bringing up a star chart of the Rim. A number of worlds were tagged as having been catalogued, but not officially brought into the Federation; beyond them, there were no tags, apart from a handful of question marks. The Survey Service had been cut to the bone long before the Justinian War. Anything could be out there, anything at all.

"Record," he ordered, straightening up. "To Emperor Marius, from Commodore Garibaldi. A dangerous situation has been uncovered..."

Chapter Nine

Captain's Court. A formal venue for military court-martials. Seven active-service Captains sit in judgement over defendants, who may be of any rank. Sometimes referred to as the Admiral's Bane, as Admirals may be judged by their subordinates.
-The Federation Navy in Retrospect, 4199

Earth, 4098

"Back again, Admiral?"

Marius nodded as he stood in front of the forcefield, clasping his hands behind his back. The captive was lying on his bunk, staring up at the cold grey ceiling, resting his hands on his chest. As Marius had ordered, a barber had been allowed to visit Blake Raistlin, ensuring he looked his best for the hearing. But no one could really look their best in the bright orange jumpsuit he'd been forced to wear. No other clothes were provided for prisoners within the Federation Penal System.

"It must be a special day," Raistlin said, mockingly. "I had my hair cut. Do you know how hard my mother and the maids had to work to get my hair cut when I was a child?"

"It's truly sad to see you never grew out of being a brat," Marius said, although he knew that was unfair. Raistlin's career had been promising, despite his exalted family connections, before he'd tried to kill Marius Drake. He should have gone into starship command and wound up commanding a cruiser, like so many of the graduates from his class. "I would have thought you'd be glad of the shave."

"No one here to be impressed," Raistlin pointed out. He swung his long legs over the side of the bunk and sat upright. "No women to charm, Admiral. Not even a guard intent on having his fun with a helpless prisoner. Not even a shower room to accidentally drop my soap. Why should I bother looking nice?"

"Your trial has finally been scheduled," Marius said. "It will take place in three hours from now."

Raistlin lifted one dark eyebrow. "And how will I defend myself in a court you have packed with your supporters?"

"You will receive a fair trial," Marius said. "It's no less than you deserve."

"And did my family," Raistlin asked, "receive a fair trial?"

"They could never have had one," Marius said. He didn't regret shooting the Grand Senators, but he hadn't been worried about putting them on trial at the time. "You will have every chance to defend yourself."

Raistlin smirked. "You must be confident I can't defend myself," he said. He stood and stalked towards the forcefield, coming to a halt just before it would have thrown him back into the cell. "Or are you merely intent on watching as I die?"

Raistlin paused. "Or do you have another reason to keep me alive, admiral?"

Marius clenched his fists. Tiffany had been right. Raistlin was a skilled manipulator, even when he was on the wrong side of a prison forcefield. His words cut into Marius's soul, even though Raistlin was nearly sixty years younger than Marius himself. But no amount of words would change the fact that he was a prisoner and about to die.

"Your death will set an example," Marius said, instead. "You will be tried–fairly. You will be judged–fairly. And you will be executed–fairly."

"How very *fair*," Raistlin observed.

"The universe isn't fair," Marius snapped. "How many of your family's atrocities would have been carried out if the universe were *fair*?"

Raistlin smiled, but said nothing.

Marius turned as a hatch opened, revealing a short grey-haired man wearing a black suit and tie, rather than a military uniform. "This is Lobe Darlington," he said. "Your defense lawyer."

For the first time, he thought he saw an honest emotion on Raistlin's face. Surprise. "You actually hired a defense lawyer for me?"

"You will be tried by a Captain's Court," Marius said. He took a moment to enjoy the younger man's astonishment, then stepped back from the forcefield. "You are entitled to a defender, if you wish, or you may defend yourself. The choice is yours."

"Thank you, Emperor," Darlington said. He had an irritatingly nasal voice, which had proven surprisingly effective in the past. The Federation's justice system might be thoroughly corrupt, but a skilled lawyer could sometimes make a real difference. "If you don't mind, I need to speak with my client."

"Of course," Marius said.

"And I further wish to register a complaint about how the guards treated me as I entered the facility," Darlington continued. "They searched every inch of my body."

"This is a high-security facility," Marius said. Normally, a Captain's Court would be held on the moon, but there was no time for him to leave Earth. "And your paperwork was left untouched."

Darlington nodded, reluctantly, as he drew an old-style notebook from one of his pockets, followed by a pen. Marius puzzled over it for a moment, then realized that the notebook would be impossible to hack. The Marines at the gates would have insisted on scanning any portable terminal thoroughly, just in case it had been rigged to explode at the right moment. A notebook posed no real threat, beyond paper cuts.

"It is still a breach of my rights," Darlington said. "I..."

"...Was hired to serve as a defense attorney," Marius said. "The security requirements are a part of that, I'm afraid."

He walked towards the door, then stepped through it, resisting the temptation to shout something rude as he left. He'd always hated lawyers, hated the way they could twist the truth into a pretzel or manipulate the jury until someone who was obviously guilty was released on a technicality. God alone knew how many corrupt officials had escaped punishment because they'd been able to pay for a good lawyer. But it was important to ensure that Raistlin had a fair trial. The Federation's legal system needed to be repaired.

Three hours later, they assembled in the courtroom. It hadn't been designed to serve as a courtroom and there had been some quick changes to allow for the procedure. A long table held seven Captains, all selected by lot, while two smaller chairs and tables had been put to one side, one for the defendant and one for the prosecutor. Captain Helen Yale saluted Marius as she entered, then sat down at the prosecutor table. Moments later, Raistlin and Darlington were escorted into the room.

"He looks better than I expected," Tiffany muttered in his ear. "Where did he get that uniform?"

Marius shrugged. Raistlin wore a commander's uniform instead of the orange jumpsuit. He considered it briefly, then decided that Darlington would have asked for the uniform, or simply brought it with him when he entered the President's House. Marius hadn't forbidden him to bring anything, as long as it didn't set off the security alarms. But it was still an uncomfortable sight.

Captain Warren, the senior Captain, tapped for silence. "Commander Blake Raistlin stands accused of treason, murder of a senior officer, attempted murder of a senior officer and obeying illegal orders," he stated. There were few of the formalities seen in civilian courts. "Commander Raistlin. How do you plead?"

"Not guilty, sir," Raistlin said.

"Duly noted," Warren said. "Captain Yale?"

Helen Yale rose to her feet. "The case before us is simple," she said. "Commander Raistlin was assigned to the permanent staff of Admiral Marius Drake as his aide. He served in this role until the defeat of Admiral Justinian, whereupon he took a gun into the CIC and opened fire, resulting in the wounding of Admiral Drake and the death of General Vaughn. These facts are beyond dispute."

She paused, for effect. "Commander Raistlin is an officer in the Federation Navy," she continued. "He was commissioned as an officer six years ago, just after the Battle of Earth, when he took the second oath. As such, he has a duty to uphold both the traditions of the Federation Navy and the structures that make the Navy work. To betray his senior officer, to call into question the trust the Navy needs to function, is the act of a traitor. Is there any defense he can make that would save him from the consequences of his actions?

"Yes! There is! He will say that he was only following orders! But the orders from the Grand Senate to murder Admiral Drake were not, could not, be legal! Admiral Drake was not a declared rebel, an enemy of the Federation. He was an officer following orders who could be legitimately recalled to Earth. There were no grounds for ordering his subordinates to remove him, let alone assassinate him.

"An officer in the Federation Navy must be capable, above all, of judging the orders he receives and determining their legality. Following an illegal order makes the officer following the order an accomplice, at the very least. It certainly does not constitute an excuse! Blake Raistlin, in choosing to follow the order, stepped well over the line. I have no hesitation in asking the court for the heaviest possible penalty for his crimes."

Yale sat down. Marius watched her for a long moment, then shifted his gaze to Blake Raistlin. The younger man was sitting there, his dark face impassive, as Darlington rose to speak. There seemed to be nothing readable in his expression,

Marius noted, not even a single trace of emotion. But Raistlin was a skilled dissembler. He'd grown up in a world where deceit was as natural as breathing.

Tiffany was right, Marius thought. *I should just have had him shot.*

"I would not claim to be familiar with the military way of doing things," Darlington said, into the silence. "Ideally, a JAG officer would serve as Commander Raistlin's advocate and defender. But I do know, civilian that I am, that the military prides itself on following a chain of command. The Admiral issues an order to the Captain, the Captain issues an order to the Lieutenant and *everyone* issues orders to the Midshipman. Would that seem an acceptable description of the chain of command?"

Marius felt a flicker of disquiet. Several of the judges had smiled, very briefly.

"The Federation is not–was not–a military dictatorship," Darlington continued. "The Federation Navy took its orders from the Grand Senate, which set the outlines for military deployments, operations and funding. It was the Grand Senate that approved the rules and regulations set out for governing the Navy, even if the rules were implemented by military officers. The orders that make up the Big Red Book, as I believe it is commonly called, come ultimately from the Grand Senate."

He paused, his gaze sweeping the judges. "I do not attempt to deny that my client drew a pistol in a...*ah,* CIC...and opened fire. That, as Captain Yale says, is beyond dispute. The case file I was given included live footage, independently verified, from the CIC's monitoring suite. There is no point in trying to deny the facts of the case.

"But what can be questioned are the motivations and legalities of the act itself."

Marius felt his eyes narrowing. They *knew* the motivations. The Grand Senate had been scared of him, scared he would take Admiral Justinian's place, even though all he'd wanted to do was save the Federation. He hadn't *wanted* to overthrow the Grand Senate, he hadn't *wanted* to make himself emperor, but they'd given him no choice. It had been fight or die, with the certain knowledge that his subordinates would be purged alongside him. What choice had he had?

Darlington continued, unaware of Marius's thoughts. "Commander Raistlin received orders from the Grand Senate, from the legal source of *all* orders," he said. "Those orders were to assassinate Admiral Drake. This is not in dispute either. Again, evidence has been presented to prove that these orders were issued, beyond all shadow of a doubt. But we must ask ourselves a very simple question. Were these orders actually *illegal*?"

Marius stared at him, astonished. Beside him, Tiffany put a hand on his arm.

"The Grand Senate is the source of all orders," Darlington said, hammering the point home. "Could the Grand Senate issue an *illegal* order? Can one of their orders be illegal by definition?"

I should have had him shot, Marius thought, coldly. He tried to ignore the thought that it was hardly too late. It would be easy to issue the orders and easier still to make sure they were carried out. He'd been careful to staff the President's House with officers and men loyal to him, or to Tobias Vaughn's memory. *It might have saved us some trouble.*

"Picture it, sirs," Darlington continued. "You are a young officer. The Grand Senate is the source of all authority. Would you be in a hurry to disobey–or question–an order from the Grand Senate?"

He paused, dramatically. "Captain Yale is quite right to note that being given an illegal order does not serve as an excuse," he said. "But were the orders actually *illegal*? *That* is the question we must answer."

Marius had to bite his lip to keep from saying something, anything. He'd never considered the possibility that someone might question the illegality of the orders, yet in hindsight it was an obvious path to take. If the orders were declared *legal*, then Raistlin would have to be freed; after all, he'd only been following orders. Even the death of Marius's best friend could be explained as an accident, rather than deliberate malice. Cold hatred burned through his mind as he forced himself to sit back and *listen*, rather than trying to sway the judges himself.

Helen Yale rose to speak. "The Grand Senate was the source of all authority," she said. "I do not believe that was in dispute. However, the fact remains that the Grand Senate had legal avenues to explore, including–at worst–declaring Admiral Drake to be an outlaw. No such judgement was made, sirs."

There wouldn't have been, Marius knew. The Brotherhood, for its own inscrutable reasons, had chosen to promote Marius as a hero. There might well have been riots on Earth if the Grand Senate had moved against him openly, which didn't bode well for Raistlin's future, whatever happened. They might just have disowned him once Marius was safely dead, assuming he survived the assassination attempt. Marius's crew would probably have killed him out of hand.

"Nor did Commander Raistlin have any reason to *believe* that Admiral Drake had been outlawed," Yale said. "The procedures for declaring someone an outlaw are very clear–and they were not carried out. Indeed, there wasn't even a note to that effect in the message Commander Raistlin received. There was *no* reason for anyone to believe that Admiral Drake was anything other than a naval officer in good standing."

That sounded a convincing argument, Marius thought. But how would Darlington respond to it?

"Except that he received orders, from a *legitimate* authority, to execute Admiral Drake," Darlington said. "That would seem sufficient grounds to assume that Admiral Drake had been declared an outlaw."

"Except that such orders have to be openly propagated to be legal," Yale snapped. "The procedure for declaring someone an outlaw, as I said, is well understood. There are no grounds for anyone to assume that Admiral Drake *was* an outlaw, then or ever."

Captain Warren tapped the table and they both fell silent. "I believe it would be best to hold a recess," he said. "Both sides will need time to reformulate their defenses, assuming they both wish to continue?"

He looked at Yale, then Darlington. They both nodded.

"Then the court is dismissed," Warren said. "The prisoner will be escorted back to his cell."

Marius managed to keep his mouth closed until they returned to his office, where he sat down in his chair and swore like a Marine on his fifth deployment to a warzone.

"That *bastard*," he said. "I should have had him shot!"

"Too late now," Tiffany said. She shrugged, then pulled up a chair and sat down next to him. "It would look very bad if you just had him shot, particularly now. You couldn't claim it was done in the heat of emotion any longer."

Marius rubbed his forehead. There were times when he felt he was doomed to always be headachy, now that he was trying to rebuild the Federation. No wonder the Grand Senate had been a load of assholes, if they'd been headachy from birth till death. Or perhaps the staggering luxury was a way of distracting themselves from the realization that they, for all their power, had less control than they cared to admit. Marius knew, all too well, just how long it took to get orders from one side of the Federation to the other. The warlords had enjoyed a kind of limited autonomy long before they'd started to rebel.

"I screwed up, didn't I?"

"Maybe," Tiffany said. She'd always been more aware of the legalities of any situation, having been trained by her father. "But if you want to make a point, if you want to prove that trials are actually fair, you have to let the process play out until the end."

"Yeah," Marius said. But the hell of it was that the judges would have their doubts. If the Grand Senate could legally do anything, could they actually issue an illegal order? And if the order wasn't illegal, what grounds did they have for holding Raistlin? "He still killed Tobias, after all."

He sat back in his chair, then glanced at the terminal. A new set of reports from the industries, warning him of production bottlenecks and work slow-downs in the wake of the collapse of the Grand Senate. The new/old managers had barely been found and sent back to work. God alone knew what would happen when they started trying to compete against newcomers to the field.

It will work out for the best, he told himself, firmly. He had to believe it. *And the Federation will be freer than ever.*

He sighed. "What's next on the agenda?"

"A deputation from Castile Sector," Tiffany said. If she was annoyed at being treated like a secretary, she didn't show it. "They want to discuss their future, now that Admiral Roper is dead."

"They supported him," Marius said. Admiral Roper–another rogue warlord–hadn't lasted long, but he'd distracted the Grand Senate from concentrating everything against Admiral Justinian. "What should we do with them?"

"You'll have to decide," Tiffany said. "And I suggest you decide quickly."

Chapter Ten

One of the unfortunate truths of military operations is that true surprise is very rare. When one side gets surprised, it tends to be because they missed something that hinted at the coming disaster and the other side got lucky.
-The Federation Navy in Retrospect, 4199

Base One, 4098

"That's the last of our squadrons, sir," Lieutenant Juneau reported. "And just in time."

General Charlie Stuart nodded, slowly. God alone knew what the Marsha had been thinking when they'd lost a starship and failed to report it to the rest of the Outsiders. No, he knew what they'd been thinking. Losing a starship was akin to losing honor and they couldn't afford to do that, not when it would be quite costly. But it had also sacrificed the advantage of surprise.

It had taken years to build up the Outsider Navy, but he was uneasily aware that the Federation still had a considerable advantage. On one hand, the chance to bring overwhelming power to bear against the Federation's Fifth Fleet was a godsend; on the other, it had the prospect of doing serious harm to his fleet while the remainder of the Federation Navy rapidly mobilized. And with a *competent* emperor on Earth, there would be none of the diversions caused by the Grand Senate. The full weight of the Federation would be brought to bear on the Outsiders.

But if we don't move, we will be discovered, he thought. The lost starship alone ensured it. It wouldn't be long before Fifth Fleet started hunting in earnest for the mystery aliens, once they'd reinforced Athena. The war would become chancier at the worst possible moment. *And if we are discovered, we will be lost.*

Charlie knew, without false modesty, that the Federation would consider them dangerous criminals at best, renegades, terrorists and traitors at worst. There would be no mercy, if they were discovered. He would be killed, along with everyone else who had been involved in building up the Outsider Federation. And both the Marsha and the Insects would be exterminated. Collectively, they were a dangerous foe. The Federation would consider them too dangerous to live.

But the timing was badly wrong, he knew. The fleet had intended to have a great deal of support on the ground. And a number of planets had revolutionary cells that were ready to liberate themselves from the Federation. But there was no time to alert the rebels. Instead, they would have to make do with what the advance agents could muster when the shit hit the fan.

No plan ever survives contact with the enemy, he reminded himself.

"Record," he ordered. "It is my belief that the current situation on Athena can only develop to our disadvantage. Governor Barany was a useful fool. This newcomer can hardly be more advantageous to us. It is my intention, therefore, to issue the start order in two days from now. We will enter the Athena System seven hours later and engage the enemy."

He took a breath. "Training schedules will slip," he added, "but I feel we are ready to move on our targets. We will have the firepower advantage, as well as some new surprises. We will give them hell."

Tapping a switch, he saved the message and then sent it to the courier boat. It would be on its way to Sanctuary within the hour, but by the time it arrived at its destination the war would already be underway. They'd assumed as much, when they'd hashed out the final steps of the plan, yet it still bothered him. He would have preferred to have the council with him when he gave the order.

Independent command, he thought, sardonically. *Every commander in the Federation Navy would give his balls for the degree of independent authority you've been granted. And that will help ensure our victory.*

He shook his head. Fifty years of careful preparation and planning, twenty years of building up a fleet that could challenge the Federation Navy...and it was all about to be tested for the first time. There had been no way to carry out proper tests, not really, and simulations could only go so far. Now...the shit was definitely about to hit the fan and he had no way to be sure that everything would go according to plan. And if it didn't...?

"All command staff, report to Briefing Room A in twenty minutes," he ordered, keying his console. "We have an operation to plan."

ꙮ

Uzi had been midway through yet another training simulation when the holograms had frozen, then blinked out of existence completely. He'd wondered, in a moment of horror, if someone had deduced his identity and sent soldiers to try to arrest him, before the message started playing through the overhead speakers. All simulations and training exercises were cancelled; trainees were to return to their barracks, while commanding officers and trainers were to report to the briefing compartment. Uzi couldn't help feeling a shiver running down his spine as he dismissed his men, then followed the other trainers through the ship. It sounded as though the Outsiders were finally ready to begin their war.

The briefing compartment was jam-packed with officers, both dedicated Outsiders and mercenaries. Uzi joined the latter, knowing the former wouldn't accept him, even though they'd be better sources of information. But it wasn't really a surprise. The dedicated had always had their doubts about those who fought for money, no matter how trained and experienced they were. And in his case, he had to admit, they were right.

He looked up and down the ranks of mercenaries, committing names and faces to the recording implant in his mind. They'd be checked against the Federation's files, when–if–he made it home, then charged with high treason for assisting aliens as well as Outsiders. He wondered, absently, if any of them were also operatives from the Federation, but dismissed the thought with some irritation. There was no way to know–and besides, he *shouldn't* know. His implants were supposed to be impossible to hack, but there was no such thing as a complete impossibility. What he didn't know he couldn't betray.

"If I could have your attention," a voice said, from the front of the room. "This will be a short meeting."

There was a long pause as General Erskine stepped up to the podium. He was a tall man, with short brown hair and a beard that had been neatly trimmed close to his skin. For some reason, the Outsiders were less worried about grooming than the Federation, something that bothered Uzi even though they were relentlessly practical. Maybe it was a sense of independence, or maybe it was just an attempt to set themselves apart from the Federation.

"The offensive will be launched in two days," the General said. "This fleet will depart from here to Target One."

Uzi kept his face expressionless, as did most of the mercenaries. The Outsiders, less used to concealing their feelings, showed a mixture of anticipation and fear. He didn't blame them for the latter. No matter how much training they'd had, they weren't ready for actual combat. They wouldn't get over the fear until they'd actually seen the elephant and spat in his eye.

But General Erskine has seen the elephant, Uzi thought. He was sure of it, even though he'd never been able to identify the man. *And where did he serve?*

"We will be starting tailored simulations tomorrow, then continuing right up until the moment the fleet hits the Phase Limit," General Erskine continued. "And some of you have to make a decision."

He looked down at the mercenaries. "We hired you to train our people as well as fight for us," he said. "I understand that not all of you were enthusiastic about fighting the Federation. If you wish to back out, you will be held on a safe world until the war comes to an end or we can release you without compromising our security. However, there will be no further chance to change your mind. You either leave now or you will remain with us until the end of the war."

Win or lose, Uzi thought. He'd stay, of course. There was nothing he could do for the Federation on a safe world, assuming the Outsiders didn't simply plan to kill them out of hand, once they were useless. It would be hard to blame them. Mercenaries went where the money was and the Federation had a great deal of money. And, if they were hired, they might prove to be chatterboxes as well.

He looked at the other mercenaries, silently gauging their thoughts. Some would be worried about fighting the Federation directly, knowing that it would mean certain death if they were captured, others would be worried about serving paymasters who might lose the war. The Federation–his lips quirked at the thought–could hardly be expected to uphold any claims made by disgruntled mercenaries who'd been fighting on the wrong side. If the Outsiders lost, any chances of payment would be lost with them.

As would any chance of maintaining the old mercenary structure, Uzi thought. The Federation had tolerated it because the alternative was driving the whole system underground–and besides, mercenaries came in handy from time to time. It would hardly be the first time he'd intercepted a Grand Senator trying to hire mercenaries for use against his rivals, or insurrectionists, or merely workers who wanted a fair deal. *They could lose everything if they're caught fighting the Federation.*

"The shuttle is already prepped for departure," General Erskine concluded. "Those of you who wish to depart may proceed to the shuttlebay prior to 1800, when the shuttle will depart for a safer place. The remainder of you can report back here in an hour for a more elaborate briefing."

Uzi checked his internal chronometer. Unsurprisingly, the elaborate briefing would take place just after the shuttle had left. Anyone who wanted to remain behind with the fleet would be held in the brig, if they balked too late. He silently calculated their chances as a third of the mercenaries headed for the hatch leading to the shuttlebay, then gave it up as a fool's effort. There was no way to calculate the odds without knowing the target.

The briefing resumed an hour later. This time, the mercenaries and the Outsiders mingled together.

"The target is Athena," General Erskine said. He ignored a handful of muttered oaths from the mercenaries. They'd known they'd be going after a big world, but not the sector capital itself. "Our objective will be to secure the facilities on the ground intact, if possible. That would have been easy if the previous governor hadn't been replaced by a military officer, one Commodore Garibaldi."

Uzi had to fight to conceal his surprise. Commodore *Garibaldi*? Was it the same Garibaldi who had delivered them to Hobson's Choice? Or was it someone who happened to bear the same name? There were millions of spacers serving in the Federation Navy. It wasn't beyond belief that the name was nothing more than a coincidence. But it hardly mattered, he knew all too well. He had to play his role to the bitter end.

And if that means firing on the Federation Navy, he thought, *I will have no choice but to obey.*

"As it is, we must expect some hard fighting," General Erskine warned. "Commodore Garibaldi may have some reason to believe we will be coming."

Uzi was tempted to ask why they were even attacking Athena, if the attack was no longer a surprise. But a check of his internal databanks revealed the answer. Athena was a sector capital because it held five Asimov Points, two of which led deeper into the Federation. In Outsider hands, it allowed fleets to stab deep into the Federation's guts; in Federation hands, it would allow the Federation Navy to mass its forces for a deep strike into the unknown. No, Athena could not be left untouched.

"We will pass over the naval side of the action," General Erskine said. "The landing plans are as follows..."

He was definitely no amateur, Uzi decided, after an hour of going through the landing places, piece by piece. There was more rote behaviour called for than he would have preferred–he knew, all too well, that rote behaviour was predicable behaviour–but there was little choice. The Outsiders didn't have many experienced officers, outside the mercenaries. And besides, who in their right mind would trust the mercenaries indefinitely?

"Remember, we're coming to liberate these people," General Erskine concluded. "I will not tolerate any abuse of the local population, whatever the cause. Anyone responsible will face immediate court martial, followed by death if found guilty. I will not sacrifice their goodwill on the altar of expediency."

Good thought, Uzi thought, coldly. He'd known commanding officers who'd turned a blind eye to their troops misdeeds, either out of a misplaced sense of loyalty or simply a desire to avoid being blamed for whatever had gone wrong. It was sour in his mouth, but he couldn't help feeling a flicker of admiration for the older man. Not everyone would have been so honest, or brutally determined to avoid disaster.

But he knew the mercenaries weren't likely to pose a problem. They'd been drilled in the Mercenary Code from the moment they joined a mercenary force. No one wanted to risk the Federation Navy coming after them for committing atrocities. The Outsiders, on the other hand, would be fired up after their first battle...and probably unready for the multi-sided chaos they were likely to encounter on liberated worlds. It was then that even the most capable force tended to commit atrocities.

He listened to the final words of encouragement, then stamped back to his cabin and spent the next hour modifying the simulation. There was no point in showing anything but complete commitment to the cause, not now. As he worked, part of his mind worried over the problem of getting word to the Federation. There had to be a way to send a warning...but, no matter how he looked at it, he couldn't find one. The starship crews were carefully isolated from the ground troops, and he didn't have the command codes to operate a ship. All he could do was wait and see what happened when they arrived at Athena.

Carefully, he started to compile everything he'd seen, heard and recorded into a single file, which he stored in his internal datanodes. As soon as there was a chance to take control of the communication system and send the message, he would, despite the risks. It was the only way he could think of to get a message back to the Federation.

But, no matter what he did, he couldn't see any way of getting a message back earlier.

There was a tap on the hatch. Cleo stepped inside, looking lovely–and tired.

"It's been a long day," she said. "But we're finally moving!"

"Yes, we are," Uzi said. He'd seen more combat than anyone else on the ship, with the possible exception of General Erskine. It was nothing to be excited about, not really. Cleo didn't realize it in her bones yet, but there was a possibility that she would be dead in three days, along with the rest of the crew. "And we have a shitload of work to do."

Cleo sat down next to him, then eyed the display. "What's that?"

"That is what the politically-correct called a multi-sided conflict zone," Uzi said. "Anyone with any sense, however, would call it a shitstorm. There are too many factions involved for us to sort out who's on what side. This faction"–he prodded the map–"might turn on *that* faction, then attempt to manipulate us into getting rid of its enemies. And *that* faction might hate us so much it launches suicide attacks, just to get at us."

"I don't understand," Cleo said. "Federation loyalists?"

Uzi shrugged. "Some of them, maybe," he said. The Federation would have some supporters, if only among those who had done well under its rule. "Others will want power for themselves, or merely fight because they don't know what's going on. Some of them will definitely fight us."

He sighed, inwardly. It would probably help the Federation if he *did* encourage atrocities. And it would be easy, too. A few words in the right set of ears and there would be an outbreak of looting, raping and burning that would ensure the locals were inclined to welcome the Federation Navy when it returned to Athena. But it wasn't something he *wanted* to do, even without the risk of being caught and exposed. It would be disastrous in the long run.

"We're their friends," Cleo said, shocked. She had no real experience of life in the Federation. She was an Outsider, after all, born in a hidden colony somewhere beyond the Rim. "Why would they fight us?"

"A beaten dog will often stay with its master," Uzi said. Psychology had always interested him. What made some men rebels, some men terrorists and some men slaves, doing nothing even as they were tortured, raped and killed by their masters? "And they may see us as just another set of masters. What we need to do, to secure our position, might well be seen as an attempt to take power for ourselves."

Idly, he wondered how the Outsiders planned to solve that problem, assuming they won the war. The Grand Senate had become a nightmare, at least in part, because of the problem of trying to run the entire Federation from Earth. It simply wasn't an easy task. The Outsiders would have the same problem, at least to some extent. They could declare the worlds to be independent, he suspected, but who would protect humanity then?

No one, he thought. The aliens would be free, ready to rebuild their forces and wreak their revenge on humanity. *And that might be what they want.*

Chapter Eleven

One of the Grand Senate's many problems was that it took months to get news from the Rim, then longer still to get orders out there, while the situation might already have moved on before the Grand Senate ever heard of it. This ensured that problems along the Rim tended to get out of hand before Earth ever knew they were underway.
-The Federation Navy in Retrospect, 4199

Athena, 4098

"There's no point in worrying now," Elf said.

Roman sighed. It had been a week since Governor Barany had been dispatched to Earth, along with a report that would ensure the only reception he got was a date with the hangman, but too much had happened since then. The security investigation had turned up too many potential problems for him to relax, ranging from hundreds of officers who had taken bribes to officers who might have connections with rebels or insurgents from across the sector. It was starting to look as though the Federation would have to relieve every last officer in the system and replace them with newcomers. And that would cause a riot.

"I thought I was used to complex systems" he muttered. Catching enough time to nap in his quarters with Elf had been hard enough. "This is a nightmare."

Elf snorted. "You grew up on an asteroid and moved to the navy, where everyone moves to the beat of the same drum," she said. "How much do you know about life on a planetary surface?"

"Little," Roman conceded. Even the largest asteroid habitat rarely held more than twenty thousand inhabitants. Even the giant asteroid settlements of Sol were spread out over several hundred asteroids. There was no room for separate factions on an asteroid–or a navy starship. "I may have underestimated the task."

"You probably did," Elf said. She sat upright, then reached for her jacket. "There will always be people with interests that might conflict with yours, even though you're meant to be in command. Their interests will lead them to oppose you. You just have to cope with them, or keep a sharp eye on their activities and prune off the most dangerous. Not everyone is a nail who needs to be struck with a hammer."

Roman turned to look at her, admiring the muscles in her arms. "So what do you advise I do?"

"Hang on, watch what happens and make it clear you intend to be a fair-minded person," Elf said. She shrugged. "Change is always disturbing, Roman, all the more so when the average person has good reason to fear that it won't be for the better. The Federation does not have a good reputation for treating the folks here very well."

"It wouldn't be so bad if they didn't work with the pirates," Roman pointed out, tartly.

"They didn't choose their governor," Elf reminded him. "In many ways, Barany was a good Governor. He didn't feel the urge to throw his weight around, like so many others, nor did he squash free enterprise mercilessly. The people who live on Athena don't give a damn about his protection rackets and his sales to people with dubious motives, Roman. They only care about what they can see...and what they can see is that the governor is better than many others they've had, over the years. Why wouldn't they be worried when you removed him?"

Roman suspected she had a point. When he'd been a junior officer, he hadn't really given a damn about anything that had happened away from his own ship. It had been, at best, a matter of academic interest. And it would have been even less so, he thought, if there hadn't been a war on. Life in the peacetime navy had been dreadfully dull, unless one had been assigned to the Rim. Every cadet had hoped for such a posting. And then Admiral Justinian had made his move.

But if he'd been unconcerned about other starships, why would the population of Athena give a damn about the smaller colonies, the ones raided by the pirates?

Human nature, he told himself. *Always concentrate on what's right in front of your face.*

"They'll just have to see how little we intend to change," he said, finally. "We're not going to slap new taxes on free enterprise, are we?"

"They don't know that," Elf explained. "And you won't be governor indefinitely. Once Earth learns of what's happened, someone else will be sent out to pick up the task. That person might be a complete bastard, no matter his intentions, as far as the locals are concerned. He might demand a total crack-down on everything that will shatter the local economy."

Roman grunted. Economics were hardly his thing, but he'd grown up on an asteroid, where everything had to be carefully regulated. If Athena was producing more than the system–or the legitimate buyers in the sector–could absorb, what would happen to the economy? Even a demand for proper end user certificates might be disastrous. It was possible, he told himself, that Athena might end up shipping supplies deeper into the Federation, but they'd face increasingly heavy competition. God knew more than a few asteroid colonies had been ruined by laws specifically enacted against them by the Grand Senate.

Emperor Marius won't be enacting such laws, he thought. But Elf was right. None of the people on the planet below had any reason to believe that, did they? As far as they were concerned, Marius Drake was just another warlord, one who had played for time and, in the end, won everything. It wasn't true, Roman was sure, but it might not matter. Perception could mean everything when people had to gamble with their lives.

Elf stood upright and paced over to the porthole, staring down at the blue-green world below the ship. After a moment, Roman stood up and walked over to join her, wrapping his arm around her waist. Part of him marvelled at how perfect her body was, not a single piece of fat or anything that detracted from her work; the remainder looked down at the planet and tried to imagine the surface teeming with life. From high orbit, it was impossible to see any traces of human civilization.

"Planets are *huge*," Elf said, as if she'd read his thoughts. "Do you know, sometimes, that the Grand Senate used to send a regiment or two of Marines to hold an *entire* planet?"

Roman choked off a laugh. A regiment was a thousand Marines, assuming full strength. And the war had left many units dangerously undermanned. Armed and armored, the Marines could practically go wherever they wanted to go, but they would never be able to hold ground, at least once they had to move on to the next target. They could secure a PDC or a city, but not an entire planet. The thought was laughable.

"They saw the star charts," Elf said. "Each of the planets look *small* on the charts, when the charts show entire star clusters and transit lanes. But when you come up to a planet and actually try to land...well, that planet becomes very large indeed, on our scale. Down below, there are millions of settlers, more than enough to develop hundreds of different factions. It is hard to grasp just how many there are until you actually immerse yourself in the planet's society."

"I know," Roman said. "There are just too many of them."

He sighed. The basic intelligence sweep had turned up hundreds of factions, from Federation loyalists to people who would support the Federation if the *status quo* remained unchanged to people who hated the Federation and wouldn't shed a tear if it collapsed into civil war. It was hard to tell just how much of the hostile chatter on the planetary datanet–Governor Barany hadn't installed any limiters at all–was real and how much was just blowing off steam. And a harsh response to someone who was essentially harmless might spark off an uprising from people who were *far* from harmless. It was difficult to know what to do.

"You will never get rid of them," Elf predicted dryly, "short of total planetary destruction and mass slaughter. And I submit, Roman, that that would not be a good idea."

Roman shuddered. Even if he had been inclined to consider it, Emperor Marius would have had his head. He'd been furious when the Grand Senate's men had slaughtered prisoners after he'd guaranteed their safety personally. Roman didn't want to think about the emperor's reaction to a destroyed planet. Too many civilian lives had already been lost in the Justinian War.

"No, it wouldn't," he agreed. He glanced at the holographic display, then noted the time and smiled to himself. There were several hours before they had to return to duty. "Come back to bed?"

Elf smiled back at him, but shook her head. "I need to get back to the barracks," she said. "There's too much paperwork to do."

"Something to mention to the emperor," Roman said, with a sigh. "A ban on paperwork. Or a return to the days when commanders had personal assistants and stewards."

"You would have no privacy," Elf pointed out, as she pulled on her uniform. "And he would probably sell his memoirs to the tabloids."

"I grew up on an asteroid," Roman reminded her. "And then I was at the Academy. What is this *privacy* concept again?"

Elf snorted. "Try sharing a barracks with a hundred sweaty smelly Marines in various states of undress," she said. "It doesn't get worse than that, really."

"So I've heard," Roman said. He ducked the pillow she threw at him with practiced ease. "I thought it would be worse in foxholes."

"Nah," Elf said. "When you're in a foxhole, and the enemy is firing at you, and mortar shells are dropping down all around you, and pieces of dirt and mud are flying everywhere...you're just glad to be there."

ꝏ

There was nothing remarkable about Athena's star from a distance. It was just another white light, burning endlessly against the inky darkness of outer space. General Charlie Stuart examined the star as his fleet slowly entered formation on the outer edge of the target system, then forced himself to sit back and relax. It would be hours before they went into action for the first time, when they would discover if the years of effort had been worthwhile or not. Until then, all he could do was wait.

"The fleet has completed its arrival, sir," Lieutenant Juneau reported. "Laser links have been established. Fleet relay communications are online and operating at acceptable levels. No reports of major malfunctions."

"Good," Charlie said. "Inform all commanding officers that stealth protocols are to remain in effect–and we will cloak in"–he glanced at his chronometer–"four hours from now, unless we receive an update from the watching spies."

"Aye, sir," Lieutenant Juneau said.

Charlie looked up at the scene as the fleet slowly settled into formation. The continuous displacement stardrive was a remarkable invention, allowing humanity to bypass the tyranny of the Asimov Point network and settle worlds that had previously only been accessible through STL travel through normal space, but it had its limitations. For reasons best known to the boffins, it couldn't be used within a certain distance of *anything* that cast a gravity field. Worse, a ship that happened to be traveling at FTL speeds when it encountered a gravity field would simply vanish. No one knew what happened to those ships; unsurprisingly, no one wanted to try and find out the hard way. The Outsider fleet had had no choice, but to come out of FTL quite some distance from their target.

But at least we're not approaching along a predictable course, he thought. War along the Asimov Point network consisted of a series of incredibly costly assaults through the points, where one side *knew* where the other had to appear and had ample opportunity to pick the assault fleet off, one by one. The sheer carnage of an assault into the teeth of enemy defenses had to be seen to be grasped, which was at least partly why the Inheritance Wars had dragged on for so long. Only the invention of the stardrive had shifted the balance of power decisively in favour of the Federation.

It had also changed the face of basic military strategy. Now, an attacker could come from anywhere. Admiral Justinian would never have managed to attack Earth if he hadn't succeeded in crossing the icy vastness of interstellar space. He couldn't have bribed his way past the defenses of the Gateway–and his rebellion would have been detected long before he was in a position to threaten the Grand Senate itself. If it hadn't taken years to cross the immensity of the Federation with stardrive, rather than Asimov Points, the war might have been won or lost years ago.

But now it presented his opponent with a tactical headache. Defend the planets or defend the Asimov Point leading back to the Federation?

"We picked up an update from the stealth ships," Lieutenant Juneau said, breaking into his thoughts. "The Fifth Fleet is assembled at Athena."

Charlie swung round to look at the tactical display. It was several hours–at least–out of date, but it was the best he was going to get until the fleet approached its target. The Federation Navy ships were clustered around the planet, apart from a handful that seemed to be escorting freighters in and out of the system. It was a tempting target, and part of him yearned to take the fleet directly to Athena, but he knew better. A direct attack on the planet might cost them the war.

"Pass the word," he ordered. "We will proceed with Plan Theta."

"Aye, sir," Lieutenant Juneau said. If she was disappointed–or relieved–she didn't show it. Instead, she worked her console, sending the signal to the rest of the fleet. "Message sent."

"We leave in one hour," Charlie added. "The fleet is to cloak prior to bringing up our drives."

He sighed, inwardly. The fleet's cloaking devices were–they thought–an improvement on the Federation's pre-war designs. But no one was sure just how far the Federation had advanced during the Justinian War. Far too many of the Grand Senate's security measures, intended to keep out the rogue admiral's spies, had managed to keep out the Outsiders as well. And besides, Fifth Fleet had a hardcore of experienced officers, tacticians and sensor operators. They'd have the instincts they needed to interpret vague flickers of energy and deduce the presence of a cloaked ship.

Good thing we're not planning to sneak up on Fifth Fleet, he thought. *That could have proven exciting–and fatal.*

"Aye, sir," Lieutenant Juneau said, again. "I should note, sir, that we have picked up no trace of sensor platforms."

Charlie nodded. Only the richest of systems could afford a network of sensor platforms at the edge of the gravity limit–and Athena, despite the Governor's best efforts, couldn't have hoped to put a comprehensive network together. Not, he knew, that it would have guaranteed anything. Earth had had a comprehensive sensor network and Admiral Justinian had waltzed right through it, without even giving a *hint* of his presence. If he hadn't tried to be clever and decapitate Earth's defenses before he arrived, he might have won the battle and the war.

"My orders stand," he said. They'd dropped out of stardrive well below the system plane, where most starships would choose to arrive for a least-time course to Athena itself, just in case the reports had been wrong and the governor wasn't so inclined to take chances with the planet's security. But then, the worst he'd ever had to fear was pirates. No pirate in his right mind would tangle with even outdated battlestations. "We don't want to take chances."

"Aye, sir," Lieutenant Juneau said.

Charlie nodded and forced himself, again, to relax. One way or the other, they were committed now. Right across the Rim, small squadrons of starships, insurgent cells and even single-person operatives were getting the command to go into action. The Federation had faced uprisings before, but never anything on this scale. Even the Inheritance Wars, as bloody as they'd been, had never been on such a scale. Maybe even the Grand Senate would have grown sick of the slaughter if they had.

"The fleet has responded," Lieutenant Juneau said. She sounded relieved, although she should have known better. Charlie had no intention of biting heads off for asking questions, particularly ones that might expose problems *before* they were used against him. "They're ready to move on your command."

"Send the signal," Charlie ordered. At the speed of light, the radio signal would still take seven hours to reach its destination. But it would beat the fleet there by nine hours. "Tell them to move at the designated time."

He shook his head slowly as the timer started to tick down to zero. The Federation had been foolish to leave so many people convinced that it was evil and utterly untrustworthy, even now an emperor had replaced the Grand Senate. There was so much hatred along the Rim that countless worlds could be trusted to simply fall into Outsider hands the moment the fleet appeared in their system. Hell, there were rebel cells within the inner worlds, cells that wanted their own independence, no matter the cost. It was just a shame they hadn't been able to subvert many officers from the Federation Navy. In the wake of the Justinian War, even contacting an officer had been deemed too risky. The Grand Senate's security measures had seen to that.

"The fleet is ready to cloak," Lieutenant Juneau said. "Sir?"

"Cloak us," Charlie ordered. He sat upright, slowly. On the display, seven squadrons of superdreadnaughts and hundreds of smaller ships slowly dimmed as they activated their cloaking devices. Beyond them, the fleet train waited. It would either join them in the system after a victory or run back to the Beyond, if the fleet lost. "And then take us into the system, as planned."

Chapter Twelve

One of the gravest threats to any system is internal subversion. An outside attack can force the system to surrender, after punching through the defenses, but internal treachery can deliver the system and its facilities into enemy hands.
-The Federation Navy in Retrospect, 4199

Athena, 4098

Corporal Mark Canty rather enjoyed the posting to *Big Brick*, as her crew affectionately called the outdated battlestation. Sure, it wasn't duty on a planet's surface, where the Marines might find themselves patrolling one day and helping to find a missing child the next, but it was surprisingly enjoyable. The station's CO might have been relieved of command for what had been termed gross incompetence–Mark had heard that it was rather worse than mere incompetence–yet the remainder of the crew seemed surprisingly welcoming. Maybe they hadn't liked their former commander very much.

It wasn't a challenging duty, either. The platoon of Marines were merely expected to rotate between the CIC and their quarters, keeping an eye on the station's crew. Mark suspected that they were merely there to remind the crew that there *was* a Federation out there, when most of them might have forgotten it since the system had been cut off by the war. There weren't enough Marines to take over and operate the station on their own, if it were deemed necessary. It bothered the lieutenant enough that he'd sent at least three messages back to the fleet, requesting reinforcements. But there were none to be had.

He stood outside the hatch leading into the CIC and tried to keep himself from dozing off. Guard duty was the worst, in his opinion; he still recalled the Drill Instructors yelling at him and his fellow recruits when they'd fallen asleep on duty. If the insurgents had discovered them, the instructors had bellowed, they would have had their throats cut before they had a chance to wake up and defend themselves. It wasn't one of his finest memories from Boot Camp. But it was hard to remain alert when the station crew seemed completely harmless.

The hatch opened, revealing a pair of officers in the bright red uniforms of the local system defense force. It made them looked ghastly, in Mark's opinion, but he kept that thought to himself. Besides, the form-fitting uniforms worn by female officers were keepers, even if they *did* prove that the system defense force didn't plan on doing any actual *fighting*. It was the little miniskirts some of the juniors wore that made him certain of it.

"Still on duty, Marine?" One of the officers asked. "Isn't it boring out here?"

"It has its moments," Mark said. They were meant to be friendly, after all. "And it could be worse."

"Very true," the officer agreed. "Good luck."

They strode off down the corridor, chatting about nothing in particular. Mark eyed their backs, then forced himself back into guard position. It *was* boring, without even the prospect of boredom being suddenly transformed into screaming terror. He heard the sound of someone else entering the corridor and tilted his head, then smiled as he caught sight of Yolanda Flanna. She was a young girl, barely out of her teens, wearing a miniskirt so short that he could see the bottom of her ass. It said a great deal about the former CO, the Marines had quietly agreed, that he'd brought Yolanda onto the station in the first place...*and* that she'd stayed on the station when he'd been relieved of duty and sent elsewhere. Playing at being a maid, and carrying mugs of coffee from one duty station to another, was better than staying with her former superior. Mark didn't blame her in the slightest.

"Hi," he said.

He'd tried to court her–all of the Marines and most of the station staff had tried to court her–but she'd been unreceptive. Maybe it was hard to blame her for that too. He was fresh out of Boot Camp, yet some of the tales told by the old sweats had chilled him to the bone. A Drill Sergeant Nasty type, ready to threaten extreme punishment for even the slightest mistake, was preferable to some of the bluebloods who occupied high command positions in the Federation Navy, the ones who took advantage of their subordinates for their own sick pleasure. Thankfully, the war had gotten rid of most of *those*.

"Hi," Yolanda said. She held up her tray, holding a dozen steaming mugs of coffee. "Would you like one of these?"

"I'm on duty," Mark said, reluctantly. Coffee sounded very nice right now. He was having quite enough trouble keeping his eyes open without it. "How strong is it?"

"Military-grade," Yolanda said. She waggled the tray invitingly. "I made an extra one for you."

Mark hesitated, then took one of the mugs. The coffee was black, no sugar, just as he'd been taught to like it in Boot Camp. Yolanda gave him a smile as he sipped the coffee–it tasted suitably foul–then stepped up to the hatch, which hissed open. Mark watched her go–she was worth watching–then sighed inwardly as the hatch hissed closed. He turned back to his post, drinking the coffee quickly before the lieutenant could arrive...

And then a sudden wave of tiredness overcame him. Before he could catch himself, before he could do anything, even trigger the emergency alert, he collapsed. He was asleep before his body hit the floor.

ஐ

It had taken months to get herself assigned to the crew, Yolanda recalled, as the CIC staff collapsed at their consoles. The former CO had been a man of very few charms and a passionate liking for sexual activities that might not have been *technically* illegal, but would still cause problems for him if they ever became public. Getting him to take her on as his stewardess–a thinly-disguised term for mistress–had been simple enough. Enduring his company long enough for her superiors to finally come take the system had been much harder. There had been quite enough days when she'd seriously considered arranging an accident for the bastard. It would have been easy. He'd never thought of her as anything beyond a pair of tits on legs.

And then he'd been removed from command. She'd almost found herself crying and laughing when she'd heard the news. He hadn't been relieved for perversions, particularly perversions that would have made him a suitable candidate for blackmail, but for gross incompetence. To be fair, he *was* grossly incompetent. But it had come far too close to ruining all her work. Thankfully, no one had questioned why she'd wanted to remain on the battlestation. They'd been so grateful for her quiet assistance that no one had bothered to insist she leave.

She sat down in front of the tactical station and started to type commands into the system. It should have been inaccessible without the proper command codes, but–thanks to the former commander's carelessness–she had access to all areas, without needing a hacking chip that might have been detected by the Marines. He'd definitely never taken her seriously. Piece by piece, she locked down the system and then started to purge the databanks. It would take weeks of effort to undo what she'd done, even if the crew realized the scale of the disaster at once. By then, the battle for Athena would have been won or lost.

Smiling to herself, she linked the battlestation into the overall planetary command net and started to upload chaos software. It had been six years since Admiral Justinian had used a similar tactic, she knew, and the results were unlikely to be wholly effective. But it would provide a distraction, even if it didn't knock out the entire system. And that was what she needed to do.

ജ്ഞ

"Commodore, this is Palter. We just picked up a FLASH alert from Asimov Point One."

Roman swore, then pushed the datapad aside. "What level of alert?"

"Priority Two," Palter said. "Someone infected the battlestation command network with chaos software. There are additional reports of shootings and uprisings on other battlestations and at least one of them has dropped out of the network completely."

"Understood," Roman said. He thought, rapidly. The Asimov Point was two light-hours from the planet itself. By now, the situation might have resolved itself–or blossomed rapidly out of control. And no one would reveal their assets on the battlestations without being sure it would be worthwhile. "Bring the fleet to full alert, then launch a spread of drones. I want this region of space quartered until we know it's clear."

"Aye, sir," Palter said.

"And dispatch a squadron of fast battlecruisers to the Asimov Point," Roman added. The modern battlecruisers were the fastest ships in his fleet, capable of even outrunning destroyers when their wind was up. "I want a comprehensive report of what the fuck is going on."

He grabbed his jacket, then walked down the corridor into the CIC. There were no red icons on the display, but several yellow icons had flickered into existence over a handful of battlestations. Thankfully, Admiral Justinian's attack on Earth had spurred the development of new defenses against chaos software, but it would still be a major headache. He would bet half his salary that Governor Barany hadn't bothered to make spreading the new techniques a priority.

Fifth Fleet should be immune, he thought. *But the local defenses might be in real trouble.*

"Crash the planetary defense network," he ordered. "We can route command authority through us."

Palter stared at him. "Sir?"

"Just do it," Roman snapped. He took a breath, forcing himself to calm down. "The planetary defense network isn't safe. If they're using chaos software, it will spread into the battlestations and starships, shutting them both down. We have to stop them before it's too late."

"Aye, sir," Palter said.

He paused. "Sir, we're picking up reports of attacks on the planet's surface. And shooting on several of the orbital stations."

Roman nodded, unsurprised. "Once the fleet is at full alert, move us away from the planet," he ordered. It was crucial that he avoided being trapped against the planet, all the more so if the orbital defenders were untrustworthy. The odds rather favored the mystery attackers having assets on the battlestations too. "And keep a direct link to the Marines on the surface."

He cursed under his breath as he sat down. Emperor Marius–he'd been Admiral Drake at the time–had told him that there would be times when all he could do was watch and wait for the situation to become clear. As a lowly captain, Roman hadn't understood what he'd been told. Now, he understood all too well. The planet was under attack, the fleet was in danger and he wasn't even sure who he was fighting.

But he was sure it was part of a larger plan.

"Send a signal to Asimov Points One and Two," he ordered. "They are to dispatch drones through the Asimov Points at once. The Federation must be warned."

"Aye, sir," Palter said.

ꕤ

Lieutenant Chas Parker disliked Athena intensely. It was rich enough to be settled, yet poor enough–and isolated enough–to dislike the thought of being part of the Federation. The locals hadn't started hurling things at the Marines yet, thankfully, but they didn't seem obliged to make them feel welcome. Indeed, Chas had the feeling that the locals were only biding their time before they turned on the Marines. It was why he had placed an entire platoon on guard duty and kept another platoon, under his personal command, in reserve.

He gritted his teeth as the hot air drifted over the warehouse complex they'd converted into a makeshift barracks for the company, ever since they'd been told there were no more suitable barracks available. The Marines had suspected that they had been deliberately placed on the edge of Athena City, far too close to the poorest and most discontented citizens on the planet. What they *hadn't* been able to decide was if they had been left there as a show of contempt, or if they'd been put there as a firebreak against an uprising from the poor. The poor had nothing to lose, after all, and what remained of the planet's government might think that having the Marines put down the riot would allow them to blame any excesses on the Marines, rather than the local security forces.

The sound of a lorry reached his ears as the vehicle lumbered into view. It was typical, a heavy-lifter designed for more primitive worlds; easy to drive, easy to repair and easy to cannibalize, if it happened to be broken completely. But it was far too close to the gate to be allowed any closer. He reached for his communicator, intending to tell the guards to fire warning shots, then the world turned brilliant white. Chas found himself on the other side of the room, stunned. What had happened?

He pulled himself to his feet, then swore as he peered out of the window. The guardpost was gone, along with the lorry. There was a smoking crater where the latter had been while–behind it–armed men were charging right at the Marine complex, firing as they came. Chas cursed–half the company was out on patrol duties, while two platoons had been meant to be getting some downtime in the barracks–then grabbed his rifle and ran out of the office. His ready platoon would have to form a line to hold the enemy back while the sleepers grabbed weapons and armored up.

"Form a line," he bawled, cursing the planetary defenders under his breath. A proper Forward Operating Base would have armor everywhere, giving the Marines plenty of room to defend themselves if necessary. Here, there was hardly any real protection at all. "And get the..."

Another explosion, far larger, cut off his words. He looked up, in time to see a second heavy-lifter drive into the compound and head straight for the makeshift barracks. The Marines on the ground opened fire, but the vehicle was rigged with heavy armor. Someone had spent quite some time planning the assault, he realized grimly, as he bellowed orders. The sleepers–they wouldn't be sleeping any longer–would have to run. No doubt the intended target had been the local defenders, with the Marines moved to the top of the target list when they arrived.

"Get down," he shouted. "I..."

The heavy-lifter exploded. Chas hit the ground, gritting his teeth in pain as the compound started to collapse around the remaining Marines. It was hopeless. They'd been caught badly out of place, without anything like enough protection to save their lives, and at least forty Marines were dead. He tongued his voder, but there was no response. By now, the fleet had to know the planet was under attack...unless the fleet was under attack too. The rebellion couldn't hope to succeed if the fleet remained intact and untouched.

He lifted his rifle as running footsteps came into his hearing, then opened fire as he saw two men in black uniforms. One of them fell; the other jumped backwards with commendable speed, then hurled in a grenade. Chas reached for it, but he was far too slow...

Darkness.

жҗ

"Roman, we have reports coming in from all over the planet," Elf said, through the command network. "Both us and the locals are under heavy attack."

Roman swore as more red icons blinked into life. He'd never liked spreading his forces so thin, but he hadn't thought there was a choice. Now, his people were paying the price for his mistake. He could deal with an uprising on the planet's surface–if worst came to worst, he could hammer the planet into submission from orbit–but he couldn't do that if the system itself was under attack from an outside force. And it had to be, because there was no way the rebels could make any permanent gains without it.

"Recall as many of our people as possible," he ordered. Two icons winked out completely, representing an outpost that had been overrun. It was possible the Marines had managed to make it out and scatter into the streets, but he knew it was unlikely. Strangers would be noticed and they would be hunted down. "And ready the fleet for action."

Elf didn't argue, somewhat to his surprise. There were *her* people down on the planet, after all. But she knew the likelihood that this was all part of a greater operation as well as he did.

"And prepare the reserves," he ordered. "We may need to try to seize the battlestations..."

"Commodore," Palter said, sharply. "I'm picking up an emergency alert from Asimov Point One. The enemy fleet has been detected."

Roman cursed under his breath. So far, the enemy had played the game perfectly. By the time his fleet reached the Asimov Point, the battle for control of the point would have been decided. He would then have to assault the point himself...and he didn't know for sure what had happened on the other side. If the enemy had been planning their attack for years, they might have attacked the defenses on both sides...

"Order the fleet to prepare to set course for the Asimov Point," he ordered. Right now, it was the most important location in the system. "And prepare to fire on the planet's industries as we depart."

"Aye, sir," Palter said.

Roman gritted his teeth against an unexpected surge of guilt. The planetary industries supported millions–but they would be a weapon against the Federation, if they fell into enemy hands. There was no point in trying to deceive himself. The unknowns wouldn't have launched their attack against the fleet unless they were reasonably confident of victory. Fifth Fleet needed to see its enemies, needed to know who the hell they were fighting, but they also needed to remain intact. His fleet was the largest in the sector.

"Take us out of orbit," he ordered. "And open fire."

Chapter Thirteen

Battles are generally won by who gets there first with the most. When the warzones are measured in light years, that takes on a new and terrifying meaning.
-The Federation Navy in Retrospect, 4199

Athena, 4098

"The troops have boarded the remaining stations," Lieutenant Juneau reported. "No major problems, sir."

Charlie smiled, relieved. Getting their own people onto the stations had been a gamble; if they'd been discovered, even a man as short-sighted as Governor Barany would have smelt a rat. But it had paid off, handsomely. There had been no message through the Asimov Point, warning of a new war, before the fleet had arrived and quashed all resistance. The remaining defenders, outgunned and completely alone, had surrendered after a brief exchange of fire.

"Have the prisoners transferred to the supply ships," he ordered. Some of the local defenders would probably want to switch sides, but the Outsiders would have to be careful. Those who refused to switch sides would be transferred to camps on Athena. They could be held there until the end of the war. "And purge the command datacores of the chaos software, then take control."

"Aye, sir," Lieutenant Juneau said.

She bent her head to her console, while Charlie rapidly reviewed the situation. They held the Asimov Point–both vital Asimov Points. What was his opponent thinking? Would he come after the fleet on the point, knowing it was the shortest route into the Federation, or would he seek to escape through continuous displacement drive? It had worked before, during Operation Retribution. And Charlie knew that Commodore Garibaldi had served during the failed campaign.

"Launch a second spread of drones," he ordered. "And then bring the fleet around. We will prepare ourselves to advance on the planet."

ꙮ

"That's at least six squadrons of superdreadnaughts, unknown design," the sensor officer said. "And over two hundred smaller ships."

Captain Antony Brooks nodded, bitterly. His squadron of battlecruisers had raced to the Asimov Point, only to discover that they were too late. Far too late. The point was surrounded by heavily-armed ships, while the battlestations had either fallen or had been subverted. It hardly mattered, in the end. All that mattered was that the fleet was trapped in the Athena System, unless it wanted to make an escape through stardrive.

"Launch drones, then hold us here," he ordered. They were well out of engagement range, but he knew better than to take chances. Unknown starships might have unknown surprises, just waiting for the officer incompetent or foolish enough to get too close. "Continue to monitor the enemy output."

"They could be drones," his XO suggested. "They might have made a breakthrough in ECM."

"Too much turbulence for drones, sir," the sensor officer said. "I think most of those ships are definitely real."

"Then keep probing their formation," Antony ordered. "We need to keep the commodore as informed as possible."

ꙮ

Roman sat, stiff and cold, on his command deck as the stream of bad news swelled to a torrent. The Asimov Point was occupied, all right, by a fleet that had no business even existing. Long-range sensors and probes warned that his fleet was heavily outgunned, while the defenses around the Asimov Point appeared to have been taken out–or subverted. Roman would have bet on the latter, given how little care Governor Barany had shown for the system's security. But there was no point in crying over an atmospheric leak now.

The tactical problem was simple enough, but impossible. Unless the enemy was hopelessly incompetent, there was no way the fleet could break through to the Asimov Point without crippling losses. And he couldn't afford to lose more than a handful of ships. The Federation Navy would be pushed back hundreds of light years if Fifth Fleet were lost...

"Outsiders and aliens," Elf muttered, in his earpiece. "Who else can they be?"

Roman nodded. The fleet surrounding the Asimov Point included a number of ships of unknown design. Even the best intelligence analysts had found it impossible to say anything *definite* about them. Were they missile-heavy or did they rely more on energy weapons? The only way to find out would be to engage them–and that risked losing the fleet. He considered, briefly, conceding the system and retreating, but he needed intelligence. They had to know what those ships could do.

"Alter course," he ordered. Thrusting right towards the Asimov Point would guarantee their destruction, but a long-range engagement would give him the chance to see what those ships could do, while allowing him to break contact if necessary. "Take us out on a firing path, then prepare to engage."

A dull quiver ran through the ship as the massive superdreadnaught altered course, while the formation fanned out to allow the fleet's full broadsides to be fired at the unknown ships. It was possible, Roman told himself, that they were actually *alien* ships, with *alien* crews, but there was no way to be sure. Would some of the Outsiders be foolish or desperate enough to teach the aliens how to build superdreadnaughts? Or had they come up with their own designs and put them into mass production?

"Enemy fleet altering course," Palter said. "They're coming towards us on attack vector."

But they could double back to the Asimov Point if necessary, Roman thought. As long as his fleet remained on the outside, the Outsiders could ensure he couldn't force his way through the point. They could dance the long slow stately dance of fleet movements for hours, if necessary, without sacrificing their position. *They have us and they know it.*

He contemplated several possible tactics, all of which would be chancy. Unless his opponent intended to let himself be bullied into making a mistake, there was no way to avoid losing the system. Hell, given time, his opponent could cut half of his ships loose to attack the planet itself, while keeping the rest on the Asimov Point. He had the firepower to make the normal danger of dividing one's forces immaterial.

"Prepare to fire at maximum range," he ordered. "And hold the starfighters for emergency launch."

༄༅

Commodore Garibaldi was playing it cool, Charlie noted, as the two fleets slowly converged. He'd expected more boldness from the younger man, although it was clear that Garibaldi had had to grow up quickly, after the Battle of Earth. Besides, even an idiot could calculate the odds and decide not to try to force the Asimov Point. Instead, Garibaldi seemed to be angling towards a long-range engagement.

Charlie smiled. It was quite alright with him.

"Long-range missiles are locked on target," Lieutenant Juneau informed him.

"Good," Charlie said. "Prepare to fire."

His smile grew wider. He'd wondered if the Federation's sudden determination to improve its missile systems had borne equal fruit, but it seemed, from Commodore Garibaldi's careful manoeuvring, that it hadn't. It didn't seem to have occurred to the younger man that he was in Charlie's missile range; indeed, that he'd been in range for several minutes. The only reason Charlie had held his fire was to allow Garibaldi to sink further into the trap. He would have no time to simply reverse course when he realized he was under attack.

"Missiles ready to fire," Lieutenant Juneau said.

Charlie sobered. This was it, he knew; this was the moment of truth. Either they fought and beat the Federation or they lost themselves to eternal slavery. Or death. The Federation would show no mercy, even though the Grand Senate was gone. He laughed at himself inwardly a moment later. The dice had already been rolled. Even if he abandoned the battle without further ado, the Federation would know it had a more dangerous enemy lurking along the Rim.

May God be with us, he thought, remembering ancestors who had been persecuted for daring to keep their religion. *And may he defend the right.*

"Activate Attack Pattern Weber," he ordered. "Fire."

"Firing," Lieutenant Juneau said. The superdreadnaught shuddered as it flushed its giant external racks, then followed up with a broadside from her inner tubes. "Missiles away."

༄༅

"Missile launch," Palter snapped. "I say again, missile launch!"

For a moment, Roman's mind refused to accept what he was seeing. The enemy had just wasted thousands of missiles? No, they wouldn't have fired unless they thought they had a reasonable hope of scoring a hit. And that meant their missiles had to have greater range than he would have believed possible. Maybe they *could* take on the might of the Federation Navy after all.

"Deploy countermeasures," he snapped. There was no time to simply reverse course, even if he'd known when the enemy missiles would reach burnout and go ballistic. "Launch counter-battery missiles, then prepare to flush our tubes."

He took a breath. "Increase speed," he ordered. "Take us straight into their fire."

Someone–one of the tactical officers, he assumed–gasped behind him. It seemed like suicide, but there was no choice. His ships were loaded with external racks too, each one carrying hundreds of antimatter-tipped warheads. One hit would be enough to destroy the magnetic chambers and blow the ships into flaming debris. He had to shoot off his missiles before the enemy attack reached his ships.

"Lock missiles on the battlestations, as a final blow," he ordered. The timer was ticking down rapidly. "And fire as soon as we enter engagement range."

"Aye, sir," Palter said. The Outsiders seemed surprised by his actions, although it wouldn't be long before they ducked back...if they could. Superdreadnaughts generally moved like wallowing pigs in mud. "Missiles ready."

Roman let out a breath. Thanks to his actions, the time to impact had shrunk sharply. "Fire," he ordered. "Launch everything we have."

He watched the missiles blazing away from his ships, then forced himself to turn and study the incoming missiles. They were impressively powerful–it occurred to him that the Outsiders might have finally cracked some of the inherent limitations of missile power cells–and precisely targeted. Most of the attack had been concentrated on his superdreadnaughts, but enough malice had been reserved for his fleet carriers to blow them into atoms.

"Signal Captain Brooks and his squadron," he ordered. "They are to disengage from their position and head for the stardrive limit. Once they cross it, they are to split up and head for Haven, Croxley and...and New Tennessee. They should be able to alert the Federation Naval Bases there, then proceed deeper into the Federation to Battersea."

"Aye, sir," Palter said. "What if those systems have already been overwhelmed?"

Roman grimaced. Most systems along the Rim were effectively defenseless. It wouldn't take more than a single destroyer to occupy them, assuming it was necessary. Most of the Rim-worlders hated the Federation with a blinding passion. The Outsiders wouldn't need to concentrate their forces against worlds that would probably join them willingly, given a chance. And besides, if they had enough ships to attack all possible targets and *still* send a major fleet against Athena, the Federation was screwed.

"They won't be," he said, hoping he sounded confident. Someone considering his possible options would certainly point to those three worlds as potential destinations. They all had Asimov Points, after all. "Send the orders."

"Enemy fleet is launching starfighters," Palter added. "They're readying themselves for antishipping strikes."

"Launch ours, configured for close-in defense," Roman ordered. "And then send the fleet carriers to the rear."

On the display, a wall of red light–there were so many missile icons that they blurred together–swept down on his fleet. Roman issued orders, instructing the fleet to reverse course and extend the range, although he had a feeling it would be futile. The enemy fleet would hardly have laid such a careful trap without making sure he couldn't escape the tidal wave of incoming missiles. But they had their own problems too now...

We'll need to duplicate those missiles, he thought, sourly. It had been a while since the last major advance from the Federation Navy's researchers–and longer still since they had developed something completely new, rather than learning from their enemies. But the Grand Senate hadn't been interested in research for the sake of research. Something might have been discovered that would have tipped the Federation's balance of power into the rubbish heap.

There's no choice, he told himself. *Those damn missiles give the bastards too many advantages.*

He gripped his armrests as the missiles entered point defense range. Thousands vanished, picked off by the unified point defense of the entire fleet, but hundreds more kept roaring towards his ships. Worse, they were definitely antimatter-tipped warheads. As they exploded, they released waves of electromagnetic interference that blinded sensors and made it harder for the survivors to be tracked. Thankfully, they didn't seem to be any *smarter* than the average Federation Navy missile head. Quite a few hurled themselves on drones and expended themselves uselessly. Others lost their locks on their targets and were picked off before they found new ones.

But hundreds still found their targets. Roman watched, helplessly, as damage mounted rapidly. It would have been worse, he knew, if they'd fired at the smaller ships. As it was, a dozen cruisers and destroyers were vaporized when they were targeted by accident. Others took significant damage. The superdreadnaught *Thunderhead* dropped out of formation, streaming plasma from a major gash in her hull, then exploded when her antimatter containment fields failed. She was followed, quickly, by the superdreadnaughts *Canopus* and *Denver.* The latter, at least, managed to launch lifepods before she followed her comrades into oblivion.

Don't think about the dead, he told himself. Most of them were strangers, but some he knew personally. *Mourn later, when you have time.*

"*Boskone* has taken heavy damage," Palter reported. There was a bitter tone in his voice as the superdreadnaught's details flashed up in front of them. "Lieutenant Walters is asking permission to abandon ship."

"Granted," Roman said. He had to check his implants to identify Walters, fifth in the chain of command. At least it wasn't quite as bad as when he'd been thrust into command of *Enterprise,* he told himself, but one glance at the screen had made it clear that *Boskone* was doomed. "Detach SAR craft to pick up the lifepods."

He took one last look at the stricken vessel, then turned back to the display. The enemy fleet was launching a second salvo of missiles, thankfully a much reduced one.

This time, the tactical officers knew their enemy. But the Federation ships were still going to take a pounding.

"Alter course," he ordered. "I want a least-time passage to the edge of the gravity limit."

"Aye, sir," Palter said.

ঌ৩

Charlie had worried about his ships and crew when the enemy returned fire. He had to take his hat off to Garibaldi; he'd taken a beating, but he'd made sure that the battle wasn't a complete curbstomp. It was almost a shame he was on the wrong side, Charlie considered, as the missiles roared down on his ships. A mind like that, willing to grasp a fleeting opportunity and use it to score a blow, was worth keeping.

He watched, grimly, as the missiles entered his point defense envelope. They'd drilled endlessly, against missiles with impossible capabilities, yet he'd always questioned how well they would do against a real opponent. Even the best possible situation would give the tactical officers and their automated servants problems that couldn't really be simulated, not easily. And some of those simulations had ended very badly.

"*Pilgrim* is gone, sir," Lieutenant Juneau reported. "*Lightning, Hawker* and *Robert Bruce* have taken minor damage, but *Kershaw* has lost one of her drive chambers and has to fall out of formation. *Peace, Freedom* and *Liberty* have all taken heavy damage and will have to be abandoned. I..."

She broke off. "*Freedom* has just been destroyed, sir."

"Order the other two to abandon ship," Charlie snapped. "We'll pick up the lifepods once the battle is over."

He watched the display, his eyes narrowing as the Federation Navy's ships altered course. It seemed that young Garibaldi had had enough of the battle and was trying to escape. Charlie didn't blame him. The missiles had to have been a surprise—no one would have come in so fat and happy if they'd known they were walking into a trap—and his ships had taken significant damage. It might have been worth it, if they'd been fighting on equal terms, but the Outsiders had significantly more firepower at their disposal.

The final tally of damage appeared in front of him and he let out a sigh of relief. It was bad, but it could have been worse. He'd feared losing so many ships—or having to send them back to the repair yards—that the second or third steps of the operational plan would have to be cancelled completely. It wouldn't have been a major hiccup, but he knew from bitter experience that delays beget more delays...and eventually they would prove fatal.

"Detach two squadrons of cruisers and order them to escort the troopships to Athena," he ordered, softly. "But caution the CO. They are not to attempt to land if the defenses are ready to resist them. If so, we can deal with the defenses later."

"Aye, sir," Lieutenant Juneau said.

"One squadron of superdreadnaughts is to remain on the Asimov Point," Charlie continued. "The remainder of the fleet is to give chase. And prepare to engage the enemy once again."

He smiled, again, as his orders were carried out. The Federation Navy ships would probably make it to the limit and drop into FTL, but they would take one hell of a beating first. And any ship that dropped out of formation, crippled and helpless, could be obliterated later, if the crew refused to surrender. Taking Federation ships and pressing them into service would tie up engineers he didn't want to waste, but they might need the hulls. The war had barely begun. It wouldn't be long before things started to go wrong.

"Fleet reconfigured, sir," Lieutenant Juneau said.

"Then take us in pursuit," Charlie ordered. Irritatingly, the Federation Navy had managed to put some distance between themselves and the Outsiders, but not enough to escape contact completely. The starfighters would see to that, he knew. "Best possible speed."

Chapter Fourteen

Operation Retribution. The first major battle between the Federation Navy and forces loyal to Admiral Justinian. Owing to incompetence (and false intelligence) the Federation Navy flew into a trap, forcing the fleet to withdraw into interstellar space and make a stand at Boskone.
-The Federation Navy in Retrospect, 4199

Athena, 4098

It's like Operation Retribution all over again, Roman thought, as the enemy fleet finally shook itself down into pursuit formation. *Except I'm in command.*

He cursed under his breath as the enemy starfighters swarmed forward. They were tiny, each one individually harmless, but as a mass they were deadly. They could catch up with his fleet, fire off their missiles and then retreat back to their carriers to rearm, re-launch and do it all over again. His starfighters would do what they could to keep the pressure off, but they would be badly outnumbered. Roman knew, all too well, that his fleet was about to take a beating.

"Deploy the starfighters in a Foster Formation," he ordered, then cut himself off. The CAG knew what he was doing and, more importantly, he didn't need someone from higher up trying to issue orders himself. "Order the point defense to be ready to engage the enemy starfighters."

"Aye, sir," Palter said.

Roman scowled as new reports came in from the sensor platforms. There was no StarCom in the system, thus no way of getting reports in real-time from more than a few light minutes away, but it was clear that part of the enemy fleet was turning and advancing towards Athens. He studied the vectors for a long moment, trying to determine if there was a way he could break off and intercept that subsection of the fleet, then decided it was useless. The main body of the enemy fleet would always be between him and his target.

"Send a signal to the planet," he ordered. It was a futile effort–the planet's defenses were in total disarray–but they had to try. "Warn them that the enemy fleet is on the way."

He looked down at his console, trying to think of something–anything–he could do other than escaping the system through stardrive. But there was nothing. Keeping the remains of his fleet intact was the top priority and even the planet, as important as it was, came second. The Federation Navy couldn't afford to lose his ships, not when it didn't even know it was under attack. Roman considered the vectors for a long moment, trying to put himself in the enemy's shoes. Where would they attack to make sure it took weeks, even months, for the Federation to discover a whole new war had just begun?

"Message sent," Palter said.

"Good," Roman said.

The enemy starfighters plunged into his starfighters...and immediately revealed one weakness. Roman's pilots were veterans, survivors of the Justinian War; the Outsiders had only trained in simulations, as far as he could tell. They were good, Roman admitted privately, but they didn't have the edge that only came with experience. It didn't seem to help that half of their pilots seemed more intent on fighting one-on-one with the Federation's starfighters than actually pressing the attack against the fleet.

Odd, he thought. *We haven't permitted dogfights like that since we worked out tactics for starfighters that actually worked.*

But hundreds of enemy starfighters broke through and threw themselves on the fleet, ducking and weaving as they entered point defense range. Dozens died as the fleet's experienced defense systems picked them off, but hundreds survived to launch their missiles into the fleet's formation. Roman cursed under his breath as three superdreadnaughts staggered, taking heavy damage from the missiles, but somehow remaining intact. *Patton* was almost certainly doomed, he suspected, as her drive compartments had been badly damaged, yet the other two might make it out. But they'd be in the yards for years.

"The enemy starfighters are breaking off," Palter said. "I..."

He paused. "Sir, correction. A third of the enemy starfighters are breaking off."

Roman frowned. The remaining enemy starfighters were *still* duelling with his starfighters, even though there was no longer any point in keeping them occupied. It made no sense. If the starfighter pilots had been roughly equal, the Outsider advantage in numbers might have made the gambit worthwhile, but the pilots *weren't* equal. And now that a third of the enemy starfighters had pulled back to their carriers, it gave the Federation the advantage. It definitely made no sense.

He shook his head. There was no point in worrying about it, not now.

"Continue on our present course," Roman ordered. So far, the enemy didn't seem intent on launching another missile barrage, but that would change soon. They'd need to cover their starfighters for the next offensive. "And tell the fighter jocks to pick off as many of the bastards as possible."

He felt a savage flicker of satisfaction as two more icons vanished in quick succession. They'd lost the battle—he was realistic enough to know that they'd lost—but at least they'd clawed the enemy before they fled. And, whatever had gotten into the enemy pilots, it had cost the Outsiders dearly. Their confidence would be badly shaken. But what had caused it?

"Aye, sir," Palter said.

ഇഠങ

Charlie would gladly have strangled the High Lord—or any other glory-seeking Marsha meritocratic aristocrat—if he'd been in reach. They'd gone over the plan for engaging the Federation Navy time and time again, but the moment the starfighters had actually encountered the enemy they'd slipped right back into terminally stupid mode and attacked the Federation's starfighters as individuals. They hadn't even given a damn for their wingmen, let alone the rest of the formation; they'd just lashed out at their targets, allowing the more disciplined Federation pilots a chance to swing the balance in their favor.

"Sir," Lieutenant Juneau said, "our fighters are rearming."

Our fighters, Charlie thought, angrily. *Or what's left of them.*

It should have been a relatively straightforward mission. Blow though the defenders, salvo missiles at the superdreadnaughts, then get out again. But the Marsha pilots had blown it, simply by living true to their code. Charlie mentally composed an angry message to the High Lord as he looked up at the display. The worst of it was the pilots who might have learned better were being picked off, one by one, as the Federation Navy took advantage of their weaknesses.

"Prepare them for a second round, then recall the Marsha," he ordered, although he had little hope that the order would be obeyed. The Marsha truly had no idea how to fight as part of a much larger force. Left to themselves, he suspected, they would never have produced anything larger than a destroyer, for fear that serving on the lower decks would deny them honor. "Tell them they have to rearm."

He cursed them again as the message went out. Even if they saw sense and obeyed orders, they'd still lost far too many starfighters. The Federation ships would have a chance to wipe out the next attack force, rather than just try to beat it off. Once again, Murphy had reared his ugly head at the worst possible moment.

"The message was not acknowledged," Lieutenant Juneau said.

Charlie gritted his teeth. Any Marsha commander who was disobeyed had the option of simply beheading his subordinates. It was stupid and wasteful, Charlie had thought when he'd first heard of it, but now he thought he understood. A successful bout of disobedience, even for reasons the Grand Senate would have accepted, was a stab against the officer's honor. But he had no intention of beheading any of the pilots...no, that wasn't true. He'd be quite happy to behead the idiots who thought that single combat in space, against more experienced pilots, was a clever idea.

But that would probably be taken as a breach of the treaty, he thought. *We need to find them some suicide missions instead.*

Gritting his teeth, he swung round to face the status display. The planetary occupation fleet was on its way and it was unlikely the Federation fleet would be able to intervene. That left them with only the planetary defenses to contend with and, although the last report was several hours out of date, it didn't seem as though the defenders had managed to pull themselves back together. Once Athena was occupied, the natural hatred of the Federation of Rim-dwellers would probably allow the Outsiders to recruit hundreds of thousands of humans. Maybe they could replace the Marsha. God knew he would have lots of empty slots in his fleet after the engagement was concluded.

"Launch the second strike," he ordered. "And tell the escorting fighters not to leave their formation, no matter what happens."

"Aye, sir," Lieutenant Juneau said.

Charlie nodded, then looked down at his fleet's status again. They'd fired off their external racks, as well as two barrages from their inner tubes. He could press the offensive, force his way back into missile range, but it would cost him dearly. Even an outright victory would leave his ships shot dry. And if the Federation Navy managed a counterattack, it could be decisive. Unarmed superdreadnaughts would be easy targets.

They don't have another fleet in the sector, he thought, slowly. It would be worth it if they could guarantee several weeks of peace. *But we didn't know their Fifth Fleet was on the way until it arrived at Athena. There could be another major formation out here, unknown to us.*

He was almost sure there wasn't. But he didn't dare take it for granted. It would take weeks to repair the damage to his ships, even if they broke off the engagement now. And what if the Federation *did* manage a counterattack?

"Once the fighters are on their way, reduce speed," he added. "We'll shadow them as they leave, but make no attempt to close to missile range."

Lieutenant Juneau looked surprised. "Sir?"

Charlie understood her confusion. The fleet would never have a better chance of engaging a sizable Federation formation on such favorable terms. But they had to think past the first battle. The Outsider Navy wasn't large enough to absorb hideous losses and keep fighting, while the Federation Navy *was.* They couldn't risk a victory so costly it ensured they would lose the war.

And besides, if the Federation ships managed to stay ahead of them, all the advantages he enjoyed from his technology would be negated.

"We've won," he said. "There's no point in fighting them to a finish."

He sighed. The downside was that it would leave the Federation Navy ships out there, ready to cause havoc along the Rim. But they would have no idea where to target to do real damage. It hardly mattered if a stage-one colony world like New Hampshire changed hands a dozen times before the end of the war. Most stage-one colony worlds could add nothing to the balance of power, not even trained manpower. And he could go after the real targets with overwhelming force.

"Aye, sir," Lieutenant Juneau said.

She paused. "The Marsha will not take that calmly," she warned. "We should be prepared for trouble."

"Understood," Charlie said.

••

"The enemy fleet is launching starfighters," Palter reported.

"Stand by point defense," Roman ordered. The Outsider pilots were *still* dogfighting with his pilots, despite the need to cover their attackers. It made absolutely no sense. Maybe they'd assumed that he would have to recall his fighters once the second attack wave was launched, but if so the tactic had cost them dearly. It wasn't as if starfighters couldn't be replaced far faster than superdreadnaughts. "And recall the starfighters once the second attack wave is in range."

He rubbed his chin as the new wave of icons came into attack range, then scattered into smaller groups as his starfighters broke off their engagements and roared after them. It was starting to look as though there were two different groups of

Outsider pilots; one set calm and disciplined, the other capable, yet undisciplined. The more he looked at it, the more puzzled he became. The rogue pilots had cost their fellows a chance at scoring a decisive victory.

Maybe their training was too short, he thought, although there was nothing wrong with the flyers individually. They were making mistakes that showed they were more used to facing simulations than real pilots, but they were learning from them. *Or maybe they were encouraged to develop lone wolf flying skills.*

"Sir," Palter said, "the enemy fleet is reducing speed."

Roman swung around and stared at the main display. Palter was right. The enemy fleet had indeed reduced speed, as if it had given up on the pursuit. That too made no sense, unless one assumed that the starfighters' losses had made the enemy commander think twice about pressing the attack. But they could still have used their missiles to pound his fleet into scrap metal...

But we would have given as good as we got, he thought, slowly. *They would have taken a beating too.*

He watched, grimly, as the enemy starfighters raced in and fell on his ships. Dozens died, as before, but dozens more survived long enough to launch their missiles towards their targets. *Invincible, Incredible, Fantastic* and *Harness* died at once, vanishing in balls of superheated plasma; *Tyrant* and *Thunderchild* survived long enough to launch lifepods before they too followed their fellows into oblivion. Losing the battlecruisers would cost him, later, he was sure. He had a feeling they would have been very necessary as the war spread rapidly.

"The enemy starfighters are falling back," Palter informed him. "Even the rogue ones are leaving."

"Have SAR teams pick up the lifepods, if possible," Roman said, absently. So far, the Outsiders hadn't fired on any lifepods, but it was quite possible they would refuse to pick up survivors. Or that the lifepods would be mistaken for weapons and picked off by automated systems before anyone realized they were harmless. God knew it had happened before, during countless wars. "And launch a set of probes to watch the enemy formation."

"Aye, sir," Palter said.

Roman watched the enemy starfighters retreating, puzzling over their actions. *Lone wolves*; there was no such thing among starfighter pilots, no matter how many movies praised the heroic loner over pilots who worked as a team. Anyone with pretensions to blowing a hundred alien starfighters out of space and then taking out a capital ship with a single well-placed torpedo was rapidly disabused of that notion. It didn't happen, not outside the movies, where a patriotic scriptwriter and gorgeous love interest could make up for anything. He'd even once been told, back when he'd served on *Enterprise*, that far too many pilot-wannabes had seen the infamous show where a pilot had smuggled his girlfriend into a starfighter and made love to her under the stars. But the starfighters were too cramped for one person, let alone two...

But it seemed the enemy had taken the movies seriously.

He shook his head. "Keep us on our current course," he ordered. "Once we're outside immediate sensor range, detach one squadron of destroyers. They are ordered to go into cloak and observe the system from the outskirts, using the sensor platforms to monitor activity much closer to the planet itself. We'll be back to relieve them as soon as possible."

"Aye, sir," Palter said.

Roman nodded, then brought up the starchart and studied it quickly. He'd had a handful of contingency plans, but he'd underestimated the Outsiders. Professor Kratman–he remembered the man's lectures on conceptual surprise with a flicker of fondness–would have his head. So would Emperor Marius. His career might have come to a sudden halt. But for the moment, all he could do was concentrate on saving as much as he could.

The enemy would try to anticipate his movements, of course. Where did they think he would go?

"Set course for Tyler's World," he ordered. It was actually several light years further into the Rim, but the Asimov Point there would allow him to skip back into the Federation, following the crazed lines of ill-understood wormholes. "We'll pass through the point there, then head to Boston."

"Aye, sir," Palter said. "Do you think they could have attacked Boston too?"

"I hope not," Roman said. The Outsiders had hurled six squadrons of superdreadnaughts at Athena. If they had enough force to attack both Athena and Boston–and be sure of victory–it might be time to consider suing for peace. But what did the Outsiders actually *want*? They hadn't made any demands, as far as he knew; they'd simply started shooting. "If they have, we're in deep trouble."

He sat back and forced himself to relax as the fleets broke contact. The sudden pause in the storm gave his crews time to evacuate two damaged ships, then scuttle them before the Outsiders could take them for prizes. Standard procedure was to scuttle ships damaged beyond repair in any case, but this time was different. The Outsiders might well be able to put any crippled starship back into service and point her at her former owners.

And if they really are playing from the Operation Retribution playbook, he thought, *they might well try to have an ambush waiting for us as we head back to Boston.*

"Signal all ships," he added. There were too many other things to take care of to let himself worry about possible future encounters. All he could do was make preparations and pray. "I want a full update on their ammunition loads. There's no hope of recovering anything from the fleet base, so we may have to conserve ammunition."

He cursed, again, the shortage of freighters. They'd assumed the fleet base would supply all their needs, but their imagination had proven inadequate. Very inadequate.

"Crossing the line in twenty minutes, sir," Palter reported. "All stardrives are on line."

"Good," Roman said. He looked up at the image of Athena's star. "We'll be back one day."

He paused. "Take us into stardrive as soon as we cross the line," he ordered. "And then stand the fleet down from battlestations."

Chapter Fifteen

Occupying an entire planet is a task beyond almost all military forces. Standard Federation doctrine, therefore, is to secure the planet's capital city and industries, then maintain a reserve force in orbit to respond to any threatening events. The remainder of the planet is left to its own devices.
-The Federation Navy in Retrospect, 4199

Athena, 4098

"Hey, you think they'll greet us with flowers?"

Uzi looked up. Lieutenant Caleb Roebuck was depressingly young and enthusiastic–and completely devoid of any real experience. His simulations showed promise, Uzi had to admit, but there was no way to know how he'd perform when the shit hit the fan.

"I think we should prepare for the worst," he said. The last report had stated that the planetary defenses had been immobilized, but Uzi had heard such reports before and they'd always been proven inaccurate. "And you should watch for signs the locals aren't too pleased to see you."

Roebuck sat down next to him as the transport shivered, slightly. "But they should welcome us?"

I was never that naive, Uzi thought, coldly. *Never.*

"You can never take anything for granted in such a dangerous situation," Uzi said, instead. "I think you have to concentrate on preparing for the worst."

"So you said," Roebuck said. "But really...why wouldn't they welcome us?"

"For all the reasons I gave when we worked our way through the simulations," Uzi said, feeling his patience start to fray. "They may fear us, they certainly don't *know* us and we look aggressive. And don't forget the Federation's loyalists, either."

He closed his eyes as he accessed the transport's sensors through his implants. So far, he had to admit, the Outsider plan had largely survived contact with the enemy. The Federation Navy was in retreat and the planetary defenses were either shut down or shooting at each other. They were certainly in no state to put up any resistance as the occupation fleet entered orbit, picking off automated defense platforms as they opened fire. Half of the automated network seemed to be dead; the other half seemed torn between several different imperatives.

Unless they're just playing dead, he thought, as he turned his attention to the communications network. *They might be hoping to lure us into point blank range.*

He kept that insight to himself as he started to interface, very carefully, with the transport's datanodes. It wouldn't have been possible at all if the transport hadn't been built within the Federation, with all the little modifications the security services insisted on including installed. The Outsiders would be aware of the danger, he suspected, but actually doing something about it without replacing the entire system would be pretty much close to impossible. Or so he hoped. Calmly, he uploaded a message into the system, then attached a supervisory program to the data package. It would move through the network like a ghost, then be uploaded into the planetary network and forwarded to the fleet...with all traces of its passage wiped as soon as it had gone.

A dull *thump* echoed through the transport as she entered orbit, her shields taking a glancing blow from an orbital weapons platform that was blown into vapor seconds later by one of the escorts. Uzi pulled himself out of the computer network, feeling his heart pounding in his chest. If someone was watching the system, he'd just revealed his existence and rough location–and there weren't that many plausible candidates for being a spy. In their place, he would simply have relieved all the mercenaries from duty until he knew the truth.

"We're launching," Roebuck said. "Here we go..."

Uzi smiled as the shuttlecraft blew free of the transport, then braced himself as the craft rocketed into the planetary atmosphere. Drive field or no, it shook violently as it fell towards the planet's surface, striking gusts of wind at high attitude while trying to evade incoming fire...if there had been any. Uzi eyed the planetary defense centers, such as they were, through the shuttle's sensors, but none of them seemed to be going active. Indeed, two of the bases that should have been in view were missing. The forward teams had done a better job than he'd dared fear.

And let us hope that gives them Victory Disease, he thought, as the shuttle rocked again. The turbulence was bad enough, but at least it wasn't incoming fire. *It won't be so easy on a world where the governor isn't such a greedy bastard.*

"We're being sent to the spaceport," Roebuck said. He sounded disappointed at the thought of not making a combat jump into the teeth of enemy fire. It always looked exciting until someone actually had to *do* one. "We have to secure the landing zones for the follow-ups."

"Good," Uzi grunted. "It gives us time to get our planetary legs."

The shuttle rocked again, then hit the ground so hard that even Uzi wondered, for a split-second, if they'd actually *crashed*. But there was no time for worrying about it. He stood up, bellowed orders, then pushed and shoved the armoured recruits through the hatch and out onto the landing strip. The spaceport was fairly average, as spaceports went; it was really nothing more than a cluster of buildings, a handful of landing pads and a few hangers for shuttlecraft. And, thankfully, it was undefended. Quite a few of the Outsider troops were in no condition to fight.

"What have I told you," Uzi bellowed, as they struggled to set up a perimeter, "about being sick in your suits?"

Four more shuttles came in to land in quick succession. Gritting his teeth, Uzi barked more orders, forming the combat effectives up in makeshift squads and then pointing them towards their targets. He took personal command of the first squad and led the way towards the main building, while Roebuck took his squad to the shuttlecraft hangers. It *was* important to secure the shuttlecraft–they'd need every shuttle they could get to move supplies down to the surface–but it also kept him out of the way. The last thing Uzi needed was a half-trained and inexperienced officer barking orders.

Or is that precisely what you need? He asked himself. *Someone who can take the blame for a screw-up?*

He crashed through the spaceport wall and into the departure lounge. Thankfully, it was almost deserted, even though it would normally be heaving with people. He snapped orders, directing his men to secure the control rooms, security officers and anything else that might be important, than relaxed slightly as he realized there would be almost no resistance. The staff had ordered the civilians to go back home, then most of the staff had gone into hiding. Only a handful of staffers were found and they were swiftly detained. They would be released once their identities had been verified.

"Mission complete," he said, with some relief. He detailed a pair of men to handle landing operations–more shuttles were coming in to land, threatening to collide with the other shuttles–then led the remainder of his squad back outside. In the distance, he could see pillars of smoke rising up over Athena City. "Sir?"

Roebuck met him outside. "We're being detailed to the advance force," he said. "They're letting us take point as we go into the city."

Uzi winced. Urban combat was *never* fun–and the download from the fleet command network, such as it was, showed that parts of the city had dissolved into riots. They would have to be put down as swiftly as possible, with minimum necessary force. On the other hand, at least there didn't seem to be any organized resistance. The remains of the Federation Marines had gone underground, or scattered into the countryside. There would be time to eliminate them later.

"Get the men lined up," Roebuck ordered. He hadn't lost his enthusiasm. "Hurry!"

Uzi nodded–salutes were forbidden in combat zones–and started to bark orders. There had been no casualties, apart from the men who had thrown up or suffered badly from the shuttlecraft's mad descent through the atmosphere. That, too, was something they would learn to overcome, in time. But for the moment it was a major pain in the arse. They would have to remain at the spaceport until they recovered–aided by the taunts of their fellows–then they could be reattached to the ground force. Until then...

He pushed the thought aside as he mustered the remaining men. In their armor, they would be protected against almost everything, at least everything civilians could muster. The Federation wasn't keen on arming civilians–the weapons might be turned against Federation officials–but the Rim had always had a progressive view of carrying weapons on uncivilized worlds. And then there were the Federation Marines. *Their* weapons would go right through the suits.

"Maintain formation–and calm," he ordered, sharply. "Do *not* respond with lethal force without my order. Do you understand?"

As soon as they agreed, he turned and led the way down the road into the city. It was an impressive sight, part of him had to admit, even though some of the buildings were clearly damaged by the fighting. The settlers hadn't waited for too long before removing the prefabricated crap and replacing it with homebuilt crap. He smiled at the thought, then activated his loudspeaker. It would give away their position, but he would have been very surprised if the enemy hadn't already known exactly where they were. The armored combat battlesuits were many things, yet they weren't *quiet*!

"RETURN TO YOUR HOMES," he bellowed through the loudspeaker. "STAY INDOORS. WAIT FOR ORDERS. RETURN TO YOUR HOMES. STAY INDOORS. WAIT FOR ORDERS."

Uzi glanced from side to side as the squad continued its advance. All he could do was hope the locals would obey orders. If they didn't, there would be a massacre.

ꕥ

Greg Easter had never worked a day in his life. It wasn't through choice. His father had been a Federation Loyalist–he'd worked for one of the big interstellar corporations–and too many people remembered the name when the younger Greg had started to apply for work. They'd either hated the Federation and its supporters or feared that Greg was part of a Trojan Horse operation to find a legalistic precedent to seize their facilities and give them to a Federation supporter. There had been no hope of finding work.

He'd grown into a bitter young man, spending most of his time drinking, smoking and gambling with his friends. Governor Barany didn't give a damn about them, personally, but he'd ensured they had the means to keep drinking themselves to death. It was obvious to anyone who thought about it, Greg considered, that the governor was no Federation Loyalist. All he cared about was money and pleasing himself. But at least he'd had a loose tie to the Federation. The Outsiders had none...

...And they would probably kill his family too.

Greg had grown up knowing that if the planet became independent, anyone with any ties to the Federation would be hunted down and killed. It wasn't a comfortable thought. Now, with armoured troopers from beyond the Rim marching through the streets, it was clear the lynch mobs would not be far behind. His father would be killed, his mother and sisters would be raped and *then* killed...and Greg himself would be killed too. He knew there would be no mercy from the rebels. Why should they show any when the Federation had shown them none?

And so he'd gathered his friends, had a few stiff drinks to boost their morale, then started to put together an ambush. It had been simple enough. They'd filled older bottles with gas, then attached rags and prepared to light them, all the while congratulating themselves on their ingenuity. Surely, no one else had thought of such a simple weapon.

He smiled to himself as the armored troopers came into view, then lit the first match.

ꕥ

There was no warning. Uzi barely registered the bottle flying through the air before it struck his armored forehead and exploded, sending sheets of flame everywhere. A Molotov Cocktail, the dispassionate side of his mind noted; a very simple and common makeshift weapon. But useless against armored suits. More flew at the squad and crashed into the suits, leaving them burning but unharmed. And the flames died away quickly as they ran out of fuel.

"Forward," he ordered. Ahead of them, his sensors picked out a number of youths, staring in disbelief as the troopers walked forward. The ambush had been so amateurish that he was almost ashamed of himself for just walking straight into it. But it was also no threat to armored men. "And take prisoners."

ꕤ

Greg had exulted when he'd seen the flames envelop their targets. He'd expected to see them collapse to the ground, burning to death. Instead, the flames faded, revealing the armored men marching straight at their position. He felt something warm and wet running down his pants as they came closer, then he turned and fled as fast as he could. His friends, shocked into sobriety by the sight, fled too. Behind him, the armored men kept marching forward, never slowing or speeding up. He didn't stop running until he reached his home and ran inside, slamming the door behind him.

ꕤ

Uzi shrugged when the youths outran the armored soldiers. They could have caught them, if they'd run, but there had really been no point. The youths weren't soldiers, or even armed with anything more dangerous than Molotov Cocktails, and the story of how they'd been effortlessly scattered would do more to discourage resistance than mass shootings.

"Shouldn't we be hunting them down?" Casey asked, as they started to walk back into the streets. "Give them a proper thrashing?"

"If you thrashed someone in a combat suit, you'd smash them to jam," Uzi pointed out, darkly. "And you would make their families mad and everyone else fearful. It would encourage resistance, I think. This way, we get to make a show of strength while not actually doing anything they can use to rally resistance."

He sighed. So far, none of the Outsiders had committed any atrocities, but how long would it be before that changed? And would his message to the Federation reach anyone who could make use of it? There was no way to know.

"But sir..."

"Do as you're told," Uzi snapped. "The objective is to take the planet as peacefully as possible, not to slaughter drunken idiots in their hundreds!"

The thought made him grind his teeth in frustration. He understood the impulse to just break out the clubs and get stuck into a mob of idiots who thought they could defy armored men–and it had been the first real encounter with *any* resistance for most of his troopers–but it had to be suppressed. Let them get mad at him rather than the locals. General Erskine would have his head, perhaps literally, if his men committed any atrocities. And then he would be completely useless to the Federation.

Watch and wait, he reminded himself. It wouldn't be the first time he'd done something distasteful–and some of the things he'd had to do had been *incredibly* distasteful–for the greater glory of the Federation. *Watch, wait and take your chance when you see it.*

The next street held a makeshift barricade, completely abandoned. Judging from its position, it had been intended to keep refugees from the inner city out of the suburbs, rather than blocking the Outsiders as they moved into the city from the landing zones. Or maybe the builders had thought they had time to block the other lines of approach too. He shrugged, then ordered his men to tear it down. Once it was gone, they could move on towards the center of the city.

And hopefully without encountering more idiots, he thought.

ജ്ഞ

"The city has been largely secured, sir," General Erskine said. His face on the display screen flickered in and out, a warning that the communications network was far from stable. "There are some minor pockets of resistance–or riots–but we have them sealed off and will deal with them, once everything else is under control."

"Good," Charlie said. "And the facilities?"

"Some are intact, but quite a few have been destroyed," General Erskine reported. "The Federation Navy took out a number of orbital installations too, as they left orbit. They must have assumed they were going to lose the system."

Charlie cursed under his breath. Athena's industry would have been a valuable prize. Not all of it had been destroyed–a glance at the report made that clear–but enough had been taken out to make rebuilding it a significant challenge. Luckily, enough had survived to ensure that Athena wouldn't need help from outside to rebuild. It would just take several years.

And by then the war might well be finished, he thought, coldly. *Either we win or they win–or we manage to compromise. The industries here might prove immaterial to the outcome.*

"And the local assets?" He asked. "Are they in place to take over?"

"For the moment, only in the city itself," Erskine said. "They took a pounding from the Marines before they scattered, sir. We can start recruiting from other locals, as planned, but that offers other risks."

"We will just have to live with them," Charlie said. "Keep a lid on any trouble, General."

"I will," Erskine said. "And good luck with the advance."

His image vanished. Charlie frowned, then turned his attention to the reports from the Asimov Points. Both of the systems leading back towards the Federation had been secured, but it wasn't clear if they'd managed to get off a warning or not. If they had, the shit would definitely hit the fan. And even if they hadn't...it wouldn't be long before *someone* realized that something had gone badly wrong. The Justinian War had taught the Federation to pay attention to vague reports of trouble from the fringe.

And then there was the Federation Navy's ships...

He sighed. They'd won this battle, but the war itself had only just begun.

Chapter Sixteen

It is a curious fact about the Federation that, in all but its final incarnation, it was determined to produce at least an appearance of following the rule of law. This tended to produce no shortage of legalistic foul play to create a veneer of legality, all of which was complete nonsense. The laws could be changed at will by the Grand Senate. Quite why they felt this compulsion, when no one was in any doubt that the Federation cared nothing for the rule of law, has never been satisfactorily explained.
-The Federation Navy in Retrospect, 4199

Earth, 4098

"It's been a month," Marius said, angrily. "A month of endless stalling, all around the same question! Are orders from the Grand Senate *legal* by definition?"

"You may have underestimated that lawyer," Tiffany agreed. They sat together in his office, looking down at the latest set of reports. She wrapped an arm around his shoulders as she spoke. "How long does it normally take to hold a court martial?"

"A week," Marius said. "The evidence is presented, the defendant and his defender make speeches...then the jury moves to immediate judgement. It shouldn't take any longer than a week at most. It's gathering the evidence that generally takes time."

He cursed himself under his breath. Deciding to give Blake Raistlin a reasonably fair trial had been a mistake. He was sure of that now. It would have been relatively straightforward to get a board to rubber-stamp an execution, or simply to have him shot along with the others after the Fall of Earth, but he'd had to make a point. And besides, he'd felt personally betrayed by Raistlin. He'd trusted the younger man to do his duty, rather than serving as a spy and assassin for his family. Instead, Raistlin had shot him.

The media was full of accounts of the trial, divided between those who thought Raistlin was innocent and those who wanted him shot out of hand. How was it, Marius asked himself, that the *media* had been the only industry to survive the fall of the Grand Senate and come out reasonably intact? But then, to maintain a facade of impartiality, the media corporations were officially owned by people with no connections to the Grand Senate. They'd simply kept their jobs and started to work without having to have everything approved, in triplicate. And several media corporations *had* been semi-independent in any case.

And they'd been joined by hundreds of others. There were thousands of would-be journalists out there and, now the regulations governing the media had been swept away, they'd started to band together to form new outlets of their own. Marius suspected, from what Professor Kratman had said, that most of them wouldn't last longer than a year, but for the moment they were creating a barrage of noise. Life had been easier, the PR staff had said, when most of the media did what the Grand Senate said. But then, it had also included hundreds of obnoxious reporters who'd managed to get in the way during the war.

And a few of them got killed by the enemy, Marius thought, with bitter satisfaction. It was hard to feel sorry for someone who insisted on the finest cabins, the finest food and then bitched whenever they picked up a tiny bruise. And tried to lure female officers into their beds. *Some of them might even have been killed by friendly fire.*

But right now the Trial of Blake Raistlin was devouring the headlines. And so was everything from the scrapping of rules and regulations to the changes in ownership of various industrial concerns. Everyone seemed to have something to say, even though most of them merely repeated what someone else had already said. It was a major headache to keep track of the babble, or what it was doing to public opinion. There were reports from some of the shipyards of labor unrest, caused by fears over the future. And those fears were being spread by the media.

Tiffany leaned forward. "Maybe it's time to bring the matter to a close," she said. "Put a limit on the defender's right to speak."

"That's not permissible," Marius said. The defender could keep raising issues forever, as long as the judges were prepared to allow it. There were so many precedents that Darlington could keep hammering home the same message time and time again, without repeating himself once. "Most court martial hearings concentrate on the facts. They don't normally need to spend months arguing over precedents."

"Then ignore the issue," Tiffany advised. "You don't need to worry about him any longer, do you?"

Marius shrugged. He didn't care to look at his own feelings, for the issue had become an obsession. Betrayal was something he'd expected from the Grand Senate, not someone who had been so close to him. And yet, in hindsight, it was blindingly obvious that Raistlin had been placed there to keep an eye on him. He should have anticipated that the younger man would be given other orders too.

"I don't know," he said, finally.

He'd always enjoyed working with younger officers, helping to steer their careers into places where they could best serve the Federation and themselves. Everyone wanted to be a captain, but not everyone was *suited* to be a commanding officer, not when the demands of commanding a starship under fire were intense. Steering someone gently away from command track was often a service to them as well as the Federation, even if they didn't appreciate it at the time. Mentoring younger officers was important–and he'd seen himself as mentoring Raistlin, as well as Garibaldi and the others. And Raistlin had shot him.

"Well, don't," Tiffany said. She poked him in the chest. "This has..."

The ground heaved. Marius blinked in shock as the lights flickered on and off, then stood up and pushed Tiffany under the heavy wooden desk. The alarms started seconds later, emergency alerts flashing through the datanet. Marius triggered his implants, searching for the cause of the upheaval, then swore as he realized that four datanodes had been taken out. Someone was mounting an attack on Earth.

He reached for the pistol he kept at his side as the doors crashed open, revealing a handful of armed and armored Marines. Marius forced himself to relax, knowing that the Marines would be on edge–and that if they'd been subverted, there was no hope for anyone. And besides, if they were, there was no point in trying to fight.

"Sir," the leader said. "There's been an explosion. We have to get you to the bunker."

"Take Tiffany too," Marius ordered, as he was hustled across the office and up to the wall. "She needs to be safe too."

The wall looked impregnable, but a hidden hatch opened when the Marine tapped it, revealing an antigravity shaft. Marius had no time to object before he was shoved into the shaft and fell into the depths of the earth. The antigravity field caught him before he hit the ground and whisked him into a bunker, where the president was expected to hide if there was ever a major attack on Earth. Given that the *last* president had been on the moon when Admiral Justinian had attacked, it was unlikely the cold gray bunker had ever been used for its intended purpose.

"Sir," the operator said. She was a thin woman, so pale he couldn't help wondering if she'd spent all her life below the earth. Her body was shaved so thin that he would have taken her for a child, if she hadn't been wearing a military uniform. It looked thoroughly unnatural. "We have an emergency situation."

"I gathered that," Marius said. It had been six years since Admiral Justinian had attacked Earth. "Give me a status update."

There was a whooshing sound behind him as Tiffany landed, then picked herself up off the ground. The operator looked as if she were about to object to her presence, then caught Marius's eye and thought better of it. Instead, she turned back to her console and brought up a system-wide display.

"There was a bomb attack outside the President's House," she said, "and a number of smaller attacks scattered over the system. Nothing nuclear or antimatter, thankfully, but most of them were precisely targeted and did considerable damage. There were also attempts to attack the datanet with chaos software, but thanks to the precautions we put in place after the last attack they all failed. As of now, the datanet is secure."

Marius took a step forward until he was looking down at the display. The attacks had been carefully targeted all right, and collectively they represented a major breach in security. It was beyond him to imagine how *anyone* had managed to carry out so many attacks, unless they'd had inside help. Admiral Justinian had done the same, six years ago. Hadn't the Grand Senate's purge been enough to sweep away all the infiltrators?

Evidently not, he thought.

He took a long breath. "Are there any reports of incoming ships?"

"None," the operator said. "I checked with both the Gateway and Titan Base. Both of them are at full alert, but neither of them are reporting trouble. The long-range sensors in Luna Orbit have gone active and are currently sweeping the system, yet nothing out of the ordinary has been detected so far. There may be no incoming attack."

Marius considered it, quickly. Home Fleet consisted of twelve squadrons of superdreadnaughts and over three hundred smaller ships, while both Earth and the Gateway were heavily defended. This time, the defenders had not been caught napping. The damage the attackers had done had been significant, but not fatal. There should be no need for a desperate defense of Earth.

"We will see," he said. "Keep me informed."

Reports came rolling in from all over the system. Each one made grim reading; the enemy, whoever they were, had targeted industrial plants as well as shipyards and even asteroid mining stations. One of Jupiter's massive cloudscoops had been destroyed, while two others had been badly damaged. Marius watched in grim disbelief, wondering how so many terrorists had managed to get through the screening program. Surely, the Grand Senate had closed off all the likely angles of attack.

They subverted a clerk somewhere in the bureaucracy, he guessed. *That rat bastard cleared them through the security net, perhaps recording that they were given the full security vetting before they were granted clearance to work anywhere. And people pay far too much attention to what's written in the databases, rather than checking for themselves.*

But there are too many people involved, his thoughts mocked him. *How can they all be checked and vetted and then declared safe?*

It was nearly five hours before he was sure they'd seen the worst of it. No attacking fleet had made its presence known, not entirely to his surprise. Admiral Justinian had attacked a fleet he'd known he'd decapitated–Marius had a suspicion he'd had someone watching the fleet from Earth, reporting on its status–but Home Fleet was intact and searching for any attackers stupid enough to infringe on Earth's defense limit. And the chaos software attack had failed completely.

He shook his head as he tried to take in the scale of the attack. As shocking as they were, the attacks on Earth were the least of it. The attacks on the industries might well be more dangerous, in the long run. It was quite possible that the attackers had hoped to cripple the Federation indefinitely. If that was the case, there might well have been other attacks...and almost certainly major trouble somewhere else. No one would have committed so much effort towards disrupting Earth–which wouldn't last, despite the scale of the damage–without having a long-term plan to take advantage of the chaos.

It could be another warlord, he told himself. There were people who would argue that *he* was a warlord, the most successful one of all. *But it could also be something far worse.*

The thought tore at his mind. He'd known–and reported to the Grand Senate–that there were rumors of at least two undiscovered races out beyond the Rim, races that might pose a threat to the Federation's security. Nothing had been reported as definite, but he'd known the Outsiders were still there, nursing their grudges and plotting revenge. The real danger had been the threat of them uniting against the Federation and fighting as a unit. And, with the Federation distracted by the Justinian War, they might have had a chance to unify and build up their fleets. It was certainly more believable than an alien race somehow managing to get enough people into place to carry out the attacks without being detected.

"Local space appears to be clear," the operator reported, finally. She hadn't given him a name, not once. "Emergency services are tending to the bomb blast victims."

Marius nodded. The attacks appeared to be over, but he knew better than to think that was the end of it. Most of the terrorists had remained undiscovered...given time, he was sure, the security staff would track them down, but until then they'd have their opportunity to unleash hell across the system. Something would have to be done.

"Summon General Ricardo and...General Thorne to the bunker," he ordered, slowly. There was no choice. Ricardo was a good man, but he would have to go. He'd been placed in command of Earth's security and he'd dropped the ball, spectacularly. "And then send a priority-one message to the rest of the Federation. Earth has been attacked and other attacks will be on their way."

He cursed as he looked up at the star chart, then paced into the barren office set aside for the president. Tiffany was sleeping in the bedroom, trying to relax. Marius didn't blame her–and besides, he wanted to chew Ricardo out in private. Or, at least, without his wife in hearing range. By the time the two officers arrived, he had worked himself up into a furious state. It would be months before much of the Federation received the alert and God alone knew what would have happened by then.

"I want to know what happened," he snarled, as soon as the door was closed and locked. "These attacks were unthinkably savage, weren't they?"

"Yes, sir," Ricardo mumbled. "I..."

Marius scowled at him. "*What happened*?"

"The attackers were completely under the radar," Ricardo said, gathering himself. He'd spent too long working for the Grand Senate to have much of a backbone. "Each of the attacks was carefully planned and aimed right at our weakest spots. They managed to..."

"They managed to do more damage than Admiral Justinian," Marius snapped. The latest reports had warned that it would be at least a year before Earth's industries were completely rebuilt. And reports through the Gateway stated that Terra Nova had been attacked too. "This is the greatest counter-intelligence failure since the Battle of Spider Bite."

"Yes, sir," Ricardo said. He didn't try to defend himself. "I take full responsibility."

"I'm glad to hear it," Marius said. Heads would have to roll. Perhaps literally. "You are relieved of duty, effective immediately. There will be a full inquiry into just how this breach of security took place and, if you are found responsible for some of the failure, you will be held fully accountable."

"Yes, sir," Ricardo said.

Marius gave him one final glower, then turned to look at General Thorne. He was a hard man, with a hard reputation and a war record that was regarded as somewhat questionable, but he *had* managed to complete his mission reasonably well. The Grand Senate had made use of him, yet that couldn't be held against him. Marius had worked for the Grand Senate too.

"General," he said. "I want you to take full command of Earth's security. A state of emergency is now in effect and all rights are suspended, understand? I want every military base and industrial node under heavy guard. No one is to get inside without being thoroughly vetted, then searched."

"Yes, sir," Thorne rumbled. One of his eyes was clearly artificial; the other was a surprisingly soft brown. "I won't let you down."

"I want *everyone* who might be even remotely involved interrogated, thoroughly," Marius ordered. "Go through *everything.* Search incoming ships, probe computer databanks, investigate even the slightest trace of dissident leanings, *everything.* I don't want you to leave even a single stone unturned."

"Yes, sir," Thorne said.

Ricardo cleared his throat. "Your Majesty..."

"I am not a *Majesty,*" Marius snapped. It sounded absurd to be called 'Your Majesty' by anyone. "*Sir* is quite sufficient."

"Sir, the economic effects of such a security sweep will be disastrous," Ricardo warned. "If even the slightest hint of dissident leanings is grounds for an arrest..."

"Investigation," Marius said. "Whoever is behind this attack has to be stopped, *now*!"

He forced himself to calm down, taking deep breaths until he could speak clearly. "This disaster happened on your watch," he added, sharply. "I trusted you to look after Earth. Instead, we've had the greatest series of terror attacks since...*ever*...and the start of a whole new war. We must eliminate these bastards before they manage to hit us again."

"Yes, sir," Ricardo said.

"Go," Marius ordered. "The board of inquiry will be organized as soon as we have a preliminary security report."

It crossed his mind that Ricardo might commit suicide, but Marius found it hard to care. The man had failed spectacularly. Even if it hadn't been his fault...he caught himself, suddenly understanding why the Grand Senate had spent so much time and effort looking for scapegoats. It was always easier to handle failure or disaster if there was someone to blame.

He shook his head, dismissing the thought. There were too many other problems to handle right now. The attacks had to signify the start of a new war...

...And, along the Rim, all hell could be breaking loose.

Chapter Seventeen

Surprise is always a deadly weapon because it leaves the enemy reeling–and, more importantly, unsure of what is going on. A naval squadron that considered itself connected to an entire navy might find itself isolated, utterly unaware of the fate of its comrades. Thus, such a squadron might seek to avoid battle even when the odds are in its favor.
-The Federation Navy in Retrospect, 4199

Tyler's Star, 4098

Tyler's Star–and Tyler's World–was among the oddest star systems known to the Federation. It had two Asimov Points, but while one of them led back into Federation space the other was a complete mystery. Dozens of ships, some of them heavily armored, had slipped into the Asimov Point...and never been seen again. The other actually existed *outside* the star's inner gravity field, something that had perplexed the Federation's researchers ever since it had been discovered. Before then, they'd *known* that all Asimov Points floated within the star's gravity field. Indeed, the best–or at least most commonly believed–theory for their existence relied on stars providing the gravity field that warped the fabric of space and time.

The system, Roman knew, had once attracted a great deal of scientific attention. There should have been two research stations orbiting the Asimov Points, one probing the mystery point and the other studying the more regular point that drifted at the edge of the star system. But now, the second research station was gone and a very familiar red icon orbited the Asimov Point in its place. There was no trace of any debris, according to the probe, but there might well not have been any to find. The station might just have been shoved into the Asimov Point to be turned into atoms by the gravity tides.

"The battlecruisers are to sneak up on that ship and take her out," he ordered. Anywhere else, there would be no need to be sneaky. Here, the picket could drop into FTL at any moment and make her escape, if they suspected trouble. "She is not to be allowed to escape."

He watched as dispassionately as he could as three battlecruisers disengaged from his fleet and crawled forward, advancing on the Asimov Point. They shouldn't be detectable, he knew; they mounted the latest in military-grade cloaking devices. And yet, the Outsiders had sprung far too many surprises already. What about an advance in sensor systems that would pick up the battlecruisers before they entered firing range? The bad guys might have a nasty surprise waiting for the Federation starships on the other side of the Asimov Point.

They can't be strong everywhere, Roman told himself, firmly. Not even the Federation Navy was strong enough to assign an entire battlefleet to every potential destination for his fleet. *And yet they have to know where I would need to go.*

He sighed, inwardly. Civilians saw the stardrive and wondered how starships could ever be intercepted on their voyage from A to B. But they didn't realize just how much time the Asimov Points shaved off interstellar journeys. It would take months for Roman to take his fleet to Boston using stardrive alone, ensuring that the war would probably be decided, one way or the other, before he linked up with any other friendly forces. No, he *had* to go through the Asimov Points...and the Outsiders would know it as well as he did. They would have a chance to lay an ambush in his path.

But where will they go? He asked himself. *And what are their objectives?*

The red icon flashed once, then vanished. "Operation complete," Palter said. "The enemy vessel has been destroyed."

Roman felt a flicker of sympathy for the enemy crew, even though they would have gladly killed him and his men, given half a chance. One moment, they'd been alone in space; the next, missiles had been fired from what was, effectively, point-blank range. They hadn't stood a chance. There had been no time to bring up either their drives or their shields before they'd been blown into atoms. And it was doubtful that any of them had been able to get into the lifepods, even if they'd thought there was a chance of being rescued by friendly forces.

"Good," he said. "The fleet will advance to the Asimov Point, then prepare to launch drones."

The Asimov Point itself was invisible, at least to the naked eye. On the display, however, it was a tight knot of gravity, twisted into a shape that was never consistent from one moment to the next. Spacers had strange dreams close to the Asimov Points, Roman had been told, although he'd never shared them himself. Perhaps it was the sense of abiding *wrongness* surrounding the points–no one had managed to prove any of the theories that attempted to justify their existence–or perhaps it was just night terrors. It was never easy to relax near an Asimov Point, even in friendly territory. There was no way to be sure that something hostile wouldn't pop out and open fire.

He recalled, once, a bull session in the barracks, back at the academy. The senior cadets, having taken on the duty of alternately supporting and scaring the hell out of the junior cadets, had whispered a tale about super-advanced aliens creating the Asimov Points. It explained why they were so strange, they'd said, and why they didn't seem to follow a predictable pattern. The one cadet who'd asked the instructors about the legend had been told, in no uncertain terms, to keep his mouth shut. Federation orthodoxy claimed that the human race was the most advanced race known to exist–and ever *would* exist. Suggesting that an alien race could have created the Asimov Points called all that into question.

"The drones are ready for launch," Palter said. "Sir?"

Roman looked up at the holographic display. "Launch the drones."

He braced himself as the drones sped towards the Asimov Point and vanished. They had neither the mass nor the shields of full-sized starships, which meant an alarmingly high number of them would simply be lost to the Asimov Point itself, let alone anything lurking on the far side. It was not beyond possibility that *none* of them would return, even without enemy action. But he needed to know what was waiting for them, if *anything* was waiting for them. Sending his ships through the point one by one was a good way to get them smashed, one by one. And none of them would know they were flying into hell until the missiles were already screaming towards their hulls.

Seconds passed...and, eventually, four drones popped back into existence. It was a better return rate than he'd dared hope, Roman knew, although the drones might still be useless. He watched, knowing there was no point in ordering his crews to hurry up, as the drones transmitted their data back to the fleet. There seemed to be nothing hostile on the far side of the point.

"Send the first formation through," Roman ordered. If there *was* a cloaked enemy fleet lurking just outside active sensor range, they might well have seen the drones pop in and out of the system. "And hold the second formation ready for immediate deployment."

The lead squadron of superdreadnaughts moved up to the Asimov Point and vanished. Long seconds passed, then a set of courier drones materialized around the point. Nothing had greeted them, the superdreadnaughts reported. The system appeared to be completely empty.

"Take the rest of the fleet through the point," Roman ordered. "And then deploy for immediate departure from the system."

The superdreadnaught shivered slightly as she passed through the Asimov Point, the display blanking out and then hastily rebooting itself. Green icons were spreading out around the Asimov Point, but there were no signs of anything hostile. There had never been any fortresses or even automated combat platforms placed near the Asimov Point, according to the files. The kind of investment that demanded heavy defenses was rarely made along the Rim.

"Local space seems clear," Palter said. "Should I ping the planet, sir?"

"No," Roman said. "Keep us well clear of them."

He sighed. There *was* an inhabited planet in the system, but it was only a stage-one colony. It was quite possible the inhabitants didn't have the slightest idea that enough firepower to destroy a thousand such colonies was passing through their system, or that the Federation had suddenly found itself fighting a whole new war. Such systems would be prizes for the winner, nothing else. They certainly couldn't contribute anything to either side.

"Aye, sir," Palter said.

"Set course for Boston," Roman ordered. Thanks to the crazy lines between Asimov Points, they were now only a week from Boston by stardrive. And there was little prospect of being ambushed, now their course was no longer predictable. "Best possible speed."

His console chimed. "Commodore, this is Briggs in Combat Intelligence," a new voice said. "There's something here I think you should see."

Roman rose to his feet. "I'm on my way." He took one final look at the empty display, reassuring himself that the fleet was alone. Or, at least, that any enemy forces within the system were disinclined to engage. "I'll be there in two minutes."

And if they had caught us, he thought, as he strode through the superdreadnaught's plain white passageways, *it might not have been a bad sign.*

The thought made him roll his eyes. It had been less than a century since the Blue Star War had taught the Federation the dangers of trying to be too clever in wartime. If the Outsiders had made the same mistake, it might have given the Federation a chance to turn the tables quickly, without having to rebuild and reinforce its forces first. But they'd clearly been careful enough to avoid spreading their forces too thin.

He stepped into the Combat Intelligence Center and nodded to Specialist Briggs. Combat Intelligence sounded like a great idea, on the surface, but Roman had learned their limitations very early on. In theory, they could intercept and decipher enemy transmissions, allowing the Federation ships to identify the enemy flagship; in practice, their insights tended to come too late to be useful. And where aliens were concerned, the insights were rarely accurate. There were even officers who believed that Combat Intelligence should be stepped down, their duties assigned to other intelligence personnel. It was one of the few cost-cutting measures that had won approval from the vast majority of naval officers.

"Specialist," he said. Intelligence officers were never in the chain of command, something that rankled badly with them and had led to more than a few fights on leave. "What do you have for me?"

Briggs cleared his throat, loudly. He was a tall man, going slowly bald on top, wearing a dark blue uniform that didn't quite disguise his growing paunch. Roman guessed–there was no time to review his file–that he'd been in the service for decades and was probably not a little resentful of his slow rise in the ranks. And he was probably too old to switch to command track. After the first battles with Admiral Justinian, anyone who might have made command material would have been encouraged to switch. The Navy had been short of skilled commanding officers.

"As always," Briggs said, "we picked up a great deal of data from the star system before we dropped into FTL. It was all recorded, then scanned for anything potentially useful. Most of it is garbage, unsurprisingly, but one piece of information in particular was very interesting."

Roman frowned. Intelligence had been known to make mistakes. No one had predicted Admiral Justinian's attempt at a coup, even though it was a potential risk. But then, Admiral Justinian had had years to lay his plans and make sure his bases were secure.

So did the Outsiders, Roman thought. *They surprised us completely.*

He leaned forward. "What did you find?"

"This," Briggs said. He tapped his console, meaningfully. "A sealed packet of data, encrypted with a Federation Intelligence code."

Roman blinked in surprise. "And you didn't bring this to me earlier?"

"It wasn't identified until now," Briggs said. His tone stiffened, defensively. "The packet wasn't designed to attract attention, Commodore. I believe it was forwarded through a number of datanodes, the escorting program clearing the way for further transmission, then wiping all traces of its passage from the datanet. If it had been specifically tagged 'Federation Intelligence' it might well have been caught in a buffer somewhere."

"Fine," Roman said. "What does it actually *say*?"

"We haven't been able to decipher it all," Briggs said. "What we have been able to decipher, by applying a standard Federation Intelligence Key, is a warning about the Outsiders and a surprising amount of tactical data and observations. There's quite a bit of data within the packet, sir. It will take some time to evaluate."

Briggs paused. "The remaining encrypted sections will need to be returned to Earth," he added, slowly. "They're impossible to decrypt without the proper key."

Roman nodded. Communications security wasn't his speciality, but he understood just how hard it could be to decrypt an encoded message. Some of them even had special functions that automatically erased the message if there was more than one failed attempt to decrypt it, no matter what the communications officers did. It annoyed him not to know what was in the sealed parts of the packet, but he would just have to wait.

"I see," Roman said. "Why were some parts of it accessible and other parts kept sealed?"

"Well, they weren't accessible without the standard key," Briggs said. He launched into a complicated explanation, which ended by noting that any Federation Intelligence officer would have access to a standard key. "I suspect whoever sent us the packet wanted to make sure that whoever got it could access the data, without being able to decrypt anything that might compromise his identity. There's precedent for that, I believe."

"Very well," Roman said. The identity of the mystery agent could wait. "Have the sealed part of the message returned to Earth. Then send my staff copies of the unsealed pieces of intelligence..."

"I should warn you, sir, that this information will betray at least one piece of data to the enemy," Briggs said. "It should be heavily restricted."

Roman's eyes narrowed...and then he understood. Presumably, the Outsiders didn't know they had a mole, even though they'd used infiltrators of their own in attacking Athena. The mere presence of the data packet, even assuming it could not be cracked without the right key, would reveal the existence of the mole. And then the Outsiders would start hunting for a spy. The thought of sending them off on a witch-hunt, with all the problems the Grand Senate's hunt for moles had caused the Federation, was amusing...but also unacceptable. It was, at the very least, well above his pay grade.

And, at worst, it will betray one of us to the enemy, he thought, crudely. The Federation Navy stressed loyalty to one's fellows, which was particularly ironic in the wake of the Justinian War. Interviews with some of the survivors had convinced Emperor Marius that most of them had been more loyal to the ideal of the Federation than to the Grand Senate...

He shook his head. No, he wouldn't betray the mole. But the data would still have to be analyzed.

"Send it to my terminal," he ordered, finally. "I'll review it personally. Keep the rest of it firmly in-house, at least until you have something to present to my command staff."

"Aye, sir," Briggs said. He sounded pleased, if only because he'd gotten what he wanted–and kept control of the data. "I'll prepare the remainder for transmission to Earth."

Assuming no one has managed to cut the chain of Asimov Points to Earth, Roman thought. It would still be two to three months before anything reached Emperor Marius. By then, who knew what might have happened. *But we have to do the best we can.*

"Good," Roman said.

He stood, walked out of the Combat Intelligence Center and down to the sickbay. There hadn't been any casualties on *Valiant*–the ship had barely been touched–but a number of smaller ships had had to tranship their wounded to the superdreadnaught, which had a considerably larger medical center. Roman winced, inwardly, as he saw the men and women lying on the beds, some so badly injured that they would have to be shipped home to a proper hospital. The stasis pods, he'd been told, were already overloaded.

"Commodore," one man called. He wore the uniform of a missile tech, but his uniform's arms had been cut away. One glance told Roman why. His arms ended in stumps. "Look! No hands!"

Roman had to conceal his horror. The thought of losing one's hands was particularly horrific. They could be replaced, he knew, either through prosthetics or vat-grown replacements, but it was still unpleasant. But visiting the injured was part of his duties. It wasn't one he could palm off on anyone else.

"I was on *Hawking*," the missile tech said. He seemed to be in good hmor, despite his wounds. Roman suspected he'd been drugged. "One moment, everything was fine; the next, pieces of metal take my hands! It was awful. Blood was everywhere. And then we just started giggling!"

"Giggling?" Roman repeated. "Why?"

The man smirked. "Do you know how hard it is to get a girl when you're a lowly missile tech?"

Roman shook his head.

"They think we're lazy buggers, the lot of us," the man continued. "Now, how can they say I wasn't injured on active duty?"

"They can't," Roman said. He shook his head, tiredly. "And you'll be back with them soon enough."

"I want metal hands," the man said. "It looks more impressive."

"It does," Roman agreed.

Silently, he moved on to the next casualty.

Chapter Eighteen

Owing to the number of known Asimov Point connections between Boston and Earth, it took no less than three months for Emperor Marius to become aware of the attacks along the Rim and the Fall of Athena. By then, the Emperor was well aware of just how much damage had been done in the Core Worlds.
-The Federation Navy in Retrospect, 4199

Earth, 4098

"Put the message on," Marius ordered, once his full cabinet had assembled in the briefing room. "Run it right from the start."

There was a pause, then a hologram of a woman appeared in front of them. A stream of data running along the bottom identified her as Senator Chang Li, the Representative from Nova Athena. Marius remembered her; she'd been the sole senator he'd met who hadn't belonged to any of the two main political factions. Just how she'd managed to get onto a committee responsible for interrogating Marius, after his unavoidable failure along the Rim, was beyond him. She shouldn't have been anything more than a lone voice, crying out in the darkness.

But she was heavily outvoted on the committee in any case, he thought, as the recording began. *The Grand Senators might have calculated that giving her the post would have looked good, without forcing them to compromise their power.*

He shrugged. The Grand Senators were dead. It was quite possible he'd never know.

"Emperor Marius," Senator Chang Li said. Her voice was oddly accented now, which puzzled him until he realized she'd been deliberately mimicking Earth's dialect when he'd last met her. The Grand Senators believed out-world accents to be a sign of barbarism, all the better to justify keeping the colonies under strict control. "We would prefer to have spoken with you openly, in person, but we would not trust you or your former masters with our safety. Besides, there is little to negotiate.

"I represent the Outsider Federation, a union of worlds from beyond the Rim that have gathered together to resist the endless advance of the Federation. I will not bore you with a recitation of the crimes committed by the Federation against innocent settlers, who have lost everything they built when the Grand Senate decided it wanted what they had. You know the crimes of the Grand Senate–and the Federation–as well as I do. I speak now of the future.

"It is our intention to liberate ourselves from your control and remove all threat of future oppression," she continued. "By the time you receive this message, you will have seen our first blows directed against your organs of control. Your network of bases along the Rim has been disrupted and your industries attacked, even within the Core Worlds themselves. The balance of power has shifted in our favor."

Marius gritted his teeth as the words rolled on.

"In hopes of ending this war with minimal casualties, we extend to you the following offer," Chang continued. "You will concede our independence from your control, now and forever. Each and every one of the worlds along the Rim will hold a plebiscite, where they will vote to remain in the Federation, join us or become independent in their own right. We will both agree to honor the results of their referendums.

"If you agree to these terms, we will have peace. There will be room for both of us to breathe and recover from the war. There will be a boom in interstellar trade and economic growth for both of us. But if you refuse, we will fight this war until the Federation is completely destroyed, for we know better than to expect mercy if the Federation wins. You may send your reply back to Athena, using the attached code. We eagerly await your reply."

There was a pause, then the holographic image blinked out of existence.

"Traitor," General Standerton Thorne growled. "She was a Senator."

"Not the most promising of recommendations," Tully agreed. "I..."

"It gets worse," Commodore Arunika said. She cut Tully off with practiced ease. "We have analyzed the recordings from the Battle of Athena and the data packet sent back to us by a covert agent. The news is not good."

She paused for dramatic effect. "We're not just fighting humans," she said. "The Outsider Federation–interesting choice of name, by the way–includes at least two alien races."

Marius fought to keep his face under control. Protecting humanity from aliens was one of the prime reasons for the Federation's existence. Even now, it was a rare alien who was allowed to leave his homeworld–or the colony world his race might have settled, before they encountered the human race. Aliens were *alien*. They could not be trusted, let alone honored with the full rights and obligations of humans. And the Outsiders were turning them into *soldiers*? Giving them access to human weapons and training? It could not be borne.

"Apparently, the aliens have been promised equality with humans, once the war is won," Arunika continued. "In hindsight, this may explain some of the rumors from beyond the Rim prior to the Justinian War. The Outsiders were working with the aliens and convincing them to unite against us."

"Never mind that now," Thorne growled. "The real question is simple. Can we win the war?"

"Unknown," Arunika said. She looked directly at Marius. "We have no real way of deducing just how strong the Outsiders actually *are*, sir. The only way we can guess at anything is by tracking their actions–and the actions they *didn't* take."

Marius frowned, then saw what she meant. "They didn't attack us while we were distracted by Admiral Justinian," he said, slowly. "They couldn't have been ready to take the offensive then."

There was no way to be *sure*, he knew, but it made sense. Admiral Justinian and the other warlords had come alarmingly close to winning the war. If the Outsiders had attacked, with the fleet they'd shown in the attack on Athena, they might well have successfully cracked the Federation into several smaller states. Or they could have quietly supplied the warlords with enough material to keep them going for much longer, without needing to show themselves...

They couldn't have been ready to move, he thought. And that led to another thought. *They might not have wanted to jump now either.*

It made sense, he decided. They'd known him—Chang Li had *definitely* known him. She'd known he wouldn't leave the Rim alone, not when he'd been so driven to eliminate the scourge of piracy. Commodore Garibaldi had been just the first step in a plan to eventually exterminate the pirates, which would—naturally—have revealed the Outsiders too. They might have been forced to mount their offensive before they were ready to move.

"It may be more hopeful than we believe," he said, and outlined his reasoning. "How many shipyards could they have produced in the time they had?"

"Unknown," Arunika said. "There are just too many variables. Did they start from scratch or did they have some pre-existing infrastructure in place already? How much trained manpower did they have? How much were they able to obtain from the Federation...?"

Marius raised a hand, silencing her.

"I know," he said. He turned to look at Professor Kratman. "Did the Brotherhood know anything about this?"

"The Brotherhood would not have looked kindly upon any friendly human-alien interaction," Kratman pointed out. "Our whole cause is to prevent aliens from ever threatening humanity again."

Marius nodded, keeping his face impassive. Even now, he had no idea just how large the Brotherhood actually was—or, for that matter, why the Grand Senate had even tolerated its existence. They might well have seen the Brotherhood as competition. But then, the Brotherhood *did* provide unbending support for anything that kept aliens under firm control, something that would have suited the Grand Senate very well.

"Then we fight," Marius said, shortly. "There's no alternative."

Tully cleared his throat. "The economic situation is not good," he said. "We may be unable to fight the war."

Marius turned to face him. "Explain."

The bureaucrat didn't look intimidated. If anything, he looked bored.

"Our economy has been badly damaged," he said. "We have suffered a number of blows to our industries, which have created new and unanticipated bottlenecks in production. My staff is currently working to devise plans to expand those bottlenecks, but it will be years before we have a workable action plan. There are just too many glitches in the system the Grand Senate left us."

Marius met his eyes. "Are you saying that we cannot win?"

"I'm saying it will be years before we can restore our production levels back to the pre-war rate, let alone increase it," Tully said. "There are just too many shortages. We need more trained manpower, for example, yet training people up to the required levels will take at least five years—and that assumes we are starting from a decent educational level."

"A dangerous assumption," Kratman observed. "Even now, Earth's schools are still very weak."

"Because they didn't want to teach the kids how to question," Marius snapped. Earth had been the only place the Grand Senate could have been challenged, politically. It hadn't taken long for the Grand Senators to ensure that the population became dependent on their handouts. And the population had rioted when their handouts had been cut. "But we're short on options."

"The war will be far more costly than you suppose," Tully said. "Even victory might break us. Their terms are not unreasonable, sir. They should be accepted."

"So will defeat," Marius said. He felt a surge of sudden hatred he had to fight to keep under control. "And if we accept their terms, Tully, humanity's unity will be shattered forever."

He glared down at the table. There could be no illusions about the Federation's popularity outside the Core Worlds. Any reasonably fair referendum would see almost all of the outer worlds either going to the Outsider Federation or demanding independence for themselves, which would leave the Federation badly crippled. Who knew what would become of it then?

And the Core Worlds were economically dependent on the outer worlds. What would happen if they lost the ability to extort resources at will? There would be a massive economic crash, further threatening the Federation's integrity. Marius privately doubted the rump Federation would survive a year, once it had lost control of the outer worlds. And it would fall all the way down into civil war.

He'd intended to solve the problem, he knew. The Core Worlds couldn't parasite on the outer worlds indefinitely. It was, if nothing else, grossly immoral. And, more importantly, it sparked countless uprisings against the Federation's authority. But it seemed he had run out of time.

"No," he said. He had not fought Admiral Justinian for six years just to see the Federation shatter anyway, even though the rogue warlord was dead. "We will not accept these terms."

Marius took a breath. "Humanity's unity is at stake, but so is it's very survival," he warned. "If the Outsiders get their wish, the human race will be grossly weakened. And if they grant aliens rights, what happens to the human race then? This cannot be allowed."

"There may be room for negotiation," Tully said. "I..."

Marius spoke over him. "There is no room for negotiation," he said. "We pledged that we would reform the Federation, not surrender to naked force and accept division, a division that would eventually lead to a second war or humanity's destruction. I will not concede anything to rebels who believe they can intimidate us into conceding to them."

He took a breath, assembling all parts of his argument in his mind. "We will go to war," he said. "We will conscript educated manpower from wherever we can get it–and we will start educating as many people as possible, pushing them into the pipeline so they can join the production ranks as soon as possible. We will train new spacers, new soldiers, new engineers...everything we need to fight the war. We will tap every last resources of the Federation and bend it to the cause of victory."

"There will be resistance," Thorne mused.

"We will deal with it," Marius said.

He turned his gaze to General Yusuf Maringa, Head of the Joint Chiefs of Staff. "How do we stand, militarily speaking?"

Maringa's dark face looked worried. Marius had originally intended to keep the post for himself, as Commander-in-Chief of the Federation's military. Maringa had only been a temporary expedient, someone who could handle the paperwork. He had never been intended to serve as a commander during a war. It was partly why the Grand Senate had largely left him alone, even when they'd been relieving–or removing–countless other military officers.

"Well, we have two fleets ready for dispatch to the front," Maringa said, after a moment to consult his terminal. "Home Fleet itself remains untouched, now we have purged the handful of affected datanodes and other problematic spots. Our prime weakness lies with Boston, sir; if we lose control of the junction there, the Outsiders will have control of five separate Asimov Points that would allow them to attack deeper into the Federation."

"And we couldn't have that, could we?" Marius asked, dryly. But Boston was still three months away, even through the Asimov Point network. The system might already have fallen, leaving the path to Earth wide open. "Move reinforcements up to the system, then start looking around for other deployable forces we can add to the roster. We'll try to hold Boston, but I also want to mount counterattacks as soon as possible. Find a few aggressive commanders and send them into the enemy's rear."

He took a breath. "And dispatch as many survey ships as you can," he added. "I want them scouting out the Beyond, looking for enemy bases. I want them found and prepped for destruction."

"Aye, sir," Maringa said.

He didn't look pleased, Marius noted. It was hard to blame him. Searching for enemy bases was a huge task, without any real guarantee of success, but it had to be done. Short of capturing an Outsider vessel with its database intact, which wasn't particularly likely unless the enemy screwed up by the numbers, there was no other way to locate the enemy homeworlds. The only real advantage the Federation had was its reasonable certainty that the alien homeworlds would be harder to hide than an Outsider base.

Marius, once again, cursed the Grand Senate under his breath. The Survey Service had been reduced to a handful of ships, left updating navigational charts of the outer worlds rather than exploring beyond the Rim. And then it had been absorbed into the Federation Navy in hopes of finding an unexplored Asimov Point that led into the rear of warlord territory. They certainly hadn't been doing their job of probing unexplored space...

But that might have caused political problems, he thought, bitterly. *Who in their right mind would want another Blue Star War?*

He cleared his throat. "We have a colossal advantage, if we have time to use it," he said. "And I will not stand for *anything* that gets in our way. Do you understand me?"

"Yes, sir," Maringa said. The others echoed him quickly. "We won't fail you."

"Good," Marius said. "Dismissed."

Professor Kratman lingered until the others had gone, leaving him alone with Marius. "You do realize that we might win the war, but lose the peace?"

Marius glowered at his former commanding officer. "Do *you* realize that we would lose everything if we accepted their terms?"

"I do," Kratman said. "And I understand what's driving you. But I think you need to understand that the Federation is alarmingly fragile at the moment. A push in the wrong direction might shatter it."

He nodded politely to Marius, then turned and walked out of the room. Marius glared at his retreating back, then looked down at the intelligence reports on his terminal. None of them made comforting reading. He was far from the only military officer to suspect that trouble was gathering itself in the Beyond, but the analysts were now trying to make up for their failure to predict the offensive by competing to come up with the most hair-raising predictions and projections of enemy strength. And, if they'd been sending memos to the Grand Senate, they might well have succeeded in alarming them into making peace.

But Marius was an experienced officer. He'd read enough intelligence reports to know when officers were doing their best to predict the enemy's capabilities–and when they were trying to cover their asses by writing down the worst possible projection, then presenting it as absolute truth.

"Bastards," he muttered.

There was no way they could accept the peace terms–and the treacherous bitch of a senator had to know it. He'd thought well of her, hadn't he? The one senator in the room who'd actually given a damn about her people. And now...the more he looked at it, the more he wondered if the Outsiders had been behind the pirates. Senator Chang Li might have been backing the people who were ravaging her worlds! It was no surprise–Governor Barany had done the same–but it was still disappointing. He wasn't sure why.

"Record," he ordered. The automated system clicked on at once. "From Emperor Marius to Commodore Garibaldi. Congratulations on maintaining your fleet in an intact state. You are hereby promoted to Vice Admiral–paperwork and other formalities to come."

He sighed. There would be other commanding officers heading to Boston–and some of them would outrank his protégée. Normally, that would be acceptable, but Garibaldi had shown an astonishing talent for coming out on top. It was worth trying to press that talent into service. Besides, he had no doubt of Garibaldi's loyalty. The others were more questionable.

Damn Justinian, he thought.

"Your orders are as follows," he continued. "I want you to prepare to go on the offensive as soon as possible..."

Chapter Nineteen

It says something about the sheer hatred of the Federation among the outer worlds that hundreds of thousands volunteered to join the Outsiders, despite knowing that the odds were–at best–even. But no one was really surprised.
-The Federation Navy in Retrospect, 4199

Athena, 4098

"I think they like you," General Stuart muttered.

Chang Li had to smile as she descended the steps from her shuttlecraft and set foot on Athena's soil. The crowds gathered just beyond the security fence were cheering loudly, as if there had been no real debate over who would win the battle for hearts and minds. Li smiled and waved at them, hoping the crowds wouldn't have reason to regret their conversion to the Outsider cause after the war. The Federation would be truly merciless if it won the war and imposed its own peace on the Beyond.

She kept waving until she reached the door, then allowed General Stuart to lead her into the building. General Erskine stood just inside, surrounded by a small honor guard. He saluted her, which she returned, then motioned for her to follow him through the corridors. Li was struck by the staggering luxury all around her as she walked, then pushed the thought aside as they stepped into a briefing room. It looked reassuringly mundane.

"The population is relatively quiet," General Erskine said, as they sat down at the table. "There have been a handful of nasty incidents, but mostly it seems as if they're waiting to see what happens, rather than rise up against us as a body. It helps that we have countless volunteers already clamouring to join up with us."

Li smiled. "Are they truly willing?"

"Most of them are," General Erskine said. "We're doing our best to vet them now, but we have colossal gaps in our system. We may end up taking them all and praying that none of them have bad intentions."

"I see," Li said. "And the remnants of the enemy defenders?"

"We think a number of Marines have managed to scatter into the countryside," General Erskine said. "Unfortunately, we have no hard numbers; the bastards managed to purge the command datanodes before we got our hands on them. The best we can do is hope they aren't in any state to cause trouble, but remain watchful anyway. There's no point in detailing forces to hunt them down right now."

He paused. "Most of the planet's industrialists have declared their intentions to seek contracts from us," he added. "I think they wish to meet with you before you depart."

"We can certainly make time," Li said. She hadn't wanted to spend time pressing the flesh–it reminded her, all too clearly, of her time in the Federation Senate–but she had little choice. Besides, she had to make it clear to them that the Outsiders had no intention of becoming just another distant master. "Is the world ready to join us openly?"

"I believe it may be a year before a provisional government asserts itself," General Erskine said. "But after that, I don't think we'd have any real objections to them joining us."

"The Federation might," General Stuart growled. "They held Boston."

Li steepled her fingers. "How bad is it going to be?"

"We need to hack our way around Boston," General Stuart said. "It will give them time to recover from the shock, particularly since they rejected our offer of a negotiated peace."

General Erskine looked up. "They just said no?"

"More or less," Li said. The response had been undiplomatic in the extreme. It was a change from the Federation's normal approach, where even an ultimatum had some conciliatory words that changed absolutely nothing. She'd once wondered if one of the Federation's diplomats had read the line about a spoonful of sugar helping the medicine go down and taken it to heart. "The response was largely unprintable. Suffice it to say they are determined to fight to the finish."

"Unless someone assassinates Emperor Marius," General Erskine said. "We should consider the possibility."

Li frowned. Assassinating Grand Senators had been a waste of time; there was always a successor, while there would also be bloody reprisals against the perpetrators of the crime. But an Emperor...Marius Drake might be married, but there were no children. Indeed, it was possible that Lady Tiffany wouldn't *want* children. Her file suggested she'd been more interested in her research than playing power games with the rest of the Grand Senate brats.

But that might not make any difference, she thought, morbidly. *She could have children grown in exowombs, perhaps. Maids would take care of them from birth till they were old enough to walk. And if she refuses, a man like Marius Drake is forceful enough to overwhelm her objections and force her to have children.*

It wasn't a reassuring thought. She knew, all too well, just how corrupt the Grand Senate had become, simply through being able to pass power down the generations without a real challenge. Emperor Marius's family might follow the same pattern, except they would have no true peers, no one who could challenge their petty cruelties. Marius himself might be a fine man–and she had to admit he was–but what would his children or grandchildren be like? She wasn't sure she wanted to know.

"We should," she said. The first wave of bombings and other attacks had shocked the Federation, but it had also galvanised the security forces to root out the moles, root and branch. It would be far from easy to get an assassin close enough to Admiral Drake to make the kill, not since the Grand Senate had already tried to kill him. "But I don't see how."

"I will consider it," General Erskine said. He paused. "But, for the moment, the war itself goes on."

General Stuart nodded, then keyed a switch. A 3D holographic starchart appeared in front of them.

"We cannot attack Boston directly," he said. "The defenses aren't much more advanced than the defenses of Athena, but Commodore Garibaldi has had ample time to make improvements, prevent chaos software from infecting the whole system and repair his fleet before we were ready to attack. Now, we might win if we stormed the system, but the cost would be staggeringly high. Our best case would see us losing a third of our fleet merely trying to break through the Asimov Point, let alone storming the planet and its orbital facilities."

Li frowned. "Don't we have supporters on the planet itself?"

"Not enough," General Erskine said. "Commodore Garibaldi has already taken precautions against another uprising."

"So we will angle our attacks, instead, against worlds closer to Boston," General Stuart said. "We will gain control of three separate Asimov Point chains, forcing Commodore Garibaldi to split his forces to cover the planet as well as the system. Eventually, we will be able to punch through and take Boston, forcing Commodore Garibaldi into a missile duel that will play to our strengths."

"Until they duplicate the long-range missiles for themselves," Li said. She looked down at the table. "How long will it take them to copy our weapons, now they've seen them in action?"

"Unknown," General Stuart said. "Assuming they don't have any samples to work from, I'd say at least six months to come up with a workable design and another six months to start mass production. But they may have a similar concept on the drawing board already, in which case the time to mass production will be considerably shorter."

"All of that assumes they are in position to keep researching newer technology," Li said. "We did hammer their production yards pretty hard."

"Not hard enough," General Stuart said. "They will be able to recover, if they have time."

"Which brings us all the way back to taking out Boston," Li added. She looked him in the eye. "We've tested ourselves against them now, General. Can we take the system?"

"I believe so," General Stuart said. "But time is not on our side."

Li nodded. The Outsiders had swept over nearly two hundred worlds, not counting the asteroid settlements and other minor habitations, but most of them were largely irrelevant to the overall outcome of the war. Their settlers might be enthusiastic, yet they brought nothing to the table. All they could really do was eliminate the Federation's supervisors and pray the Outsiders won the war. The Federation would not be merciful if it returned to the sector to discover that countless investments had been destroyed, or nationalized.

She sighed. The Federation would not be merciful. It was practically becoming a refrain.

We won the first battles, she thought. *But now the Federation is alert and knows we're out here. The next battles will be far harder.*

"Then you may commence preparations to take the system at once," she said. "But remember not to risk everything on one blow."

General Stuart nodded. "Understood," he said. "We won't let you down."

ꙮ

"This isn't a bad place to take leave," Lieutenant Caleb Roebuck said, without irony. He and Uzi sat together in a cafe, drinking beer and watching as their subordinates had their fun. "I could spend a few years here."

Uzi had to smile. "I suppose you could," he agreed. "But there really isn't anything remarkable here."

Roebuck looked disbelieving. The spaceport strip consisted of nothing more than a dozen brothels, five gambling halls–they would have been called casinos, Uzi had heard, but there was a tax on casinos that didn't apply to gambling halls–and at least thirty places to eat, drink and pick fights. He didn't have the heart to tell Roebuck that there were places for shore leave on Earth where hundreds of thousands of spacers could be catered for at the same time, then pushed out when they ran out of money. There was no shortage of ways to separate a spacer or a soldier from his money and the people who ran the shore leave facilities knew all of them. By Earth's standards, the spaceport was really quite small.

"But tell me," Roebuck said. "Who are they?"

Uzi followed his gaze. A pair of near-naked women, wearing nothing more than silver thongs, stood there, smiling cheerfully at spacers and soldiers alike. They couldn't have been more obviously prostitutes if they'd carried signs around, although they had a certain innocence that suggested they were part-timers, rather than dedicated prostitutes.

"They're probably part-timers," he said, finally. "They're often inexperienced."

Roebuck gave him a sharp look. "Part-timers?"

"The wages here aren't very high," Uzi said. "When a large number of ships arrive in orbit and their crews come down for shore leave, the young girls often come to the port and offer themselves, in exchange for a few credits. They book a hotel room and service three or four spacers a day, then they stagger off home and clean themselves as best as they can. Some of them find they like it and join the brothels, others swear never to do it again until they really, really, really, really need the money. And some of them die on the streets"

"I...they're just..." Roebuck swallowed and started again. "But why?"

Uzi felt a sudden urge to shock the younger man. "Why do they do it? Because they need money. And why do they die?"

He smiled, humorlessly. "The brothels have rules," he said. "You can have just about anything you want, as long as you book in advance. Get your kicks by slapping girls? You can find a girl willing to be slapped by you for a few extra credits. But step over the lines you paid for? You can expect to be yanked off the girl by a security guard and tossed naked into the streets."

Roebuck looked sick.

Uzi went on, enjoying himself. "But the girls who come for a day or two have no protections," he added. "They're innocents, too. They don't realize that someone might want more than a quick blowjob or a hasty screw in a hired bedroom. Some of them are beaten, some try to back out when they realize they're actually selling themselves for money...and some are killed by the brothel owners. They don't like the competition."

"That's...that's awful," Roebuck said.

"It could be worse," Uzi said. "I was once hired to train soldiers on one side of an insurgency. Their leaders had a habit of kidnapping women from the other side of the insurgency and raping them, then telling the poor bitches they had a choice between working for them or going back home. And most of them stayed with the kidnappers, even though the choice was quite genuine. They could have gone home if they'd wished."

Roebuck's eyes widened. "*Why?*"

"Because their menfolk would have killed them for daring to be raped," Uzi said. "You see, they felt that a proper woman simply couldn't be raped. They genuinely believed that to be true. So, by definition, any woman who was actually raped was not a proper woman and had betrayed her family. She had to die."

"And this was tolerated?" Roebuck asked. "The Federation let it happen?"

"The Federation was backing the side that was trying to crush those bastards," Uzi said, just to see what sort of response he got. To Roebuck–and the other Outsiders–the Federation was the source of all evil. "It never bothered to just crush them from orbit."

There were other tales he could tell, he knew, but he kept them to himself. The mercenaries had been forced to blend in with the locals, even share some of their pursuits. And some of them had made looting, raping and burning seem almost normal.

Roebuck shook his head. "We're fighting to stop it," he said. "We won't let it continue."

"I'm glad to hear it," Uzi said, dryly. "You do realize there's a contradiction there?" He smiled, then explained when Roebuck looked puzzled. "You talk about freeing the colony worlds from the iron grip of the Federation, allowing them to develop in their own way," he pointed out. "But at the same time, you're wanting to stop cultural practices that would be a great deal worse without the Federation's interference. For every world birthed from a decent culture, Lieutenant, there is one birthed from a nightmare that was booted off Earth, centuries ago. And which ones do you consider worth protecting?"

Roebuck looked down at his hands. "I don't know," he admitted. "But...but the Federation is a monster."

"I don't think that is in dispute," Uzi said. The Grand Senate had committed more than its fair share of atrocities. "But tell me...can you form a government that large without committing monstrous acts of your own?"

"I thought you were on our side," Roebuck said.

"I'm a mercenary," Uzi countered. "I'm on the side of whoever pays me."

It was true enough, he thought, even as Roebuck twisted his lips in disgust. To an idealist, the mercenary must seem the lowest form of being. But to a practical man, idealism itself was a weakness. No amount of idealism could bring warmth and security to a family. Only money–cold hard cash–or power could ensure either.

"Bah," Roebuck said, finally.

He rose, dropped a credit on the table, then stalked off. Uzi watched him go, wondering what–if anything–would result from his gentle prodding. It was just possible that Roebuck would grow dissatisfied with the Outsiders, perhaps even be ready to be turned into a double-agent. Or he might rationalize his way through the contradiction and convince himself that he was still on the side of bright, unvarnished good. Uzi had met far too many people who talked themselves into believing that anything they did was justified, because it was in the name of the greater good.

The waitress–a young girl wearing a long dress buttoned up to her neck–strode over and picked up Roebuck's abandoned glass. Uzi finished his glass with one long swallow, then passed it to the girl, making sure to keep his eyes on the swell of her covered breasts. The girl looked nervous as she scurried off, taking the credit with her. Uzi allowed himself a cold smile, taking a moment of amusement in the whole situation. She'd probably been harassed by just about everyone who came in for a drink, even though her clothing suggested she was off the market. Shaking his head, he stood and walked out of the door.

He heard the sound of someone gagging in an alleyway and peered inside, allowing his gaze to adapt to the gloom. A girl was on her knees in front of a man, who was zipping up his fly with practiced ease. The girl herself was spitting out the remains of his semen...She, Uzi decided, was definitely a newcomer to the whole game. Even the most man-hating whore would know to pretend it tasted sweet.

Too young, Uzi thought, feeling an odd flicker of sympathy. He was good at judging ages and the girl, he thought, was only seventeen at most. Perhaps younger. It wasn't uncommon for girls to take tailored hormones in hopes of boosting their bodies, even when they were too young to handle it. The growth of the girl's chest, out of proportion with the rest of her body, suggested she'd definitely had something done to it.

The client glanced at him, nodded in an almost friendly manner and strode off down the alleyway. Uzi watched him go, then looked at the girl. The despair in her blue eyes would have been comical, under other circumstances. It was very definitely her first time on the streets. She'd probably thought she'd known what it was like until she actually did it. And then she'd had a very nasty surprise.

And, he told himself, *isn't that just like the Outsiders*?

He could have her, he knew. She was a whore. He could pay for her. But, after everything he'd said, it wouldn't have felt right. The thought bothered him–a conscience, after all this time? But he pushed it aside.

Reaching into his pocket, he produced a coin and tossed it to her, then turned and walked away.

Interlude One

From: *The Chaos Years* (5023)

The defeat of the Federation at Athena, the attacks against Earth and the flight to Boston effectively cost the Federation control of the Rim. Independence-seeking rebels on countless worlds threw the Federation's control of everything from vital industrial nodes to Asimov Point junctions into doubt. The Federation, already weakened by the Justinian War, staggered under the blows. It seemed as though the collapse of central authority would not be too far away.

It still possessed overwhelming power. But all of its power meant nothing when the system itself was failing. The Grand Senate had weakened the bonds of loyalty that had allowed the Federation to survive the Inheritance Wars. Now, countless star systems thought more of independence, even of joining the Outsider Federation, rather than remaining loyal to the Federation. What had the Federation done for them? The benefits its rule brought were more than matched, even exceeded, by the downsides of being forced to submit themselves to the Grand Senate. What sort of security could anyone hope for when the Grand Senate could take whatever it wanted, whenever it wanted?

The Outsider Propaganda, thus, fell on fertile soil. Combined with the victories won by the fledgling Outsider Navy, it came close–very close–to convincing the wavering worlds that its success was inevitable. Everyone knew, eventually, that another stunning victory might convince rebel groups to strike while they had a chance, perhaps even throw the Federation off their worlds. And if that happened, it would prove fatal to the Federation's cause.

As Commodore–later Admiral–Garibaldi struggled to hold the line and keep possession of vital junctions which would be desperately needed once the Federation Navy mounted a counterattack, Emperor Marius fought to gird the wavering Federation for war. But it was not easy. The Federation was in disarray...

...And, as Emperor Marius strove to keep the Federation intact, his actions made matters worse.

Much worse.

Chapter Twenty

One of the strangest contradictions of the Asimov Point network is that it can allow certain star systems to become chokepoints, while denying the enemy the ability to simply travel interstellar space to their destination. But if there happens to be a separate chain running near the vital chain, a raider can slip in through the cracks.
-The Federation Navy in Retrospect, 4199

Taurus, 4100

"Transit complete, sir."

Captain Scott Palter nodded, tersely. *Spartan* was his first command, after serving as Commodore–now Admiral–Garibaldi's tactical officer. It wasn't lost on him that his promotion had come about as a direct result of the desperate need for experienced officers–or that he could lose his first command as quickly as he'd gained it, if he screwed up. The Federation Navy couldn't afford mistakes any longer.

"Cloak us," he ordered. There had been no point in trying to move through the Asimov Point cloaked. The device would have fluctuated when they made transit, allowing them to be spotted by any watching eyes. "Run a full sensor sweep, then move us to the RV point."

"Aye, sir," the sensor officer said.

Scott nodded, watching the display through cold blue eyes. Taurus was a disputed system, disputed in the sense that neither side felt able to divert the ships and fortifications needed to actually *hold* the system against determined attack. It possessed three Asimov Points, none of which had been particularly heavily defended before the war, and a planet whose inhabitants took as little interest in the outside universe as possible. Surprisingly, the Federation had honored their wish to be left alone. Scott had read through the files, but there had been nothing to suggest *why* the Federation had acted so badly out of character by leaving the population to themselves. Perhaps someone had shovelled out huge bribes, once upon a time.

Or there's something else here that bears investigation, later, he told himself, as his ship headed towards its destination. *Something one of the Grand Senators sought to conceal from the others.*

He shrugged, then studied the tactical display. There was almost no activity in the system at all, at least as far as his passive sensors could tell. No one seemed to be mining the asteroids, let alone setting up other colonies or industrial nodes. It was odd, given the potential value of the system, but it would have to be explained later. Perhaps someone had been saving it for development when the sector received more investment, only to see the investment faded away when the Federation started to contract. Or...

"We're in position, Captain," the helmsman reported.

"Hold us here," Scott ordered. "Deploy passive sensor platforms, then link us to them."

He smiled to himself, grimly. There had been two battles fought in the system; once when the Outsiders had punched through to take control of the Asimov Points, then another when a squadron of Federation Navy battlecruisers had responded to the attack and chased the makeshift defenders back out of the system. Since then, it had been largely abandoned, but ONI swore blind that the Outsiders were using it to run supplies down to the forces besieging Boston. Admiral Garibaldi had ordered Scott to do what he could to interdict the supply lines.

We should mine the Asimov Points, he thought, although he knew it would be largely pointless, only dangerous to independent freighters. *Give them something to worry about as they make their way to Boston.*

But the Admiral wouldn't allow it. The minefields could and would be swept, unless they were covered by fortresses and mobile units, and there were nowhere near enough of either to allow Taurus to receive its own battlefleet. It would only delay the Outsiders, not deter them altogether. The only real way to stop them, or at least force the bastards to divert more strength to their convoy escorts, was to ambush them as they made their way towards the front...

"Captain," the sensor officer said. "I'm picking up ships transiting Point Beta!"

"Show me," Scott snapped, rising to his feet and striding over to the officer's console. It felt strange to sit on a bridge and know it was his, but there was no time to enjoy it. "What do we have?"

A line of red icons emerged from the Asimov Point and settled down into a standard formation. "Twelve freighters," the sensor officer said, "and a single battlecruiser."

Scott felt his eyes narrow. Standard Federation Navy doctrine–and there was no sign the Outsiders disagreed–called for lighter units to escort convoys, although there hadn't been a major war on when that doctrine had been devised. Smaller units were more flexible than battlecruisers, he knew, and less likely to be needed elsewhere. Were the Outsiders merely trying to kill two birds with one stone by using the battlecruiser as an escort while it made its way to the front, he asked himself, or were they up to something else? Could it be a trap of some kind?

Or, he asked himself, *are they shipping something so important they detailed a whole battlecruiser as escort?*

"The freighters," he said. "Is there anything odd about them?"

"They appear to be standard *Polaris*-class bulk freighters," the sensor officer said. "I can't get a read on their drive fields to ID them properly, sir."

And that might well be meaningless, Scott thought. *If they liberated the ships from us, they might well have fiddled with the drive fields to make identifying them from a distance impossible.*

He peered down at the screen, thinking hard. The *Polaris*-class freighters were common; maybe not the most common freighters in the galaxy, but there were certainly hundreds of thousands of them plying the spaceways. But they had their flaws, he recalled from his Academy days; they were rarely used by anyone outside the larger shipping firms. They needed a proper orbital station, complete with heavy-lift shuttles, to unload, making them utterly cost-ineffective for anyone else. The independent shippers, and those who tended to stage-one colony worlds, considered them little better than junk.

But they could be turned into Q-ships, or troop transports, with a little effort... and *that* might explain the enemy battlecruiser.

"Move us into firing position," he ordered, as he watched the enemy ships. The Outsiders weren't wasting time, he noted with abstract admiration; as soon as they assembled, they started to head towards Point Charlie. Federation Navy officers could hardly have done as well. "And prepare to flush everything towards the freighters."

The tactical officer glanced up. "Sir?"

"There's no point in a missile duel with that big bastard," Scott said. "All we can do is get our blows in and then vanish into the darkness."

The thought didn't please him. Assault cruisers had been designed for sneak attacks, not going head-to-head with battlecruisers. There were times when he suspected the *real* reason he'd been given *Spartan* was because she was expendable. The Federation Navy had built her and her sisters when they'd been trying to fill holes in their line of battle, after all. They might have their advantages, but they didn't have the throw weight to compete with anything larger than a medium cruiser. Their only hope was to land the first punch and then vanish.

Unless the battlecruiser's crew isn't alert, he told himself, but one look at the display suggested otherwise. The cruiser was sweeping space carefully, not ambling along as if it didn't have a care in the world. They were as alert as any crew could reasonably hope to be, if they weren't at red alert. Scott would have been impressed if they hadn't been the enemy.

He cursed the Grand Senate under his breath. If the numbers had been even, if the Outsiders had faced the Federation on even terms, he had a feeling the Federation would have lost by now. The Outsiders were far more motivated; they had grudges to pay off and family to protect, unlike the Federation Navy's officers. Even now, with one of their own ruling the Federation and the old patronage networks shattered, the Federation Navy was demoralized and unsure of itself. But the successful defense of Boston–so far–might convince the older officers that they had a chance to win...

Assuming we get more supplies shipped forward, he thought. Before he'd been promoted, he'd seen enough to know the Federation Navy was being pushed to the limits, simply reinforcing the forces at Boston. The Outsiders had done too much damage too quickly and the Federation had reeled under the blows. *And then perhaps we can take the offensive.*

The console chimed. "Captain," the sensor officer said, "they will enter firing range in twenty minutes."

"Hold us here," Scott ordered. It was the moment of truth. Drives and weapons stepped down, there should be nothing to betray their presence to the prowling battlecruiser. But if the enemy had pulled off an unanticipated advance...he pushed the thought aside, then watched as the battlecruiser swept closer. "Stand by all weapons and drives..."

The battlecruiser's sensors swept over them, then faded into the distance. Scott let out a breath, although he knew better than to relax completely. If *he'd* been in command of the battlecruiser and picked up traces of a cloaked ship, *he* might have held his fire until they were practically at point-blank range, obliterating the cloaked ship before she even knew she was under attack. But instead, the battlecruiser proceeded onwards. Behind her, the line of freighters came on.

Pity there's no time to take them intact, Scott thought. It was probably futile anyway. The Outsiders fought desperately to avoid being taken prisoner, thanks to the Grand Senate's treatment of prisoners in the last war. Only a handful had fallen into Federation hands, mainly through being knocked out or stunned before they had a chance to kill themselves. Given half a chance, Outsider crews activated antimatter scuttling charges and blew themselves up, rather than surrender. It was a major headache for ONI, which needed prisoners desperately...

Maybe they have a point, Scott thought. *Being ONI's test subject would not be a pleasant experience.*

He glanced over at the sensor officer. "Can you pick out anything new about them?"

"No, sir," the sensor officer said. "They're fully-laden, but nothing else."

Pity they don't advertize their cargo on their hulls, Scott thought, with a flash of amusement. *It would make this so much easier.*

He cleared his throat. "Lock weapons on the freighters," he ordered. He waited for the tactical officer's nod. "Fire!"

Spartan shuddered as she flushed her external racks, then her internal tubes. At the same time, her cloaking device dropped, revealing her to enemy sensors. Scott watched the enemy battlecruiser–it was probably his imagination, but he could have sworn the enemy ship *jumped*–as his ship opened fire. Despite his surprise, the enemy CO reacted quickly and swung his ship around. But he wasn't moving in pursuit.

"Bring up the drives," Scott snapped. "Get us out of here!"

The enemy battlecruiser flickered on the display, then unleashed a spread of missiles. Scott watched, perplexed; the enemy might have fired at extreme range, even for them, but they could have fired a far larger barrage if they'd wanted to. Instead of pursuing his ship, the enemy CO was attempting to cover the freighters. But he'd been caught badly out of position and there was no time to get back into place. One by one, the freighters died as the missiles slammed home. There were no survivors.

Scott gritted his teeth. The enemy CO must have realized it was futile quickly, because he altered course and drove his ship right towards *Spartan*. His missiles were already closing in rapidly, leaving the assault cruiser at severe risk of being crippled. Scott braced himself as his point defense weapons opened fire, sweeping most of the missiles out of space. A handful managed to get close enough to detonate, but two wasted themselves on decoys. The remainder slammed into the ship's shields, shaking the entire ship.

"Rear shields down fifty-seven percent," the tactical officer reported. "No major damage."

"Take us back to Point Alpha," Scott ordered. The enemy CO was clearly out for blood. There was no point in allowing a long stern chase, when it would give the enemy CO all the time he needed to take *Spartan* apart. "And send a standard alert message to reinforcements."

He glanced at the angry red icon and hoped like hell the enemy officer fell for it. The standard message was well known, both in and out of the Federation Navy. There would be no room for misinterpretation. He'd know that Scott was signalling for help, but would he know there was no one in the system–or on the other side of Point Alpha–to come to Scott's assistance? The only way to find out was to try.

"Missile separation," the tactical officer reported.

Scott blinked. Given enough time, the battlecruiser would overhaul *Spartan* and hammer his ship into scrap metal. There was no point in firing missiles at extreme range; hell, there was a good chance the missiles would burn themselves out long before they entered attack range and threw themselves against his shields. Was the commander so desperate to extract revenge, knowing his career had just gone down the sinkhole, or was he merely intent on punishing *Spartan* for her insolence? There might be some advantages, Scott had to concede, in ensuring *Spartan* never made it home.

But you'll know you lost the ships, Scott thought, darkly. *And I bet your superiors will be even less forgiving than ours.*

He watched the missiles, as dispassionately as he could, fight to get into attack range. They were faster than any starship, but their drives were far more limited. Scott felt a flicker of relief as he realized most of the missiles didn't have a hope of getting to his ship, despite their speed. The enemy CO had to be frustrated as hell.

Or is it an alien commander? Scott asked himself. *One of their allies?*

There was no way to know. The Federation would never have tolerated giving starships, let alone warships, to alien powers. But, given how much the Outsiders had done, it would be hard to decide what their leadership was actually being executed *for.* Scott might have been lukewarm on the subject of defending the Grand Senate–he'd seen how baleful an effect it had on the Navy–but he understood the importance of keeping aliens under tight control and supervision. Aliens just couldn't be trusted.

The thought made him smile. *How are the Outsiders enjoying their allies now?*

"Coming up on the Asimov Point, sir," the helmsman said.

"Take us straight through," Scott ordered. He keyed a switch on his console. "All hands, brace for violent transition; I say again, all hands brace for violent transition."

"Missile separation," the tactical officer snapped.

Oh, now you're just throwing good money after bad, Scott thought, mockingly. *I...*

Spartan hit the Asimov Point at speed. For a long moment, there was nothing...and then Scott's stomach churned so violently he thought he was going to be sick. The noise–and smell–behind him told him that some of his crew hadn't been so lucky. Transiting through an Asimov Point at anything above a slow crawl was not recommended, no matter the situation. Older crewmen were at particular risk of shock, followed by death. The cynic in him wondered if the rules had been written by older Admirals.

"Transit complete, sir," the helmsman said. He sounded badly shaken, but at least he'd kept his lunch where it belonged. "Our drive fields took a pasting."

"Take us away from the point, then cloak us," Scott ordered. If the cloaking device had been disabled, and the enemy ship came after *Spartan*, they were dead. There would be no way to escape the battlecruiser's grasp. "And shut down all non-essential equipment. We have to be a hole in space."

Seconds ticked by, slowly. There was no sign of the enemy ship.

"Captain, this is sickbay," Doctor Cullen said. He didn't sound pleased. "I have seventeen crewmen here, all suffering from jump shock."

"Put them in stasis," Scott ordered. It sounded heartless, but there was no time to worry about the crew, not now. "Are there any other problems?"

"Not yet, but there will be," the doctor said. "And you'll have to pay to have the entire ship cleaned."

Scott heard someone chuckle behind him. It was hard not to swing his chair around and reprimand the mocker, even though he knew the doctor was right. Statistically, he knew, a violent transit would have at least half the crew throwing up, or slipping into jump shock. An IG inspection of his ship as it was, reeking like a pirate hulk, would probably have resulted in his immediate court martial. But there had been no choice.

"The enemy ship hasn't come through," the sensor officer said. "They must think we have allies on this side."

"Let us hope so," Scott said. *Spartan* was in no condition for a fight, even against a tiny gunboat or destroyer. "But it is dangerous to come to a conclusion about what the enemy is thinking and then accepting it as gospel truth."

He forced himself to relax as reports flooded in from all over the ship. There would be weeks of repair–fortunately, none requiring a shipyard–before *Spartan* was fully operational once again. Quite a few crewmembers would probably require treatment for delayed jump shock once the tension of battlestations wore off and it came crashing home. But the mission had been a success; *Spartan* had destroyed all twelve freighters and left the enemy escort thoroughly humiliated. The Outsiders would have to replace whatever it was they'd lost before resuming their assault on Boston.

And Admiral Garibaldi will be pleased, he thought. *Very pleased indeed.*

Chapter Twenty-One

It is a perverse irony that the lot of the average worker in the Federation grew worse after the destruction of the Imperialist Faction in the Grand Senate. The Conservatives were not, of course, intent on respecting workers' rights; they saw to it that strikes, slow-downs and protests were banned. But it was the Liberal/Socialist Faction who did the most damage...

-The Federation Navy in Retrospect, 4199

Sol, 4100

The funeral was a short one, but then they always were.

Lucy Roster looked around as the manager's speech came to an end, seeing her own tiredness and frustration reflected in so many eyes. She'd worked for years, battling the educational system on Earth, to earn a chance to actually start making a living for herself. And she'd been good, too. Working in a factory wasn't for everyone, but she'd done well. Her children would have a chance to enter employment at an advanced level. They would certainly never grow up on Earth.

But now all of that was threatened.

She rubbed her eyes as the workers left the compartment, leaving the body behind. They'd all liked Gary King; he'd been one of those people with a talent for befriending everyone, no matter how reclusive or unpleasant they were. But he was dead now, killed in an accident, an accident everyone had known was inevitable since they started working sixteen-hour shifts, trying to produce as much as possible for the war. They'd cut so many corners, and taken on so many undertrained staff, that it was a minor miracle that Gary King had been the only one to die. And he'd been a *trained* worker!

Cold hatred flared in her breast as she caught sight of a handful of interns, laughing and joking as they slipped away from the crowd. Bastards! They didn't have the experience, let alone the training, to work in the factory complex, but the workers had been forced to take them on anyway and try to teach them what to do. It was impossible! They didn't have the grounding they needed to understand what they were doing–and, without that, all they could do was work by rote. And God help them if they ever ran into a problem they hadn't trained to face...

She saw her own reflection in the glass as she pushed open the door to the drinking hole and flinched. Her long hair was turning grey; her face, once pretty, was tired and worn. Her husband had barely seen her over the past three months; her children, no matter how much she loved them, had been sent to boarding school. Once, she'd worked a nine-hour day and gone home to be with them. Now, she spent her few sleeping hours at the factory, trying hard to relax before she had to go back to work.

The other workers looked just as worn–and angry–as she felt. They were an odd lot, she'd discovered the day she first joined them; some looked tough, their muscles showing clearly against the tight uniforms, while others looked dignified and young. But they were a close-knit bunch, despite appearances, and they'd taken Gary's death badly. She took a glass from the table and chugged it down in one gulp, gasping as the liquid hit her stomach. The still the workers operated within the factory might produce alcohol, but it tasted like paint stripper. And *that* would probably be better for her health.

"I just heard from Gary's wife," John Rawson said. He was an older man, with a badly scarred face, but he was one of the kindest men Lucy had met. "There won't be any insurance—or pension!"

Lucy stared at him, suddenly completely sober despite the alcohol. "No pension!"

She wasn't the only one to be shocked. They'd been told, when they took on the job, that their relatives would be looked after, if something happened while they were working and they didn't make it out. Building stardrives was not a safe occupation. And, as far as she'd known, the pension system had survived both the Justinian War and the destruction of the Grand Senate. Her children would be cared for if she died. It was the sole reason she'd stayed on the job, rather than emigrating to some colony world along the Rim.

"And she won't be allowed to stay in her apartment," Rawson continued. "She will have to go back to Earth."

The anger broke. Men and women shouted questions, then snapped at one another, fueled by the alcohol. Lucy sat there, stunned. To lose her life was bad enough, but to die for nothing? To see her children go back to Earth? She knew, all too well, what would happen to anyone unlucky enough to grow up on humanity's homeworld. The smug faces of the interns, too dim to comprehend the forces they used to build the stardrives, drove it home. And to think the interns were the *lucky* ones! Whatever the media might say, Lucy knew from bitter experience that the average citizen on Earth was lucky to live more than fifty years. Life was cheap on Earth.

"It's bad enough that we have to work more and more hours," she said. They'd all worked longer and longer hours as the war raged on. "But what will happen to our children when we go?"

The anger grew stronger. She was far from the only one to have kids—or the only one to remain in her job, purely because it provided the funds to look after her children. And yet, what would happen to her kids when she died? The apartment and boarding school weren't the best on the moon—she didn't earn enough to move her family to a higher level—but it was infinitely preferable to life on Earth. The thought of her daughter being taken by one of the gangs and sold as a whore was sickening. And to think that was one of the *better* options for life on Earth!

She felt rage welling up within her—rage, and a sense she could go no further. That none of them could go any further. That there was no point in working herself until she collapsed and died on the job, if a simple accident didn't kill her, if her children wouldn't be protected. Once, she'd loved the job. Now, she hated it with every fibre of her being.

"No more," she said. "We can't go on like this!"

There was a loud roar of agreement.

"Then we strike," John Rawson said. "We have to make a stand now!"

"But strikes are illegal," Gayle Henderson pointed out. "We could be arrested and exiled and..."

"And what difference would it make?" Rawson thundered. "We're practically in jail already!"

Lucy shouted her agreement with the rest of the workers. She'd once heard, during the mandatory classes on workers' rights, that the Socialist Faction had guaranteed their rights so there was no need for any independent unions or anything else that might protect them from exploitation. Why, the speaker had said, such independent unions might not have the clout to save their members from a fate worse than death–being sacked. But it hadn't taken her long to realize that the political faction that claimed to represent her did nothing for her, or for anyone else. It was designed to keep them under control.

And it worked as long as we were relatively happy, she thought. *But now we're pissed.*

She took another glass and drank it, then stood up. "Strike," she called. "Let us be heard!"

"Not just us," Rawson said. He jabbed a finger at men he knew to have friends in other factory complexes. "Get them *all* to go on strike!"

"Shouldn't we sort out our demands first?" Gayle asked. "They have to know what to give us."

"Good point," Rawson said. "What do we *want*?"

ꟹ

It was early morning before Gayle Henderson managed to break free of the mob and make her way back to her bunk in the worker barracks. They weren't comfortable–although they were heavenly compared to some of the places she'd lived in the past–but they did help keep the workers under control. Or they had, she acknowledged, as she reached for her terminal and brought up a game screen. Right now, everyone was so angry that they weren't thinking through their actions, something not helped by the copious amount of alcohol they'd drunk.

Idiots, Gayle thought, as she opened the game. No one would think twice about her owning a terminal, or playing games when she wasn't on duty. But it was also a way to get a message out without using one of the public systems. The factory's managers didn't know she was there and she wasn't about to let them know. She had to warn her superiors before the strike got out of control.

She wasn't blind to the need for change. The workers did have a point–and more, besides. Gayle had enough experience to *know* just how dangerous the workplace had become, over the past two years. Cutting safety procedures and adding more working hours hadn't gone well together. And cost-cutting had been just plain spiteful. But she knew the needs of the war against aliens came first. The strike couldn't be allowed to get out of hand.

Quietly, she tapped in her message. The security forces would be alerted. And then...

Let us hope it is settled quickly, Gayle thought. *Or it could become really bad.*

ꟹ

Lucy had taken two painkillers, but her head still throbbed unpleasantly as she followed Rawson and two other workers–elected representatives–to the manager's office. She'd barely met the man, but she'd heard that he was more interested in meeting the monthly quota for producing new stardrives than helping his staff. But he was an improvement on some of the other managers, she'd been told by the visitors from other factory complexes. One of them was so dim he'd honestly believed his factory was producing weapons, rather than navigational systems.

Rawson tapped on the hatch, which opened. Manager Pimlico looked up, surprised. He was short and stout, compared to any of his workers, wearing a pair of glasses balanced on his nose. It was fashionable, Lucy suspected–correcting eyesight was not a difficult medical procedure–but she had no idea why anyone would find it attractive.

"I wasn't informed you were coming," Pimlico said, softly. "Why are you here?"

"We are presenting our demands," Rawson said. He produced a sheet of paper from his jacket and laid it on the desk with a flourish. "We're going on strike until these quotas are met..."

"Strikes are banned by law," Pimlico objected. "You should know better than to risk being noticed, not now."

"The current conditions are intolerable," Lucy said, quietly. She regretted it a moment later, as Pimlico's eyes locked on her face. His gaze was distant, rather than threatening, but there was something about it that chilled her to the bone. "Being arrested doesn't seem so bad compared to having to go on working here."

Pimlico's face didn't change as he picked up the paper and read it, quickly. "A return to normal working hours. Wages adjusted to keep pace with inflation. An end to quotas. An end to the apprenticeship system. Guaranteed pensions and housing for the families of workers killed on the job. An end to effective imprisonment...?"

He quirked his eyebrows at Rawson, who explained.

"We used to be able to go to parts of the moon for day trips," he said. "It allowed us to stretch our legs and get out and about, making the rest of our time here bearable."

He waved a hand to indicate the grey walls. Everything was grey in the factory, apart from the workers themselves. The sheer monotony alone probably contributed to the growing accident rate. It was sheer luck that Gary King had been the first to die.

Pimlico's face darkened, but he didn't rise to the bait. Instead, he read on.

"The right to form your own union, the right to make representation to the government..."

He shook his head. "Don't you know there's a war on?"

"Yes, we do," Rawson said.

He took a breath. Only someone who knew him very well–and Lucy did–would have been able to see just how carefully he was controlling his temper.

"We understand that there's a war on," he said. "The news channels have spent hours telling us how horrific our fate will be, if the aliens win the war. We understand! But we also understand that we simply cannot go on like this!"

"If nothing else," Lucy added, quietly, "there will be a far more serious accident soon that might well shut down the plant completely."

Pimlico pinned her with his gaze. "Is that a threat?"

"It's a prediction," Lucy said, sharply. She drew herself up to her full height and met his gaze. "Right now, *sir,* we are tired and worn. And tired and worn people make mistakes, mistakes they would never make if they had enough sleep to function properly. Gary King made a mistake and it killed him. It could easily have been a great deal worse. We found, afterwards, that several safety measures had not been reset. If Gary had been a little less lucky, we would have had power surges throughout the entire plant."

"The insurance doesn't cover death by carelessness," Pimlico pointed out.

Lucy felt her temper snap. "DON'T YOU GET IT?" She yelled at him. "GARY DIED BECAUSE HE WAS FUCKING TIRED AND IN NO STATE TO CROSS EVERY T AND DOT EVERY I!"

"Then take more care," Pimlico said. "Our policy is not to pay out if the worker is responsible for his own death."

Lucy clenched her fists. The policy didn't cover death by carelessness, true, but how could Gary have been anything else, given how tired he'd been at the time? She knew, all too well, that it could easily have been *her* who had made the fatal mistake, her husband mourning her death, her children sent back to Earth to grow up in the ghetto...

Rawson growled, deep in his throat. "Are you rejecting our demands?"

"I am," Pimlico said. "And I must inform you, furthermore, that if this highly illegal action is not stopped at once..."

"Strike," Rawson said. "We are off the job. And we will remain off the job until our demands are met. Not agreed too, sir, but met. We will accept nothing less than your full compliance with our demands."

Pimlico opened his mouth, as though he was about to say something, but Rawson didn't give him the chance. He turned and strode out of the room, followed by Lucy and the others. The door hissed closed behind them, cutting off whatever Pimlico might have been trying to say.

"Well," Rawson said, as they made their way back to the common room. "That went better than I expected."

Lucy laughed. "Now what?"

"Now we start spreading the word," Rawson said. He smirked. "It will take them several hours to decide what to do about us, probably more. By then, we need to present them with a major problem. One factory alone won't be a big headache, not for them. Several hundred factories, on the other hand..."

He allowed his voice to trail off, suggestively.

"And we kick out the interns," Lucy added. "They might be on the wrong side."

She shrugged. "And even if they're not, they can't help us," she added. "They're too used to doing what they're told."

ജ്ഞ

Alone in his office, Giles Pimlico rubbed the side of his head. Headaches had been part of his life since he'd been promoted to fill the gap in management–the previous manager had vanished a week after Emperor Marius took control, for no reason Giles had been able to determine–and they showed no sign of going away. And, now he was caught in a bind, it was worse than ever before.

He had to fill his quota. That had been made clear to him when he'd been promoted. There was a quota and he had to fill it, or else. Success would mean further promotion–and there were new slots for an experienced manager opening all the time–while failure would mean, at best, a permanent career freeze. At worst...well, he'd heard rumors about what happened to those who failed Emperor Marius. He didn't really believe the emperor could kill a man merely by wishing him dead, but there was no shortage of soldiers or assassins who would quite happily kill a middle-ranked manager for the emperor, just to make a point.

And, to fill his quota, he'd cut everything he could. Costs had to be saved, somehow; production had to be increased, somehow. Balancing the two had become a nightmare and he had a feeling he'd finally failed. His superiors would be less than pleased with him.

But that wasn't the only problem. He had to help train newcomers, who might take some of the pressure off his workers. But the only way to train newcomers was to take them on as interns, who learned on the job. It was frustrating–he understood it was frustrating–but he had no choice. He had to do as he was told...

...And so did the workers. Only they weren't. Part of him almost envied them for deciding to take a stand, even though he knew it was not only futile, but selfish. It wasn't just his career–and theirs–that was at stake. The war itself was at stake. And, if the rumors were correct, the emperor wouldn't let them stand in his way. The war had to be won.

He thought of his wives and family, then reached for the terminal. The only thing he could do now was call his superiors. *They* would have to decide what to do.

Chapter Twenty-Two

In making sure that the workers had nowhere to take their complaints, the Socialist Faction ensured that trouble built up and up until it finally exploded. Ironically, their system worked; the Socialist Faction was a dead duck by the time disaster struck.
-The Federation Navy in Retrospect, 4199

Sol, 4100

"So we have another riot on our hands," Marius said, sharply.

"No, sir," General Thorne said. "We have a strike."

Marius met his eyes. "Explain."

"The workers at the Fredericksburg Stardrive Plant have gone on strike," General Throne said. "They're refusing to go back to work until their demands are met. And the strike is already spreading, even though we cut communications as soon as we heard what was happening. We have strikes developing in a dozen other plants on Luna."

"I see," Marius said.

Professor Kratman leaned forward. "And what do they actually *want*?"

General Thorne eyed him suspiciously. "I fail to see why their demands are important."

"Answer the question," Kratman growled. It might have been decades since he'd set foot on a command deck, but he still knew how to command. "What do they *want*?"

"Basically, an end to the emergency procedures and protocols," General Thorne said. He produced a datapad from his belt and passed it to the Professor. "We can't grant any of them without risking production levels."

Marius winced. Production was a long-running battle between the different factions in his cabinet, particularly with the war well underway. The Federation Navy needed everything from new starships to fortresses and other weapons, as well as an endless supply of new recruits and spare parts. And creating new training camps for crewmen had, in its turn, created new problems too. The only force that seemed to be adapting successfully to the new regime was the Marine Corps, which had its own training methods.

And they don't need to know so much about what they're doing, Marius thought. *But experienced officers in the Navy do.*

He pushed the thought aside, then looked at Tully. "You have something to say?"

"We should consider giving them what they want," Tully said. "The emergency measures were successful in producing some material, but in the long term they risk doing considerable damage to the Federation's infrastructure."

"We cannot give in to blackmail," General Thorne countered. "And this *is* blackmail! They will accept our surrender, then make some more demands until they find something we literally *cannot* give them."

"I think you're overreacting," Tully said, coolly. "Right now, this is a minor problem. If you overreact, it could become a major problem."

Marius felt his head starting to pound, again. There were just too many problems to handle one at a time. If the Outsider War hadn't begun, there would have been time to rationalize the Federation's industry, along with its educational system and just about everything else. But the Outsider War demanded their fullest concentration, which meant reforms had to fall by the wayside. They couldn't surrender. All they could do was hang on desperately and wait for the tide to turn.

He looked up, towards the holographic starchart in the corner. Hundreds of stars were marked either red, for enemy territory, or yellow for status unknown. It was clear–and he reminded himself, again, that the map was months out of date–that the Outsiders were moving to surround Boston. It wouldn't be long before Roman Garibaldi faced a full-scale assault on the system. Only desperate fighting along the borderline had prevented one from taking place already.

Or they will advance down and try to isolate Boston, he thought. *It might just be workable...*

Professor Kratman cleared his throat. "Giving them most of what they want wouldn't be impossible," he said. "They might be open to negotiation."

"They're *not* open to negotiation," General Thorne snapped back. "They said as much themselves."

"That's a common bargaining tactic," Kratman countered. "You deliberately ask for more than you actually want, in hopes of getting it–or of allowing yourself to be talked down to what you actually want, allowing your opponent to feel they've won the argument."

"These people aren't skilled bargainers," General Thorne said. He turned to face Marius, keeping his voice under tight control. "They cannot be allowed to spread the word over the solar system, sir."

Marius took the list of demands and read it, quickly. Some were reasonable enough, others were impossible to grant without slowing down production considerably. And if that happened, the knock-on effect would be terrifying. It was possible, he supposed, that they could handle the delays, but what would it do to the war?

"These people have been influenced by Outsider propaganda," General Thorne continued, angrily. "They have got to be stopped."

Kratman cleared his throat, loudly. "Is there any proof of that?"

"There's no proof that anyone has been distributing propaganda on Luna," Tully offered. "They tend to concentrate on the other parts of the Core Worlds. Luna is too close to Earth to be easily subverted."

Marius had his doubts. The Outsiders were skilled propagandists. Allied with hackers, who had been abusing Earth's tired datanet for years, they could get their propaganda into inboxes all over the Solar System. So far, it hadn't produced any nasty surprises on Earth itself...unless Tully was wrong and there *was* some propaganda being distributed on Luna. It was unlikely that anyone receiving it would report it, thanks to the Grand Senate. Anyone who had received messages from Admiral Justinian's faction had been arrested on suspicion of being a spy.

He pushed the thought aside too, then sighed.

General Thorne was right. This could not be allowed to spread, not when it might destroy the Federation's abilities to resupply its forces. Whatever the justice of the demands, there was no way he could honor them. After the war, he promised himself, something would be done. But there was no way they could submit to demands now.

"They have to be stopped," he said, softly. "What options do we have?"

"I have an elite battalion of Special Security Soldiers on their way now," General Thorne said. "On your command, they will storm the central complex and capture the ringleaders. The remainder will be offered amnesty if they go straight back to work, without delay, while we put the ringleaders on trial."

"There is a strong probability of damaging the facility if you attack," Professor Kratman pointed out. "And what will you do if arresting the ringleaders *fails* to stop the strikes? Are you going to save the factories by calling in kinetic strikes? Force the workers to work by shooting them?"

"We cannot grant their demands," General Thorne said, sharply. "The only alternative is to break the strike before it spreads out of control."

"Then do it," Marius said. "Dismissed."

"I think you may come to regret that," Professor Kratman said, once everyone else had left the room. "You catch more flies with honey than vinegar."

"There isn't time," Marius reminded him. "What happens if this slows down production or stops it completely?"

He cursed the Grand Senate, once again, under his breath. The Senators had intended to make sure that their clients got most of the contracts, so there hadn't been any real competition between the Federation's industries. And this had ensured there was almost no slack at all, no way to meet unanticipated demands for everything from starships to spare parts. It was difficult to believe that the war might grind to a halt for lack of...the widgets used to channel power through a starship's datanodes, for example...but it was quite possible. Much of the pre-war stockpiles, such as they were, had been used up in the war against Admiral Justinian and the other warlords.

And much of it is outdated now anyway, he thought. The Federation had not had time to supply the latest in defensive technology to worlds along the Rim, allowing the Outsiders a string of easy victories *We need new material, not the old shit.*

"I have no answer," Kratman said. "But you may find yourself holding the rock and being battered over the head with it, at the same time."

Marius had to smile. "That is an absurd metaphor," he said. "But I take your point."

He shook his head. There was no alternative.

༺༻

"We've just been joined by another factory," Rawson called. "The Stalker-Lawson Complex just went on strike! So much for the blackout!"

Lucy smiled, despite her growing fears. The factory's communications systems were top-of-the-line, but someone had locked them out of the Luna datanet, leaving the factory completely isolated. And some of the workers who had headed to other factories had failed to return. She knew it was a dangerous mission, but not *that* dangerous. It was quite possible they'd been arrested...

And Pimlico was gone. By the time they'd checked his office, after moving into the factory compound and sealing the exits, it had been too late to detain him. Lucy had been almost disappointed when she'd seen his quarters; she'd expected vast luxury, but the only luxury Pimlico had allowed himself was a large portrait of a brown-haired teenage girl, wearing a long white dress. Lucy had puzzled over it, wondering if it showed one of Pimlico's wives or daughters, then decided it didn't matter. They'd swept the room for any unpleasant surprises, then sealed it. There was no point in leaving it open for just anyone to enter.

"But Shasta didn't return," another man said. "Where *is* he?"

"I don't know," Rawson answered. "But I do know we won't win if we give in to our fears."

Lucy yawned. It said something about their condition that half of the workers, having dragged mattresses into the factory, had settled down to sleep despite the racket. As important as it was to build barricades, they were just too tired to do anything else. Even with Rawson in command, there wasn't much to do, just wait and see what happened. There were few weapons in the factory and Rawson had ruled out trying to build any. Not everyone had been happy with his judgement.

She thought, longingly, of her two sons. Were they still in boarding school? She'd heard stories about how the Grand Senate had treated their own sons and daughters; it was hard to imagine, but would the emperor lash out at her children? Cold fear crept into her heart as she settled down on one of the mattresses, wondering if she'd made their lives a great deal worse...what if they were used as hostages? Or worse?

There had been no response to their demands, not even when they'd tried to put them out on the datanet. Pimlico had said something, even if it had been a flat refusal. Why hadn't the government said anything? Rawson had speculated that the lack of response meant the question was being pushed up and up the line until it reached someone willing to make a decision, but he didn't know for sure. None of them knew for sure and the sheer tedium of not knowing was getting to them. They'd had certainty in the factory; now, they were waiting for...

A loud explosion echoed through the complex. Lucy jumped to her feet, just in time to see black-clad men storming into the compartment, smashing through the barricades with contemptuous ease. She turned and fled, running through the corridors as she heard the sound of stunners behind her, trying to make her escape before it was too late. But she turned a corner and ran into another group of armed men. One of them knocked her to the ground, then rolled her over, yanked her hands behind her back and cuffed them roughly. Another put a foot on her back and kept her pressed firmly against the floor until she could barely breathe and tears were forming in her eyes.

"Up, bitch," one of them snapped. The foot was removed, just in time for one of the men to grab her by the arm and pull her up, then press her against the wall. Strong hands searched her pockets, removing her tools, terminal and the photographs of her family she kept in a small wallet. "You're under arrest."

Lucy opened her mouth. "I..."

"Quiet," the man ordered. "Do not say a word until you are spoken to."

He pressed her back against the wall, then waited. It felt like hours of fear and shock before he finally took her arm and half-pushed her down the corridor, back towards where they'd planned the strike. A dozen bodies lay on the ground, limp and helpless. She stared at them with growing horror, wondering if they'd all been killed, before she realized they'd merely been stunned. No one in their right mind would use energy or projectile weapons in the factory, not unless they wanted to cause more damage. She caught sight of Rawson lying on the ground and winced, bitterly. He'd broken his nose when he fell, leaving blood staining the floor.

She was shoved out of the door and into a large armored transport. The other female workers followed her, either cuffed or stunned; the latter were dumped onto the floor of the vehicle before the hatch banged closed, leaving them in darkness. Lucy had to bite her tongue to keep from asking questions, knowing they'd be overhead. It wasn't easy, particularly when one of the girls started to cry. None of them had ever been arrested before. They hadn't really thought they would be arrested for striking, let alone so violently. In hindsight, Lucy wondered why they hadn't anticipated the possibility.

The vehicle hummed to life, then shuddered. It was disconcerting as hell to know they were traveling somewhere, either through the underground tubes linking the Luna settlements together or out on the surface, beyond all hope of rescue. She tried to time the journey, but swiftly gave it up as futile. By the time they reached their destination, she knew they would be completely disoriented. And that was probably the point.

There was a dull thud, then nothing. The hatch opened a moment later, revealing two incredibly ugly women in black uniforms. Lucy couldn't help thinking of the notorious Blackshirts before she was dragged out of the vehicle, then dumped on the ground. One of the women cut the clothes away from her body, then dragged her into the next room. The door slammed closed behind them, leaving her completely alone with the woman.

"Get one thing through your head," the woman snarled, leaning so close to Lucy that she could smell the woman's breath. "You're mine now, understand? I can do anything to you and no one will give a shit. Do exactly as you're told and you'll have an easier time of it. If you resist, we can do anything to you to break your resistance—anything at all."

Lucy staggered backwards. It took her two tries to speak clearly.

"I have rights," she said. "I demand..."

The woman backhanded her, hard enough to send her falling backwards. Her bare ass hit the ground hard enough to hurt, and she tasted blood in her mouth. She spat it out and looked up, helplessly. Even with her hands free, she doubted she could have fought the prison guard on equal terms.

"You seem to have missed something," the guard said. "You have been arrested under the terms of the Emergency Powers Act, which forbids strikes, outright sabotage or any other form of activity that hinders the war effort. You have no rights left to you. Your only hope is to cooperate fully and hope it is taken into account when your case is put before a judge."

She paused, then snapped on a pair of rubber gloves. "Now," she added, as Lucy stared at her hands in disbelief. "We will commence the search."

"I'm naked," Lucy pointed out. "What do you expect to find?"

The guard smirked. "Nothing," she said. "But I think you will be less uppity when I'm finished."

ꟹ

"Operation complete, sir," General Thorne said.

Marius looked up from the report on shipbuilding programs. It had to be gone through, but it didn't make for pleasant reading. Admiral Garibaldi was likely to have fewer ships sent to him over the next five months, while the Federation struggled to devise newer designs that might match the Outsiders, one-on-one. Marius hated to admit it, but the Outsiders had definitely benefited the most from the Justinian War. The Federation had been diverted, true, yet it had also learned a great deal about how modern technology worked in combat without paying any of the butcher's bill for the lessons. Their designs, in greater numbers, might have proved stunningly decisive.

"Good," he said. Allowing General Thorne to build a new security force had caused him some sleepless nights at the time, but it had definitely proved its value. Besides, the Marines were overworked and needed at the front. "And the prisoners?"

"We have fifteen ringleaders in custody," General Thorne informed him. "The remainder have been interrogated, then released under supervision. They have been warned that they will be expected to give evidence, if necessary. In addition, they have been tagged and will be arrested if they try to leave the settlement."

Marius nodded. The Grand Senate's method for dealing with upper-class criminals had its uses, even if it had primarily been abused before the Grand Senate had been destroyed. But then, the Senators hadn't wanted to be too harsh to their relatives. It would have caused unacceptable levels of blowback.

"We can hold the ringleaders for the moment," General Thorne added. "But word of what they did is already spreading. We may need to give them a trial."

Marius groaned. "The last time I gave someone a trial, it was a nasty mistake," he said. "Have them and their families shipped somewhere safe—somewhere they can't do any harm. And then have a complete blackout placed on the news."

"Aye, sir," General Thorne said. "It will be done."

And let us hope, Marius thought, *that will be the end of it.*

Chapter Twenty-Three

The trap confronting the Federation could be best described as a man caught between two fires. If he jumped one way or the other, the fire would get him; if he stayed where he was, the fires would eventually kill him anyway. In the end, the Federation could no longer maintain the balance.

-The Federation Navy in Retrospect, 4199

Boston, 4100

"Excellent work," Roman said.

Captain Palter beamed. "Thank you, sir."

Roman smiled–it was obvious that Palter had expected to get in trouble for having his ship damaged - then dismissed him with a wave of his hand. The report was heartening at a time when it was becoming clear that the noose was tightening around Boston and the Outsiders had successfully gained control of three of the seven Asimov Points in the system. They could launch a three-pronged attack at any moment, if they felt inclined to take the risk, or merely launch a massive assault through one of the points. The Blue Star war had exposed the folly of trying to be clever when launching several separate assaults at once.

And it might be the best thing they could do for us, Roman thought, as he looked up at the display. Red stars surrounded Boston, each one occupied by the enemy. It looked intimidating, even though he knew that most of the occupied systems were irrelevant to the war. *We'd have a chance to smash each of their assaults individually.*

He looked up as Midshipwoman Haze entered the compartment. She looked terrifyingly young–part of his mind insisted she was too young to go to the Academy, let alone serve on a starship–but she was enthusiastic and competent. Besides, *he* could hardly talk about people being promoted young. If it hadn't been for the war, he'd be lucky to have made commander by now. Indeed, given his lack of political connections, he might well have stayed a lieutenant indefinitely.

"Admiral," Haze said, "the other admirals are waiting for you."

"Great," Roman said, without enthusiasm. They'd be complaining about the lack of formalities, he knew. Before the war, it could take hours to welcome one admiral aboard another's flagship. Now, he'd cut the formalities out completely. "I'm on my way."

He took one last look at the display, then turned and walked through the hatch. The flag deck had been expanded to allow for a new briefing room, suitable for senior commanding officers and their staffs. Roman privately disapproved of it–the design came from the Grand Senate–but having some facilities might keep his subordinates happy. They'd be complaining otherwise, he knew, and while Emperor Marius might dismiss their complaints, others might not. He sighed–he'd never realized that being an admiral also meant being a politician–and walked into the briefing compartment. As always, the sheer luxury of the compartment caught him by surprise.

"Ah, Roman," Admiral Ness said. He sounded suspiciously jovial as he poured himself a glass of expensive wine. "Glad you could join us."

Roman kept his expression blank as he sat down at the head of the table. The briefing compartment was rated secure, ensuring that no one was allowed to enter without his specific permission. He'd heard complaints, the first time, from officers unused to fixing their own coffee, but he'd ignored them. Honestly, it wasn't as though pouring coffee into a mug was so difficult. Getting out of bed was harder, he'd told himself after the first set of complaints, and the officers did that all the time.

"Thank you for coming," he said. "We have much to discuss."

He settled back and surveyed the table. Admiral Ellison Ness was older than him, older than Emperor Marius, with a reputation for being reliable, but lazy. It had worked out in his favor, Roman had to admit, as he'd survived the Grand Senate's purges and maintained command of his battle squadron. His weakness, Emperor Marius had said in a private letter, was that he had no initiative at all. He would sooner respond to an enemy attack than mount an offensive of his own. And he was so wedded to the idea of precedence that he was mortally offended by the idea of Roman, who was his junior by a good seven decades, being his superior officer.

Beside him, General Yaakov looked grim. He had been an Imperial Marine before transferring to Fortress Command, after suffering nerve damage that had been impossible to fix by the time he'd reached medical help. Elf spoke highly of him—and she was a good judge of character—but there was something about him that bothered Roman. Perhaps it was the awareness that there were injuries that couldn't be healed, even by the Federation. Yaakov's scarred face was a warning of what could happen to anyone else, if they got unlucky.

And Admiral Baumann was a total non-entity, her face so bland and colorless that she was almost invisible. She'd spent the Justinian War as a logistics officer, rather than a line officer, and done a good job. But there had been something of a cloud hanging over her after the Grand Fleet had occupied Earth. Roman was surprised she hadn't been purged, if she'd been untrustworthy; instead, she'd been sent to Boston to handle the logistics. She'd been doing a good job, Roman knew, but he had his doubts. He'd assigned a pair of Marines to keep an eye on her, just in case.

But Emperor Marius vouched for her, he thought. *I should trust his judgement.*

And then there were the commodores...

It had been a great deal easier when he'd been the only commanding officer in the fleet. Roman sighed, then activated the holographic display. The starchart appeared in front of them, glowing red icons winking into existence, surrounded by tactical notes from recon probes. It wasn't a reassuring sight.

"Admiral Baumann," Roman said. "Would you please give us a rundown of the logistic situation?"

Admiral Baumann cleared her throat. "Owing to events in the Core Worlds, we will be unlikely to receive any heavy reinforcements for the next six months," she said. "Stockpiles of supplies are at sufficient levels, but again, we are unlikely to see any increase in the flow coming here from the Core. In particular, our supply of the newer design of missiles is badly limited..."

Roman nodded as she droned on, cursing the Grand Senate under his breath. If they'd spread missile-production capabilities out a bit more, the fleet wouldn't be having so many supply problems. And if they'd treated the workers better, perhaps so many of them wouldn't have signed up with the Outsiders and sabotaged their own workplaces. The thought of losing the war because they ran out of the weapons to fight it was galling, but it was a problem that had to be faced. Logistics, more than anything else, would make or break the war.

"Well, Admiral Baumann has made it quite clear," he said, once Admiral Baumann had finally finished her report. "We are in some trouble."

"I suppose that's one way to put it," General Yaakov said. His voice was completely unemotional, thanks to the nerve damage he had suffered. "If we lose this system, the Outsiders won't run into any serious opposition until they reach the Core Worlds."

Roman nodded. Once Boston fell, once the Outsiders had access to the Asimov Point network that made up the core of the inner worlds, there would be too many angles of attack for them all to be guarded. The Federation Navy would harry them, of course, and try to lure them into ambushes, but they would face the age-old problem of trying–and failing–to be strong everywhere. And some of the inner worlds had industrial bases of their own, as well as rebellious populations. The Outsiders would find themselves growing much stronger as the Federation weakened.

"General," he said. "What is the security situation here?"

"Acceptable," General Yaakov informed him. "We have most of the battlestations under our direct command, with the former local defense force crews scattered over the system, once they passed a lie detector test. We weeded out several hundred agents who planned to sabotage the defenses, once the Outsiders launched their attack. For the moment, I'd say we were fairly safe from internal problems, at least in space.

"On the planet, it's a different story," he added. "Boston always had a strong pro-Federation party, but some of our security measures have alienated the locals, while the underground has managed to remain hidden. We may have problems if the Outsiders ever manage to take the high orbitals."

Roman didn't doubt it. The Outsiders were good at getting their people into place to cause mayhem–and the Federation hadn't done anything that might have made it harder, like offering concessions to the locals. But Emperor Marius had stood firm against all such demands. The unity of the human race was the Federation's reason for existence. Nothing, but nothing, could be allowed to threaten it.

A few minor concessions wouldn't threaten it, he thought, grimly. But he already knew the emperor wouldn't agree with him. Too much latitude, in his view, had been granted already.

Roman tapped the table. "This is the situation as I see it," he said. "We will face a major attack on Boston within the next six months, probably sooner. Does anyone disagree with that analysis?"

No one, not even Admiral Ness, said a word. They'd all seen the reports. The Outsider fleets were massing at a dozen different stars, mustering their forces for an advance that could only be targeted on Boston. Roman knew the assault was coming. The only real question was *how* it would come.

"We cannot afford to lose Boston," he continued. "Therefore, it is my intention to lure the enemy into a trap."

He keyed a switch, altering the starchart. The plan had been born in his mind when he'd started looking for a way to strike back at the Outsiders that didn't involve weakening the defenses of Boston. After some careful thought, he'd brought a handful of analysts into the scheme and ordered them to war game it out in simulations. The good guys had won more often than not.

But anything can happen, he reminded himself. *No battle plan ever survives contact with the enemy.*

It was no comfort, he knew, to realize that the enemy commander probably felt the same way too.

"This is currently termed Plan Omega," he said. "On the surface, five battle squadrons and escorts will leave Boston with orders to target Goldstone, a world we know to be serving as a logistics hub for the Outsiders. However, we also believe that Goldstone is no longer a priority for them after they captured two Asimov Points that allow them to move supplies down to the front with a reduced chance of interception. They are unlikely to be unduly worried by us attacking the system."

Admiral Ness leaned forward. "That will take five battle squadrons away from Boston for at least two months," he objected. "Even following the least-time course, they won't be back for far too long."

"Officially, that's true," Roman agreed. "And, if we were right about how important Goldstone is to them, the risk would be worth taking."

He paused. It had taken longer than he cared to admit to find a target that looked reasonable, while offering the enemy the option to disregard the assault, if they saw fit. Anywhere else wouldn't be reasonable or would be *too* reasonable. But Goldstone fit the bill perfectly.

"You said officially," General Yaakov said. "Do I assume correctly that you have something else in mind?"

"Unofficially, the battle squadrons will travel to Heart's Ease and go FTL there," Roman said. "But instead of heading to Goldstone, they will head to here"–he tapped an icon on the display–"and wait.

"The enemy will not fail to note the departure of the fleet," he added. "They have too many spies in the system for the fleet's departure to pass unnoticed. We can make sure that rumors of their destination are spread too. Indeed, as far as everyone outside this room and the analysts are concerned, the fleet's destination *will* be Goldstone. The enemy will pick up on it and draw their plans accordingly. They will launch their long-awaited attack on Boston."

"And they'd face a significantly reduced defense force," Admiral Ness pointed out."

"No, they won't," General Yaakov said. His voice was as unemotional as ever, but his face twitched into a cold smile. "The ships sent to Goldstone will be nearby, ready to intervene if necessary."

"Correct," Roman said. "We will trap the enemy fleet and blow hell out of it. If nothing else, we will hold the system *and* give the enemy a very bloody nose for their pains. We will win time for the Federation to get its industrial might into gear and start out-producing the Outsiders, then crush their fleets and invade their space."

"Assuming they take the bait," Admiral Ness said. "They might decide to defend Goldstone instead."

"In which case they will be unable to assault Boston," Roman countered. "We might not have the chance to smash their fleet, Admiral, but we would have time to keep strengthening our own defenses. Time, if our agents are to be believed, is not on their side."

"It isn't on ours either," General Yaakov grumbled.

"We could lose everything," Admiral Ness objected. "The timing could be screwed up..."

"Yes, it could," Roman agreed. On the surface, the plan lacked any adherence to the KISS Principle–Keep It Simple, Stupid. But he'd worked through it with the study team, eliminating as many problems as they could. At worst, the fleet he dispatched from Boston would spend two months lurking outside the system for nothing. "But we are short on options."

"I cannot believe the emperor would approve a plan that involves daring the enemy to attack you," Admiral Ness continued. "I believe a full Council of War should be called..."

Roman slapped the table, hard. Now, he understood why Admiral Ness had never been considered a threat. The man didn't have the drive to *be* a warlord in his own right, let alone an emperor. He'd been considered safe...but, right now, *safe* was the last thing the Federation needed.

"A council of war is only required when there is no designated senior officer," Roman said, sharply. They were also called when the senior officer needed to cover his ass, but he kept that thought to himself. The plan was his and he would bear the blame, if any, for its failure. Given what was at stake, he could hardly blame the emperor for ordering Roman shot if the plan failed spectacularly. "I am the senior officer in this system and I intend to put this plan into action."

He took a breath. "Besides, the emperor is a skilled officer in his own right," he added. "I am sure he would approve the plan."

"Then ask his approval," Admiral Ness said. "Send a message requesting permission to proceed."

Roman met his eyes. "How long does it take to get a message from here to Earth? And to get a reply?"

"Four months," Admiral Ness said. "Assuming there are no delays..."

"Precisely," Roman said. "By the time we obtained the emperor's approval, the Outsiders might have already launched their assault on Boston. We have to move now or remain here, fists bunched, waiting for the inevitable attack. And that attack will be launched at a time and place of the enemy's choosing! We need to recover the initiative and we need to recover it *now*!"

He paused, watching Admiral Ness to be sure the message was sinking in. It was quite likely the bastard would send a message back to the emperor anyway, expressing his concerns...or he might not, knowing that he would look stupid—at best—if Plan Omega succeeded and the Outsiders took a beating. And besides, if the plan failed, they would probably all end up dead.

"As far as everyone else is concerned, we will be attacking Goldstone," he said. "Commodore Lopez"—he nodded towards the silent officer—"will take command of Task Force 5.2, which will be charged with carrying out the assault. The battle squadrons need some reorganization, which will serve as an excuse for leaking the target. I'll have sealed orders prepared for your subordinates, which will be opened as soon as the fleet departs Heart's Ease."

"Yes, sir," Commodore Lopez said. He was a tall officer, only a year or two younger than Roman. And he'd served well in the Justinian War. "When do you want us to depart?"

"Ideally, within two weeks," Roman said. "The haste will provide another excuse for leaks, I hope."

"Or they may feel you're overdoing it and suspect a trap," Admiral Ness said.

"They'll see the fleet depart," Roman said. There were just too many freighters, mining stations and other settlements within the system for his peace of mind. One or more of them would definitely be keeping the system under observation, assuming the Outsiders didn't have a recon squadron specifically dedicated to Boston. It was what he would have done. "And, at that point, they will have a chance to decide if they want to cover Goldstone or attack Boston."

He smiled. The Outsiders had the advantage of internal lines; if they believed the attack on Goldstone was real, they could muster forces to block it quicker than Commodore Lopez could reach the system. They'd have plenty of time to make up their minds. But if they wanted to attack Boston instead, they'd never have a better chance. Goldstone was utterly immaterial compared to Boston.

"I expect the true objective to remain a secret," he warned, as he rose to his feet, "We cannot afford a leak."

And I will know, he added silently, *which one of us spilled the beans.*

Chapter Twenty-Four

One must remember that the Federation's idea of a fair trial was not, by any definition of the term, actually fair.
-The Federation Navy in Retrospect, 4199

Earth, 4100

"Well," a voice said. "This is a bit of a cock-up, isn't it?"

Lucy looked up. She had no idea how long she'd been in the dark cell, naked, alone and very afraid. They'd fed her once, a bowl of something soft she wouldn't have fed to a cat, and she'd dozed off shortly afterwards. It hadn't occurred to her that the food might have been drugged.

She had to cover her eyes against the glare from outside. "Who...who are you?"

"I'm the only friend you have," the man said. He stepped into the cell, allowing her to see him properly. "Right now, you're in very deep shit."

Lucy gathered herself as best as she could. Somehow, it seemed pointless to cover herself, after the *very* thorough search she'd been forced to endure. The man didn't even seem to look at her properly, keeping his eyes fixed firmly above her head. She wasn't sure if it was an attempt at kindness, however misplaced, or a gesture of contempt. There was no way to know.

"I want to speak to a lawyer," she said. "I have a right to speak to a lawyer."

"I'm afraid that isn't true for anyone held under emergency powers," the man said. He stepped to one side, then held out a hand. "Would you please come with me?"

Lucy eyed him darkly as she took his hand and allowed him to help her to her feet. Her entire body felt weak; even if she'd been able to overpower him, she had a feeling there was no way out of the complex. Outside, the walls were gunmetal grey, solid metal. There was no sign of anyone else, not even other prisoners. And, when she listened, she could hear nothing apart from a rattling old air recycler. It was not a reassuring sound. By the time they reached a small office, she was thoroughly unnerved.

"Please, take a seat," the man said. He waved to a stool in front of a metal table, then walked around it and sat down. Once Lucy had sat, he reached into a drawer and recovered a terminal. "There are some documents here. I want you to be reasonable and sign them."

"I'd like to read them first," Lucy said. She knew the dangers of signing anything without reading it first. "If I can..."

She paused. "And what is your name?"

There was a flicker of hesitation. "You can call me Dan," the man said, finally. He passed her the terminal, then looked into her eyes. "I suggest you sign them now."

Lucy read through the document, page by page. It was horrifyingly simple; she confessed to having deliberately slowed production, an act of treason when the Federation was at war, fighting for its life. The final page was nothing more than heartfelt begging for her life in florid tones. If she hadn't been in jail, she would have found herself unable to believe that *anyone* would beg for mercy like that. But maybe it happened anyway...

"I'm not going to sign this," she said. "We didn't have a choice..."

Dan held up a hand. "Let me be blunt," he said. "You were caught in the act of outright sabotage, no matter the words you use to justify it. We have enough evidence against you to skip the trial and move directly to the sentencing. You *will* be found guilty and, because this is a case of treason, you *will* face the maximum penalty. Do you know, incidentally, what the maximum penalty is in cases of treason?"

Lucy shook her head.

"You will be killed, of course," Dan said, "but it doesn't end there. Your family will be killed as well, just for daring to know you."

"My kids," Lucy said. "You can't kill them!"

"It is the fate reserved for traitors," Dan said. "Your kids are young. The emperor may commute their sentences to life imprisonment, or exile to a colony world so primitive that they think stardrives are nothing more than the products of over-simulated imaginations. I would prefer not to think about what would happen to young boys, out along the Rim. Even if they find a decent foster family, they will never have a chance to be anything more than dirt poor."

"You *bastard*," Lucy said.

Dan didn't bother to deny it. "You have to make a choice," he said. "Sign the confession and you–along with your family–will have your sentence commuted to lifetime exile. You'll spend the rest of your life on a colony world, but you'll be alive and living with your family."

"You just made it sound so attractive," Lucy snarled.

"Oh, it is," Dan said. "You'll be going as colonists, you see, not indentured criminals. You will have a chance to live your life..."

He paused, then met her eyes. "Or you will spend the next few days in this complex, then you will be executed," he added. "There will be no escape, no last-minute reprieve. Sign the confession or die, along with your family."

Lucy forced herself to think. She'd never really thought what could happen to her if she ran afoul of the security forces, not even when the Grand Senate had been tightening its grip on society. Now, she was naked, alone and facing death...and her family was facing death beside her. The thought of her two little boys being hung was horrific, but so was the thought of them being exiled to the Rim, without her. There were rumors about what happened to children on the Rim. She'd always assumed they were lies, but Dan's words gave them a sudden–terrifying–credence. What if they were...?

Dan watched her, emotionlessly. Somehow, that was worse than having him leer at her body, or even force himself on her. And he could have, she knew. To him, she was nothing more than a piece of meat; no, *less* than a piece of meat. She wasn't really *human*. He could do anything to her, undeterred by anything resembling a conscience. And he could do the same to her children, or to her husband.

She took the terminal, paged back to the start, and signed her name.

"Thank you," Dan said. There was a glimmer of amusement in his voice. "Now, you have to record a message."

Lucy looked down at the table, broken. "A message?"

"A message," Dan said. His voice hardened. "One to be broadcast everywhere. And *do* try to make it sound convincing."

ꝏ

"Only two of the strikers held out," General Thorne said. "I believe we can simply exile or execute them now. The remainder have already signed the confessions."

"Good," Marius said. He'd been dreading the prospect of another show trial. "Have the ones who signed confessions sent into exile, as planned. The remainder can be shipped to the nearest penal world."

"Yes, sir," Thorne said.

He nodded, then left the chamber. Marius rubbed the side of his head, feeling the headache abate slightly. Decisive action always felt good, even though he knew that breaking the strike was only the start of what he needed to do. The strikes couldn't be allowed to resume...he sighed, then glanced at the preliminary report. It would be at least two weeks before the striking complexes returned to full production, assuming nothing went badly wrong. There would be knock-on delays that would impinge upon military readiness.

But it can't be helped, he thought, grimly. *There's no alternative, but chaos.*

ꝏ

Tiffany Drake–she had abandoned the endless series of names she'd been given as a minor scion of the Grand Families after the coup–had never wanted to be much of anything. There was no point in trying to be ambitious when she would either get whatever she wanted, just by asking for it, or be denied it simply because her father wasn't a very prominent member of the Grand Families. Indeed, it was why she had been ordered to marry Admiral Marius Drake in the first place. She was very definitely an aristocrat, with a bloodline that could be traced all the way back to the earliest years of the Federation, yet she brought no influence or power to her husband.

And if I had, she'd reflected often enough, *I would have been married off long before the war began.*

She hadn't expected to *like* Admiral Drake, let alone fall in love with him. And, if she were pressed, she would have found it hard to explain *why* she'd fallen in love with him. He was nothing like the sensitive young men held up as the ideal on Earth, although neither were many of the male aristocrats of her generation. But they had earned their prominence through choosing the right parents, while Admiral Drake had cut his way to the top through sheer brilliance and iron determination. It was easy to see why the Grand Senate had feared him, a thought that never failed to make Tiffany smile. If they hadn't tried to kill him, she knew, Drake would never have rebelled.

And besides, there was work–real *meaningful* work–for her to do now.

She'd *known* she would either become a trophy wife or an old maid. Indeed, being an old maid seemed preferable to being married off to anyone. But now she had real work to do, real problems to tax her brain. It didn't bother her that most of the Grand Families were gone–she'd never liked the ones she'd known personally anyway–when it allowed so many people to flourish. A meritocracy would allow people to rise to the level they deserved, not the one determined by their birth. And she knew she could do well, if given a chance...

The door buzzed. Unafraid–she knew just how heavily the President's House was protected–Tiffany used her implants to send a command to the door, ordering it to open. She lifted her eyebrows in surprise when she saw Professor Kratman standing there. It wasn't that she disliked the man, merely that he'd seemed to have his finger in too many pies. And he was a member of the Brotherhood. *That*, more than anything else, suggested he had an agenda.

"Professor," she said. There was no call to be rude. "What can I do for you?"

"I was hoping we might have a word," Professor Kratman said. "There is a matter we should discuss."

Tiffany's eyes narrowed, but she motioned for him to enter the office as she signaled the maid, who brought tea and cakes. She knew how to be a good hostess, thanks to her father, although she had rarely had a chance to practice. Her family had never hosted any of the great galas, not when they'd been so unimportant. Now...it amused her to think that many of the families who'd snubbed her would be begging for favors, if they were still alive. But most of them were dead or exiled.

"I hope this isn't a suggestion about providing a heir," Tiffany said, once the maid had withdrawn. "We talked about it and decided to wait."

"Those people have always given me the creeps," Professor Kratman said. His eyes had followed the maid, warily. "How do you *know* they're not listening to you?"

"You trust in the control implants," Tiffany said. She disliked the idea of stealing someone's ability to control themselves too, but she knew what the maid had done before her arrest. There were some people who could never be trusted to walk free. "This is the President's House, after all."

She poured tea, then passed Professor Kratman a cup.

"The president was powerless for centuries," Professor Kratman observed, as he took the cup and an almond finger. "Do you think he wasn't watched by the Grand Senate?"

Tiffany shrugged, sending her red hair cascading down in waves to her shoulders. "I fancy they considered him nothing more than a harmless boob," she said. "The president might have been elected by popular vote, but I agree, he was always powerless."

She took a sip of her tea, then leaned forward. "Why have you come here, Professor?"

Professor Kratman met her eyes. "Does your husband still confide in you?"

Tiffany blinked. "Yes," she said, surprised. "We talk."

"I do wonder if your husband is having problems," Professor Kratman said. "I knew him as a young midshipman, you see."

"I know," Tiffany said, darkly. She didn't need the reminder that Marius Drake was decades older than her. Large age gaps were far from uncommon, in an era where rejuvenation technology could keep a man or woman physically young for decades, but theirs was an extreme case. "And your point is...?"

"Your husband is under a great deal of stress," Professor Kratman said, softly. "I believe he truly intended to reform the Federation, then hand power back to a reformed Senate. But the war has changed things. Your husband may well break under the stress."

"Marius is the strongest man I know," Tiffany said, stiffly.

"That is not in dispute," Professor Kratman reassured her. "But few men have faced such levels of stress in their lives. The Grand Senate, whatever its flaws, had control of a structure that ensured its orders were obeyed. Your husband has the people who are loyal to him and no others."

"He has me," Tiffany said.

"He needs you," Professor Kratman said. He paused. "Have you noticed the new security agencies?"

Tiffany's eyes narrowed. She'd only met General Thorne once, but she hadn't liked him. The man had given her the creeps, even though she wasn't sure why. He hadn't treated her with anything other than respect and yet he'd still bothered her.

"The Grand Senate did the same, when it felt threatened," Professor Kratman said. "It established new security forces, mainly to keep an eye on the older ones. Your husband, intentionally or otherwise, is doing the same. And, historically, those forces have a tendency to grow in power as time goes on."

"True," Tiffany agreed. "There were some forces that grew more powerful after Admiral Justinian went to war."

She shuddered at the memory. The Blackshirts had started life as the Grand Senate's security forces. By the time they'd been crushed by the Grand Fleet's occupation of Earth, they'd mustered an impressive record of atrocities and even managed to remove a handful of military officers on spurious grounds. And the political commissioners had proved even more of a headache. Marius had told her, more than once, that their interference had cost the Federation Navy battles it should have won.

"But Marius isn't like that," she protested. "He wouldn't stamp on people for breathing."

"No man can hope to master all the details of running a single planet, let alone something the size of the Federation," Professor Kratman warned. "He can't even begin to give certain issues all the attention they deserve, or even the minimum they need to be kept stable. I know of a dozen issues that have slipped through the cracks and others that can only be fixed once peace returns to our part of the galaxy. The recent strike on the moon may only be the first to take place."

"But the strike was broken," Tiffany objected. "And they signed confessions."

"There are limits to how many strikes can be crushed without shooting ourselves in the foot," Professor Kratman warned. "Losing even a relatively small number of experienced workers might cause us long-term problems. The strikers may realize that if enough of them strike, we can't crush them."

He shook his head. "But we are getting away from the point," he warned. "There's a very real risk of your husband losing control completely–or doing something very dangerous. The strikers were effectively forced into signing confessions, then exiled. I believe General Thorne would have gone much further, if necessary. What will happen when the next piece of faecal matter hits the fan?"

Tiffany met his eyes. "What are you asking me to do?"

"Be with him, support him, try to help him," Professor Kratman said. He shook his head in irritation. "We are caught between several different fires, Lady Tiffany, and our ability to deal with just one of them is hampered by the others. The Federation needs time to breathe and the Outsiders, damn the lot of them, aren't likely to let us rest. And, given your husband's growing impatience and frustration, something very bad might happen."

"I see, I think," Tiffany said. "And what does the Brotherhood have to say about all of this?"

"The Brotherhood is torn," Professor Kratman said. "Human unity is our goal. On the other hand, there's a point beyond which fighting is essentially pointless. We could win the battles, but lose the war."

Tiffany nodded. "Like the Grand Senate," she said. "Someone else might see a chance to take power for themselves."

"It's a possibility," Professor Kratman agreed. "Whatever we may think of the coup, and of your husband's role as emperor, it cannot be denied that he has proven that *yes*, it *is* possible to take power by force. I suspect several other admirals have not failed to take note."

"Then have them removed," Tiffany snapped. There was no logic in leaving the potential rogues in place, was there? Who knew what they might be cooking up, away from the emperor's oversight. "Get rid of the bastards!"

"They might refuse to be recalled," Professor Kratman said. "And they wouldn't listen to me, in any case. And I don't know if your husband would agree with me. He has great faith in the Federation Navy."

"Admiral Justinian rebelled," Tiffany said. "And he wasn't the only one."

"No, he wasn't," Professor Kratman said. He finished his tea, then rose. "Take care of your husband, please. We're going to need him."

Chapter Twenty-Five

One of the simplest problems with trying to lure the enemy out of place is that the enemy may miss the lure entirely–or mistake it for something else.
-The Federation Navy in Retrospect, 4199

Galen, 4100

"I trust," Chang Li said, "that your new flagship meets with your approval?"

"It is an improvement," General Stuart agreed, dryly. His previous flagship had been badly damaged in a brief skirmish with a Federation Navy squadron, an encounter that might have been personally disastrous if reinforcements hadn't arrived in the nick of time. He was still unsure if it had been a deliberate ambush or a stroke of bad luck. There was no way to be sure. "But the new crew requires more training."

He sighed, then sat back in his chair. The display showed a hundred stars in green, all occupied by the Outsiders, surrounding Boston, which glowed a grim defiant red. It was absurd, in the days of the stardrive, to think that a single system remained so vital, yet there was no way to avoid it. As long as the Federation Navy held Boston, the ultimate end of the war remained in doubt.

"We're expanding facilities as fast as we can," Chang Li assured him. "But the Marsha are insisting on adding more manpower of their own."

Charlie gritted his teeth. "I suppose you can't tell them to stuff it?"

"Not without causing a diplomatic incident," Chang Li said. "And we don't need the distraction right now."

"We don't need to lose so many starships either," Charlie countered. The only realistic use for the Marsha, he was coming to believe, was kamikaze missions. They seemed to enjoy the prospect of hurling their lives away for a tiny goal, even though any objective observer of the situation would raise eyebrows, at the very least. "The bastards cost us too much."

"We need them," Chang Li said.

"They're also a propaganda nightmare," Charlie added. They'd had to deploy Marsha troops to a number of worlds and the results had been hellishly predictable. Right now, the Marsha were fighting an insurgency on several worlds and losing. "The Federation takes advantage of their presence to claim we intend the destruction of humanity."

"I know," Chang Li said. "But what can we do?"

Charlie understood her frustration. Once it had recovered from its surprise, the Federation Navy had reminded the Outsiders why it was considered a deadly enemy. The Federation hadn't contested every world, but it had made sure to destroy anything the Outsiders could use before withdrawing, right down to tiny asteroid mining complexes. And, in many places, it had withdrawn factories and small industrial nodes too. The irony was chilling; the deeper the Outsiders advanced into the Federation, the longer it took for them to draw supplies from their bases. Several star systems had changed hands more than once because the force that took it, the first time, hadn't been able to hold it against a quick counterattack.

"We have an opportunity," he said. "We may be able to knock the Federation back on its heels."

Chang Li leaned forward. "Show me."

"Intelligence has been our one real advantage since the fighting began," Charlie explained, as he altered the starchart. "If our intelligence sources are to be believed, the Federation Navy has finally twigged to Goldstone's role in our supply lines–or, I should say, its former role."

"I see," Chang Li said. "And they intend to try to cut it?"

"I believe so," Charlie said. "If they got a fleet there prior to one of our convoys passing through the Asimov Points, they would be in a perfect position for a major ambush. It might prove decisive...if we were still using that route. As it is, this gives us a chance to attack Boston while some of her defenders are elsewhere."

"It would still leave a fleet in our rear," Chang Li pointed out.

"It would," Charlie agreed. "But that fleet wouldn't be able to strike anywhere dangerous, even assuming it knew where to go. They'd eventually run out of supplies, if they didn't try to head back into the Federation."

He scowled. As much as he hated to admit it, he would have sold his soul for a straight answer to a simple question. Just how many of the 'secret' bases beyond the Rim were known to the Federation Navy? It had been two years since the war had begun and everything he'd heard about Admiral Garibaldi indicated he wasn't a man to sit on his hands. By now, the Federation would certainly have dispatched a small armada of scoutships far beyond the Rim. Who knew what they had found?

Statistically, it was unlikely they'd find much, he knew. The main bases and shipyards were all carefully concealed, even established–in one case–in the trackless depths of interstellar space. But they might attack a smaller settlement and capture someone who could lead them to a bigger settlement, then so on until they located one of the major bases. Or they might simply concentrate on G2 stars until they located one of the alien homeworlds, then bring their full might to bear against its defenses. And both of the main homeworlds had flimsy defenses, compared to Earth. Or Boston, for that matter.

Chang Li smiled. "And what do you have in mind?"

"Attack Boston with everything we can muster," Charlie said. "We've been trying to cut the system off or isolate it, but it hasn't been successful. The Federation has managed to keep control of its supply lines. This way, we would be hammering the system directly."

"It would still be heavily defended," Chang Li pointed out.

"We wouldn't be trying to secure the high orbitals," Charlie said. It was a regrettable decision, particularly as he knew there were insurgents on Boston intent on liberating their world as soon as the Outsider Navy arrived, but unavoidable. "We'd merely concentrate on the Asimov Points themselves. Boston herself can be left to wither on the vine."

"That won't go well with the Assembly," Chang Li admitted. "They will be pissed."

Charlie felt a flicker of sympathy. Chang Li had been moving from liberated world to liberated world, trying to cajole the governments–provisional, in many cases–to send representatives to the Outsider Assembly. It hadn't been a great success; the newcomers were either fearful of Federation retaliation–after all, the Federation knew where *their* worlds were–or more fire-eating than any of the older representatives. The thought of leaving Boston in Federation hands, even if the system itself was held by the Outsiders, would horrify them. And the Council might not disagree.

"Boston is heavily defended," he said, instead. "However, her defenses cannot impinge on anything outside her orbitals. We gain nothing from attacking the system–besides, the enemy commander might surrender without further ado."

"You don't know that will happen," Chang Li said. "We may treat prisoners well, but still..."

"And they may not believe it," Charlie said. "They don't know just how well we treat prisoners."

The thought was infuriating. He had offered to exchange prisoners, during a brief lull in the endless taking, losing and retaking of star systems, but the Federation Navy had flatly refused. There was no way to know if the Federation Navy was simply reluctant to admit how few prisoners it had managed to take–or if something sinister had happened to those prisoners. The Grand Senate would not have hesitated to tear information out of their brains by force, if necessary, but he thought Admiral–Emperor–Drake would treat prisoners better. But then, the emperor did seem to have decided that the war against the Outsiders was effectively a holy war. *He* had no interest in peace on any but the Federation's terms.

"And they keep refusing our peace envoys," Chang Li added. "There's no way to end the war, short of total victory."

"And that might destroy us," Charlie said. "Or them."

Chang Li nodded. "Our own industry is working desperately to catch up with the Federation, but we're still suffering critical shortages," she warned. "Whatever happens, we are going to have to slow the tempo of operations soon."

"Then we throw everything at Boston," Charlie said. "If Intelligence is correct, taking Boston will knock the Federation so far back on its heels that it will need years, at best, to fix the damage and rebuild its forces. Emperor Marius will have to concentrate forces to block our advance to Earth, which will allow us to raid deep into their territory. We would win..."

"Assuming there's anything left of us," Chang Li said. "Can you assign the Marsha a major role in the operation?"

"Of course," Charlie said. He gave her a grim smile. "I already have several ideas for expending as many of them as possible."

Chang Li looked torn between rebuking him for the casual racism and giving him an understanding look. In the end, she shrugged.

"They really need to grow up," she said. "And, along those lines, have you given any thought to targeting the Snakes?"

"I would strongly advise against trying to liberate the Snakes," Charlie said, flatly. "It would be a public relations disaster."

"The Assembly is torn," Chang Li admitted. "Do we move to forgive or..."

"It doesn't matter," Charlie said, cutting her off. "The Snakes are the one alien race *everyone* hates, without exception. They're not too primitive to know how badly they've been screwed, or too ethereal to give much of a damn about us, but they are humanity's first real non-human enemy. Blowing away the battlestations in orbit around their world will convince a great many fence-sitters that the Federation, for all of its crimes, is a better defender of human rights."

He sighed. "Make the really big changes after you win the war," he advised. "There's no time for a colossal spat right now."

"That's what I told them," Chang Li said. She smiled. "Can you come up with a solid military reason for rejecting the concept?"

Charlie frowned. "Their world is too deep within the Core Worlds to be raided safely," he said. "Besides, we'd need to devote a major battle squadron to the task, given how heavily defended the world is, and that would mean weakening our forces elsewhere."

He rolled his eyes. It said something about the level of paranoia the Snakes caused in humans, at least in the Grand Senate, that they had *still* been adding refinements to the fortifications surrounding the one known remaining Snake-populated world, even though the Snakes themselves had been reduced to a Bronze Age-level of technology. There wasn't a hope in hell of the Snakes managing to break the blockade without outside help. And even if they *did* get outside help, he would have bet half of his salary that the Federation had placed an antimatter bomb on their world, just to make damn sure the Snakes never escaped.

And they're not even that dangerous, he thought, wryly. *The Federation just intends to keep them alive as a potential threat, without letting them become a real threat.*

"I think that's the best justification," he added. "Freeing the Snakes now might cost us the war in more ways than one."

Chang Li nodded. "Very well," she said. "And now...*can* you take Boston?"

"I think we have no choice," Charlie said. "What happens if the Federation manages to get back on its feet?"

He knew the answer to that one, alright. His most optimistic estimate gave the Federation a colossal advantage over the Outsiders–at least five to one–assuming they managed to match the Outsider technological advances. The Outsider Navy would be forced back into the Beyond, then the Federation would start searching for their homeworlds and destroying every single one it located. And that would be the end.

"We lose," Chang Li said, flatly.

She rose to her feet. "I have to get down to the planet in an hour," she said. "I have yet another meeting with the leaders, then I have to be on my way back to Athena. It will not be fun."

Charlie nodded in sympathy. Galen's population seemed sympathetic, but they were only two short hops from Boston and they knew, beyond a shadow of a doubt, that the Federation would take a brutal revenge if they defected openly. For the moment, they were stalling and playing for time, hoping one side would actually win the war before they had to make a final decision. Part of him wanted to condemn them as cowards, part of him understood their fears all too well. They were right at the front line of the war, with the added disadvantage that anyone caught defecting from the Federation would be punished harshly.

"Good luck," he said. "I'll escort you down to the shuttlebay."

"Thank you, General," Chang Li said. "Overall, how are the crews coping?"

"Reasonably well, but the thrill of having overrun Athena has paled," Charlie said. "We've shown we can best the Federation, but we haven't managed to actually win or even force it to the negotiation table. Right now, we're well-prepared for a drive on Boston, but our morale will take a catastrophic hit if we lose."

"Then you'd better not lose," Chang Li said.

ꕥ

"They say we're definitely moving, this time," Captain Roebuck said.

Uzi shrugged. One of the disadvantages of being a mercenary, even with two years of loyal service, was that no one told him what they thought he didn't need to know. In his experience, they also tended to not tell him information he really *did* need to know, even when he was genuinely being a loyal–and well paid–servant. There had been so many false starts to the long-planned attack on Boston that he wasn't taking any rumors seriously, until they were confirmed.

"That's good, I suppose," he said. Roebuck had been promoted, unsurprisingly. The promotion rates were quite high, for those who survived. Some of the mercenaries had muttered about that, but they knew the score. The Outsiders weren't fool enough to promote mercenaries who weren't anything, apart from hired hands. "And do we have definite instructions?"

"Not yet," Roebuck said. "Merely an order to be ready for departure at forty-eight hours notice."

Uzi smiled, mentally cataloguing the steps they would need to take to ensure the entire unit was ready to go. Roebuck might not have been manipulated into questioning everything he was told by his superiors, which would have been the first step towards turning him into a source, if not an active agent, but he had grown to trust Uzi. Uzi planned to take ruthless advantage of that in the future.

"I think we can make it," he said. Roebuck's transfer to the Outsider Naval Infantry–Uzi had pointed out that ONI was already taken, but the Outsiders had been unimpressed–had given him all manner of access, including some levels the Outsiders hadn't realized anyone could access without proper security clearances. "Is it just us?"

"Just the Naval Infantry," Roebuck said. "The other groundpounders are going to remain here."

"And keep the planet under control," Uzi said. It was hard to be sure, but he suspected the planet's provisional government was playing a double game. The threat of bombardment could be used as an excuse, if the Federation won the war. It wouldn't save them from execution, though. "The locals do seem to like us."

"Mostly," Roebuck said. He looked worried. Keeping track of men running in and out of the brothels was a minor nightmare, particularly when there were elements on the planet who were very unfriendly. "But I will be glad to leave."

"I understand," Uzi said. "I'll call back the men, then keep them confined to barracks and running endless drills. The experience will do them good."

"And keep the equipment functional," Roebuck agreed.

Uzi kept his face impassive. Compared to some of the stupid greenie lieutenants he'd had to take by the hand and turn into officers, Roebuck wasn't too bad. Even with Uzi's strictly limited help, he was turning into a capable young officer. But he was on the wrong damn side. There would come a time, Uzi knew, when he would stick a knife in Roebuck's back, even though he would regret it.

There's no choice, he told himself, as he reached for his terminal. *It has to be done.*

He contemplated the possibilities as he sent the signal, recalling the regiment to the barracks. The Outsiders didn't like to admit it, but they'd effectively duplicated the Federation Marines, although on a smaller scale. They'd never really needed to hold down vast tracts of land, after all. The Naval Infantry were designed to take and hold fortifications in space, or even board starships, not land on planetary surfaces. And that meant...

They plan to punch through one of the Asimov Points, he thought. *Unless they plan to force the defenders to surrender...*

"Make sure everyone is ready for deployment," Roebuck said. "I have a good feeling about this one. It might be the *real* offensive we've all been waiting for."

Uzi kept his face impassive. In his view, the longer the offensive was delayed, the better.

"And once we take Boston, we can move on to Earth," Roebuck continued. "And that would be the end of the war."

"There are more defended systems between Boston and Earth," Uzi pointed out. "The offensive would have to punch through them, one by one."

"But Boston is the big one," Roebuck said. "We could win this war! Next year, we could be walking down the streets of Earth!"

"I've seen Earth," Uzi said. "It wasn't much to look at, really."

And besides, he added silently, *Earth's fall will not end the war.*

"Sourpuss," Roebuck said, lightly. "Earth's fall will bring down the emperor. And then all we will have to do is mop up the remains."

"I hope you're right," Uzi lied.

Chapter Twenty-Six

The downside of the Federation's control (directly or indirectly) over the media was that no one believed a word the official media said. Unsurprisingly, when rumors started to spread rapidly, they were believed.
-The Federation Navy in Retrospect, 4199

Earth, 4100

Jonathon Small disliked his job.

It wasn't the food he hated, although a few years serving synthetic burgers to students had left his hands stained and greasy. Having a steady job was worth any amount of suffering–and besides, he and his fellows were allowed to finish the remaining meals after the diner had closed for the night. It might have left him fat, smelly and generally bad-tempered, but it *was* a steady job when there were almost none to go around. His wages ensured his family didn't have to crawl to the civil servants for everything they needed, no matter how simple.

It was the *students* he hated. Many of them were bright young things, handsome or beautiful, without a single original thought in their brains. If, of course, they had brains. He had his doubts, because not a one of them seemed capable of stringing two thoughts together without a textbook from some overpaid teacher in front of them. And, he knew, most of them would graduate and then discover they couldn't find a job. Who the hell wanted someone with a degree in liberal arts when Earth's infrastructure was falling apart? The pretty young girls and handsome young boys would spend the rest of their lives in poky apartments, collecting dole from the civil servants and breeding the next generation of moronic idiots who thought they knew everything.

Maybe the girls will go on the game, he thought, as he eyed one particular table, crammed with young girls in their late teens. The girls were even stupider than the boys, in his opinion; they tended to cling to their opinions, even when confronted with proof they were completely wrong. He still recalled one of them asking him, in all sincerity, if he didn't feel exploited by his employers. Of course he did, Jonathon had thought, although he'd merely muttered something under his breath and then asked if she wanted fries with her burger. But at the end of the day, he was actually earning something and the students in front of him were living on the government's teat.

But this time things looked different. More and more students were cramming their way into the diner, ordering plates of food and drink and then debating, in their earnest manner, something that had happened on the moon. It was just as absurd, in Jonathon's view, as when he'd overheard students discussing the merits of Admiral Justinian's war against the Federation and the Grand Senate. No matter what the students thought, the war would be won or lost...and nothing would change for the average citizen. There would merely be a different boss right at the top. And he'd been right. Emperor Marius had taken over, in the end, and what had changed for Jonathon? Nothing.

He rolled his eyes in disgust, then walked behind the counter and frowned. Patty was sitting behind the rows of machines, crying. Jonathon winced–Patty was young, barely older than the students–and too sensitive for the job. If her father hadn't been owed a favour by someone in the civil service, she probably wouldn't have gotten the job. She was really too young and pretty to survive as a waitress. Between being leered at when she was behind the counter and being groped when she was serving food, it was unlikely she would survive very long. But she didn't have many other options, unless she wanted to become a whore. The brothels were always looking for fresh meat.

"Go find the next few bags of fries," he told her. She was young enough for him to feel almost fatherly towards her, although she was five years older than his oldest son. "I'll take the food out to the little bastards."

He watched her scurry off–her trousers were really too tight, but the workers weren't allowed to change anything without written permission from headquarters–and then picked up the tray of food. The students probably didn't realize it, he suspected, but they were actually eating the diner out of cheap reprocessed food. He'd already asked his boss to put in an emergency order for more foodstuffs, yet they'd be unlikely to arrive in time. They might have to close the diner early for the first time in years.

Balancing the tray with the ease of long practice, he strode out into the eating zone and sighed as he realized that someone had spilled a large milkshake on the floor. The little bastards hadn't even bothered to tell the overworked staff that there had been a spill, even though the staff could lose some of their wages if inspectors saw the hazard before it was mopped up. He gritted his teeth and walked up to the table, then announced the contents of the tray in a loud voice. The students were debating so earnestly that he had to repeat himself twice before they heard him and started to claim their food.

One of the students–a loud girl wearing a shirt so tight her breasts were threatening to break out–caught his arm, fortunately just after he'd emptied the tray. "What do you think of it?"

Jonathon had to fight to keep the irritation off his face. Being sneered at by his superiors was always easier to handle, if only because his superiors had worked to earn their ranks. The students, on the other hand, always looked down on him, as if working for a living was somehow a bad thing. The lucky ones would be joining him in a year, he was sure, no matter how much they sneered now. And the unlucky ones would be buried in the crapper.

"Of what?" He said, somehow managing to keep his voice civil. These were trying times and a single complaint could cost him his job. "I haven't heard of anything."

"There was a strike on the moon," a male student said. The disdain in his voice was so strong that Jonathon had to resist the temptation to punch him in the face. "The pigs broke it up and arrested the leaders."

Jonathon shrugged. He'd never heard of any strike–or of the cops being involved. Pigs indeed–didn't the students realize that their lives would be much worse without the campus police? There were places barely a mile from the university where he wouldn't dare go without an armed escort, where looting, rape and murder were daily occurrences. The pretty girls in front of him would be torn apart if the madness ever slipped into the campus, no matter how socially just they considered themselves to be. And their boyfriends wouldn't stand a chance.

"I wouldn't know anything about it," he said, instead. He picked up several empty boxes–the students were too occupied with their debate to shove them into the waste bins–and a half-eaten burger that someone had abandoned. It was hard to blame whoever had been trying to eat it. Jonathon knew, all too well, just what went into the burgers. "My job is merely to serve food."

"He's one of the exploited," another student whispered, too drunk or too stupid to keep his words low enough so they couldn't be overheard. "He dare not say a word."

"We're going out on strike ourselves," the first student said. She took a breath, which did interesting things to her chest. "Why don't you join us?"

Jonathon studied her for a long moment. Judging from her appearance, her family was almost certainly middle-class. It was unlikely in the extreme she would be anywhere near the campus if her family was upper-class. Her perfect face, soft appearance and complete lack of concern over her clothing–what little there was of it–all added up to a disgraceful naivety about the universe. But he knew there was no point in trying to lecture her. She didn't want to hear anything that disagreed with her worldview.

"Because someone has to serve the food," he said, reminding himself why his sons weren't going to go to university. They were going to become tradesmen instead. "And because I have work to do."

"That's true," another student said. "You can serve us food while we're on strike."

Jonathon nodded politely, then left them to their plotting.

"There's some shouting outside," Patty said, when he got back around the counter. Another line of students had appeared and were ordering takeaway, even though it cost an extra credit to eat outside the diner. "I think there's going to be trouble."

Jonathon rubbed his ears. A lifetime of working in the diner–at least it felt like a lifetime–had left him deaf in one ear and hard of hearing in the other. It had its uses, particularly when his wife felt like nagging, but it was irritating. Now Patty mentioned it, though, he could hear someone shouting outside the diner. It almost sounded like they were chanting something over and over again, but he couldn't make out the words.

"They're calling the students to strike," Patty said. "For Great Justice or something like that."

"Get the cash out of sight and into the safe," Jonathon ordered. "And then stay behind the counter. If rioters get in here, hit the screens and jump into the back."

Patty blinked in surprise. "What about the students?"

Jonathon snorted. "What about them?"

ꕥ

Being a Campus Policeman was not an easy job, Constance McNamee considered. The students might not be as violent as people unfortunate enough to live in the lower-class parts of the city, where the police only went in armed squads if they went at all, but they could be incredibly argumentative. And they could get away with one hell of a lot, if they were careful or hired the right lawyers. Staff weren't permitted to exclude or expel students for anything less than a truly dire crime, which meant that the campus policemen had very little effective power. She'd lost count of the number of times an open and shut case had become a multi-sided nightmare, thanks to political interference. It was a wonder to her that so many students kept coming to university. Didn't they realize just how dangerous it could be?

She heard the shouting as she walked down the streets, students chanting demands into the air. Protests were one thing–and fairly common on campus–but this sounded different, nastier. She gritted her teeth, then clicked her radio and started to make a report as the students came into view. They looked furious about something, but what?

No change there, she thought, darkly. She'd once harbored the thought that university was supposed to be about education. Instead, the students seemed to spend half of their time getting drunk or chasing sexual relationships, while the rest of their time seemed to be spent on one political cause or another. She had never had any idea why the Grand Senate tolerated it. But then, the students were hardly a political threat. They didn't have any weapons, for a start.

"Freedom for strikers," one of the students yelled. "Strike! Strike! Strike!"

The mob swelled as more and more students emerged from campus buildings and joined the crowd, picking up the chant as it grew louder. Constance felt cold fear running down her spine as the mob advanced towards her, one hand playing with her stunner as the other fiddled with her radio. The students, damn them, had managed to convince the campus authorities to ban lethal weapons on campus, which hadn't seemed a problem until now. But the more realistic part of her mind knew that a loaded gun wouldn't have made a difference.

Her radio bleeped. "Constance, pull back," her supervisor ordered. "There are mobs forming everywhere. It looks as though every damn student in this whole damn campus is out on the streets."

"Or trying to hide," Constance said, as she caught sight of a group of students distributing drugs and alcohol to the strikers. "They won't want to be caught up in this..."

"No, they wouldn't," her supervisor agreed. "Get out..."

"Kill the pig," someone yelled.

Constance looked up, just in time to see the mob changing course and bearing down on her with terrifying speed. Some of them might have their doubts about attacking a campus policewoman, but they were being pushed on by the people behind them. And when it was over, they would have nowhere to go. She turned and ran, as fast as she could, but the mob grew louder and louder. And then she sprinted around a corner and ran straight into another mob. There was no way out.

She reached for her stunner, but it was already too late.

ᘓᘐ

"But damn it, Tony," the dean protested. "You have to do something!"

Director Tony Kingworm looked up, meeting the dean's eyes. "Like what?"

He sighed inwardly as the dean started to splutter. If only they'd been allowed to set up headquarters somewhere else. He could have barred the dean from entering during a crisis...but they'd been forced to set up their headquarters in the admin building. The dean, as soon as he'd heard about the budding riot, had come down the stairs and into Tony's office. He hadn't had a moment of peace since.

"Like...like *something*," the dean said. "Do *something*!"

Tony rose to his feet. "Right now, I've lost seven officers," he said, sharply. He'd seen mob violence before, back when he'd been on the streets. It was unlikely that any of the officers had survived. "Your damn students are rioting and tearing the place apart. And you have persistently denied me the tools I need to deal with them."

"Then...then *get* the tools," the Dean said. "Just...do *something*."

It was unlikely, Tony knew, that his career would survive. Losing control of a university campus would look very bad on his record. He'd have to apply to serve as a colonial marshal or something along the same lines, if he wished to stay in law enforcement. There certainly wouldn't be such a cushy posting in his future. But if his career was doomed, he might as well go out in style.

"Very well," he said. He reached into his desk and produced a stunner. "If you'll just look this way."

The dean's mouth dropped open. A moment later, Tony pressed the trigger and the dean crumpled to the floor.

"Leave him there," Tony ordered. He walked over to the display, mounted on the wall. "I want you to pull all of the officers out of the campus, then concentrate them at the security guardposts."

"Yes, sir," the dispatcher said. "But what about us?"

"Seal the building," Tony said. He had no illusions. Main Building was no castle. It was incapable of standing off an attack from a horde of insane students. If the students attacked, he and his men would be rapidly overwhelmed. "We'll see about getting out through the roof, if possible."

He cursed under his breath. The students might just stop rioting in a few hours and go back to classes–they'd certainly done that before–but the speed at which the riot had spread suggested otherwise. This was no spur of the moment reaction, he was sure. Someone had done a great deal of planning and preparation in advance. The bastards were already smashing security monitors, both the overt bulky cameras and the smaller, well-hidden sensors. It pointed to treachery. No, it pointed to outright subversion.

"Contact the planetary security command," he added. "Tell them we need reinforcements."

He'd been briefed on the dangers of Outsider propaganda, back when the Outsiders had first shown they were capable of reaching all the way to Earth to make their anger felt. Some of the students were intelligent enough to realize they were in a trap, after all, and seek some way to get *out*. Backing the Outsiders might seem a way to escape...and besides, the Outsiders did have a point. Earth hadn't been free before Emperor Marius, let alone after him.

Stupid bloody students, he thought. *And they're about to learn just how unpleasant the world can be.*

ഌ◌ശ

Jonathon watched, grimly, as a pair of students entered the diner. They were swaggering, deliberately showing off their power, hoping to intimidate the staff. He felt cold ice flowing through his body as they waved the other students out, then marched up to the counter and smiled at him. They had no doubts at all about their cause.

"We want food and drink, now," the leader said. "One hundred burgers..."

"We're almost out," Jonathon said. The last report had told him that the transport had reported heavy delays. He suspected that was something of an understatement. The riot had made it impossible to deliver to the campus. "You won't get half that..."

The leader snarled at him. "You will send us the food," he snapped. "I..."

Jonathon hit the emergency button. Solid metal bars dropped into place, sealing off the staff section from the rest of the diner. The students looked shocked, then stamped out of the diner, banging the door closed behind them. Moments later, the howling mob started to pour through the door and trash the eating zone.

Patty caught his arm as rocks and glass bottles started slamming into the bars. "They can't get in, can they?"

"I hope not," Jonathon said. The howling was growing louder. He'd always known the students believed in conspiracies, but he'd never realized how absurd they were. What sort of idiot thought that food was still delivered, even in the midst of a riot? "But all we can do is wait and see."

And pray, he added, silently. The bars were starting to rattle ominously. *If they break in, we're dead.*

Chapter Twenty-Seven

This was unfortunate as rumors were never very accurate. The original police action on the moon netted several hundred strikers, most of whom were released without charge. By the time the rumors reached Earth, they claimed the military had shot several thousand strikers and raped thousands more.
-The Federation Navy in Retrospect, 4199

Earth, 4100

"I don't think you should be taking those," Tiffany said.

Marius scowled at her, then softened. "I keep having headaches," he said, tiredly. "What do you think I should take?"

"I think you should rest," Tiffany said. She'd been more solicitous recently, something that pleased and annoyed Marius in equal measure. It was nice to have someone caring for him, but Tiffany had her own work to do. "You're pushing yourself too hard."

Marius snorted. For better or worse, the buck stopped with him. That had been true since his first command, years ago. Now, he was emperor and he had to oversee everything personally. He just didn't have enough subordinates he could trust to handle their responsibilities without supervision.

"I don't have time," he said. A holiday sounded nice–he hadn't had a proper holiday since before the Justinian War; besides, they hadn't had a proper honeymoon either–but where would he find the time? Somehow, he knew it wouldn't be easy. "There's too much to do."

Tiffany stepped up behind him and began to rub his back, her fingers stroking his skin. It felt good, so good that Marius wanted to relax into her ministrations, but he knew there was no time. He'd condemned enough senior officers for spending time with their mistresses instead of doing their duty that he didn't feel right about enjoying himself. Besides, he had yet another set of meetings to attend. Everything had been so much simpler when he'd been in command of the Grand Fleet. His crew had known their jobs and got on with them.

And Blake shot me, he thought, sourly. The betrayal still hurt, even now. *I guess he knew his job too.*

The communicator bleeped. "Sir?"

Marius heard Tiffany grunt in irritation as he stepped away from her and walked over to the communicator. "Yes?"

"There's trouble on Earth, sir," the operator said. "I..."

"Define trouble," Marius said. It was irritating as hell to know that his subordinates were nervous about bringing him bad news–but then, the Grand Senate had been known to shoot the messenger. They hadn't been the only ones either. "What is happening?"

"There's a riot, sir," the operator said.

"A riot," Marius repeated. He allowed his voice to darken. Couldn't anyone tend to anything these days without asking him for instructions? "And this is important enough to call me?"

"General Thorne requests a meeting, sir," the operator said. "He's already on his way."

"Very well," Marius said. "Show him into my office when he arrives."

"You have to come back here afterwards," Tiffany said. "I have some other ways to relax you."

Marius shook his head. "I have too much work to do," he said. "And none of it can be passed down to someone else."

He kissed her on the cheek, then stepped through the door and into his office, pulling on his dressing robe as he walked. It wasn't what anyone expected an emperor to wear, he was sure, but the Federation didn't really *have* a proper uniform for a supreme ruler. The Grand Senators had always worn suits and ties, each one made by designers who charged more than an admiral earned in a year for each suit. Marius had suspected, when he'd looked at the books, that it was just another attempt to prevent outsiders from trying to run for election and overturn the system. Chang Li had been the only successful outsider–in more ways than one–for decades.

And she was a treacherous bitch, he thought, nastily. Forgiveness wasn't one of his virtues, not when the whole Federation was at stake. *How long was she planning our downfall?*

He sat down at his desk and pressed his hand against the terminal, allowing it to scan his ID implant. A long list of documents appeared in front of him, all demanding his personal attention and signature. Everything, he noted with some irritation, from personal files to industrial production plans for the next five years. Replacing the infrastructure the Outsiders had destroyed was a long hard chore.

And the Grand Senate burned out too much of our infrastructure, he reminded himself. *Were they that confident that they could win the war in time to save themselves?*

There was a person who might be able to answer. But Marius had no time to face him.

"Sir, General Thorne is here," his aide said.

"Then show him in," Marius ordered. "Please."

General Thorne looked tired, Marius noted, as he was shown into the room. But at least he was reliable, unlike so many others. He saluted Marius curtly, then sat down on the other side of the desk and rested his hands on his lap.

"General," Marius said. "What's happening?"

"A major series of riots, student riots," General Thorne said. "These were clearly planned in advance."

Marius cursed under his breath. "The Outsiders?"

"Almost certainly," General Thorne said. "They knew about the strike, somehow, but the rumors were vastly inflated."

"I thought we had that under control," Marius said.

"We did," General Thorne countered. "As far as we can tell, word didn't move from Luna to Earth...but somehow it reached Earth anyway. And then the riots began."

Marius groaned. "I see," he said. He reached for another pill and swallowed it, without bothering with water. "What's the current situation?"

"We have riots on twelve separate campuses, sir," General Thorne said. "They started at more or less the same time, too. That *cannot* be a coincidence."

"Evidently not," Marius said. The pill wasn't working. His head felt as thick as ever. "And are they under control?"

"We have the campuses sealed off, sir," General Thorne reported. "But they have managed to get word out into the datanet. We may see other riots soon."

Marius gritted his teeth. Earth's datanet was unusual in many ways; unlike any of the others, it included large sections that were almost completely outside government control. There were archives of data dating back thousands of years in the datanet, some harmless pornography, but others considered politically dangerous. The Grand Senate, for all of its power, had failed to bring the datanet to heel. And students, for all of their general ignorance, tended to make the best WebHeads. They probed the datanet for hidden sections, then infested the uncontrolled cores and made them theirs.

"Bastards," he said. "What do they actually *want*?"

"The first set of demands were for the release of the strikers," General Thorne said. "After that, their demands became a little more extreme. Right now, they want free elections, free unions, a resumption of government-backed social programs... and quite a few other things, all of which would cost us dearly if we attempted to implement them."

"Idiots," Marius said. What sort of moron thought the Federation would be inclined to just roll over and give them whatever they wanted, if they rioted? The Federation hadn't submitted to the Outsider demands and the Outsiders were invading Federation space with a huge fleet. "I assume you have a plan to deal with them?"

"Yes, sir," General Thorne said. "I have four regiments of security troops on their way to each of the campuses. On your command, they will storm the campuses and deal with the students. They will go into detention camps and be held until we have established their role in these events, then you can deal with them as you see fit."

"Good," Marius said. Students. Why hadn't they done something useful with their lives, like joining the Navy? Or emigrating to a world that could actually handle them? Or even taking vocational training? "I think we'll add them to the list of involuntary emigrants."

"Yes, sir," General Thorne said.

"After that, we should take a long hard look at just what role the universities play in our modern society," Marius added. He'd left them alone because many of the students had parents who were actually working, which made sending their children to university all the more inexplicable. "And start expanding the vocational training courses."

He sighed, cursing—yet again—the Grand Senate. There just weren't enough trained people to serve as teachers for the vocational courses, which meant that expanding the whole system was going to take time, longer than he cared to admit. If there hadn't been a war on, perhaps it could be done at a calmer pace, but there *was* a war on. And they had to win the war. Defeat would mean the end of human unity...

God help us, he thought.

"See to it," he said, out loud. "And then inform me when the operation is completed."

He watched General Thorne leave the office, then looked down at the endless stream of documents he had to read and sign. Some of them, thankfully, had summaries at the front, but others were just too detailed for him to read quickly. Didn't the writers realize he didn't have *time* to parse out every last detail? He wrote an angry note at the bottom of one particularly lengthy report, then closed the terminal and rose to his feet. The longer he stayed in the office, the greater the chance he'd snap at someone who didn't deserve it. He changed quickly, then walked towards the door.

The door hissed open as he approached and stepped through, then hissed closed behind him.

"Sir?" His aide said. "I..."

"I'm going for a walk," Marius said. "Stay where you are."

He shook his head as he walked through the door, nodded to the Marines, then started to wander through the President's House. It had been a long time since it had served as any form of administrative center and it showed; there were large art galleries that had been left completely untouched, while the former offices had been closed down years ago. Marius wandered down a long deserted corridor, looking at paintings so old that half of them had no known origin, then made his way to the elevator. It pinged open on his approach, then took him down into the basement. The guard in front of the prison cell looked up, then jumped to his feet and saluted as Marius approached.

"As you were," Marius ordered. "Open the door."

The hatch hissed open, revealing the cells. All but one of them were empty.

"Admiral," Blake Raistlin greeted him cheerily. "My trial seems to have been abandoned."

"There's a war on," Marius growled. "But somehow I'm sure you know that, don't you?"

"I'm in a cell," Raistlin said. As always, his voice was faintly mocking. "The only amusement I get comes from being bent over the bunk by one of the guards."

"There are never less than three guards supervising you whenever you are taken to the shower," Marius snapped, refusing to rise to the bait. "And they wouldn't abuse you, whatever happened."

"One could argue that being locked up indefinitely without a trial is cruel and unusual punishment," Raistlin pointed out. "Or to have a trial suspended for no valid reason..."

Marius smiled. "Correct me if I'm wrong," he said, "but weren't there a great many officers held on Luna without trials by the Grand Senate?"

Raistlin's eyes narrowed. "I thought you claimed to be better than us," he said. "I've been in better hotels, if you happened to think you were giving me a holiday..."

Marius cut him off. "Tell me," he said. "What were your people *thinking*?"

"I imagine power, sex and money, perhaps not in that order," Raistlin said. "Or did you have something specific in mind?"

"We're trying to expand training opportunities for people," Marius said. "There's no shortage of work, but there's a major shortage of people trained and able to actually *do* the work. We need to train more people as fast as possible..."

He shook his head. "But how many of those people will never be trained properly because the facilities to train them don't exist? What were your people *thinking*?"

"They probably felt they didn't want anyone to question their power," Raistlin said. "And I dare say it worked for hundreds of years."

"The Outsiders think differently," Marius said. "I shudder to think of what would have happened if Admiral Justinian hadn't given us due warning of what we might face, in the future. The Outsiders would have held a definite tech advantage when they fell on us."

"Then you owe us," Raistlin said. "Without the Grand Senate, you wouldn't be ready for war."

Marius's eyes narrowed. "Explain."

"The Grand Senate fucked around with Admiral Justinian," Raistlin said. "So he rebelled. His rebellion pushed you to prominence, but it also got rid of a shitload of deadwood in the Federation Navy's upper ranks. And it also forced the Federation to start developing new weapons and tactics, which gave you a better base for facing the Outsiders."

Raistlin smiled. "See? You owe us."

"I will not even *try* to unpick that...that piece of insane troll logic," Marius said. "And I will *certainly* not believe you intended it to happen. It was a fuckup from start to finish."

"True," Raistlin agreed, without heat. "But you have to admit you did well by it, *Emperor*."

He stood, then prostrated himself on the ground, banging his head off the hard metal floor.

"All Hail Marius, the Great Emperor of Humanity," he said. "Supreme Master and God of the Universe..."

"Get up," Marius snapped. He'd never liked watching people prostate themselves, certainly not to other humans. "You're making a fool of yourself."

"It isn't like I have much else to do," Raistlin pointed out. He made kissing sounds as he rubbed his head on the floor. "And besides, what do I actually have to look forward to? You won't keep playing with me for the rest of my natural life. One day, you'll actually grow tired of trying to nail me legally and simply have me shot."

"I dread to imagine how many people have pissed on that floor," Marius said. "These cells weren't actually cleaned for years before you moved in."

Raistlin looked up. "They made me clean it," he said. He paused. "Is the condemned man allowed to make one last request?"

"Get off the floor first," Marius growled. He watched as Raistlin obeyed, then leaned forward. "What do you want?"

"A woman," Raistlin said. "Or a man. I'm not fussy."

"I know," Marius said. Raistlin had cut a swath through the younger crewmen on board Marius's flagship, both male and female. Marius hadn't been sure if it was sex appeal–Raistlin was handsome and charming, even in jail–or if it had been the prospect of using his connections to help someone's career. "But I think not."

"You could think about it," Raistlin said. "I might become more cooperative if I got laid."

Marius rubbed his temple. The pain had faded, for a time, but it was coming back.

"I don't need to think about it," he said. "You're a prisoner. You're a prisoner because you shot me on my own flagship."

"And that is what this is about," Raistlin said. "It isn't because you want to kill me legally, admiral, and because you want a fig leaf of respectability for your decision. It's because of your injured pride. You can't abide the thought of being betrayed, even though you have betrayed the entire Federation."

"It betrayed me," Marius snapped. "Your whole damned family tried to *kill* me!"

"Injured pride," Raistlin repeated. "They never gave a damn about you. You were just in their way, just someone who needed to be used, handled and then discarded when you were no longer necessary."

Marius stepped forward until his face was almost touching the forcefield. "And where would the Federation be if I were dead?"

"The Grand Senate would have found a solution," Raistlin said. "A political compromise, if necessary."

"You would have sold out the entire Federation to keep your power?" Marius demanded. The idea of breaking the Federation, even surrendering the outer worlds, was beyond contemplation. No thought of separation could be tolerated. "You would have sold out all of *humanity*?"

"Of course," Raistlin said. "The business of power is power. And, admiral, I think you've discovered that all too well."

Marius stepped back, fighting to hold on to his temper. "I could have you shot..."

"Then *do it*," Raistlin shouted. "End this farce!"

"You will be tried," Marius said. "And then you will be condemned to death..."

"You've been trying for the past two years," Raistlin said. "There are just no legal grounds to kill me." His voice became a sneer. "I was only following orders from my lawful superiors."

"Damn you," Marius said.

He turned and walked through the door, leaving Raistlin alone. The thought gnawed at his mind as he stepped into the elevator, then returned to his office. A blinking light on the terminal told him that new papers had arrived, in his absence. He was going to be working all night, just to clear them all.

Or maybe I should just sign them all, without reading them, he thought. But he'd rejected proposals before, knowing they would be damaging to the Federation. He needed more trustworthy officers, but there just weren't that many people he trusted. Raistlin had done far more than just put a bullet in him, he knew. He'd destroyed Marius's ability to *trust*.

He opened one document and looked down at it. Blake Raistlin's death warrant. There were emergency powers he could invoke, if necessary, in signing the warrant. But that would mean giving up all hope of nailing the young man legally. And that would undermine the base of his regime. What protection was there if someone could be executed–legally–without trial?

And he was laughing at me, Marius thought. He popped another pill, absently. *And he was right.*

Chapter Twenty-Eight

Trying to be clever, in a military operation, is asking for trouble. Trying to appear clever, on the other hand, is sometimes quite promising.
-The Federation Navy in Retrospect, 4199

Boston, 4100

"Sir," Lieutenant Thompson said, "Commodore Lopez is in position."

"Good," Roman said. It had been an edgy two weeks. Commodore Lopez might not have reached Point Theta before the Outsiders attacked, which would have made life on Boston *interesting*, to say the least. Admiral Ness had repeated the point time and time again in planning sessions, leaving Roman wondering if he could legally strangle the bastard and get away with it. "Continue to monitor the Asimov Points."

He looked up at the display, feeling cold tension clutching at his heart. There were three Asimov Points that led directly into enemy territory, while two more could be seized in short order if the Outsiders wanted to avoid his strongest defenses. The more he thought about it, the more he envied the tacticians from the First Interstellar War, before the stardrive had been invented. *They* had always known where their enemy had to attack, even if they hadn't known *when*. But the stardrive had changed the tactical situation completely. An attack could come from any direction.

"Check the StarComs," he ordered. They'd taken a leaf from Admiral Justinian's playbook and rounded up all the StarCom units they could find, then established them at the different Asimov Points. Roman would have an instant alert as soon as the attack began, allowing him to move his forces to counter the enemy offensive. "I want the system to ping each platform every ten minutes."

He shook his head, understanding–finally–why so many pointless orders had come down the chain when the fleet had been guarding Asimov Points in the past, waiting for an attack that might–or might not–come. The commanding officers had done all they could; now, all they could do was wait and worry. *He* was just the same, he admitted now. He'd reached the point where he could do nothing, apart from trusting his subordinates and waiting.

"Belay that order," he said, softly. "Just ping the system once every half hour."

It was hard, very hard, to resist the urge to pace the CIC as he waited for something to happen. The Outsiders had to know, by now, that a large subsection of Fifth Fleet had departed Boston–and, if their intelligence was as good as ONI believed, they had to know the fleet's official destination. Elf had tested the strands of intelligence and informed him, once her Marines had returned to the fleet, that the 'secret' was common knowledge. Roman sighed as he sat back in his chair. The Outsiders *had* to know where Commodore Lopez was heading...

And so they should be coming here, he thought, as he stood. He couldn't stay in the CIC indefinitely or he would drive his subordinates mad. *But do they have something else in mind?*

He shook his head as he walked through the hatch. The Outsiders might smell a rat, no matter how tempting the bait. If so, they wouldn't attack; they'd try to go somewhere else. But where? There was nowhere else they could go without risking their hold on countless star systems, not when Federation Navy raiding squadrons were still poking through the warzone, looking for vulnerable targets. One raid could convince wavering planets that the Federation was far from dead. And then...

There's no point in going over it time and time again, he told himself. *You've done all you can.*

He reached his cabin and stepped inside. It was empty, of course. Elf had been spending much of her time training with the Marines, particularly the FNGs from Mars. Their training had been curtailed, she'd complained, just to get as much manpower as possible out to the front. She had to keep working with them to ensure they were ready. And they would be needed soon.

Roman sighed again, then lay down on the bed and closed his eyes. There was nothing he could do, but rest–and make sure he was ready for the moment the shit hit the fan. Because it would, he knew. And then he would know for sure just how well his plans worked when they encountered the enemy.

ꕥ

Commodore (Fortress Command) Tanya Osborne didn't like the plan. She hadn't liked the idea of sending so many battle squadrons on a wild goose chase to Goldstone, nor had she liked the *real* plan when Admiral Garibaldi had briefed her on it, two weeks ago. To set her fortress–and the other ten heavy fortresses orbiting Asimov Point Delta–up as a target was far from *her* idea of a good plan, even though she knew they would never have a better chance of giving the enemy a bloody nose. Indeed, if she hadn't been aware that the admiral was a close friend of the emperor, she would have made an official complaint.

She paced her command deck, throwing irritated glances at the display whenever the Asimov Point emitted the faintest flicker of a gravity pulse. Being so close to the point struck civilians as dangerous, but Tanya had been an officer long enough to know that almost anything the point might spit out–naturally–could be handled at this distance. The real danger lay in transiting the point...and no one in their right mind would try to power an entire fortress through the chink in space/time. And then there was the prospect of an enemy fleet attacking the system...

The last report from her probes had shown nothing, apart from layer upon layer of mines and a thousand automated weapons platforms, covering the point against an offensive from the Federation Navy. The Outsiders weren't focusing their resources on a fixed defense, which would have been admirable if it hadn't been so irritating. Everything they wasted on a fixed defense couldn't be expended on building a giant war fleet and sending it out to wreak havoc on the Federation. But she couldn't fault their logic. The Federation had immense supplies of fortress components stored in reserve, even if they'd used many of them to seal the points against Admiral Justinian. It was unlikely the Outsiders had anything comparable.

They wouldn't have wanted to rely on them, she thought. *Not in the Beyond.*

She smiled at the thought. Her brother had been a survey officer, before the survey service had been effectively disbanded. But now he was back in uniform and poking through the Beyond, looking for targets the Federation Navy could reach. And there was a good chance he would find undetected and unguarded Asimov Points. There was no way the Outsiders could locate *every* point in their backyard without a thorough survey of their own...

Ping!

"Report," she snapped. "What do you have?"

"Commodore," Midshipman Peter Quigley reported. "We have drones transiting the Asimov Point."

"Order the CSP to intercept," Tanya ordered, as red icons sparkled to life on the display. "Sound Red Alert."

She watched, grimly, as several of the icons flashed out of existence. The Outsiders had probed the Asimov Point routinely, of course, but this time they were expending hundreds of probes. Some of them would get back, no matter how many the CSP managed to pick off before they reversed course and vanished back into the Asimov Point. And then the Outsiders would have the tactical data they needed to plan their offensive.

"Signal the Admiral," she ordered, as her fortresses woke up. "Inform him that all hell may be about to break loose."

"Aye, Commodore," Commander Janelle said. There was a long pause. "All fortresses report battlestations, Commodore. They're requesting permission to launch additional starfighters."

"Denied," Tanya said. The Outsiders probably hoped she'd do just that, forcing her starfighters to exhaust their life support packs before the battle began. "Order them to place the starfighters on launch warning, two minutes."

"Aye, Commodore," Janelle said.

The last red icon disappeared from the display. Tanya forced herself to sit calmly, knowing they were about to know, beyond a shadow of a doubt, just how effective the admiral's plan had actually been. Either the enemy would take the bait...or they would stand off, leaving the front stalemated. But even that would give the Federation an advantage. The Outsider technological superiority would not last forever.

"No contacts," Quigley droned. "No contacts..."

"Inform me if anything changes," Tanya ordered. Had she ever been that young? "Until then, wait."

But we can't wait indefinitely, she thought. *And the bloody bastards know it.*

ꙮ

"The drones have returned, General," Lieutenant Juneau reported.

"Put the data on the big display," General Charlie Stuart ordered. There was a moment's pause as the tactical computers crunched the raw data, then uploaded it onto the display. "I think we have a target."

He sighed, inwardly. Point Delta had much to commend it, but unfortunately the Federation officers could probably see the advantages too. It was the closest Asimov

Point to Points Alpha and Beta, which led further into the Federation, while it was quite some distance from Boston itself. Any attempt to intercept his fleet as it moved through the point would require Admiral Garibaldi to leave Boston and face Charlie, well away from the planet's defenses. He was mildly surprised that Garibaldi hadn't moved all of his mobile units to Point Delta, although he couldn't have *assumed* the Outsiders would attack that point.

And if he had, we would have attacked somewhere else, Charlie thought, ruefully. The long-range sensors on the probes hadn't located the Federation's Fifth Fleet, but Charlie hadn't expected anything else. *Perhaps through Point Gamma...*

"General," Lieutenant Juneau said. "The Marsha are requesting permission to advance."

Charlie hesitated. One way or another, despite the absence of several Federation Navy battle squadrons, they were about to make a leap into the unknown. The entire war could be determined by who won or lost the Battle of Boston. He couldn't wait to tear into the enemy, but at the same time his caution warned him to be careful. The Outsiders couldn't afford a victory that left most of their fleet shattered and broken...

But leaving Boston alone was the first step to accepting eventual, inevitable defeat.

"Order the assault drones to commence the first advance," he ordered. "And prep the communications drones for transit. They are to signal as soon as they pass into Boston."

"Aye, sir," Lieutenant Juneau said. "And the Marsha?"

"They are to move once the drones are through," Charlie said. If they wanted to get stuck into the enemy, he wouldn't stop them. Besides, it might teach them that the most important thing on the battlefield was not honor, but victory. "And then ready the first assault formations to proceed."

ജ്യ

Roman jerked awake as the alarm sounded. "Report," he snapped. He swung his legs over the side of the bed and stood. "What's happening?"

"We have probes being reported at Points Delta, Echo and Foxtrot," Lieutenant Thompson reported. "All three Asimov Points are being probed, but no actual warships or assault drones yet."

Roman splashed water on his face, hastily. All *three* Asimov Points were being probed? It was odd, to say the least. Coordinating it would be a bitch, even assuming the Outsiders had managed to round up enough StarComs to copy Admiral Justinian's favorite trick. Unless they *had* found a new way to send signals at FTL speeds...if they had, the war was within shouting distance of being lost. They'd have a colossal advantage in flexibility while the Federation had to struggle to coordinate its forces across multiple light years...

He shook his head. Everything they'd seen—and everything they'd picked up from intelligence operatives—suggested the Outsiders had the same problems as the Federation, not a mythical FTL communications system. There was no need to panic.

They'd probably timed the probes...unless, of course, they planned to repeat the assault on Sapphire. But that would be suicide...

Unless they have far more ships than we think, he told himself. It didn't seem likely. If the Outsiders had enjoyed such towering supremacy, they would have taken Boston in their first push into Federation territory, cutting Roman off at the knees. *No, only one of those assaults is real. But which one?*

He grabbed his jacket, then ran up to the CIC. This time, at least, he had real-time data from each of the Asimov Points, but the enemy probes seemed to have stopped. It puzzled him for a long moment–the enemy knew they had to move fast, if they hoped to catch the Federation on the hop–and then he dismissed the thought. There was no point in wondering just what the enemy was doing...

Maybe they decided the fortresses were too hard a target, he thought. It was reasonable; no matter what technical advantages the attacker had, charging through an Asimov Point was always a meatgrinder. Admiral Justinian had certainly found out as much, during the Battle of Boskone, and the Outsiders had learned from that war.

But there was a nastier possibility. *Or maybe they're looking for us...*

He looked over at Lieutenant Thompson. "Is the fleet ready to depart?"

"Yes, sir," Lieutenant Thompson said. "The 45th Cruiser Squadron is experiencing delays, but her CO estimates that she will be ready to depart in ten minutes."

Roman nodded. "Hold the fleet here," he ordered. The moment the real assault began, he would take the fleet towards the Asimov Point, but until then he couldn't move. There was a very real danger of being caught out of position. "Anything on the planet's surface?"

"Not yet, sir," Lieutenant Thompson reported.

"Good," Roman said. He reached for his headset, then placed it over his ears. This was a private call. "Elf?"

"Roman," Elf said. She sounded tired and irked, although it wouldn't have been clear to anyone who didn't know her very well. "There's no sign of trouble yet. I've deployed platoons of Marines to reinforce General Yaakov, though. There's no way of knowing what the local insurgents will do when the attack begins in earnest."

"They'll do their best to take the defenses down," Roman predicted. They'd done everything they could to secure the planet-side facilities, but there were too many weak points for his peace of mind. "Inform the crews that I want the orbital fortresses put into lockdown, right now. We cannot afford to take chances."

"Understood," Elf said. "Roman...don't worry about it. Right now, the enemy is coming to you, as you planned."

"Thank you," Roman said. She was the only person he'd confessed his doubts to, when the plan had first been drawn up. "And good luck yourself."

"Thank you," Elf said. "You have a good plan. Now all you have to do is keep it alive in the face of the enemy."

She broke the connection. Roman returned the headset to its compartment, then forced himself to think rationally. The enemy was doing...what? They'd probed three Asimov Points and then stopped. If nothing else, it had wasted a few thousand drones. Maybe they could afford the losses–or thought they could–or maybe they had something else in mind? But what?

ꕥ

Tanya could *feel* the tension rising on her command deck as the seconds ticked away, with no sign of an enemy attack. The crew were starting to question themselves, wondering if the enemy was just waiting for them to relax or if they had merely intended to force the fortresses to battlestations without any actual plan to attack the system. Both were equally bad, Tanya knew; the former would have her crew on edge, while the latter would force them to lower their guard. But there was nothing she could do without making the problem worse.

"Automated Platform Series Alpha through Gamma are reporting ready," Midshipman Quick reported. "They're on full alert."

"Platforms Golf through Mike are reporting ready," Midshipwoman Jones added. "They're on full alert."

"Excellent," Tanya said. How had her crew become so young? Or how had she become so old? She'd barely seen anything of the Justinian War, apart from the first assault on Earth. But she'd been on the Gateway and only seen the battle from a distance. It galled her to realize that some of her crew had more experience than she. "Keep the platforms ready to engage the enemy."

She sighed, inwardly, as the seconds kept moving onwards. What was the delay? Logically, the enemy should have attacked with minimum preparation and reconnaissance, perhaps even none. This way, they were just giving her time–far more than she needed–to bring her fortresses to battlestations. She knew better than to believe it, but it was really terrifyingly easy to start wondering if the enemy merely wanted to annoy them. If so, they were succeeding nicely.

"The CSP is reporting overstretch," Lieutenant Janelle said. She sounded peeved, much to Tanya's irritation. If she'd wanted excitement, she should have gone into command track and aimed at starship command. "The CAG is requesting permission to withdraw them to their bases, then launch a replacement flight."

"Launch the replacement flight first," Tanya ordered. The enemy had to know she wouldn't panic, didn't they? There were few surprises in assaulting an Asimov Point. It was definitely starting to look as though the real objective had been to force her to alert her crew, then waste time and resources responding to a non-existent threat. "And then bring back the CSP..."

"Incoming," Midshipman Quigley snapped, as red icons flared into existence. "I have multiple drones transiting the Asimov Point! Tactical computers assess them as assault drones; I say again, tactical computers assess them as assault drones."

"Launch starfighters," Tanya snapped. This was no mere probe, then. A hundred assault drones had interpenetrated and vanished in flashes of radiation, but there were hundreds more, just getting their bearings before they attacked. "All batteries, commence firing!"

Chapter Twenty-Nine

The main advantage gained by the defender during an Asimov Point assault is that he knows where the enemy must appear. But the attacker's advantage is that he gets to choose the time of his assault.
-The Federation Navy in Retrospect, 4199

Boston, 4100

Tanya sucked in her breath as the assault pods oriented themselves and opened fire, spewing cargos of missiles towards her fortresses. They were largely short-range missiles, but it didn't matter. They'd find their targets before their drives burned out. Her starfighters were picking off as many of the missiles as they could, but there were just too many of them. The remainder simply continued towards the fortresses.

"All hands, brace for impact," she snapped, as the missiles entered point defense range and closed in. "I say again, brace for impact."

The tidal wave of missiles roared down on her fortresses, blazing through a web of deadly point defense fire. Hundreds died, but hundreds more survived as they entered engagement range and slammed home. The fortress rocked violently as a dozen antimatter warheads slammed against her shields, the lights flickering and flaring as power was hastily diverted to the backup shield generators. Tanya held the armrests of her command chair and prayed, silently, as the missiles hammered her command. A single failure at the right–or rather the wrong–time could shatter her fortress, followed by the datanet link holding the defenses together.

"Commodore," Lieutenant Janelle reported, "the drones are screaming past the defense line."

Tanya's eyes narrowed. The enemy had launched communications drones through the Asimov Point as well as assault pods. And that meant...what? They had to be trying to communicate with someone inside the system, because there could be no other explanation for expending so many drones, but why? Did they have an entire assault fleet lurking on the edge of the system, just like Commodore Lopez? Or were they hoping to coordinate an assault through multiple Asimov Points?

They're not stupid, she told herself. *They have to have something in mind.*

She activated her implants, linked her mind into the fortress's datanet and ran through the figures. It would take hours to get a message from one Asimov Point to another, unless the enemy had somehow managed to build a miniaturised StarCom and fit it on a drone. Somehow, she doubted it; even if they had managed to solve the problem of making it small enough, they'd be insane to send it into an enemy-occupied system. No, there was something else at work, but what?

"Commodore, a second wave of assault pods is transiting the point," Midshipman Stevenson snapped. "They're spewing out missiles now."

Tanya nodded. That, at least, was more conventional. The starfighters prowling around the point were doing their best, but they were taking losses. Unsurprisingly, the antimatter the enemy was using for warheads was sweeping space clean of starfighters, ensuring that few starfighters survived their attempts to take out the pods. And the missiles were also wiping out the minefields, piece by piece. She'd known the mines wouldn't last long, but watching them die without harming the enemy in the slightest was more than a little galling.

She watched, grimly, as a second wave of missiles fell on her fortresses. The enemy didn't seem to have had time to conduct any assessment of their earlier strikes, because the missiles went after targets at random rather than trying to hammer the fortresses that had already been badly damaged. That was a relief; the fortresses were designed to soak up missile hits, but the sheer immensity of the barrages was doing real damage. Two of her fortresses had lost some of their shields, while three more had taken minor damage. It looked as though her network of automated platforms were also taking a beating. By the time the enemy started launching warships through the point, she might not have anything left to stop them.

"New contacts," Midshipman Quigley warned A wave of red icons appeared on the display. "They read out as freighters..."

Tanya leaned forward, puzzled. There was no point in sending twelve freighters through the Asimov Point. Her starfighters were already swooping down to engage... realization dawned and she reached for her console to call them back, but it was already too late. Space flared with brilliant light as the freighters dropped their containment fields, allowing the antimatter in their holds to touch matter. The resulting explosion was truly staggering. Even at a distance, the sensor network took one hell of a battering, while the starfighters were literally swatted out of space. Mines were detonated or simply knocked out of commission.

"The sensor network has been weakened," Lieutenant Janelle said. "I'm having to reboot large segments of the datanodes and..."

Her voice trailed off. New red icons appeared on the display.

"Incoming ships," Midshipman Quigley said. "They read out as gunboats, small shuttlecraft and bulk freighters...*correction*! The freighters are small carriers. They're launching fighters now."

"Contact Admiral Garibaldi, inform him that we require additional starfighter cover," Tanya ordered, although she knew it would be too late. The enemy ships were already launching starfighters, while the main body of the Federation fleet was light hours away. "And inform him that this appears to be the main axis of attack."

The gunboats roared towards their targets as another wave of missile pods appeared in their wake, then started to spew missiles into space. Tanya gritted her teeth as the missiles launched, targeted–once again–on her fortresses. The point defense network, badly weakened, kept firing, taking out as many missiles as they could. But there just wasn't enough firepower to make a difference. Her fortress rocked violently as missiles slammed home, knocking down her shields. Three more fortresses vanished in tearing flashes of light, their containment chambers failing as the missiles detonated against their armoured flanks and wiping them out of space. The remaining fortresses had all taken heavy damage...

Five thousand dead, part of her mind noted. The enemy gunboats were closing in, launching missiles towards the automated platforms as they entered engagement range. *There will be more dead soon.*

She sucked in her breath as yet another wave of red icons appeared on the display. This time, they were small cruisers, their sensors already probing space for possible targets. If the Outsiders hadn't damaged her defenses so badly, the cruisers wouldn't have lasted long enough to orient themselves, let along scan local space and send their results back to their commanders. But now, they had all the time they needed to check on the results and send a message home. It wouldn't be long before the battle-wagons started to transit the Asimov Point, then secure local space.

"Commodore, the shuttles are closing in," Lieutenant Janelle reported. She sounded puzzled, as if she didn't understand what she was seeing. "They're scattering..."

Tanya frowned. It didn't quite make sense...

"They're launching assault troopers," she said. She keyed her switch, then checked the firearm at her belt. "All hands, prepare to repel boarders. I say again, all hands prepare to repel boarders."

She cursed under her breath. Boarding actions were rare, almost unheard of outside adventure stories and bad movies. The enemy would have to gamble she wouldn't blow the fortress, just to prevent it falling into enemy hands. But if they succeeded, they would have taken possession of a useless hulk. She'd definitely have time to purge the command network, if nothing else...

"And send a signal to Admiral Garibaldi," she added. On the display, a green icon representing a fortress flashed and vanished. Another two thousand men and women had just been wiped from existence. "Inform him that we will continue sending updates as long as we can."

ꕥ

"Admiral," Lieutenant Thompson said, "there are smaller attacks at the other two Asimov Points."

Roman cursed under his breath. The enemy was trying to be clever, which he'd expected, but there was something about the timing that bothered him. At least the assault on Point Delta was too strong to be anything other than the main assault... unless the Outsiders were far stronger than he had believed possible. No, the assault on Point Delta had to be the main assault. And that meant...what? Why was the enemy probing the other Asimov Points?

He stared down at the display for a long moment, then understood. The Outsiders *hadn't* anticipated the StarCom network. They'd launched three assaults, two of them feints, just to distract him, believing that he'd hear about the assault on Point Gamma first. And he would have done, if he hadn't been using the StarComs. Instead, he knew which of the assaults was the real one.

"Set course for Point Delta, best possible speed," he ordered. By the time they arrived, the enemy would likely have secured the Asimov Point and started to advance into the system, probably heading for Point Alpha or Point Beta. But they would have to take out his fleet before declaring victory. "And contact Commodore Lopez. I want him to bring his fleet to alert status now."

"Aye, sir," Lieutenant Thompson said.

Roman sat back in his chair and forced himself to relax.

ꙮ

Uzi smiled to himself as the fortress loomed up in front of him. She was colossal, a giant box-like structure crammed with missile tubes and directed energy weapons. The Federation Navy's Fortress Command had constructed thousands of similar fortresses, then broken them down into prefabricated structures that could be assembled quickly, if the need arose. It had come in very handy for the war against Admiral Justinian, allowing the Federation to seal off Asimov Points that had been left undefended. Now, they served a similar purpose as the Outsiders pressed the offensive into the Federation.

He landed on the armoured side of the fortress, then activated his sensors. Two-thirds of the force had made it through the maelstrom outside, the remaining troopers wiped out by enemy fire or antimatter discharges. It would probably have been more, if the enemy had realized the Outsiders would attempt to board the fortresses. But there was no time to waste. He checked the formation, then sent a single command: Find the hatches and get inside, whatever it took.

"Hatch located," one of the troopers sent. "We're breaking in now."

Uzi nodded, then followed the advance unit as it broke through the airlock and into the station. The atmosphere started to explode out of the station as they opened the second airlock, then stilled as the inner compartment vented completely. Uzi wasn't too surprised, although some of his men sounded alarmed. The innards of the fortress would have been secured, with airlocks and tubes sealed tightly shut. Even if the hull was breached, the remainder of the fortress would have remained pressurized.

But the lack of resistance troubled him.

"Seal the hatch, then press onwards," he ordered. One team was already trying to hack the fortress's datanet, through an uncovered set of datanodes, but he would have been astonished if they actually succeeded. The Federation had learned a great deal about improving its computer security, in the wake of the Justinian War. "And watch for ambushes."

He led the way towards the command deck himself, trusting Roebuck to handle the assault on the power cores. No resistance materialized until they made their way through a second airlock, whereupon they ran into an enemy-held position. The fortress crew were armed, he noted, although it was clear from their tactics that they'd never had any proper combat training. But that wasn't really a surprise. The Marines would have been deployed to Boston, just to make sure the planet stayed loyal. There would only be a handful left on the fortresses.

Unhooking a grenade from his belt, he threw it along the corridor, then lunged onwards as the grenade exploded. A handful of bodies lay on the deck, damaged beyond repair by the grenade. He felt a moment of cold disdain as he saw one of the bodies–what sort of idiot didn't even wear protection when there was a very real chance of the entire fortress venting?–and then dismissed the thought. No one in their right mind would have anticipated the Outsiders actually storming the fortress directly...

"This is Roebuck," a voice said. "The power cores are heavily defended."

"Unsurprising," Uzi said. They'd drilled time and time again, but it seemed that most of their assumptions had been wrong. "Hold the line. We'll try and break into the command core."

The resistance grew stronger as they forced their way up the corridor. A pair of IEDs claimed two of his men, while a third fell to a sniper who'd hidden herself in a tube and opened fire the moment his men came into view. Uzi glanced at her body, then led the way up to the command core itself. The solid metal hatch seemed to glare at them as they paused, then fixed explosive charges to the hinges. Uzi braced himself as they sought cover, then triggered the charges...

ฆ

Tanya watched, grimly, as her fortress fell to the enemy. They'd probably had plenty of time to study the layout–the basic design had been standardized for years–and they hadn't wasted any effort. Her computer network was under siege–thankfully, she'd primed it to seal off contaminated sections before the enemy could use them to overwhelm the entire system–while two enemy parties were advancing through the interior. One of them was heading right for the command core...

The entire compartment shook violently as the hatch was blown off its hinges, allowing the enemy to charge into the room. Tanya considered drawing her pistol and going out in a blaze of glory, before deciding otherwise. There were young men and women in the compartment who deserved to live, assuming the Outsiders were telling the truth when they claimed to treat prisoners decently. Besides, resistance would only get them all killed, for nothing. She tapped a switch, triggering a core dump, then kept her hands in view as the armored men advanced forward.

"Get away from those consoles," the leader snapped. "Hands in the air!"

Tanya obeyed, as did her subordinates. The Outsiders searched them roughly, removed their weapons and then bound their hands behind their backs. She forced herself to relax, remembering everything she'd been taught in the dreaded Conduct After Capture course. If dealing with humans, the first few moments of captivity were always the most dangerously unpredictable. Being captured by aliens was much worse. There were plenty of reports of humans being dissected by their captors, or simply tortured through ignorance...

They were marched into her office, then placed against the wall and told to wait. They obeyed–they had no choice–as the Outsiders checked the datanet. It didn't take them long to discover that it had been purged, leaving the fortress completely useless. Tanya watched them as they spoke in hushed voices, wondering if they would take their frustration out on her people. It was quite possible they'd be willing to make her people pay...

"Get them to the shuttles," the leader ordered, finally. "And then blow the hatches completely."

No, Tanya thought. Blowing the hatches would decompress the entire station. If some of her people had managed to avoid capture–and she had a large crew–they would die when they ran out of oxygen. She tried to think of something she could say to prevent the Outsiders from venting her command, but she couldn't think of anything. The fortress was no longer hers.

She grunted as she was hauled to her feet, patted down again, then pushed towards the hatch. Her crew followed her–at least the Outsiders were professional, she noted–their faces desperately worried. Who knew what would happen to them once they reached the POW camp? Even if the Outsiders treated them well, they might never return to the Federation...

...And if they did, she asked herself, would they be blamed for being taken captive?

There was no way to know. All she could do was wait and see.

ꕥ

"Three of the fortresses have been secured," Lieutenant Juneau reported, as the latest flight of drones returned through the Asimov Point, "but two of them had their systems purged. The third almost destroyed itself. The engineers believe the self-destruct system jammed when the boarding parties attempted to hack the system. They think the station should be abandoned."

"See to it," Charlie ordered.

"But the other fortresses are useless," Lieutenant Juneau said. She sounded shocked. "We won't learn anything from them."

Charlie shrugged. It wasn't a surprise. Attacking the fortresses had always been a gamble, one that might well not have paid off. It had, to some degree; they'd taken upwards of three thousand prisoners. But he'd wanted the fortress computer records too.

And the weapons would have come in handy too, he thought. *We could have held the point, if necessary...*

He shook his head. "Order the first battle squadrons to proceed through the Asimov Point," he ordered. "Then dispatch two transports for the prisoners. They can be shipped back to Athena for interrogation, then moved to the detention camp."

"Aye, sir," Lieutenant Juneau said.

Charlie smiled, then sat back in his chair. The assault, so far, had gone about as well as he'd dared hope. The Marsha had done their bit–and other assault units were hitting the other points, hopefully keeping the Federation's defenders unsure which one was the main axis of attack. But now, there would be no mistaking the true assault. His fleet would be impossible to miss, once it slipped through the point.

And then we will see just how well they prepared for us, he thought. On the display, the first superdreadnaughts vanished as they entered the Asimov Point. *Because we have quite a few surprises up our sleeves.*

Chapter Thirty

As always, the main problem with launching a major attack remains one of coordination. This is why the Federation's tactics were often simple in the extreme–and why the Blue Star War went so badly wrong.
-The Federation Navy in Retrospect, 4199

Boston, 4100

"They're coming through the Asimov Point, sir."

"I can see that, boy," Captain Ward growled. "Get your head out of your ass and give me a detailed breakdown."

Lieutenant Carmon looked down at his console. Admiral Garibaldi had given *Dasher* strict orders; she was to remain near the Asimov Point, close enough to monitor the starships as they made transit, without revealing her presence to the enemy. A network of sensor-stealthed platforms hung nearby, linked to the cloaked ship through laser transmitters, feeding data into her computers without forcing her to use her own sensors. Several of the platforms had been blinded by the assault on the Asimov Point, but enough remained to allow *Dasher* to carry out her assignment.

"Nine battle squadrons, sir," Lieutenant Carmon said. "Plus at least fifty-seven cruisers, mostly Type Alpha or Type Beta, and one hundred and nine destroyers. Nine of them read out as ex-Federation Navy designs."

"Probably captured or surrendered by traitors," Captain Ward muttered. He was known for being a hard-ass–and for being the Federation's most loyal supporter. "Can you get a precise ID?"

"Not at this range, sir," Carmon said. "They're not broadcasting any IFF signals."

Captain Ward grunted. "Keep monitoring them," he ordered. "They will betray themselves eventually."

Carmon watched as the enemy fleet shook itself down into formation, then started to move away from the Asimov Point. A small flotilla of cruisers remained at the point, guarding the Outsider rear, although they couldn't have stood up to a serious offensive. The destroyer recorded everything she saw, then forwarded the data to Admiral Garibaldi. It would be his task to intercept and destroy the enemy fleet.

"Pull us back from the point," Captain Ward ordered. The enemy fleet wasn't even *trying* to be stealthy. It was sweeping space with hundreds of high-powered sensors, looking for any traces of cloaked ships. "We don't want to be spotted out here."

"No, sir," Carmon agreed.

ઉ૦૭

"They're leaving a small detachment at the point," Lieutenant Thompson reported. "But the remainder of the fleet is setting course for Point Alpha."

"Move us into interception position," Roman ordered, coolly. So far, so good. The enemy had blasted through the Asimov Point with fewer losses than he'd hoped, but otherwise everything had gone according to plan. "Detach...detach the 67th

Battlecruiser Squadron with orders to cloak, then make its way around to Point Delta. I want the enemy ships blasted off the point as soon as possible."

"Aye, sir," Lieutenant Thompson said.

Roman forced himself to relax as *Valiant* picked up speed, heading towards the planned interception point. The enemy CO would have good reason to feel confident, even though it would be clear, to him, that Roman was planning to fall back on Point Alpha. Indeed, there was little choice. Roman's ships were outnumbered and a straight missile duel would be disastrous. His only real hope was to rely on the fortresses covering Point Alpha for additional firepower.

His headset buzzed. "Picking up reports from the planet," Elf said. "There are riots forming in a dozen cities. I think the word got out."

"Joy," Roman said, sarcastically. "Do they pose a security threat?"

"Not at the moment," Elf said. "They may be a diversion..."

"Keep an eye on it," Roman said. General Yaakov was in charge of handling the planet; hopefully, he would follow orders and be gentle. There had been quite enough incidents to give the Outsiders all the propaganda they could possibly want to make the Federation look bad. "But as long as it isn't a major problem, don't worry about it."

He leaned back in his command chair and tried to project an impression of jaunty unconcern as the display updated. The enemy commander wasn't trying to be clever...absently, Roman wondered if his opponent knew where Roman actually *was*. There was still no explanation for the communications drones the enemy had fired into the system, unless they'd been used to trigger the assaults on Point Echo and Point Gamma. It was quite likely that the Outsiders had a handful of survey ships in the system, watching the Federation's every move. They'd be able to draw real-time data–or as close to real-time as possible–without breaking the known laws of science.

But there was a time when drive fields would have seemed impossible, he reminded himself, *and FTL an unattainable dream. It hasn't been that long since we escaped the tyranny of the Asimov Points...*

"Admiral," Lieutenant Thompson said. "The enemy fleet is launching drones."

"Understood," Roman said. "Keep an eye on them, but don't panic. They need data too."

He ran through the calculations, once again. The tutors at the Academy had warned him, time and time again, not to try to be clever. Now, he saw exactly what they'd meant. The time delay between his fleet, the enemy fleet, Boston and the various Asimov Points ensured that managing the battle would be tricky. It was incredibly hard to say, for sure, what the enemy could see. Or, for that matter, what any prowling spy ships might have told them. In some ways, he was grateful the enemy wasn't trying to hide...and yet, was the large fleet he could see the diversion? There was no reason for the diversion to be smaller than the main offensive.

"Check with Points Echo and Gamma," he ordered. "Are there any signs of a major assault?"

"No, sir," Lieutenant Thompson said. "The attacks were savage, but oddly uncoordinated."

Roman sucked in his breath, then forced himself to relax. It would be hours before the two fleets entered engagement range and, by then, he would have worn himself out. All he could do now was watch and wait. And pray.

ꕤ

"The enemy fleet has been located," Lieutenant Juneau reported. A mass of red icons blinked into view on the display. "They're blocking our course to Point Alpha."

"They won't have a better chance to hurt us and they know it," Charlie said. The long hours of nothing as they'd crawled across the system had been nerve-wracking, but they were finally about to engage the enemy. "Launch a second flight of drones, then prepare to engage. The Marsha can take the lead."

"Aye, sir," Lieutenant Juneau said.

Charlie watched as the display started to update itself, drawing data from the drones before they were picked off by prowling starfighters or point defense weapons. The enemy fleet was stronger than he'd anticipated–seven battle squadrons instead of the six intelligence insisted remained at Boston–but he still had a major advantage, even without the advanced weapons. There were no grounds for refusing an engagement, particularly if he could prevent the Federation Navy from falling back on Point Alpha.

"Order the Marsha to begin the offensive," he ordered. Two years of bloody warfare had taught the aliens some lessons, but they remained barbarian warriors at heart. The Federation Navy would tear them apart, yet their deaths would win the Outsiders some time to get their own offensive into play. And besides, they might hurt the Federation before they died. "And then place our starfighters on full launch alert."

"Aye, sir," Lieutenant Juneau said.

ꕤ

"Sir, the enemy fleet is launching gunboats," Lieutenant Thompson reported. She broke off, shocked. "Sir, their drives are radiating hot."

Roman's eyes narrowed. No amount of shielding, at least not any level mounted by such small craft, could hope to protect the crew. The drive field would be spitting out enough radiation to ensure the crews would be dying already. They had to be insane–or desperate–but it might have paid off for them. Even missiles would be hard-pressed to match their speed before they died.

"Launch starfighters," he ordered, grimly. On the display, the gunboats were already streaking towards his ships. "And inform me when the enemy enters missile range."

He smiled to himself, humorlessly. The Outsiders didn't know it, but they were about to get a very nasty surprise. He might not have *many* long-range missiles, yet the ones he did have came with a modification of their own. And to think it was something they owed to Admiral Justinian...

The gunboats closed in, firing as they came. Their flight patterns were surprisingly eccentric, although, with the radiation no doubt already affecting the crews, perhaps he shouldn't be too surprised. Roman watched grimly as they unleashed missiles towards his starfighters, then exploded in blinding flashes of light as they were picked off, one by one. They weren't just carrying missiles, he realized, as the wave of gunboats reached his point defense envelope and started to close in. There was enough antimatter crammed into the small ships to give his capital ships a very bad day.

And the antimatter blasts will damage our datanet, he thought, grimly. *But at least we have some time to prepare.*

He pushed the thought to one side as the gunboats started to ram their targets. One struck a superdreadnaught, damaging its shields; the others went after smaller crafts, one successfully blowing apart a battlecruiser by slamming into its shields and knocking them down. Dozens more died as they were picked off by point defense, particularly as they dropped into attack formation. They didn't seem to have mastered the art of constantly flying evasive patterns, like starfighter pilots. Roman was fairly sure the enemy ships weren't piloted by humans. Even the most fanatical human wanted his death to mean *something*...

"Contact Commodore Lopez," he ordered, as the last gunboat died. Two of his superdreadnaughts had taken minor damage, but the remaining heavy combat ships were intact. "Order him to commence Operation Sword."

"Aye, sir," Lieutenant Thompson said.

Roman nodded. The Outsiders were on the verge of entering missile range, but would they open fire as soon as they could or would they wait, diminishing his chances of shooting down the missiles before they reached their targets? *Roman* would have waited; the Outsiders, however, might have other thoughts. It all depended on how many missiles they could fire at a time...

"Enemy ships entering firing range," Lieutenant Thompson said. "They're sweeping us with targeting sensors, but they're not actually firing."

"Not yet," Roman said. They'd probably fire just outside *his* missile range—or what they thought his missile range to be. It was what they'd done before, with the additional problem that he was trying to fall back on Point Alpha, rather than lunging forward to force himself into missile range. "Update our firing patterns, but hold fire until I issue the order."

"Aye, sir," Lieutenant Thompson said.

ꕥ

"The Marsha did better than predicted," Lieutenant Juneau observed.

"Noted," Charlie said. The Marsha had loved the idea of sprint-mode gunboats, even if the crews would probably have died before their bodies could be recovered. But they hadn't cared. To them, dying in battle, with their hands around the enemy's throat, was the ultimate achievement. "Have you locked missiles on target?"

"Aye, sir," Lieutenant Juneau said. "However, I have been unable to locate the enemy flagship."

Charlie nodded, unsurprised. The Federation Navy rotated the datanet through every ship in the fleet, ensuring a considerable degree of redundancy. Losing the command ship would cause nothing more than momentary hesitation, while the new commander was informed that he was now in command. But specifically targeting the command ship was impossible, unfortunately. The tactic worked so well that the Outsider Navy had copied it for itself.

"Target their superdreadnaughts," he ordered. If nothing else, they had to crush as many enemy battle squadrons as possible. They'd never have a better shot at their hulls. "And fire in two minutes."

"Weapons locked," Lieutenant Juneau said.

Charlie waited for the seconds to tick down, then braced himself. "Fire!"

The superdreadnaught shuddered as she unleashed her external racks, hurling five hundred missiles towards the Federation Navy. Her fellows followed moments later, unleashing their own broadsides. Charlie looked up at the display, as yellow icons seemed to merge together into a cloud of death and destruction, and prayed they would be enough. Two years of production had just been expended in a few seconds...

"General," Lieutenant Juneau snapped. "The enemy ships have just opened fire!"

ꕥ

"The enemy ships have opened fire," Lieutenant Thompson said. She paused. "They just fired their external racks."

"Odd," Roman commented. *He* would have flushed both external racks and internal tubes, just to ensure he didn't lose a ship when a missile detonated an antimatter warhead. Were the enemy holding back? Or were they planning something? Or...did they have fewer long-range missiles than he'd believed? "Return fire."

Valiant shook violently as she opened fire. Unlike the Outsiders, Roman had fired both internal and external missiles, although their throw weight wasn't quite a match for the enemy ships. Upwards of forty-five thousand missiles were flying towards his ships, enough to wipe them out of space if the point defense didn't manage to weaken the missile swarm before it reached its target. He'd fired thirty thousand missiles himself...

"Launch gunboats," he ordered. The enemy ships seemed to flinch, but–unless they had made a colossal improvement to their drive systems–they didn't have a hope of getting out of missile range before it was too late. "And push the point defense forward."

He braced himself as the cloud of red icons bore down on his ships. No matter what precautions he'd taken, it was all too clear that he was about to take a beating. Hundreds of thousands of lives would be lost. And all he could do, he knew, was pray it would be worth it.

ꕥ

Long-range missiles, Charlie thought, numbly. *They built long-range missiles of their own.*

He turned his gaze to the sensor display as it updated, rapidly. The missiles didn't seem to be as efficient as the Outsider designs, but quantity had a quality all its own. His point defense would kill many of them, yet quite a number would get through and hammer his ships...

"Engage them as soon as they enter weapons range," he ordered. There was no choice, not really. They certainly didn't have a hope of getting out of range before it was too late. "And then close to engagement range."

ꕤ

"The gunboats are engaging the missiles," Lieutenant Thompson reported. There was a pause. "I can confirm the missiles are armed with antimatter."

"Surprise, surprise," Roman muttered. If nothing else, one missile's explosion might take out several other missiles nearby. He hoped for a chain reaction that would break the entire attack, but it didn't seem as though they were going to be lucky. "Keep firing."

He smiled to himself, despite the situation. Gunboats didn't serve many purposes in war; indeed, the only time the Federation normally deployed them was as part of an assault force passing through an Asimov Point. They were large enough to survive transit and small enough to be rated expendable. However, Roman had fitted several hundred gunboats with point defense weapons and targeting systems that would allow them to engage missile swarms, hopefully from a safer distance than any starfighter. It seemed to be working, he decided. The Outsiders weren't the only innovative people in the galaxy...

"Missiles entering attack range," Lieutenant Thompson said. Hundreds were picked off, but thousands survived. "Sir..."

"Brace for impact," Roman ordered, quietly.

The missiles slammed home. Roman watched as damage reports spread rapidly through the fleet; *Mountbatten*, *Powell*, *Jellicoe*, *Bismarck*, *Muhammad* and *Caesar* were blown into vapor, while *Spruce* and *Tirpitz* were badly damaged and fell out of formation. The enemy seemed to be targeting superdreadnaughts specifically, which allowed his smaller ships to cover them without worrying about their own protection, but there were just too many missiles to take them all down. *Valiant* shuddered twice as missiles slammed into her shields, then vibrated as the helmsman angled her weaker shields away from the enemy fire...

"*Denver* is reporting major damage, sir," Lieutenant Thompson said. "She's..."

She broke off. "*Denver* is gone, sir."

"Noted," Roman said. He glanced at the display, then gritted his teeth. "Keep us falling back on the Asimov Point."

ꕤ

"Sir, the missiles are emitting odd radiation," Lieutenant Juneau reported. "They're...*Jesus Christ*!"

Charlie had barely a moment to realize what was happening before his superdreadnaught *screamed* like a gored bull. Admiral Justinian had designed missiles intended to channel the fury of an antimatter warhead into a single deadly beam; the Federation had taken the concept and improved upon it. What did it matter if the missiles were destroyed within milliseconds of activation, the designers had asked, if most of the blast went in the right direction? It was the old concept of a laser warhead, scaled up to eleven. And the Outsiders were taken completely by surprise.

"*Hope*, *Light*, *Charity* and *Admiral Anderson* have been destroyed," Lieutenant Juneau said. "Twelve other superdreadnaughts have taken significant damage..."

"I see," Charlie said. They'd been hurt worse than he'd expected, all the more so because he hadn't anticipated long-range missiles. The warheads hadn't been the only things the Federation had scaled up. But he still held the missile advantage, even if the Federation Navy *was* falling back on the Asimov Point. "Continue firing as soon as we enter normal missile range."

He smiled, darkly, as the two fleets converged. The battle was far from over...

"Picking up a signal from Point Delta," Lieutenant Juneau said. "Enemy ships destroyed all but one of the guardian squadron. The Asimov Point is no longer secure."

Charlie felt sweat trickling down the back of his neck. There was no point in taking out the guardian squadron, unless the enemy had something up their sleeve. But there was nothing on the far side of Point Delta, apart from Outsider fortifications. They'd just detached a squadron of ships from their main body, for what?

"Continue the advance," he ordered. He was jumping at shadows. If he broke off now, it would leave the Federation in possession of the system. "And fire as soon as we enter engagement range."

Chapter Thirty-One

If, however, someone manages to solve the problem of coordination, the enemy commander will never know what hit him.
-The Federation Navy in Retrospect, 4199

Boston, 4100

"They're continuing the advance, sir," Lieutenant Thompson said.

Roman shrugged. He'd expected as much, even though the enemy CO probably knew the Asimov Point was no longer secure. There was no real reason to break off and retreat to Point Delta, at least as far as the enemy CO could see. They'd be giving up their sole chance to inflict real damage on Roman's fleet if they retreated...or so they thought.

"Keep us falling back," he ordered. The enemy would be within standard missile range in three minutes, unless they reduced speed sharply. By then, he wanted to be able to call on the launchers orbiting Point Alpha. "And get me a direct link to Commodore Lopez."

"Aye, sir," Lieutenant Thompson said.

Roman keyed a switch. "Record," he ordered. It was a shame they couldn't open enough bandwidth over the StarCom to allow for a proper conversation, but it hardly mattered, not when he could simply record a message. "Commodore Lopez. You are ordered to begin Stage Two once you receive this message. I say again, you are ordered to begin Stage Two once you receive this message."

He closed the connection, then looked up. "Send the message," he ordered. "And then start the timer; two minutes, thirty seconds."

"Aye, sir," Lieutenant Thompson said.

The display suddenly sparkled with angry red icons. "Admiral," Lieutenant Thompson added, "the enemy ships have opened fire."

"Return fire," Roman ordered. The timing wasn't perfect; the enemy had managed to open fire before he could call on the fortresses for additional protection. "Order the fortresses to launch their starfighters, then stage them out here to support us."

"Aye, sir," Lieutenant Thompson said.

Roman checked the timer. One minute, twenty-seven seconds to go.

ඞ

"The enemy ships have opened fire," Lieutenant Juneau reported. "They're targeting our lighter ships."

Charlie frowned. *That* was odd. Oh, he could see the point–the fewer point defense platforms, the better–but he couldn't understand why the enemy were wasting their fire. Right now, their only hope lay in killing as many superdreadnaughts as possible...or on trying to break contact and escaping. Combined with the loss of Point Delta, it was either an attempt to rattle him or a sign the enemy had something else up their sleeves.

"Continue firing," he ordered. They were almost close enough to go to rapid fire, whereupon the Federation ships would be rapidly smashed. But they should be clawing him back before they died. "And launch a flight of probes. I want to know what's out there."

He forced himself to sit still as the superdreadnaughts continued firing. The enemy kept their odd firing pattern, stripping away his smaller ships one by one. It was actually quite impressive, in a way, but worrying. The one thing he'd learned about Emperor Marius's protégée was that he was far from stupid, yet he was being stupid now. Or acting stupid. Why?

It looked like a certain victory. The Federation ships would be unable to reach the Asimov Point before most of them were killed. He could bring up the Marsha suicide squads and break through the defenses, then obliterate the fortresses and punch deep into the heart of the Federation. The access to the inner Asimov Point lines alone would prove decisive. Countless wavering worlds would switch sides, turning on their Federation garrisons and surrendering their industrial plants to the Outsiders. Victory–total victory–would be within their grasp.

So why were the enemy practically handing him a victory?

"General," Lieutenant Juneau snapped. "I'm picking up incoming ships!"

Charlie swung around and stared at the display. Red icons–*new* red icons–had popped into existence, advancing on his formation from the rear. The Federation Navy had crafted a trap, he realized numbly, as the tally of incoming ships started to click upwards. Five whole battle squadrons, nearly a hundred smaller ships and...several large ships of unknown design and capabilities. They couldn't exist. But they did.

The fleet they sent to Goldstone must have doubled back, he thought, with a sudden sense of bitter sickness. He'd never thought that anyone would dare uncover a priceless world merely to lure an enemy fleet into engagement range. Hell, Admiral Garibaldi had already sacrificed over fifty *thousand* lives just to prime the trap. *He must be out of his mind...*

He forced the thought aside. "Emergency orders," he snapped. Now, stripping away the smaller ships made sense. "All ships are to alter course to..."

The new fleet opened fire.

ꕥ

Roman watched, feeling cold exultation, as Commodore Lopez opened fire. His ships had been loaded with long-range missiles too, but that wasn't the only surprise. The engineers had bolted countless missile pods to the hulls of bulk freighters, giving the Commodore a throw weight well above anything the enemy might expect. By now, a new tidal wave of missiles–a full Weber–was raging towards the Outsider Fleet. The enemy ships were attempting to evade, but it was far too late. They were going to take one hell of a beating.

"Reverse course," he ordered. The Outsiders had noticed Commodore Lopez a minute or two too early. They'd have a chance to get back to Point Delta or, more likely, head for somewhere they could drop into FTL. "And continue firing."

ჩ ☙

Charlie sat, stiff and cold, on his command deck as the missiles closed in. The enemy had timed it perfectly, catching his fleet between missiles coming from two different vectors. He had no choice, but to turn to face the newcomers, which left his flanks exposed to missiles from the old force. And that meant he was definitely about to take a pasting. Losing the smaller ships would *really* hurt.

"Continue firing," he ordered, although he knew it was pointless. The battle was lost; the only thing he could do, really, was pull out of the system as fast as possible, leaving any stragglers behind. "And order the Marsha to launch attacks on the enemy fleet."

He braced himself as the torrent of missiles slammed home, the impacts sending shocks through his command chair. A dozen superdreadnaughts died instantly, their shields battered down by multiple missile hits, while several more fell out of formation, streaming plasma from their damaged hulks. He hoped–prayed–that the Federation was willing to take prisoners, as there was no way he could stop and pick any survivors up before the advancing enemy overcame him. Fifteen more were badly damaged, badly enough that one or two additional hits would either cripple or destroy them. And his smaller ships had been almost completely wiped out. The only really intact survivor was a single battlecruiser.

"The *Prometheus* is to detach herself from the fleet," he ordered. His voice was so cold it sounded like someone else speaking, even in his own ears. "She is to fly directly to Point Delta and make transit, if that seems possible. If so, she is to head directly to Galen and report to the commander there."

He gritted his teeth. Chang Li was there, along with representatives from a dozen worlds that might join the Outsider Federation. They wouldn't now, he was sure, not after the Outsiders had taken a terrific bloody nose. It might not prove decisive–the Federation would need time to recuperate itself, then locate Outsider homeworlds–but it would certainly prolong the war. And, no matter how long it took the Federation to find the worlds in the Beyond, they would have no difficulty targeting Galen, Athena or any of the other worlds in the Rim.

We could lose most of our gains, he thought, bitterly. *And that would be disastrous.*

"The battlecruiser has left the fleet," Lieutenant Juneau reported. "She's on her way."

Charlie nodded. The Federation had destroyed the pickets at Point Delta. Presumably, their ships were still there. Would there be time for the battlecruiser to get through the Asimov Point before she was intercepted? Or would the forces guarding Point Delta's far side come through long enough to cover her retreat?

"Send a signal to the captured fortresses," he ordered. "The crews are to evacuate at once."

He took a breath. "And send another signal to the fleet," he added. "The main formation is to proceed to the closest point we can activate the stardrive. Any starship that falls out of formation, including this one, is to be abandoned."

Lieutenant Juneau looked up at him. "Sir?"

"Do it," Charlie snapped. He had to save as many ships as possible, even if it meant abandoning vessels that might be salvageable, if they had time. "And enter the order into the fleet's log. The responsibility is mine and mine alone."

ꙮ

"I don't understand," Roebuck said. The new orders had come in while they'd been sweeping the captured fortress for useful intelligence. "Why do we have to prepare to leave?"

"The battle is going badly," Uzi said. It was impossible to tell what was going on, at least through the sensors mounted on the small fleet of shuttles. The fortress's own sensors had been ruined beyond immediate repair. "And the CO wants us to haul ass out of here before the feds catch up with us."

Roebuck stared at him. "Are you being defeatist?"

"Merely practical," Uzi said. "There is no point in refusing to accept bad news when it arrives, just because you don't want to believe it."

Roebuck snorted, then stalked off to organize the evacuation. Uzi watched him, thinking hard. Was it possible that he could arrange something that would allow him to remain behind? There was enough intelligence stored in his implants to give the Federation a very real chance of ending the war within a year or two. He'd set up a data dump on the fortress, but there was quite a strong chance they'd be ordered to blow it to atoms before they left. And most of the prisoners were already on their way to a detention center, further into enemy-held space.

Not a chance, he thought, finally.

They'd found almost nothing on the station; at least, they'd found nothing of use. Some of the men had found porn stashes, which had made Uzi roll his eyes, and another had located a hidden still. It was hardly surprising–life on a fortress could be boring, most of the time–but Roebuck had ordered both the porn and booze destroyed. He, like many of the Outsiders, was oddly prudish at times. But then, easy access to porn probably helped distract the Federation's population from contemplating the finer points of the Constitution and how badly the Grand Senate had subverted it over the years. *And* it kept the crew from growing too bored.

He smirked at the thought, then hastened down to the shuttles, where the handful of remaining prisoners were waiting. They'd clear out as soon as the fortress was empty, then head back through the Asimov Point. And pray the enemy didn't feel like ending their flight today.

The enemy, he thought. He *was* a Federation agent, after all. *After all I've done, being killed by my own side would be the height of irony.*

ꙮ

"Sir," Lieutenant Thompson said, "a number of enemy ships are attempting to surrender."

"Order them to shut down shields, weapons and main power," Roman ordered, glancing at the display. There was no way he was going to refuse to take prisoners–they needed intelligence, if nothing else–but he couldn't afford to risk being stabbed in the back. "The Marines are to board the ships, then take the crews off as soon as possible."

Elf will organize it, he thought, as he turned his attention back to the enemy fleet. Whoever was in charge had managed to re-orient his fleet far too quickly for Roman's peace of mind, then set course for the edge of the gravity limit. He'd make it too, Roman suspected, although the Federation Navy would harry his ships until they dropped into stardrive and vanished. The more ships that were destroyed here, the fewer he would have to destroy later on.

"Continue the advance," he ordered. "And concentrate on crippling as many ships as possible."

A report from Point Delta popped up in his display and he frowned. The enemy battlecruiser, free of the need to stick with the fleet, had made it to the point and passed through at high speed. Her crew would be vomiting on the deck, Roman knew, but it was worth it. They'd made their escape before the Federation Navy could do more than fire a few ineffective shots at them.

And they'll warn their fellows that we won the battle, he thought. *And how will the Outsiders react to that?*

He considered it for a moment, then pushed the thought aside. His starfighters were closing in on the enemy ships, savaging their defenses as the next wave of missiles advanced towards them with deadly intent. It would be enough, Roman was sure, to give them a very hard time indeed. And even if it wasn't...

A wave of enemy missiles came back at his ships, only to be picked off almost at once by the gunboats. Their rate of fire had slacked noticeably, Roman saw; they'd probably started to shoot themselves dry. The Federation Navy was all too aware of just how easy it was to run out of missiles, even with an entire fleet of superdreadnaughts. Logistics, as always, were far more important than mere tactics. Hell, he was on the verge of shooting himself dry too. And that raised new problems.

"Halt the pursuit as soon as we reach ten percent of our weapons load," he ordered, sourly. He disliked the idea of abandoning the chance to hammer the enemy as much as possible, but running out of missiles would be disastrous, if the Outsiders managed to launch another attack before he'd reloaded his ships. "And then take us back to Point Delta."

"Aye, sir," Lieutenant Thompson said.

ꕥ

"General," Lieutenant Juneau said. "We're about to fire our last rounds."

Charlie gritted his teeth. The energy weapons were effectively unlimited, but they couldn't reverse course and enter energy range without ensuring their destruction. There was no sign the Federation ships had run out of missiles–at least, they were firing them off with abandon–and he didn't dare take the risk of a knife-range duel that could go either way. He could cripple the Federation's fleet, but the Federation could rebuild faster than the Outsiders, even if it couldn't match their technology.

The only way out was to keep going and hope he could repair and reload his fleet before Admiral Garibaldi capitalized on his victory.

"Sir," Lieutenant Juneau said. "The Federation ships are falling back."

Charlie frowned. The Federation ships had reduced speed sharply, ceasing fire and recalling their starfighters. For a moment, he wondered if it was a trick, an attempt to lure his ships back for the kill. But as the distances grew longer, he realized they were–for some reason–being allowed to depart without further interference.

"Take us out of here as soon as we cross the line," he ordered, quietly. "And then get me a complete report on the fleet's status, estimated repair time and everything else we might need."

He wouldn't keep his job, he was sure. No matter how well he'd served in the past, his career would never survive a defeat on such a scale. And nor should it. The Federation had sometimes kept admirals on active duty who had more political connections than they had brain cells, but it had always regretted it. There was no way the Outsiders would make the same mistake. A minor failure was a learning experience; a major failure could not be overlooked.

"We'll enter FTL in ten minutes," Lieutenant Juneau reported. "Sir, several of the fleet's vessels are unable to activate their stardrives."

"Ship their crews over to working ships, then scuttle them," Charlie ordered, tiredly. At least the Federation Navy was unlikely to intervene. "There's nothing else we can do."

Ten minutes later, it was all over.

ꙮ

"They purged their computer databases," Elf said, four hours after the remains of the enemy fleet had vanished into FTL. "But we recovered several thousand crewmen. One of them, I suspect, will talk."

Roman smiled as she sat down next to him. "And Admiral Ness?"

Elf had to bite down a very unmilitary giggle. "He was composing a long statement for the emperor on how the defeat was all your fault and claiming that you refused to listen to his properly cautious advice."

It took Roman a moment to put it together. "He was predicting our defeat?"

"Yup," Elf said. "And he held a destroyer at Point Beta, so he could get his ass out of the system if Fifth Fleet was smashed by the Outsiders. What a charming asshole."

"What a pity he didn't send the report before we won," Roman mused. Emperor Marius wouldn't be too pleased to receive a report claiming a victorious battle was actually a defeat, particularly once Roman's official report arrived. "I dare say we can give him command of some of our prizes and send them back to Earth, along with a proper report. That should get rid of him, if nothing else."

"True," Elf said. She paused. "I believe the governor was making noises about a party on Boston, Roman. Do you want to attend?"

Roman shook his head, quickly. "I think not," he said. "There's no shortage of matters to attend to now, I'm afraid."

"You need the rest," Elf said. "Your subordinates can handle the repair and reloading efforts."

"But a party on the surface would be no rest at all," Roman said. "I'd sooner sleep here."

"Then *sleep*," Elf said. "Or should I knock you out to make sure you actually rest?"

Chapter Thirty-Two

But the aftermath of victory can be sometimes worse than defeat.
-The Federation Navy in Retrospect, 4199

Earth, 4100

"I wasn't expecting to see you here, professor," Grand Senator–*former* Grand Senator–Rupert McGillivray said.

"I wasn't expecting to see you here at all," Kratman answered, dryly. The other Grand Senatorial mansions had been closed down, with the intention of turning them into museums when peace returned to the galaxy. "Why are you still here?"

"The emperor didn't evict me from my home," McGillivray said. "I think he knew about my connections."

Professor Kratman nodded as he sat down. Grand Senator Rupert McGillivray had been the last of the Imperialist Faction, the only one to remain in the Grand Senate after the Blue Star War. It was an open secret, now, that he'd only kept his place through his Brotherhood connections and his value as a mediator. And, of all the Grand Senatorial Families, he was the only senior member not to be dead or exiled to a penal world. That, too, had come as a result of his Brotherhood connections.

"I think he also considered you harmless," Kratman said, as McGillivray showed him into the sitting room. It was–unsurprisingly–luxurious, the walls covered with paintings of the great heroes of the past, but there was dust everywhere, save for a pair of comfortable chairs. "Can't you get the help these days?"

"The emperor banned the practice of turning criminals into slaves," McGillivray said. He clicked on a kettle, then readied two mugs of coffee grains and milk. It had once been vanishingly rare to see a Grand Senator do any form of menial labor. "I don't know if he suspected something or if he merely hated the whole procedure on principle, but I've practically been left alone in my house."

Kratman shrugged. Turning criminals and rebels into slaves had suited the Grand Senate just fine–and it had also suited the Brotherhood, who had sometimes used implanted slaves as spies. McGillivray had owned hundreds of them, all with varying degrees of independence, who watched the guests they served with unblinking eyes. But now they were gone. The only implanted slaves left on Earth, at least officially, were those who served Lady Tiffany.

"Fewer mouths to feed," Kratman said. He watched as McGillivray poured coffee for them both, then added a generous slug of whiskey. "And fewer watching eyes."

"True," McGillivray agreed. He stirred the mugs, then passed one of them to Kratman. "It is nice to see you again, professor, but something tells me this isn't a social call."

He sat down, holding his mug in his hands. "What can I do for you?"

Kratman took a moment to study McGillivray. Like many of the Grand Senators, his physical appearance suggested he was roughly forty, but in truth he was well over a hundred and fifty years old. Now, his hair was finally starting to grey, either because he'd chosen to forgo further regeneration treatments or because he simply couldn't afford them. McGillivray had never been wealthy, at least not compared to the other Grand Senators, and he no longer had a faction to call his own. It was quite possible that he was coming to the end of the line.

"I assume you've been watching the world go by," he said, carefully. McGillivray might have been retired, but he could still draw on reports from the Brotherhood. "What do you think is going to happen to us?"

"I think we're going to have a rough time of it," McGillivray said. He took a sip of his coffee, then leaned forward. "The riots have yet to be brought under control."

Kratman nodded. The first set of rioters had been squashed, hundreds of thousands of students rounded up and marked for exile, but it had come at a price. Many of their parents objected to seeing their children manhandled, let alone sent away from Earth, never to return. There were just too many to be handled roughly themselves, while they tended to include the most productive sectors of Earth's economy. Their objections could not be ignored.

And, in the meantime, other riots had started to spring up.

The emperor was starting to see conspiracies everywhere, Kratman knew, but he might well have a point. Someone was coordinating the riots, making them spring up and do some considerable damage before the security forces responded, then encouraging the rioters to melt away into the background when the security forces finally arrived. The ones stupid enough to stay and try to fight had been captured and interrogated, but all they'd been able to say was that they'd received orders from people who had kept their faces hidden. It hadn't been enough to help the security forces track down the ringleaders.

"That's one problem," Kratman agreed. "And the second would be our infrastructure. The disaster on AMP Thirty proved that, I think."

"True," McGillivray said. His eyes narrowed as he considered the possibilities. "Unless it *was* sabotage. Professor. Antimatter production plants are known for endless safety requirements"

Kratman shook his head. AMP Thirty had been given quotas for antimatter production well in excess of what could be produced safely, then ordered to get to work. There had been no survivors, but the datastream from the production plant had suggested that there had been a failure in the containment systems, milliseconds before the explosion. They'd been lucky as hell the production plant hadn't been located on a planetary surface–score one for the environmentalists–or billions would have died. As it was, the blast had been picked up across the entire solar system.

"I think it was a single component breaking down under the strain," Kratman said. He gathered himself, then pressed on. "It isn't the only place in danger of suffering a major failure."

McGillivray nodded, impatiently. "So we're working our people and infrastructure to death," he said. "Have you tried bringing this to the emperor's attention?"

"I've tried," Kratman said. "He doesn't want to hear it."

McGillivray smirked. "Classic father-son relationship," he said. There was an amused note to his voice. "No son wishes to hear the father was actually right about something."

"He isn't my son," Kratman snapped. The thought wasn't a pleasant one, because it dragged up painful memories. His children had died long ago; his wife had moved out to the colonies after their deaths, separating peacefully from him. "And you know it."

"You were his first CO," McGillivray said. "You were meant to be a father to your men."

"I got most of them killed at Sapphire," Kratman muttered. His ship had been lucky, as absurd as it seemed. Few other ships had survived the battle. "And he was just a midshipman at the time."

"He would have looked up to you," McGillivray said. "He certainly wouldn't have asked you to serve on his cabinet if he hadn't trusted you."

Kratman took a breath. He'd raised sensitive subjects before, during his stint at the Luna Academy, but–whatever the cadets might think–there was no real danger. Even the Grand Senate's Oversight Committee had to admit that talking about problematic policies and military disasters helped the cadets prepare for the future. But... he knew, beyond a shadow of a doubt, that he was about to cross the line into outright treason. Or, at least, something Emperor Marius would probably consider treason. The precise legal definition of the term wouldn't matter, much, if the emperor decided to press charges.

"Tell me something," Kratman said. "What do you think of the emperor?"

McGillivray met his eyes. "I think he's a driven man," he said, slowly. "But what do *you* think of the emperor?"

"I think he's losing it," Kratman said, shortly. "There are quite a few worrying signs in his behavior."

"Like what?" McGillivray asked. "He always struck me as a stable man."

Kratman sighed. "Too many to count," he said. "You realize that Blake Raistlin is still alive? The trial was suspended when the Outsiders started the war; Raistlin himself is still held in the cell under the President's House. Emperor Marius visits him, from time to time, even though he is determined to send the treacherous bastard to the firing squad."

McGillivray's eyes narrowed. "What do they talk about?"

"Fucked if I know," Kratman said. He sipped his coffee, appreciating the sour taste. "The guards are Marines, from Vaughn's former unit. They may not hear what the emperor says to the prisoner and vice versa, but if they do they will never tell."

He cursed under his breath. If only Vaughn had survived the war! The relationship between him and Marius Drake had been strong, perhaps the only true friendship Drake had allowed himself. But Blake Raistlin had killed him, removing someone who could have talked the emperor into seeing sense. Even Lady Tiffany didn't have the years of companionship Marius Drake had shared with his oldest friend.

"And that leads us to a different question," McGillivray said. "Why hasn't the emperor simply ordered him executed?"

"I wish I knew," Kratman said. "I think that the idea of nailing the bastard legally has become an obsession."

He ran his hands through his white hair. "There are other problems," Kratman continued. "I have...I have some reason to believe that the emperor is becoming dependent on painkillers. Just minor ones so far, but that won't last. Sooner or later, he's going to move on to something stronger."

"That isn't a good sign," McGillivray said, slowly.

"No, it isn't," Kratman snapped. He scowled down at the carpeted floor. "He's utterly determined to defeat the Outsiders, whatever the cost. I think he's forgotten everything, but the determination to win. In the meantime, the Federation's society–already precarious–falls apart, while large parts of our infrastructure decay into uselessness."

"Or disaster," McGillivray said. His voice was very calm. "We could win the battle, even the war, but still lose the peace."

"I think so," Kratman said. "I gave the problem to a set of analysts, with strict orders to keep their mouths shut. Depending on the assumptions they feed into the computers, Rupert, we would be looking at a total economic collapse within five to ten years."

McGillivray stared. "It can't be that bad!"

"If anything, that's optimistic," Kratman said. "I can show you the figures, if you'd like, or give you a general overview."

"The overview," McGillivray said.

"We have too many shortages in too many places," Kratman said. "Freighters, for example, are now in short supply because thousands of them have been pressed into service to haul military supplies from one end of the Federation to the other. Admiral Justinian and the other warlords didn't help with that either, as they captured every freighter they could too. And the Outsider raiding squadrons have been wiping out entire convoys, while the pirates have been snatching up individual ships..."

Kratman shrugged. "In short, we're running out of everything that makes the economy work," he added. "Some star systems have even reported shortages of HE3 and antimatter because our production has been diverted towards the needs of the war. I have a feeling that quite a few systems have effectively dropped out of the Federation, simply because they have not been contacted for years. God knows if they can sustain themselves in the long run."

McGillivray sighed. "The Grand Senate wanted the colonials to remain dependent," he said, darkly. "They didn't listen to me."

Kratman nodded. Centuries ago, a rogue physicist had predicted that–one day–the Asimov Point network would reboot itself. The points would change, rendering existing star charts useless and forcing each star system to fall back on its own resources, at least until the Federation could start probing its way through the reformed network. The nightmare had seemed so persuasive that the Grand Senate had authorized a project to ensure that each and every colony world, no matter how young, could fend for itself. But, over the decades, the priority had faded to the point where the Grand Senate had actively tried to keep colony worlds dependent as long as possible. They'd even started shipping in food from other star systems when it wouldn't have been hard to start sowing seeds on the new world.

It was insane. But it had suited the Grand Senate perfectly.

"So we have a war we cannot win without destroying ourselves," McGillivray said. "I trust you have attempted to warn the emperor?"

"He is determined to win the war," Kratman said. "The idea of accepting a truce, of granting independence to the Outsiders, is utterly impossible for him to accept."

"It would have been impossible for us too, once," McGillivray reminded him. "We support the unity of mankind."

"Not at the price of *destroying* mankind," Kratman snapped. "What good is the Brotherhood without the human race?"

"And, assuming we did grant the Outsiders independence," McGillivray asked, "where would that leave the Federation?"

Kratman sighed. The emperor had raised the same question. If the Outsiders gained independence, with their technological advantages, how long would it be until they were vastly more powerful than the Federation? Ten years of peace and military development might ensure the next war would be short and decisive. And there was little hope the Federation would be able to match the Outsiders, even though it had a far greater industrial base. The Outsiders had too many other advantages.

But there was no guarantee the next war would be fought at all.

"I think we have to put the future off until it arrives," he said. "Right now, we may see the entire Federation collapse into ruins. What will *that* do to our chances of survival if another alien race arrives on our borders?"

McGillivray stood up and started to pace the room. "I understand your concerns," he said. "Now tell me, professor; what can we do about them?"

And that, Kratman knew, was the five hundred thousand credit question.

"The Grand Senate had ways to remove a Grand Senator who was unstable or completely insane," McGillivray said. "It happened, on occasion. Not something we ever told the public, of course."

"Of course," Kratman agreed. "But how do we remove an emperor?"

They exchanged glances. The Grand Senate, for all its flaws, rested on a social structure that allowed for Grand Senators to be replaced by successors, if necessary. But there was no new emperor waiting in the wings to replace Emperor Marius. Even if Lady Tiffany became pregnant–and Kratman knew she had no intention of becoming pregnant until after her husband stepped down from his role–it would be years before the child was old enough to assume power. And his ascent would be challenged. Emperor Marius had a proven military record. The child's sole claim to power would be having the right set of parents.

"There's no one else who can take his place," Kratman said, slowly. "And there are no procedures to force him to step down."

"Then we consider assassination," McGillivray said. The Brotherhood had assassinated politicians and alien sympathizers in the past, although few of the deaths had ever been traced back to those responsible. "Can't we remove him by force?"

"He's guarded by an entire regiment of Marines," Kratman said. "They're loyal, both to the emperor and the memory of their former commanding officer. I doubt any assassin could get through the defenses and into striking range without being intercepted. Even a nuke would be hard-pressed to do real damage to the President's House."

"Admiral Justinian smuggled a nuke into Navy HQ," McGillivray mused.

"He had the right access codes and a great deal of luck," Kratman reminded him. "Procedures were tightened up, considerably, after the Battle of Earth. The Grand Senate closed all the easy access ways to the planet, let alone their personal mansions..."

He sighed, bitterly. The insistence on inspecting every starship that entered the system was yet another nail in the economic coffin. He didn't want to think about just how many man-hours–to say nothing of credits–were being lost, simply through forcing the starship crews to hold for boarding and thorough searches. And then there were the complaints about the security officers molesting the crews...

And how could I blame any starship crewman, he asked himself, *for refusing to return to Earth?*

"So we can't talk him into standing down," McGillivray said, "and we can't remove him by force. Where does *that* leave us? Stuck."

"Not quite," Kratman said. "I'm hoping to find an excuse to go out to Boston, sooner rather than later. I'd have a chance to talk to Admiral Garibaldi."

"Who happens to be our beloved emperor's protégée," McGillivray sneered. "He'll report you for treachery. And if he doesn't, we'll just end up with *another* emperor or a civil war."

"I wasn't going to urge him to launch a coup," Kratman said. "He may be the only one who can talk the emperor into bringing the war to a close, before it's too late."

"Good thinking," McGillivray said. "But tell me...do you think it may already be too late?"

"I hope not," Kratman said. If he'd believed it was truly hopeless, he would have booked passage to a stage two or stage three colony world somewhere out of the way. There would be a fair chance of living out his final years in peace. "But we have no choice, except to play our last card."

"I'll start seeing what other options there might be," McGillivray said. "But you do understand our resources are limited?"

"I know," Kratman said. "I..."

His terminal beeped. He pulled it off his belt and glanced at it.

"There's been a major battle," he said. "And we have been victorious, although there aren't many details. I've been summoned back to the President's House."

"Then go," McGillivray said. "Let me know when you find out what actually happened."

Kratman nodded, then rose and left the room.

Chapter Thirty-Three

But the problem with victory is that it can lead to victory disease. Put simply, victory disease is the sense that one is invincible, completely unbeatable. It makes it impossible to rationally calculate the odds of future victories, let alone the course of the war.
-The Federation Navy in Retrospect, 4199

Earth, 4100

"This is a very interesting report, Admiral Ness," Marius said, coolly. "A very interesting report indeed."

He eyed the Admiral for a long moment, knowing that it had been a mistake to send the older man to Boston. Admiral Ness didn't have the determination to become a warlord, true, but he didn't have the courage of his convictions or even the ability to support his superiors either. Marius didn't blame Ness for resentment–his superior officer had been nearly seventy years younger than him–yet he couldn't condone an officer trying to undermine his superiors.

"This report states that Operation Sword is doomed to failure," Marius said. "That Admiral Garibaldi took too great a risk in sending five battle squadrons away from Boston in an attempt to lure the enemy into a battle. That the inevitable end result is the loss of Boston to the Outsiders. Is that correct?"

"Sir," Ness said. "I..."

Marius spoke over him. "And here," he said, picking up a terminal, "is the official report from Admiral Garibaldi, General Yaakov and several other officers. All agree that Operation Sword was a great success and the Outsiders took a major bloody nose. Which of them should I believe, Admiral? Or are you implying that seven officers worked together to send me a pack of lies, complete with faked sensor data?"

Ness paled. "Ah...Your Majesty...I..."

"...Have nothing better to do with my time but write reports undermining my superior's position," Marius said, overriding the older man with effortless ease. "I would expect you to admit you were wrong, once or twice in a while. It isn't the end of the world. Hell, it isn't even the end of your career."

He met Ness's eyes. "Is there any reason why I shouldn't order your immediate dismissal from the Navy?"

Ness lowered his gaze. "I did what I thought was right," he said. "And if I was wrong, I..."

His voice trailed off. Marius was unsurprised. Ness was a bureaucratic warrior par excellence, capable of putting the cat among the pigeons with a single memo to the right pair of eyes, or citing obscure rules and regulations to justify sitting on his ass and doing nothing. It almost made up for his lack of connections, which might well have saved his career when Marius started his purge. Quite a few officers with aristocratic connections had been thrown out of the Navy without ceremony.

"You were wrong," Marius said. He nodded to the Marine, standing by the door. "You will be taken from this room to a small office. There, you will have a day to decide if you wish to resign from the Navy or face a Board of Inquiry into professional misconduct in the face of the enemy."

Ness opened his mouth, but the Marine caught his arm and led him out the door before he could say a word. Marius laid a small bet with himself that Ness would resign–a Board of Inquiry would note that Ness had been completely wrong, then pass judgement against him–and then turned to face his cabinet. They looked as pleased as he felt by the victory. Even if the Outsiders managed to regroup in time to prevent minor counterattacks from shoving them back into the Beyond, the losses they'd taken made their eventual defeat inevitable.

"Well," he said. "This has been a good day."

He nodded to Captain Sitka Rani, who stepped forward.

"We're still studying the raw sensor records," she said, as she activated the holographic display. "However, based on our preliminary studies, we can confirm the destruction or capture of sixty-seven superdreadnaughts, while the remainder all took damage from minor to significant. The enemy actually scuttled a number of their ships before they left the system, leaving us with quite a few hints as to just how much damage they took. They presumably could not enter FTL."

She paused, her dark eyes flickering to Marius's face. "Our losses were, as of the last count, thirty superdreadnaughts, ten fortresses and dozens of smaller ships," she continued. "The death toll was in excess of fifty thousand spacers."

Marius winced. The butcher's bill for an assault on a heavily-defended star system was always shockingly high. Losing the fortresses alone had cost Roman Garibaldi dearly, all the more so as he'd deliberately lured the enemy into attacking his command. Marius understood, in a way, what had driven Admiral Ness. In peacetime, such tricks could not be tolerated. But this was war.

And all necessary means are to be embraced to win as quickly as possible, Marius thought, coldly. *The sooner the war is ended, the better.*

"Overall," Sitka concluded, "the battle was a success. Probes through Asimov Points Delta, Echo and Gamma revealed an enemy in disarray. That was, of course, weeks ago."

Marius nodded. By now, Roman Garibaldi might have launched a counterattack that had pushed the enemy back to the Rim, or he might have lost Boston System if the Outsiders had managed to throw a second attack in through the undefended Asimov Point. Still, the victory would give new heart to the Federation and discourage unrest and outright rebellion. Given time, they could win the war. And then there would be time to breathe.

He cleared his throat. "We need to take advantage of this as quickly as possible," he said. "I believe we should immediately move to...liberate the worlds occupied by the Outsiders."

"Those worlds, in many cases, willingly joined the Outsiders," General Thorne pointed out, dryly. "We will need to put together a much larger pacification force to ensure that unrest is kept under control."

Marius nodded. It was almost a shame that the old pacification units had been disbanded, their troopers dumped on penal worlds. *They'd* known how to deal with unrest. He'd been appalled at their sheer brutality, years ago, but that was then. Now, he understood precisely why the Grand Senate had needed their servants. Brutal repression was the only way to buy time to rebuild the Federation into something workable.

"Start recruiting at once," he ordered. Recruitment centers had already been opened, but they would have to be expanded as quickly as possible. What did it say about the pre-war Federation when one couldn't even recruit enough thugs in time to make a difference? "And have them prepped for their journey to the Rim."

"Yes, sir," Thorne said.

"Admiral Garibaldi will require reinforcements," Marius continued. A thought occurred to him and he smiled. "I intend to detach four battle squadrons from Home Fleet and take personal command, once the reinforcements are ready. My wife will remain on Earth, with full powers in my absence."

Lawrence Tully coughed. "Emperor...are you seriously planning to leave Earth?"

"Yes. Yes, I am," Marius said. "Do you require my constant supervision?"

Tully looked irked. "With all due respect, Emperor, our new government is *dependent* upon you," he warned. "You are the center of government. Your absence will weaken the framework we have been building over the past two years..."

"Would you like a towel," Marius interrupted, "to wipe my shit off your lips?"

He stormed on before Tully could say a word. "This government is intended as a temporary measure," he said. "I do not intend to remain emperor forever, Comptroller. The government should be capable of operating without me, at least for a few months."

"The civil service has been badly damaged by the war–the wars," Tully said. His face had gone completely blank. "It may not survive your absence."

"Then make sure it does," Marius said.

He sighed, inwardly. Part of him knew it was stupid to leave Earth, but he wanted–he needed–a break from it all. The Grand Senators, fuck the lot of them, had had holiday worlds they could visit if they needed a vacation where their every whim was catered to by pleasure slaves. But the Grand Senators had had families who could take up the slack, if necessary. Marius only had Tiffany and, as much as he loved her, he had to admit that she lacked his experience in military affairs.

And besides, it might be good to remind the Federation's population of his military skills.

"My wife will have full authority in my absence," he said. "And I will be leaving some of you behind to advise her."

There was a long pause. It was finally broken by Professor Kratman.

"This victory will certainly knock the Outsiders back," he said. "It gives us an opportunity to gather ourselves and take some of the pressure off our industries. We could lower production demands and start fixing problems..."

"Out of the question," Marius said. He hadn't forgotten the lessons of the Inheritance Wars and he was surprised that Kratman *had*. The Colonial Alliance had slowed production before the Battle of Athens, believing the Federation Navy was effectively stalemated. They'd been disastrously wrong. "We cannot afford to slow production until the war comes to an end."

The Professor met his eyes, reprovingly. "Then we will risk more disasters like the loss of AMP Thirty," he said. "And each successive disaster will cause more disasters, more delays in production, more long-term headaches for the Federation."

Marius's hand twitched. He wanted a pill. He wanted one desperately. But he couldn't take one in front of his cabinet...

"We will have time to breathe when we have won the war," he said. "There can be no other threat on such a scale out there, can there?"

There was no answer. But then, there didn't need to be. No one had really understood the sheer scale of the Outsider threat until they'd attacked the Federation. If there was yet another hostile alien race out there, the Federation might have no warning until the shit hit the fan. And a third war would take the Federation apart at the seams.

This one is already trying to do just that, he thought, bitterly. *Yet another reason why we need to end this as soon as possible.*

The thought led to another one. "I want to have the prisoners from the battle shipped to Earth," he said. "They will be interrogated, then executed."

"Of course, sir," Thorne said. "Would you prefer a public execution or private?"

"That would cause them to retaliate against *our* prisoners," Kratman snapped. "They have hundreds of thousands of our people held prisoner, ready to be slaughtered if we massacre *their* prisoners."

"We don't know they've been taking care of our prisoners," Thorne snapped back. "I..."

"They sent us as much evidence as they reasonably could," Kratman said.

"Faked," Thorne insisted. "Keeping so many prisoners alive would strain them to the utmost!"

"They know better than to engage in mass slaughter," Kratman thundered.

Thorne took a breath. "Are you *defending* them now?"

Marius slapped the table. "*Enough*," he snapped. His head was starting to pound. "I will not hear my cabinet arguing so savagely. Do you understand me?"

"Yes, sir," Thorne said.

"The prisoners must not be slaughtered," Kratman insisted. He didn't seem cowed by Marius–but then, he'd known Marius as a snotty young midshipman. "They can be held on a penal world until the war is over, *then* you can consider their final disposition."

"But they need to be interrogated," Thorne injected. "Sir..."

"They will be held on Mars, after interrogation," Marius ruled. He looked from face to face, desperate for the meeting to come to an end. "Are there any other issues we should raise?"

"Just one," Tully said. "I believe we should cancel the plan to exile the student rebels."

Marius swung around to glare at him. "Why?"

Tully looked down at the table. "Because their parents are quite important to the economy," Tully said. "*And* the Civil Service. Resentment on their part might have quite unfortunate effects."

Maybe I can find a use for Ness, Marius thought. *Keeping the paper-pushers in line.*

He shook his head, a moment later. Ness might not be a potential traitor, or warlord, but he was simply unreliable.

"Very well," he said, instead. "Hold them here, but do not exile them."

He rose to his feet, unable to wait any longer. "Dismissed," he said. "I will discuss your specific dispositions during my trip to Boston later."

The cabinet dispersed. Marius watched them go, then walked through a side door into one of the smaller officers. He'd never been able to work out what the president had *done* in the office, but there was a large cabinet to one side, crammed with expensive bottles of alcohol. Some of them cost more than he'd made in a decade of serving as an admiral in the Federation Navy.

He sighed, then reached for a bottle at random and poured himself a glass. The reddish liquid smelt faintly of roses. Shaking his head–he'd never been a wine snob–he lifted the glass to his lips, silently toasted Roman Garibaldi and Fifth Fleet, then took a long sip. The wine tasted oddly smoky against his tongue, but it wasn't unpleasant. He finished the glass and poured himself another one.

"You shouldn't be drinking so much," Tiffany said, as she stepped through the other door and smiled at him. "You have far too much work to do."

"I know it," Marius grunted. He tossed back the second glass, then placed it in the wash basin and strode through the door into the living room. "But I also have a victory to toast."

"I heard," Tiffany said. "Roman did well."

"The boy was always lucky," Marius agreed, although he knew that luck had played only a minor role in the battle. He turned as she followed him into the room. "Did you hear the bit about you taking command on Earth?"

Tiffany's eyes narrowed. "Are you sure you want me to stay in command here?"

"I need someone I can trust absolutely," Marius said. "There aren't many people here who are devoted, first and foremost, to the Federation itself."

He sat down on the sofa, rubbing his forehead. Tully was the consummate bureaucrat; he'd keep the system running, but he wouldn't consider the greater good of anything above the system itself. Professor Kratman was more interested in theory than reality; he might be right about the dangers of pushing the economy as hard as he was, but the real danger lay in losing the war. And Thorne was more fixated on keeping a lid on potential troublemakers than anything else. Together, under his leadership, they could accomplish much. But separately, none of them could handle ultimate power.

Tiffany walked around behind him, then started to massage his neck. "I'll miss you," she said, as her fingers undid his jacket. "You'll be gone for...how long?"

"At least seven months," Marius said. "It will be quite a long time for you to hold supreme command, but you can do it. Besides, anyone who gives you real trouble will see me returning with an entire fleet behind me."

He smiled. Home Fleet was *his*. He'd replaced some of the officers with his personal loyalists, while giving the crewmen shore leaves and other special treatment, ensuring that no attempt to foment a mutiny could succeed. Anyone who had ambitions to replace Tiffany as Regent of Earth would have to subvert Home Fleet, then somehow devise a counter to Fifth Fleet. And, of course, the superdreadnaughts under Marius's personal command.

"Stand up," Tiffany ordered. She removed his shirt as soon as he obeyed, then started to work on his trousers. "You need to relax."

"I have work to do," Marius protested, half-heartedly. "I..."

Tiffany walked around the sofa, then shrugged off her dress and stood naked before him. Marius felt a sudden lump in his throat, reminding himself just how lucky he'd been to have Tiffany given to him. The Grand Senate had thought Tiffany would help control him, or betray him if he plotted rebellion. Instead, they'd become true lovers and allies.

"I think you can wait," Tiffany said, firmly. She stepped forward and pushed him down to the floor, then straddled him. "And besides, if I'm not going to see you for nearly a year, I want something to remember."

ꕥ

The emperor looked surprisingly cheerful, Professor Kratman noted, as he was shown into the emperor's office. He was sitting behind a desk, smiling to himself, as he read a set of readiness reports from Home Fleet. But then, he had good reason to be cheerful, Kratman knew. Home Fleet, as the Federation Navy's reserve formation, was ready to deploy at a moment's notice.

"Professor," Marius said. "Thank you for coming."

"You're welcome," Kratman said. "What can I do for you?"

"You'll be accompanying me to Boston," the Emperor said. "I imagine there will be talks with the Outsiders, once they realize their defeat is inevitable. You will assist me with the talks."

Kratman kept his expression under tight control. He'd expected to have to argue the emperor into allowing him to travel to Boston. Instead, he was being given what he wanted on a silver platter. It was enough to worry him more than he cared to admit.

"Yes, sir," he said, softly. "Dare I hope you plan to give them more than their lives if they surrender?"

"We'll see," the emperor said. "But it depends on just how quickly they are prepared to bend the knee."

"Yes, sir," Kratman said. There would be time to convince the emperor to moderate his demands later, on the flight to Boston. "It will be my pleasure to serve."

Kratman noticed a sheet of white paper on the desk and frowned. "What is that?"
"An execution warrant," the emperor said. He gave his former CO an odd little smile, then held the paper out for inspection. "Blake Raistlin will die today."
"Oh," Kratman said.

Interlude Two

From: *The Chaos Years* (5023)

There is an old analogy about political systems that are too closely interrelated for peaceful separation to be achieved. Two scorpions are confined within a small bottle, too small for both of them. But the scorpion that strikes first is unlikely to kill its opponent before it is stung itself. The outcome is mutual destruction.

For the Federation and the Outsiders, the analogy could not be more precise.

The Federation could not surrender its grip on the out-worlds. Nor could the out-worlds passively accept Federation domination indefinitely. Indeed, the Outsiders had fled the outcome of the last major interstellar war over who ran the Federation. The war bred ruthlessness on both sides because, intentionally or otherwise, the war aims were thoroughly incompatible. Emperor Marius saw the Federation as a holy cause; it could not be sundered, whatever the cost. But the Outsider leadership saw the Federation as the source of all evil. There could be no compromise.

For both sides, the Battle of Boston brought change. The Federation saw the victory as heralding the eventual reunification of the human race. There was no incentive to compromise. But the Outsiders saw the victory as a foretaste of eventual disaster. And, in desperation, they started to consider other ways to win their war.

And yet, the Federation was staggering. Cracks in its society, some caused by the Grand Senate, others by the Justinian War and Emperor Marius's coup, only widened as the war raged on. The Federation needed a period of time to breathe. Instead, it lurched from one crisis to another, then another and another, until it could no longer cope. The victory at Boston came too late, in the end, to prevent the Federation facing the ultimate disaster...

...And, for Emperor Marius, the choice between winning the war or salvaging something from the ruins of a once-proud civilization.

Chapter Thirty-Four

But for those who lost, the shock of defeat could force them to face facts and change their tactics.
-The Federation Navy in Retrospect, 4199

Sanctuary/Nova Athena, 4101

Chang Li had to fight to keep her face impassive as General Charlie Stuart was shown into the Council Chamber. His uniform had been taken from him and replaced with a bland jumpsuit that might as well have been sackcloth and ashes. The long interrogation sessions that had followed the news of the defeat had left the general looking thoroughly unwell; he stood between two armed Marsha, his pale face suggesting he was on the verge of collapse.

He didn't deserve such treatment, Li knew. He'd fought well and hard for the Outsider Federation. But there had been no choice. The Council wanted more than just a full investigation, no matter how hard she'd struggled against it. They wanted blood. In hindsight, thousands of people were arguing that Boston had been a trap... and that General Stuart, the man who had argued for the battle, had deliberately sent his fleet into a meatgrinder.

They think he's a traitor, she thought. *And they want him to die a traitor's death.*

She felt her lips quirk into a bitter smile as she surveyed the councilors. None of them could hope to make amends with the Federation, not now. They were either descendants of those who had fled the Inheritance Wars or aliens–and her, of course. The Federation probably considered her a traitor, all the more so for plotting against them while seated on Earth as a member of the Senate. But the other members had slowly withdrawn from the Outsider Council.

It was hard to blame them, she knew. Their worlds stood naked, exposed to the Federation's counterattack. It wouldn't be long, if the reports from Earth were true, before Emperor Marius himself led an offensive into the Rim. And it would be almost completely unstoppable, at least until the damaged starships were repaired and rearmed. The Federation, its pride stung, would attack with savage force, clearing as many Outsider-occupied worlds as possible. And they would make great gains before the Outsiders rallied.

If we can, the pessimistic side of her mind noted. They'd expended far too many starships in the Battle of Boston, for nothing. *We may not have time to replace our losses before the enemy attacks.*

"General Charlie Stuart," the mediator said. "You have been summoned before us to account for the defeat at Boston. Do you have anything you wish to say before we consider your case?"

Li gritted her teeth. It wasn't a fair trial. How could it be? They wanted blood–and they didn't much care *who* bled, as long as someone did.

"I was the person who believed there was a window of opportunity to attack Boston," General Stuart said. His voice sounded broken. "I was wrong, as you know, and I accept full responsibility for the failed offensive. There is nothing else to say."

Li winced, inwardly. General Stuart hadn't been the only person involved–and he wasn't the only person who could claim a share of the blame. *She'd* signed off on the plan to attack Boston, as had most of the Council. The Marsha, in particular, had been very enthusiastic about the plan. It was odd, but perhaps unsurprising, that they seemed the least inclined to seek a scapegoat for the disaster. Their honor code left them convinced that a failed offensive was still better than standing on the defensive.

"Then we must consider your punishment," the mediator said. "Is there anyone who would speak in your defense?"

General Stuart shook his head. He'd been offered the chance to call witnesses to the stand, but he'd declined to summon anyone. It might well have damaged their careers too.

Li hesitated, then rose to her feet. "I believe we have to consider all the facts," she said, shortly. "There were no voices who believed the attack on Boston was a mistake. No one argued against launching the invasion of the system. And, because of that, we cannot hold General Stuart solely responsible for the disaster."

There was a clicking sound from Insect #342. "These facts must be accepted and learned from," it said, through the translator. "The defeat has left us in a dangerously exposed position. There is no time to judge one person when the whole is threatened."

"Agreed," High Lord Slant said. The Marsha leaned forward. "He launched a powerful offensive and did his best to win."

"But he lost," one of the human representatives snapped. "He could have taken the system and opened the way to the Core Worlds. Or backed out when it was clear the Federation Navy was up to something. Instead, he stayed in the system too long to escape, after it became clear that the Federation had laid a trap."

"I take full responsibility," General Stuart said. "The blame is mine."

"Then I propose that General Stuart be sent to command the defenses of Nova Athena," Li said, shortly. "It will be a demotion, but it will also give him the chance to learn from his defeat..."

"But he could have planned to betray us," the representative snapped. "He should be stripped of all honors and exiled."

"He was interrogated thoroughly," Li snapped back, feeling her patience coming to an end. "He didn't intend to betray us to the Federation. I suspect we allowed our desire to break through into Boston and take control of the Asimov Points to blind us to the risks involved in the assault."

She paused. "I call for a vote," she said, as General Stuart shot her an unreadable look. "All in favour of Nova Athena?"

"All in favor," the mediator said, once everyone had raised their hands. "General Stuart is hereby assigned to Nova Athena as her system defense commander. Good luck, general."

He waited for General Stuart to be escorted out of the chamber, then keyed a switch. A young black-haired woman, wearing the uniform of an Outsider general, stepped into the chamber, She carried a small terminal under her arm and looked, thankfully, confident. Li wasn't sure if her confidence was based in reality or not, but the Council needed to believe they could win. Or at least force the Federation to come to terms.

"General Wilson," the mediator said. "You are the new commander of the Outsider Navy. Do you believe we can still win the war?"

"I believe it will be very difficult," General Wilson said. Her accent suggested she'd spent time in the Federation, before joining the Outsiders. "However, we still have some advantages. Most notably, our bases are hidden from rapid detection."

"There are still vulnerable worlds," Councilor Blunt insisted. "Every world we liberated from the Federation is now at risk!"

"Yes, they are," General Wilson said. "But, realistically, few of those worlds contributed more than trained manpower–at best–to the war effort. Athena and Nova Athena are the only worlds that possess considerable industrial bases of their own. I believe we should harry the Federation Navy as it advances back into the Rim, but avoid a pitched battle short of either of those two worlds."

"You appear to be gambling that the Federation has not located any of our homeworlds," Blunt said. "What if they choose to strike directly beyond the Rim?"

"Then we will lose the war," General Wilson said. She pressed her hands together, as if she were in prayer. "We simply do not have the resources, at the moment, to cover every possible target. The last set of reports from our agents on Earth confirm that Home Fleet will be detaching a sizeable force to reinforce Fifth Fleet. Added to what Admiral Garibaldi has under his flag, he will not run into anything big enough to do more than delay him until he reaches Nova Athena."

Wilson paused. "And I believe Nova Athena will be their prime target."

Li swallowed. "Because of me," she said, when she trusted herself to speak. "They'll target my homeworld because of me."

"I believe so," General Wilson said. She tilted her head, allowing strands of black hair to shroud her face. "They consider you the prime mover behind the Outsider cause, Councilor. Targeting Nova Athena will not only undermine your status, but prove that we cannot protect even the homeworld of one of our leaders."

"I see," Li said. "And what do you propose we do?"

"We repair our ships, then prepare to meet them at Nova Athena," General Wilson said. "We would probably be better off declining to defend Athena itself. There are too many rebels on the ground."

"Then see to it," Li said, after canvassing opinions. "But what if we can't defend the world anyway?"

"We fall back," General Wilson said. "Right now, Councilor, ships are more important than planets."

Li nodded. "And that leads us to another problem," she said. "Should we attempt to offer peace terms to the Federation–again?"

"The Federation didn't accept peace terms when we were riding high," Councilor Hammock sneered. "Why should they accept them when they think they're winning?"

"Because it might prevent mass slaughter if they have to batter through our worlds, one by one," Li suggested. "We don't know what terms they would offer us."

Councilor Hammock rose to his feet. "It seems to me, Chang, that you have good reason to worry about your homeworld," he said. "That fear is driving you to consider surrendering to the federal bastards. Have you forgotten, so quickly, that we cannot trust anything they might say? They might demand we surrendered our ships one day, then move in and take over completely the next, once we rendered ourselves defenseless. We cannot trust a word they say!"

Li's face burned with embarrassment–and rage.

"I understand you've had a shock," Hammock said. "We've all had a shock. We didn't expect a major defeat, while our early victories only made the defeat seem worse by comparison. But we have not yet been beaten. There will be time to strip naked, bend over and spread for them once we've been hammered into the ground. Until then, I intend to continue to fight."

"I wish I was surprised at your attitude," Li said, when she had managed to calm herself enough to speak. "But we do have to consider the worst. A single peace envoy..."

"...Would be seen as a sign of weakness," Hammock said. "They would think they had us on the run, that we would surrender completely if pressed harder. Let us win another battle, let us give them a bloody nose...and then we can try and talk peace. We might win better terms."

"There would be no better terms," High Lord Slant said. "The Federation will not allow us to exist."

Of course not, Li thought. Aliens with guns–and grudges. The Federation's nightmare, all the worse for the knowledge that humans had provided those guns, as well as training and starships. *You'll be lucky if you just get forced back to your homeworld and blockaded.*

"Then we fight," Hammock said. "This is no time to lose our nerve."

ꕤ

They'd given Charlie a small compartment–marginally bigger than a prison cell–and a gun with a single bullet in the chamber. He'd found himself playing with it, wondering just who had bothered to show such contempt–or a backwards gesture of mercy. The Marsha, perhaps; they might have supported his attack on Boston, but they also thought highly of ritual suicide. They might have given him the gun as a sign of respect, not contempt.

He pushed the thought aside as the hatch opened, revealing Chang Li.

"Councilor," he said. He rose to his feet, then gave her a tired smile. "What can I do for you?"

"I wanted you to live," she said, eying the gun in his hand. "Who gave you a weapon?"

"I don't know," Charlie said. He still had nightmares over just how many people had died under his command. Hell, the entire Outsider cause might have died under his command. "I don't know if I should thank you or hate you."

"Stick with thanking me," Chang Li said, bluntly. "Your successor believes that Nova Athena might come under heavy attack."

"There aren't many other targets that would absorb more than a destroyer squadron or two," Charlie muttered. "You and yours did a good job at turning Nova Athena into an economic powerhouse."

Chang Li nodded. Nova Athena's population had been lucky. Their founders had managed to avoid most of the debts and obligations that would have bound them to the Grand Senate. It hadn't allowed them to escape entirely, but it had given them a chunk of independence they'd used ruthlessly. And yet, they'd come to hate the Federation as much as anyone else along the Rim.

And why would they not? Charlie asked himself. *They were as oppressed as anyone else when push came to shove.*

"I want you to take command of the defenses and build them up into something impregnable," Chang Li said. "The Federation *cannot* be allowed another victory."

"And I won't be allowed command of the defense fleet," Charlie pointed out. "It would destroy your career if you tried to give me command."

"You'll have command of the orbital fortresses," Chang Li countered. "And that will give you influence, I suspect. Use it ruthlessly."

"Of course," Charlie said. He sat down on the bunk, then placed the gun on the table. "What happened to my crew?"

"Most of them have been dispersed through the fleet," Chang Li said. "You accepted the blame, so they were released without charge. I thought you knew that, Charlie."

"I haven't had much time to ask questions," Charlie said. He shook his head, ruefully. "If we win this war, councilor, we must come up with a formalized method of handling these cases."

"There wasn't time to come up with any formalities," Chang Li said. "You were lucky not to be put in front of a wall and shot out of hand."

"I know," Charlie said.

Chang Li looked at him, her dark eyes wistful. "General," she said slowly, "do we have a hope of actually *winning*?"

"I don't know," Charlie admitted. "There are just too many variables. Can the Federation sustain a war economy long enough to break us? Can *we* sustain the war economy long enough to break *them*? Can we come up with a silver bullet that will instantly render the Federation Navy obsolete—or will they come up with something new themselves? We can't dismiss it entirely, councilor."

He shrugged, expressively. "I think we'd be lucky if we managed to hold Nova Athena, or any other world the Federation knows how to find," he added. "We might be better off trying to withdraw behind the Rim entirely, then working hastily to build up a new fleet."

"I don't think we have that option this time," Chang Li said. "The Federation let us go years ago, after the Inheritance Wars. They won't make the same mistake twice."

"Probably not," Charlie said. "Do you have any other thoughts?"

"Just this," Chang Li said. "Make damn sure you give them a bloody nose if–when–they attack Nova Athena. Another defeat will ruin us."

ᘓᘐ

"They didn't have to send us here," Roebuck muttered.

Uzi nodded in agreement. He shared his CO's feelings, although for different reasons. Nova Athena was an interesting world, one of the logistic hubs for the Outsider Navy, but it was also a long way from the war front. There was no way he could get a message back to Earth from Nova Athena, not without risking his cover. And to think sending them to Nova Athena was a gesture of kindness!

"We could have gone to one of the threatened worlds," Roebuck continued. "Or even been assigned to the fortresses covering the Asimov Points, or..."

"It's a chance to relax," Uzi said, despite his own irritation. "Soldiers need regular downtime or they start making mistakes."

And Nova Athena would have been ideal, if he'd been a loyal Outsider. There was no security threat on a world that had tried to maintain a distance from the Federation ever since it had been founded, no risk from Federation loyalists or terrorists trying to pay off old grudges. Hell, there were beaches, pretty women, cold drinks...everything a soldier could want to forget the war existed. He'd lost track of half of his men the day after their arrival, something that didn't bother him as much as it should. The peace and quiet of Nova Athena was seeping into his soul.

"I know that," Roebuck said. "But what about downtime somewhere closer to the front?"

Uzi smiled. He'd reviewed the data and he was fairly sure Nova Athena would be on the front lines very soon. There weren't that many worlds the Federation could hit, after all, unless they'd managed to get lucky and found a planet hidden beyond the Rim. His fingers touched the medal he'd been given, after boarding the fortress and taking the crew prisoner. The Federation would want revenge for that stunt soon enough.

"I think we will be back at the front soon enough," he said, standing up. "And I think you need to get laid."

Roebuck gaped. "I...I beg your pardon?"

"There is a club down there crammed with nubile young women, all of whom want to spend time with a hero from the fleet," Uzi said, as he pulled Roebuck to his feet. "I think a few hours in their company would help you to relax."

And it would, he knew, as he nudged Roebuck down to the club. There *were* women down there and they were *easy*. But it would also distract Roebuck from his duties, allowing Uzi a chance to plot himself. And who knew what would happen when–if–the Federation Navy arrived?

We need a way to get to the fortresses, he thought. *But how are we going to get that before it's too late?*

Chapter Thirty-Five

However, one victory is meaningless unless it leads to further victories–and eventual total victory.
-The Federation Navy in Retrospect, 4199

Boston, 4101

"And thank God *that's* over," Emperor Marius said, once they were in Roman's stateroom and the hatch was securely locked. "I'm sure I said *something* about not being given the proper respect."

"The crew wanted to see you, sir," Roman said. "And besides, regulations are regulations."

He studied the emperor as covertly as possible while he poured them both tea. It had been two years since he'd laid eyes on his mentor and the change shocked him more than he wanted to admit. Marius Drake had always struck him as being a little vain; now, his grey hair was shading to white and there were dark rings under his eyes. His body was thinner than Roman recalled, while Emperor Marius's hands twitched nervously as he reached for the cup. Roman couldn't help wondering just what had happened on Earth while he'd been commanding the desperate defense of the Rim.

"Regulations," Emperor Marius snorted. "You should know better than to follow them *all*."

Roman smiled. There were no regulations for greeting the emperor, if only because the Federation hadn't had an emperor until the Grand Senate had been overthrown. He'd passed the question over to his protocol officer, who'd modified the standard greeting party for a Grand Senator and added a rendition of the Federation's anthem. There was no way he wanted to omit the proper respect for his mentor–and besides, the crew wanted to see their emperor. But if he'd known just how exhausted Emperor Marius clearly was, he would have thought better of the formal greeting.

"I'm sorry," Roman said, sincerely.

"Don't worry about it," Emperor Marius reassured him. He sipped his tea, then settled back in his chair. "You have no idea how good it feels to be back at the front."

Roman lifted an eyebrow. "There's no real danger of death right now," he pointed out. "The enemy has barely shown itself, apart from laying mines on the far side of the Asimov Points. They certainly haven't attempted to attack the system again."

"Good to hear it," Emperor Marius grunted. He waved a hand to indicate the superdreadnaught. "Here, everyone knows their place; everyone knows their job. On Earth, there are so many competing factions that keeping them all going in the right direction is a major headache. And there are days when I wished that treacherous bastard had put a bullet through my head."

Roman honestly didn't know what to say. He'd known Blake Raistlin; hell, he'd trained alongside him at the Academy. Raistlin had never struck him as a bad person, even though his family connections would probably ensure he gained his first captaincy by the time he turned thirty. It had seemed odd that he'd been assigned to Admiral Drake's staff, but Roman hadn't really thought anything of it. The war had screwed up all their careful plans for advancement. And then Blake Raistlin had tried to kill the admiral.

"He's dead, now," Emperor Marius said. "To hell with the trial, I decided. I had him shot."

"I see," Roman said. "Good."

He honestly wasn't sure what to feel about that either. Raistlin had been...if not a friend, then at least an acquaintance. Their backgrounds had been too different for true friendship, but Roman had always thought he could rely on Raistlin. And yet... in the end, Raistlin had betrayed the bonds of trust that kept the Navy together. He had to be punished–and to be seen to be punished–for his crime.

But Roman couldn't help feeling a flicker of regret.

"Never mind that," Emperor Marius said. "Are you and your girlfriend still together?"

"Yes," Roman said, puzzling over the abrupt change in subject. "We've stayed together, even during the worst of the fighting."

"Good, good," Emperor Marius said. "It's always good to have someone to lean on when the shit hits the fan. On Earth, the shit hits the fan every day."

He looked down at his shaking hands. "I don't know how long I can hold everything together, Roman," he admitted. "The Federation was coming apart at the seams even before the Outsiders launched their invasion. Now...we may win the war, but lose everything."

Roman frowned. "We could consider offering them terms," he suggested. "Maybe grant them automatic stage-three or stage-four status, as Federation member worlds..."

"That would be taken as a sign of weakness," Emperor Marius said. His hands shook so badly he had to put the cup down before he spilled it. "We cannot afford anything other than a complete victory, Roman. The Federation would shatter otherwise."

"The Federation might shatter anyway," Roman pointed out.

"Damned if we do, damned if we don't," Emperor Marius said. "I fought hard to keep Admiral Justinian from taking power or tearing the Federation in half. Now, I'm damned if I will let the Outsiders do the same."

The emperor paused. "What's the current status of Fifth Fleet?"

Roman hesitated, gathering his thoughts. "I have six battle squadrons in reasonable fighting trim," he said, recalling the days they'd struggled to repair and rearm the ships. He'd had nightmares about the Outsiders launching a second attack before he was ready to meet them. "I've also got three hundred smaller ships; the only real weakness, sir, is in starfighters. We took heavy losses during the later stages of the battle."

"They always take the brunt of it," Emperor Marius grunted. "But then, I suppose you learned that on *Enterprise*."

Roman nodded. Technically, *Enterprise* had been his first command, after everyone above him in the chain of command had been killed. He was certainly entitled to wear a star representing *Enterprise* on his collar, as an independent command. But the fleet carrier's design had been more than a little impractical and she'd been retired from service shortly after the coup. Part of Roman still regretted losing the chance to return to her command chair.

"They do," he said. Starfighter pilots were often jerks, but their odds of survival were quite poor. It was hard to blame them when a single mistake might lead to their instant death. "I was planning to draw fighters from the fortresses, if necessary."

"Probably a good idea," Marius said. He reached into his pocket and produced a secure chip, which he plugged into the desktop terminal. "I have been working on operational plans."

He smiled, humorlessly, as a starchart appeared in front of them. "We still don't know the location of any major worlds or bases beyond the Rim," he said. "Their alien allies, if the autopsies are to be believed, come from a world not too different from Earth. We'll find it eventually, I believe. Until then, there is only one world deserving of our attention. Nova Athena."

Roman wasn't surprised. Most of the Outsider-occupied worlds were unlikely to be able to stand off a single destroyer, let alone Fifth Fleet. They could be left to wither on the vine, at least until the major worlds had been occupied and the enemy fleet destroyed. But there *were* a handful of worlds that helped provide war materials for the enemy forces. Nova Athena was top of the list.

"One of their leaders comes from there," Emperor Marius added. "How long was she sitting in the Senate on Earth, absorbing information and planning her moves against us?"

He went on before Roman could say a word. "Going after Nova Athena helps solve several problems at once," he said. "It forces the enemy back on the defensive, it cripples some of their industry, it may provide clues we can follow to locate their other bases...and it proves their leadership cannot defend their homeworld. If they stand and fight, Roman, we will crush them. But if they run, they look like cowards."

Roman nodded. Boston had received envoys from a dozen worlds in the sector, worlds that had been occupied by the Outsiders. The planetary governments were looking to find a way to switch sides that didn't result in them being butchered by one side or the other. He had been quite happy to listen to them, knowing that local support might make the reconquest easy. And if Nova Athena were to be taken, the trickle of surrenders might become a flood.

"It would work," Roman said. "Unless they have more ships on the defensive than we believe."

"They would have sent them to Boston, if they had them," Emperor Marius said, flatly. He leaned forward, jabbing a finger at one of the stars. "They knew they needed the biggest hammer they could muster to take you on."

"We should still be careful," Roman said.

"We will be," Emperor Marius assured him.

The emperor keyed a switch. "The interesting fact about Nova Athena is that the system has absolutely no Asimov Points," he said. "Or, at least, none we've managed to detect. It's possible the locals didn't bother to do more than a basic survey–given the political situation, they might not have *wanted* to locate any Asimov Points."

Roman didn't blame them. Nova Athena might have evaded most of the funding options for new colonies, but–by Federation Law–Asimov Points belonged to the Federation. If they'd located one, they would have had to surrender a great deal of political power to the Grand Senate, which wouldn't have hesitated to use it ruthlessly until Nova Athena had been turned into yet another dependency. As it was, they'd managed to remain largely off the sensor display until they'd established themselves solidly. The Grand Senate might have intended to take over, but doing it legally would be a major problem.

Or would have been a major problem, Roman thought. Now, the precise post-war status of Nova Athena would depend on the man sitting across from him, sipping tea and looking thoroughly unwell. *They're not going to have an easy time of it.*

"We will proceed through Point Delta, then split the fleet into two formations," Emperor Marius continued. "You will take your battle squadrons to Salam, whereupon you will cross the gulf of interstellar space and enter the Nova Athena System. I will take my ships to Yankee and make the crossing from there. This will not only give us a chance to sweep two successive Asimov Chains clear of enemy presence, but make it harder for them to predict our course."

"They would probably suspect our target in any case," Roman said, slowly. It struck him as too complex a plan to be practical. "Shouldn't we operate as one unit, sir, and reduce the risk of having both fleets defeated separately?"

There was a flicker of anger on the emperor's face, which faded almost as quickly as it had come. "The scouts report minimal enemy presence in all of the systems," Emperor Marius said. "We will have the option of smashing those ships and minor fortifications without risking losses to ourselves, while gaining control of both chains, which would allow us to threaten a number of different worlds. They would not be *sure* we intended to head for Nova Athena...and, in any case, we would be blocking any attempt to move ships back from the occupied worlds to our target."

That was true, Roman thought, as he studied the starchart. The Asimov Chains ran through a number of vital systems, systems the Outsiders had probably designated as nodal systems for rapid reinforcement of any threatened planet. There was no way to be *sure* how many starships they had on hand for immediate deployment, but he had to admit that they wouldn't be able to get them to Nova Athena without punching through one or both of the onrushing fleets.

But it still struck him as an alarmingly complex plan.

"I have brought additional freighters crammed with supplies," Emperor Marius added, as he clicked off the display. "Your fleet train is ready to move?"

"Always," Roman said. He'd learned that precaution during the advance on Admiral Justinian that had ended the Justinian War. "They're on three hours notice to move."

"Then we will launch the offensive in one day," Emperor Marius said. "Your remaining ships and fortresses should be capable of holding Boston."

"I hope so," Roman said. He'd had replacement fortresses towed from the other Asimov Points to Point Delta, but there had been no time to replace the mines and automated weapons platforms that had been destroyed in the battle. The supplies of prefabricated platforms had been tapped out. "In any case, they would need to smash the fortresses covering all of the Asimov Points to secure the system."

"All war is risk," Emperor Marius said. He sighed. "I have to meet with people on Boston, Roman, or I would have stayed here longer."

"I understand," Roman said. Once, it would have been a pleasure to host his mentor. Now, he wasn't so sure. "Are you going to meet with the planetary representatives?"

"We'll see what they have to say for themselves," Emperor Marius growled. He made to rise to his feet, then stopped. "There is one other matter we have to discuss."

Roman shivered. There was something in the way Emperor Marius had said it that sent chills down his spine. "Yes, sir?"

"The prisoners," Emperor Marius said. "I want them transferred to the POW transports and shipped back to Mars. They may be able to tell us things we need to know."

"I would prefer to keep them here," Roman said, carefully. He'd heard rumors about what happened on Mars during the Grand Senate's tenure. The prisoners were lucky if they were *only* violated by mind-probes, their secrets ripped out of their brains one by one. "They're being held under standard POW conventions..."

"And *I* would like you to send them to Mars," Emperor Marius snapped. The anger was back, stronger this time. "They are not legitimate prisoners of war, Roman."

"I took them under the standard conventions," Roman said. He reminded himself that he'd faced death bravely as a young officer and forced himself to meet his mentor's bloodshot eyes. "Their ultimate disposition can wait until the end of the war."

Emperor Marius glowered at him. "Are you defying me?"

"They have thousands of our people held prisoner," Roman said. The envoys had made that clear, to the point of providing evidence that the POWs were alive and reasonably happy. "I don't think we should mistreat their prisoners, sir, or our people will be mistreated in turn."

Roman paused. "And every one of them who might know something useful has a security implant," he added. "I don't think we can get anything out of their heads, sir. The implants would kill them if they detected any form of enhanced interrogation. None of them are talking freely."

"There are ways around those implants," Emperor Marius growled. "Roman..."

"We shouldn't take the risk," Roman pleaded. "Sir, we *will* locate their bases and we *will* destroy them, but we don't have to become monsters in the process. The survey ships will find one of their worlds or we'll take a navigational database intact or we'll find *something* we can use as a guide..."

Marius glared at him. Roman forced himself to hold his eyes.

"I hope you're right," Marius snapped, finally. "But I think you're wrong. The prisoners will stay here."

The emperor rose, then marched towards the hatch and stopped. "I will be hosting a dinner tonight for the commanding officers," he added. "You will, of course, attend. Your girlfriend is also invited."

The hatch hissed open. Emperor Marius stepped through. The hatch hissed closed behind him.

Roman let out a long shuddering breath as he rose on suddenly weak legs. There was sweat trickling down the back of his neck. He hadn't felt so close to death since his first real taste of combat, on *Enterprise.* And yet, Marius Drake was his mentor, even a friend. There seemed no reason to be so scared...

Two years. Two years of absolute power. Had that been enough to change the man he'd known into a growling tyrant? He'd never heard Marius Drake show any traces of self-pity before, even when he'd been deprived of command unjustly. Operation Retribution would have succeeded brilliantly if Admiral Drake had been in command, but the Grand Senate hadn't trusted him. It hadn't been the brightest idea. He'd been loyal to them right up until the moment they'd tried to kill him.

And his hands were shaking, Roman thought. *What did that mean?*

His terminal bleeped. "Admiral Garibaldi, this is Professor Kratman," a voice said. "I would like a moment to talk to you, if that is acceptable."

"Sure," Roman said, shakily. For once, he had relatively little to do. He'd cleared as much of his schedule as possible to meet his former mentor, while his staff could handle most of the issues facing the fleet. "Give me twenty minutes, then come find my stateroom."

He clicked off the starchart–the emperor had forgotten to take his datachip with him–and then stepped into the washroom. His face was pale, while sweat prickled on his forehead and his uniform was stained. Cursing under his breath, he stripped, showered and dumped the uniform in the wash basket, then hastily donned a spare one. He wasn't sure he wanted to meet his former tutor, not after seeing how badly Marius Drake had changed, but he suspected there was no choice. Besides, maybe Kratman knew what was wrong.

"Elf," he said, keying a switch. He kept his voice briskly formal, even though she was his lover. They tried hard to keep it professional outside their quarters. "We've been invited to dinner tonight, but I need to talk to you first. Come to my stateroom in one hour."

And maybe you will know what's wrong, he thought, grimly. *And how best to fix it.*

Chapter Thirty-Six

The old saying about even paranoids having enemies is, unfortunately, accurate. However, paranoia tends to lead to seeing enemies even in the most unlikely of places.
-The Federation Navy in Retrospect, 4199

Boston, 4101

"It's good to see you again, Roman," Professor Kratman said. "It's been quite some time."

"It has," Roman agreed, studying his former tutor closely. He looked little different from Roman's recollections; short white hair, an angular face and sharp blue eyes. The suit he wore was very unmilitary, but he hadn't been a formal naval officer for years. "And time has been kind to you."

Kratman didn't mince words. "You saw the emperor," he said. It wasn't a question. "What did you make of him?"

Roman scowled. "What is *wrong* with him?"

"Marius Drake is a military commander," Kratman said. "A very good military commander."

"I didn't know that was in dispute," Roman said, tartly.

"A military has a relatively simple structure," Kratman explained. "Orders are issued from the top to lower ranks, who carry out their orders. Certain officers have a great deal of leeway in *how* they carry out their orders, others have very little freedom of operation. The point is that everyone knows where they stand at all times."

Roman wasn't sure that was entirely true, but held his peace.

"The civilian universe is a very different beast," Kratman continued. "Instead of–pardon the term–an absolute dictatorship, lesser ranks have priorities of their own that might not jibe with upper ranks. A corporation will do what is best for itself, rather than the Federation as a whole; a person will act in his own best interests, rather than any mythical greater good. You understand the problem?"

"I think so," Roman said, slowly.

"The Grand Senators had patronage networks that stretched from the very heights of society to the lowest depths," Kratman said. "They could and did get things done; they'd designed a social structure that supported their primacy. The emperor, by contrast, does not have any support network outside the military. His ability to make his will felt is dependent on deadly force because he has few other tools at his disposal."

Roman met his eyes. "What does this mean?"

"A military unit is well understood," Kratman said. "But a civilian structure is often less organized. The emperor has been trying to treat the Federation's economic system like a military unit, one that can be ordered about at will."

Kratman paused. "The system was broken before the coup," he said, "but there has been no time to make reforms. Instead, we have been straining every muscle to produce as much war material as possible, which has been causing some structures to simply break down. Workers are going on strike because they can't handle it any longer, we're suffering disasters because infrastructures have broken under the strain... and so on, and so on. Worst of all, perhaps, the bureaucracy has proven resistant to attempts to curb its power."

"And so the emperor is under a great deal of stress," Roman mused.

"Worse than that," Kratman said. "He's become alarmingly dependent on painkillers, I believe, and quite possibly alcohol. I have been monitoring his behavior as closely as possible over the last two months; he's definitely in a downward spiral. Mood swings, sudden fits of anger...it all fits a very dangerous pattern."

Roman bit down the urge to say something that would have earned him a record number of demerits, back at the Academy.

"His obsession with beating the Outsiders has blinded him to some of the dangers," Kratman warned. "Others, I believe, he has simply dismissed, intending to handle them after the war is won. For one thing, he has been creating new security forces on Earth. Those forces, as such forces tend to do, have started to mutate out of control. Brutal repression has become the order of the day."

"I don't believe it," Roman said. But he'd *seen* the change in the emperor. The man he'd respected and admired had become a warped shadow of his former self. "I don't *want* to believe it."

"Neither do I," Kratman said. "And I took my life into my hands to come talk to you."

Roman's eyes narrowed. "It can't be that bad..."

"It is," Kratman said. "Do you know how many journalists have been disappeared in the two months before I left Earth?"

"...No," Roman said. "The Marius Drake I knew wouldn't have allowed people to be snatched off the streets and taken away."

"I doubt he knows," Kratman said. He cleared his throat. "There are just too many demands on his time, Roman. He simply cannot handle everything put in front of him. I suspect General Thorne ordered the journalists imprisoned, either for questioning the official line or simply because he wanted to establish himself as a power. The old Blackshirts will have nothing on a force that acts completely without restraint."

Roman shivered. "And what do you want *me* to do, if you came here at great personal risk?"

"Talk to him," Kratman said. "I believe he will listen to you, if no one else. But if not...you might want to start thinking about contingency plans..."

"To take power myself?" Roman snapped. Cold anger flashed through his mind. "You want me to betray the man who put me here?"

"If necessary," Kratman said.

"No," Roman said. He forced himself to calm down. "I am damned if I will betray him."

"You have to consider the good of the Federation," Kratman said. "What will happen when something *big* breaks? Or an uprising occurs on Earth itself? Or the economy, what's left of it, collapses into nothingness? We are already on the brink, Roman, of reaching the point of no return. There will be nothing left of the Federation to save!

"We need this war to end," he insisted. "Even if we have to admit the Outsiders might have a point, even if we have to grant them concessions, we need the war to end. The Federation simply cannot support it any longer."

Kratman took a breath. "We have reached the end of the line."

Roman forced himself to think calmly, logically. He had more sympathy with the Outsiders than he cared to admit, even before he'd heard about the new security forces. He'd grown up on an asteroid, after all, and he knew how intrusive the Federation could be. There was definitely something to be said for pruning the bureaucracy as far back as possible. And yet he'd thought Marius Drake would handle it.

But he can't prune the bureaucrats if he needs them at the same time, Roman thought. *And if they resist being pruned, he will need to concentrate on dealing with them...and he can't, because he has so much else to do.*

But the thought of turning against his mentor was horrific. Admiral Drake had picked him out for rapid advancement, supported his career, even taken advantage of his determination to do the right thing. The thought of betraying the emperor... Roman shook his head, reluctant to take that step. He was no Grand Senate lackey, ready to betray in exchange for a small price; he was a Federation Navy officer, loyal to his superior. And, a day ago, he would have said his superior was deserving of such loyalty.

He looked down at his hands, recalling–to his horror–how the emperor's hands had twitched and shaken. That was *not* a good sign. He'd seen drug addicts before, on Boskone and several other shore leave hubs, and they'd barely been able to function. It started small, Elf had told him, but the addict rapidly needed more and more drugs just to hit the high. Or, perhaps, to avoid the pain. Indeed, if someone was dependent on painkillers, their body would produce pains to encourage them to take the drugs.

"I don't know," Roman said.

The thought was maddening. He knew how to be decisive in combat, when a moment's hesitation could mean the difference between life and death, but he didn't know how to turn against his mentor. And how could he? Emperor Marius needed help and support, not a knife in the back. Part of him wanted to call the Marines and have Professor Kratman thrown into the brig. The rest of him feared the professor might have a point.

Kratman rose to his feet. "I suggest you think about it," he said. "But you should know, from my lectures if nothing else, that there are few easy choices in politics."

"Fuck off," Roman said.

Kratman nodded, then stepped through the hatch.

ꕤ

Dinner with the emperor was far worse than Roman had dared fear. He'd never liked formal dining affairs at the best of times, but some of the officers the emperor had brought with him were worryingly sycophantic. They seemed to have decided that Roman was high in the Emperor's favor, so they spent far too much of their time kissing his ass. After the third captain had congratulated him on his great victory, in flowery tones that were normally reserved for Officer Readiness Reports, Roman was ready to kill the next one who dared try to flatter him.

No wonder the emperor is having problems, he thought, as the stewards served the first course. *If he has people flattering him every day, he won't know what to believe.*

He gripped Elf's hand under the table, then ate, watching the emperor all the time. There were more worrying signs, now he knew to look for them. The emperor was drinking heavily...and not just expensive wines. Someone–as always–had set up a still on *Thunderbird* and the emperor had been helping himself to their produce. Roman made a mental note to have a word with the ship's commanding officer, then dismissed the thought as futile. Captain Abrams didn't look like the sort of man who would dare defy the emperor.

Blake Raistlin had bragged, once, of dinners his family had held for their fellow Grand Senators. Roman had felt sick when he'd explained that half the food was wasted, wondering why *anyone* would indulge themselves so badly. He'd been raised to waste nothing, after all. But now, he thought he understood. It wasn't about the food, it was a display of status, of demonstrating that they could afford to buy and waste the finest foodstuffs from all over the Federation. The emperor–or his protocol staff–were doing the same.

He felt sick at heart as the fifth course was served. Marius Drake had once eaten the same rations as his men, the same meals in the Wardroom as were served in the Mess. Now, he was stuffing himself with delicacies, along with his subordinates. And drinking so much Roman was mildly surprised he hadn't fallen face-first into his plate. It wasn't a good sign either.

By the time the dinner finally came to an end, Roman just wanted to get away.

"Check the shuttle for bugs," he ordered, once they had disengaged from *Thunderbird.* He'd decided to fly the craft himself, rather than risk having a third pair of ears in the shuttle. Elf had raised her eyebrows when he'd asked her to bring her security kit with her, but she'd done as she was told. "See if we're safe to talk here."

"It looks safe," Elf said, after sweeping the shuttle. "I can set up a jammer too, if you want."

Roman shrugged. The jammer would probably disrupt the shuttle's control systems too.

"You saw the emperor," he said. "What did you make of him?"

"Someone on the edge," Elf said. "Why?"

"He's not the man he used to be," Roman said. He'd already told her about his meeting with the emperor, then Professor Kratman. The professor himself had not been in evidence at the dinner, somewhat to Roman's surprise. It might have been a long time since Kratman had served as a commanding officer, but he was still permitted entry to the wardroom. "And I don't know what to do."

He sighed. Federation Navy regulations admitted of only one way to remove a commanding officer who was showing signs of instability. The ship's doctor had to conduct an exam, then–if he or she thought the captain was not in a fit state to command–relieve him of duty, at least until higher authority had a chance to take a look at him. It was rarely used in practice, Roman knew; there had to be very strong reasons for believing the captain unfit, as the Admiralty frowned on anything that weakened the captain's authority over his ship.

And there were no grounds for removing an admiral–or an emperor–at all.

He considered the problem as he guided the shuttle back to *Valiant*. The standard procedure if there were grounds for concern was to send a message to Earth, detailing the complaint and requesting permission to relieve the commanding officer. Offhand, Roman couldn't recall if *any* of those complaints had been heeded. The Admiralty might have taken a dim view of subordinates relieving captains, but they positively *hated* the idea of anyone questioning admirals. In this case, the message would go to Emperor Marius or whoever he'd put in command of the Admiralty on Earth. There was no chance he'd receive permission to do anything more than stand in front of a Board of Inquiry.

The only other way to handle the problem was to call a Captain's Board. If there was no way to contact the Admiralty–which had happened, more than once, during the Inheritance Wars–the senior captains could pass judgement on their superior. But careers had been wrecked through participating in such a meeting, even if the admiral had been cleared. The Admiralty had always taken a dim view of such proceedings, technically legal or not.

Elf nudged him. "I think you'd be better off trying to counsel him," she said. "This might be a holiday for him."

"We're splitting up tomorrow," Roman reminded her. He wondered, suddenly, if the idea of splitting the fleet had been the emperor's–or had it come from one of his subordinates? Had someone wanted to minimise Roman's influence over the emperor? "There won't be time to talk to him."

He docked the shuttle at the hatch, then passed through the security scan and walked into the ship. A Midshipman manning the desk jumped, then hastily got to his feet and saluted. Roman concealed his amusement–he'd had boring duties too, when he'd been a midshipman–and returned the salute. The young man's hand twitched towards his communicator, ready to call the captain and inform him that the admiral had returned, before he caught himself. Roman nodded politely to him, then stepped through the hatch. It was technically against regulations for anyone to report the admiral's progress, but one sign of a happy ship was officers willing to skirt that regulation for a decent commander.

They said nothing else until they were in his cabin. Elf ran another security sweep as Roman poured them both glasses of water, then swallowed a sober-up pill. The effects, as always, left him feeling a little queasy, but sober. He'd drunk more than he cared to admit at the dinner.

Better to call it a feast, he thought, morbidly.

"Interesting," Elf said. "I found two bugs; audio and visual."

Roman felt cold ice running down the back of his neck. "Where?"

Elf pointed towards the light fitting. "Not a good place to hide them," she noted, dispassionately. "Anyone with real experience of warships would know better than to put them somewhere they could interfere with the datanodes. And they definitely weren't there yesterday."

Roman watched as she removed both of the bugs, then glanced around to see what the bugs would have seen. One of them would have monitored the bed; the other would have monitored his desk, although he rarely worked in the cabin. He felt a sudden flush as he realized the bugs would have recorded their nightly activities, then a wave of anger so strong it shocked him. Who would dare to bug his quarters?

"Amateurs," Elf said. She dropped the remains of the bugs into a secure box, then stuck it in her uniform jacket. "There's a reason Marines tend to do surveillance and counter-surveillance duties onboard ship. These bugs would have triggered the alarms as soon as they started to signal, I think. They should have stuck them somewhere else."

"But who?" Roman asked. "And why?"

"Who? Probably the emperor's security staff," Elf said. Only someone who knew her well would have heard the anger in her voice. "And why? They may have wanted to keep an eye on you. I'll have your office swept too, I think. Routine bug sweeps are part of our work, in any case. Damned fools didn't even know it."

Roman nodded. The Outsiders had shown themselves to be quite inventive when it came to sneaking bugs onto starships. A handful of subverted officers had done more damage than a thousand long-range sensor probes. But they'd all been caught, in the end; he'd just kept the sweeps going as a matter of routine. Emperor Marius would have known it, too. Oddly, it was the one hopeful sign. Whoever had placed the bugs hadn't discussed it with the emperor first.

"Bastards," he snarled. He had hoped to spend the night in bed with her. Instead, they would have to talk and plan instead of sleeping together. "What the hell do we do now?"

"You try to talk to the emperor," Elf said. She paused. "It's all you can do, for the moment."

"Very well," Roman said. Kratman had been right. Some of the emperor's subordinates were acting without his permission, but using his authority. God alone knew where it would end. "But I don't know what else to do."

"Consider the worst case first," Elf advised. She tapped the bed, firmly. "But do it tomorrow morning. You're in no fit state to think and plan now."

Chapter Thirty-Seven

The only way to make a complex plan work is to break it down to as many simple pieces as possible.
-The Federation Navy in Retrospect, 4199

Spinner/Nova Athena, 4101

"Captain," Lieutenant Regis said. "I'm picking up activity near the Asimov Point."

Captain Teresa Robbins nodded, unsurprised. The Asimov Point led directly into the Boston System, where the ill-fated offensive had met its doom. She'd expected to see the Federation Navy sooner or later; indeed, she was surprised it had taken so long.

"Move us away," she ordered. "Send an emergency signal to the platforms, then start downloading data into the drones. We may need to launch them soon."

"Aye, Captain," Regis said.

Teresa smiled, then turned her attention to the display. There was nothing unconventional about the assault on the Asimov Point; the Federation Navy had deployed the standard assault package of missile pods, small craft and gunboats, sweeping their way ruthlessly through the layers of mines placed around the Asimov Point. Hundreds of missiles died, but none of the smaller craft were harmed. Teresa cursed under her breath, yet she'd known–without fixed or mobile defenses–it was only a matter of time before the Asimov Point fell to an unimaginative attack.

Pity we didn't have time to set up fortresses of our own, she thought. There had been plans to convert asteroids into fortresses, but the need to keep moving had put all such plans on the backburner. *We might have been able to give them a very nasty surprise before they won.*

The last of the mines flashed and died, leaving space clear. Moments later, the first flight of heavy cruisers appeared, sensors probing local space for possible threats. Teresa wished, bitterly, that she'd *had* something that could be used against them, but there was nothing. Instead, all she could do was watch as the heavy cruisers moved off the point, only to be followed by what looked like an endless tidal wave of superdreadnaughts and smaller ships. There was enough firepower entering the system, she saw, to crush almost any system between them and her homeworld. For the first time, she began to consider the possibility of defeat.

"Keep moving us back," she ordered, as the Federation ships spread out. "And then send a signal to the platforms. The enemy is on its way."

ꕥ

"Local space is clear, Admiral," Lieutenant Thompson reported. "The enemy didn't bother to try to cover the mines."

Pity, Roman thought, although he wasn't surprised. Given the disparity in firepower, any attempt to cover the mines could only have one outcome–and the Outsiders knew it as well as himself. *They'd save their strength for the final battle.*

"Raise the emperor," he ordered. It felt strange to hold tactical command, but know there was a superior officer in a nearby ship. He wasn't even sure why Emperor Marius had allowed him to retain command, unless it was a gesture of favor. "Inform him that we are ready to proceed with phase two."

He took a moment to survey the display. The Spinner System had been classed as useless until two new Asimov Points had been discovered, both leading further into the Rim. There were no gas giants and only one reasonably-sized world, a rocky planet that bore more resemblance to Mars than Earth. It was inhabited by a religious sect that wanted to keep itself to itself and took no interest in the affairs of the Federation. Given how useless their homeworld was, the Grand Senate hadn't bothered to press the issue. Roman found it hard to blame them.

The Outsiders hadn't done much, either. There were a handful of radio sources near the Asimov Points, but nothing else. They hadn't attempted to mine the asteroids, set up industrial nodes or anything else that might have benefited the system in the long run. But then, there had been no point. Spinner was simply too close to the front to be given anything, save for a handful of limited defenses.

"Launch two probes towards the planet," Roman ordered. "We may as well..."

"Signal from *Thunderbird*," Lieutenant Thompson interrupted. "The emperor is ordering you to proceed with phase two."

Roman nodded. He didn't like the idea of splitting the fleet, even if there was something to be said for preserving his formation from the sycophants infesting the other formation. The amount of crawling they'd done as he fought to get the fleet ready for departure had been staggering. Why couldn't the emperor have picked crawlers who were actually *competent*?

"Signal the fleet," Roman ordered. "Phase two begins...*now*."

ꙮ

"They're splitting their fleet," Lieutenant Regis said.

"It looks that way," Teresa said. Five battle squadrons were heading towards Point Beta, while six more were proceeding towards Point Charlie. Each of them had more than enough firepower to blow through anything they were likely to encounter in the nearest systems. "Send an update to the platforms, then bring us about and set course for Point Charlie."

"Aye, Captain," Lieutenant Higgins said. He paused. "Where do you think they're going?"

Teresa felt her lips thin. Informality was not something she encouraged on her command deck, even when the crew members were largely reservists from merchant ships.

"I think they're heading for the Rim," she said. There were several possible targets, some more likely than others. "Right now, they can go pretty much wherever they want to go."

ꙮ

Marius settled back in his command chair as Task Force 5.2 started its long trek towards Asimov Point Beta. There was nothing in the system worth his attention, so he pulled up the files and started to read through the survey reports from the probes

Admiral Garibaldi had sent out after the Battle of Boston. The first serious problem would come when his ships punched their way into the Von Doom System. There were a handful of captured fortresses there, according to the scouts.

He pushed his concerns aside as he relaxed. *This*–command of a fleet, where everyone knew their place and did as they were told–was what he was born to do. There were no pettifogging bureaucrats trying to tell him what to do, no whiners coming up with nothing but excuses; hell, the political commissioners the Grand Senate had appointed were gone too. He could sit back and issue orders, in the certain knowledge they would be obeyed. It was nothing like being emperor on Earth.

"Sir," Commander Ginny Lewis said, breaking into his thoughts. "Our drones are reporting a complete absence of defenses at Point Beta."

"Lucky for us," Marius said. He smiled again, brightly. There had been no defenses in the Spinner System prior to the war and the Outsiders, it seemed, hadn't had time to do more than fortify Point Alpha. "Launch a flight of sensor probes, just in case, then detail half of them to head through Point Beta."

Commander Lewis frowned. "Wouldn't that reveal our presence?"

"They are unlikely to be in any doubt of our presence," Marius pointed out. There had been no starships detected within the system, but he would have been astonished if there wasn't a cloaked picket somewhere nearby, watching their every move. As long as her commander was careful, there was no real chance of being detected. "And besides, we want them to know we're coming. It might encourage them to surrender."

He rubbed his hands together with glee as he settled back in his chair. This was *precisely* what he'd wanted. Why the hell hadn't he stuck someone else in the emperor's chair on Earth and retained command of a fleet for himself? But who could he have trusted with so much power? The only people he thought wouldn't be corrupted by it were too young or too innocent...like Garibaldi.

The thought made him sigh. Garibaldi was young...too young, really, for his post. But he'd done well...and besides, there were few other candidates with the skill he actually trusted. And yet, he was naive in some ways, despite his girlfriend's constant presence. Too naive, perhaps...

Marius understood–*God,* he understood–why someone would want to treat POWs in line with the conventions, even if they weren't precisely legal combatants. It was the decent thing to do. But sentiment had no place in a war. They couldn't afford to let their feelings distract them from finding the most effective way to smash the enemy flat, whatever the cost. He would arrange for the POWs to be treated well, or as well as possible, but he wouldn't shrink from doing whatever had to be done to get intelligence out of their heads. The sooner they knew where to find the Outsider bases, the better...

And there was a voice. "Emperor...*Emperor*?"

Marius jerked upwards. Had he fallen asleep on the command deck? Midshipmen had been busted all the way down to the bottom for falling asleep on duty, if their commanding officer hadn't taken the semi-legal step of sending them to box with the

Marines. And his head was throbbing and...

He paused, confused. When had his head started to hurt?

"I'm calling the doctor," the woman's voice said. It took Marius a moment to remember she was Commander Lewis. "I..."

"Don't," Marius croaked. He forced himself to sit upright, then reached for the pills he'd stuffed in his uniform pouch. They were alone, at least. Thank heaven for small mercies. "Don't mention a word to anyone."

"But sir..."

"I said *don't mention a word to anyone,*" Marius roared. The mere effort of shouting left him badly drained. It was all he could do to swallow two pills, without slumping back in his chair. The compartment seemed dimmer, somehow. "There's nothing they can do for me."

Commander Lewis looked pale, but determined. "What...what can I do to help?"

Marius could think of one answer to that–he'd felt much better since Tiffany had made love to him–but refused to say it out loud. "Just say nothing about it, to anyone," he said. If he was lucky, no one else would ever know about the attack. "I mean it. Don't say a word."

He forced himself to stand, cursing his wobbly legs. Normally, any officer who'd suffered...whatever the hell it was he'd suffered...would be relieved of duty by the ship's doctor. Part of Marius would even have welcomed it. But who could relieve an emperor?

"I can help you to your stateroom," Commander Lewis offered. "I..."

"Stay here and continue to monitor Point Beta," Marius ordered. Perhaps it *had* been a mistake to split the fleet, after all. Garibaldi could have assumed command when they launched the next assault through Point Beta. "Call me when we are ten minutes away from the Asimov Point."

He sighed as he forced his tired brain to think. Captain Watson was a solid, unimaginative officer. Marius had reviewed all of the commanding officers assigned to Home Fleet, looking for signs they wouldn't be tempted to do anything stupid. Watson could handle the assault, if necessary, but he couldn't make long-term decisions. Besides, some of the other commanders would object to taking orders from a mere captain.

You picked them, a mocking voice said. It took him a moment to realize that he was imagining it. *You wanted men who wouldn't try to overthrow you.*

"Inform Captain Watson that...that I will be testing his abilities by allowing him tactical command of the offensive," he said. It was the only way he could allow someone else to hold command, without admitting his weakness. "There will be opportunities for the other commanders later."

He nodded to her, then stumbled out of the hatch and into his stateroom. It was larger than he remembered–but then, the last time he'd commanded a fleet, Tiffany had accompanied him. Now, he was alone. He staggered, then somehow managed to remain upright until he reached the bed. It was all he could do to lie down and close his eyes.

Not good part of his mind noted. Falling asleep on the command deck was a worrying sign at the best of times, let alone in the midst of a war. *Not good at all.*

ꙮ

Nova Athena, Charlie had discovered, was what all Outsider worlds wanted to be. Her limited independence from the Federation had allowed her to develop a thriving and innovative economy, which–thanks to various embargos by the Federation–had benefited the black market far more than anyone else. The only downside was the lack of Asimov Points, which automatically added an extra tariff to shipping in and out of the system. But the locals didn't care. It just gave them an extra barrier between themselves and the Grand Senate.

"They split their fleet," Commander Johan said. "Why?"

"To keep us in doubt," Charlie said. The tactic was obvious, all the more so as there was only one target that required so much firepower to squash. "They're coming here."

The reports were clear enough, even though they were out of date by several days. Both fleets were moving, slowly and patiently, through Asimov Point Chains, advancing steadily towards systems that were close to Nova Athena, in realspace. They would cross realspace then, Charlie was sure, and attack with maximum force. With a little effort, they could even coordinate their forces to launch a joint attack.

But they might not need to launch a joint attack, he thought. Without an Asimov Point to hold, Nova Athena could be attacked from almost any direction. *They could tear apart much of the infrastructure without ever having to engage the defenses.*

"You can't be sure," Commander Johan said.

Charlie smirked. "I bet you the last we'll see of those fleets, until they arrive here, will be in Salam and Yankee, respectively. They're the closest locations to Nova Athena, in realspace."

He shook his head. There was little humor in this situation, nothing to smile about. Eleven battle squadrons would smash the planetary defenses, even if they did take losses–and the system would be doomed. He knew better than to expect any mercy. The Federation would land troops and keep the planet firmly under control, at least until the end of the war. And her infrastructure would be pressed into service, supplying the Federation's war machine.

"Start the evacuation plan," Charlie ordered. There had been no attempt to expand the industries in the system–they'd known it was a prime target–but they hadn't evacuated the workforce, not when the workers had been reluctant to go. There was no choice now. "I want as many people as possible out of the system by the time the shit hits the fan."

"There will be protests," Johan said, carefully. "Wives and families..."

"I know," Charlie said. There were nowhere near enough transports in the system to take the families, along with the workers. They would have to be put on the backburner, for the moment, despite the risk of the Federation taking them hostage. "Deal with it. We cannot risk allowing people who actually know how to think falling into enemy hands."

He sighed. The Federation had used rote learning, more and more, as its educational infrastructure worsened. It had seemed easier to compensate rather than to try to fix the problem at the source. But Nova Athena had managed to produce hundreds of talented and innovative workers who were capable of actually understanding what they were doing and even improving it. They could not be allowed to fall into enemy hands.

"I'll do my best," Johan said, finally. "And the defense plans?"

Charlie nodded. The only hope was a defense of Nova Athena itself, even though it meant the remainder of the system would be left exposed. Some facilities would have to be destroyed, he knew; others would, hopefully, not draw fire, if only because the Federation would want them for itself. But they would have to be destroyed if the system fell, he knew...

"We'll have to defend the planet," he said. "There's nothing else to do."

ꕥ

Under other circumstances, Uzi would have admired how Nova Athena was responding to an imminent attack. Normally, civilians panicked, while uniformed paper-pushers weren't too far behind. There were riots in the streets, upswings in petty crimes and plenty of conspicuous consumption. Instead, the workforce was being peacefully evacuated, while the remainder of the population was buying guns and settling in for a long insurgency. It wouldn't do more than smash up the planet, Uzi knew, but it would make them feel as though they were doing something worthwhile.

Now, though, he needed to think of a way to damage the defenses before the shit hit the fan, but he hadn't been able to find one. The Outsiders had known the dangers of chaos software before Admiral Justinian had deployed it on Earth; their computer systems were secure, when they were interlinked at all. Indeed, the system was actually designed to allow them to share data without risking contamination. It might not work so well when the battle actually started, but it was definitely making pre-battle sabotage impossible.

He gritted his teeth as he escorted another line of workers to the shuttlecraft, which would take them to the transports waiting in orbit. Part of him marveled at how much discipline the civilians were showing–he'd seen trained soldiers who showed less self-control–but he kept working away at the problem. There just wasn't any way for a single person, no matter how capable, to actually make an impression. Unless...

The plan slowly took shape in his mind. It would depend, of course, on where he was stationed by the time the attack began. The Outsiders didn't seem to know quite what to do with the space-trained troops. In their place, Uzi would have sent them elsewhere, but instead they'd been deployed to the planet. Maybe, just maybe, it would give him a chance to strike a blow for the Federation.

And if it didn't, he told himself, he could make contact with the occupation forces and return to where he belonged.

Chapter Thirty-Eight

For defense planners, FTL became a nightmare. An attack could come from any vector at all, without any hope of detection.
-The Federation Navy in Retrospect, 4199

Nova Athena, 4101

"The emperor beat us here, sir," Lieutenant Thompson said.

"I didn't know it was a race," Roman muttered, testily. It would have been *nice* to beat the emperor to Nova Athena, but the Outsiders had put up an unexpected fight in the Salam System and Roman had paused to smash their defenses before proceeding to the edge of the gravity limit and entering FTL. "Hail *Thunderbird,* Lieutenant, and inform the emperor that we are ready to proceed."

Moments later, the emperor's face appeared in the display. Roman sucked in his breath when he saw just how haggard the emperor looked; his face was pale and worn, his hair was lanky and there was an unpleasant glint in his eye. And, Roman noted almost absently, he was leaning forward so that everything beneath his collar was concealed. It didn't look like a good sign.

"Sir," Roman said, formally. "I've uploaded a tactical report to you."

"I'll review it later," Emperor Marius said. His voice was harsh, as if he were having trouble breathing. "I'm forwarding an operational plan to you, based on the intelligence from probes and scoutships. You'll notice I've given you the place of honor."

Roman studied the details as they appeared in his display. The plan was simple enough; Task Force 5.1 would advance on the planet, while Task Force 5.2 would cover their rear. And yet, there was something about it that set alarm bells off in Roman's head. Task Force 5.2–the emperor's command–would be called upon to do very little, unless the Outsiders put up a real fight. That was so unlike Marius Drake that Roman was almost tempted to call him on it. Whatever else could be said about his mentor, he was no coward, neither morally nor physically.

"I expect your career to be boosted by this," Emperor Marius continued. "Try not to fuck up."

"No, sir," Roman said, carefully.

He kept his consternation hidden as best as he could. It didn't make sense. Emperor Marius was practically giving him the credit for the operation on a silver platter. He wasn't the sort of person to steal credit–he'd certainly never tried to take credit for Operation Sword–but it would certainly look odd for him to stand aside when they were both on the scene. It was either blatant favoritism or something worse.

"Then pass the word to your ships," Emperor Marius ordered. "The operation will begin in one hour from now."

"Yes, sir," Roman said. "I look forward to it."

The emperor's face vanished. Roman looked at the empty display for a long moment, then brought up the data from the scoutships. Nova Athena hadn't changed much since the last scout mission, seven months ago; the only real change was the appearance of three battle squadrons in orbit around the planet, along with an additional number of fortresses. Clearly, the locals had long-term plans for independence that might not have taken the Outsiders into consideration. But the data attached to each of the icons positively tagged the superdreadnaughts as having escaped Boston, after the trap had been sprung. It was quite likely they'd withdraw as soon as they saw the incoming fleet.

It would be hard to blame them, Roman thought. *They'd be outgunned by my task force alone, unless they have something else up their sleeves.*

He tapped a switch, forwarding the operational plan to his ships. There was nothing particularly complex about it, thankfully; the fleets would drive on the planet, pinning the enemy starships against a target they had to defend. They might retreat–Roman was *sure* they would retreat–but that would leave the planet exposed. In that case, the fleet would pick its way through the fortresses until the planet surrendered. The only real problem with the plan, he decided, was the risk of accidentally striking the planet itself with missiles designed for ship-to-ship combat. The damage to the planet's ecology would be severe.

Serves them right for not moving into space, the old RockRat in him thought. Like most people who had been born on an asteroid, he'd never really cared for life on planets. *Planets are not safe.*

"Signal the fleet," he ordered, after checking the timer. "We will advance in forty minutes."

"Aye, sir," Lieutenant Thompson said. "Under cloak?"

Roman had wondered about that, but the emperor's plan didn't call for using the cloaks. Instead, he wanted to make a stately procession that would allow the Outsiders plenty of time to see the force bearing down on them–and, if they had any sense at all, surrender before it was too late. The only downside was that it would give the superdreadnaughts far too much time to bring up their drives and escape, but one look at the data suggested that sneaking up on them was unlikely to work. There were so many sensors orbiting Nova Athena that it was unlikely a cloaked ship could escape detection.

We could still get a lot closer without being detected, he thought. *But the emperor wants to give them plenty of time to see us coming.*

Roman shook his head. "No," he said. Given how many active and passive sensors Nova Athena had scattered around the system, it was unlikely they would last longer than an hour before they were detected. "Let them see us coming."

He settled back in his command chair and waited, impatiently, for the timer to count down to zero. In hopes of distracting himself, he reviewed the records of the emperor's march to Yankee...and swiftly discovered something else that didn't fit. The emperor had made four assaults through Asimov Points and, in all cases, had passed tactical command to one of his subordinates. There was no explanation attached to the records, but the more Roman thought about it, the more it bothered him. Marius Drake was not the sort of man to give up command, not willingly. And there was certainly no excuse for placing command in the hands of inexperienced officers, particularly ones who had been promoted more for being harmless than competent.

And what, Roman asked himself silently, *is wrong with the emperor?*

"Admiral," Lieutenant Thompson said. "The fleet is ready to depart."

"Then bring up the drives and take us in," Roman ordered. He made a bet with himself about when they would be detected, then pushed the thought aside. "Take us straight towards Nova Athena."

ꟸ

Charlie started awake as klaxons echoed through the underground complex. "Alert, alert," a robotic voice droned. "Enemy ships have been detected; I say again, enemy ships have been detected."

Cursing, Charlie reached for the terminal and clicked it on. Red icons appeared at once, well away from Nova Athena. It would be seventeen hours–at least–before they arrived in orbit, he saw; they didn't seem to be trying to hide their destination. But then, there could have been no real doubt, no matter how they feinted. The only real surprise was that the Federation fleet seemed to be operating as two separate units.

"Shut that bloody klaxon off," he snapped, hitting his wristcom. There was no point in bringing the orbital defenses to full alert, not when it would be hours before the enemy ships entered firing range. The attackers probably hoped his crews would be exhausted by the time the battle began. "And then launch a spread of probes towards the bastards!"

He forced himself to calm down, then reached for his trousers and hastily pulled them over his pants. Sleeping in his underwear was an old habit, one he'd never quite lost. He cursed again as he pulled on his jacket, knowing all too well that he should go back to bed. But he wouldn't be able to sleep, now he knew the enemy were on their way. The hammer was finally about to drop.

There was a tap at the door. "Commodore Thayne's compliments, sir," the young ensign said when he opened it, "and he has sent you coffee and ration bars."

"How very kind of him," Charlie growled, as he took the tray. Thayne had made it clear that *he* thought he should be in command of the defenses, even though he'd never seen a shot fired in anger in his life. Sending coffee and food was a clever little trick intended to keep Charlie out of the CIC for a while longer. "Tell him I'll be down in the CIC in ten minutes."

He swallowed half of the coffee in a single gulp–Nova Athena's coffee was simply too sickly-sweet for his tastes–then took a bite of the ration bar. As always, it tasted suspiciously like cardboard. Sending him a ration bar was a non-too-subtle jab at his insistence that REMFs should share at least *some* of the hardships of the men and women on the front line. He rolled his eyes at the pettiness of people who had spent the war in peaceful billets, then sobered. Nova Athena was about to become the new front line.

Dropping the cup in the basket for washing, he strode out of his office and down towards the CIC. Armed men were everywhere, guarding every door, even though he knew it was pointless. Federation Marines were not about to drop out of nowhere and attack the hidden defense complex. As far as the Federation knew, the nerve center of the defenses was on a different continent, buried under the desert. They knew nothing about the *real* CIC, concealed under a giant mountain. The locals intended to keep the base operational even if they lost control of the high orbitals and had to submit to occupation.

"General," Commodore Thayne said. He nodded towards the giant holographic display. "As you can see, we have a *situation*."

"So we do," Charlie said. He allowed his eye to wander over the consoles–and the pale-faced men and women manning them. They'd held regular drills, planning for everything from a minor raid to a major offensive, but the crews had never faced a real threat. Now, their homeworld was about to start fighting for its life. "And our status?"

Thayne looked annoyed at Charlie's apparent unconcern. "We have eleven battle squadrons bearing down on us," he said, sharply. "I think this is a major offensive."

"You don't say," Charlie murmured. He reached out and clasped the other man's shoulder before he could start spluttering in outrage. "There is no point in panicking, commodore, or in overreacting. The Federation will not be here for"–he glanced at the display, then quickly calculated the time difference–"fifteen hours, perhaps more. There is plenty of time to prepare our defenses."

Charlie walked over to the command chair and sat down. "Contact Admiral Jalil," he added. "I want him to stand by to activate Defense Plan Theta."

Thayne's mouth dropped open. "But...but that plan calls for them to retreat!"

"Yes," Charlie agreed. For once, he understood the younger man's outrage. The thought of retreating without firing more than a handful of shots was unpleasant, to say the least. "There is no choice."

Charlie shrugged. "Given the disparity in firepower, commodore, there is nothing to be gained by keeping our superdreadnaughts tied to the planet. They will merely be destroyed, allowing the enemy to rip the rest of the system apart, if they desire. But it also calls for them to fire a long-range barrage at the enemy first, before leaving the system. That will give us time to prepare blows of our own."

Thayne looked doubtful. "I hope you're right," he said. "This really doesn't look good."

"No," Charlie agreed. "It doesn't."

He tapped a switch, then looked up at the display, silently calculating vectors. "Have your Alpha Crew get some rest, commodore," he added. "The Beta and Delta Crews can man the stations for the next twelve hours."

"Aye, sir," Thayne said.

"And have them launch a spread of probes," he added. "I want to make damn sure that nothing is trying to sneak up on us."

Thayne frowned, his moustache twitching unpleasantly. "Do you think that's a possibility?"

"They're not even trying to hide their presence," Charlie pointed out. Indeed, the Federation Navy didn't seem to be using ECM, which would have made it harder to get an accurate count of their ships at such extreme range. "They may want us staring at them, commodore, which will blind us to the other threat. If, of course, there *is* another threat."

Commodore Thayne scurried off, leaving Charlie to study the display and think. The sheer lack of concern for security the Federation Navy was showing was appalling; if his subordinates had revealed so much about themselves to civilian sensors, he would have beached them on the spot. His sensor crews were absolutely positive, he saw, that he was staring at the ships that had forced their way into both the Yankee and Salam systems, then started their journey across interstellar space. Somehow, they'd managed to carry out a two-prong offensive without the timing slipping or something going badly wrong.

It would be impressive, he thought sourly, *if it wasn't aimed at me.*

His display chimed. "Councilor," he said, as Chang Li's face appeared in the display. "You should board a ship. Get the hell out of here."

"I won't leave my people," Chang Li said. "Whatever happens to them, General, I will endure it too."

Charlie wished he was in her quarters, standing next to her. He could have knocked her out, then had her shipped to the superdreadnaughts and taken out of the system. There was something to be said for a politician who was prepared to stand with her people, but Chang Li simply knew too much about the Outsider Union to be allowed to fall into Federation hands, where she would be made to talk. There were ways to get around the implants, if necessary.

"You'll be taken prisoner, then interrogated," he said. "They certainly won't *talk* with you."

"I won't let myself be taken," Chang Li insisted. "General, I won't leave. I'll kill myself if there is no other choice."

"Go," Charlie urged. "You can't do any good here."

Chang Li shook her head. "What are our chances of victory?"

"Lousy," Charlie admitted, after activating the privacy field. He doubted any of the crew manning their consoles thought there was any real chance of victory, but it would hurt morale to hear their CO say it out loud. "They have enough firepower to smash our mobile units, then punch their way through the fortresses. I've got one idea in mind, but it may not be activated in time to save us."

And they may not fall for it, he added, in the privacy of his own mind. *The Federation Navy has plenty of tricky officers now, after nine years of near-constant war.*

He met her almond eyes. "You need to go," he urged. "Please."

"I have to stay," she said. "The Outsiders will carry on without me."

"I hope you're right," Charlie said.

He ran through his options, quickly. Did he have time to send troops to seize Chang Li, then put her on a starship? Yes, he did. She'd hate him, afterwards, not without reason. He might well not survive...no, that was a joke. Given the sheer size of the fleet bearing down on Nova Athena, he was either about to die or be taken prisoner. And, as he knew too much himself, suicide would be his only reasonable option.

"Good luck, Councilor," he said.

Her face flickered out of existence. Charlie sighed inwardly, then keyed a switch. There was one unit of experienced soldiers near the capital, helping with crowd control. They would have to do the mission, then leave the system. There was no other option. Without Chang Li, the Outsider Federation might fall apart. And that would be the end of the war.

He switched channels and linked into the starfighter command. "I want you ready to deliver a long-range attack," he ordered. There were no carriers in the system, unfortunately, but the fortresses still carried their regular complement of starfighters. They'd been lucky that the pilots hadn't been redeployed to fill empty carriers, after Boston. "The gunboats are to move up in support."

"Aye, sir," the planetary CAG said. "Do you wish us to coordinate our moves with the superdreadnaughts?"

"Yes," Charlie ordered. He did his best to sound confident. "Give them a bloody nose."

He shook his head as he closed the channel. There was no way to avoid one simple fact, not when the Federation Navy had superior firepower and numbers–and, perhaps, the iron determination to end the war.

Most–perhaps all–of the pilots were about to die.

ꕥ

"The general wants us to do *what*?"

Roebuck looked stunned. Uzi, who had received more morally-questionable orders in his life than he cared to remember, felt almost as stunned as his nominal superior looked. He'd been ordered to assassinate terrorist leaders, massacre innocent prisoners, train insurgent groups so they could be squashed once they showed themselves and carry out fake attacks on Federation interests, but he'd never been ordered to stun a politician and carry her out of the firing line...

He smiled to himself as Roebuck started to issue orders, then checked the download. The superdreadnaughts would be leaving orbit in two hours, giving the troops more than enough time to secure the prisoner...no, the politician. There was something about the way those words went together that made him smile again. They could take Chang Li easily enough–they had codes that would get them into Government House–and then transport her to a shuttle. And then...

There would be plenty of opportunities for sabotage then, he was sure. And, once the Federation Navy arrived, he could go home.

Chapter Thirty-Nine

Long-range engagements are, almost always, inconclusive.
-The Federation Navy in Retrospect, 4199

Nova Athena, 4101

"Their superdreadnaughts are leaving orbit," Commander Lewis reported.

"I can see that," Marius growled. *This* was one operation he couldn't leave to his subordinates, even if Roman Garibaldi held tactical command. The various commanding officers had bickered–they thought he didn't know–over which one of them was favored. "Project their course for me, then add in known and suspected missile range engagement envelopes."

He studied the display as the icons appeared in front of him. The enemy fleet wasn't heading directly for Task Force 5.1, but it would pass through extreme engagement range before heading away from both formations. Marius juggled the vectors in his head, then decided the enemy fleet intended to merely fire a single barrage before nipping back out of range and running for its life. Not a bad tactic, he noted, if rather cowardly. It was heartening in a way, he decided, as he turned his attention back to Nova Athena. It suggested the Outsiders were becoming alarmingly sensitized to losses.

"Place us in backstop position," he ordered, after a moment's thought. The Outsiders would be unable to engage Task Force 5.1 without running the risk of entering Task Force 5.2's missile range. With a little bit of luck, all three battle squadrons would be smashed before they could escape. "And prime starfighters for launch on command."

He settled back in his chair, forcing himself to think clearly. "Belay that command," he added. It had been poorly thought out. "I want the starfighters primed when the enemy fleet is twenty minutes away."

"Aye, sir," Commander Lewis said.

She'd been very good to him, Marius knew, even though he'd snapped at her more than once. He'd forbidden her from talking to the ship's doctor, but she'd provided cushions, comfort and almost everything else he needed to keep going. The headaches had faded for a while, then returned as they made the long trek from Yankee to Nova Athena. He was more determined than ever to complete the battle, then hopefully bring the war to an end. Part of him was honestly not sure how much time he had left.

His head swam at the thought. Somehow, he managed to force himself to sit upright and remain calm.

There was a bleep from the display. The enemy fleet had altered course. And reduced speed. Marius frowned, then watched as the tactical computers updated their predictions; this time, the enemy fleet looked ready to brush up against Task Force 5.2, rather than Task Force 5.1. Marius smirked to himself, even though he knew it would make it harder for them to return fire before the enemy scampered out of range. Forcing the enemy to react to one's tactics was the first step in taking the initiative for one's self.

"We will continue on our present course," he said. The enemy could stall for three hours, at most. Then they would have to decide if they wished to break contact or fight and die with the planet itself. Marius was expecting the former. "And hold our course and speed."

He smiled, darkly. The last few hours had seen sensor probes, civilian freighters and even a handful of scoutships moving towards the fleet, peering towards its hulls with active sensors. They'd all been destroyed; Marius honestly wasn't sure why they'd bothered. The fleet wasn't trying to hide anything; indeed, Marius was hoping that the sight of eleven battle squadrons bearing down on their planet would convince the Outsiders to surrender.

And if it doesn't, he thought darkly, *there will always be the violent option.*

ꕥ

"What happened?"

"We lost power," Sanderson said. He was the most experienced soldier in the troop, save for Uzi himself. "The main power core just went offline."

Uzi concealed his amusement as he made a show of checking the diagnostics. "The primary power core failed," he said. There hadn't been much time to run pre-flight checks on the shuttle, which was partly why his little piece of sabotage had worked so perfectly. "The log says it was replaced, but I think someone in maintenance must have pocketed the new unit and left the old one in place."

"Fuck," Roebuck swore, as the artificial gravity gave out and they started to drift into the air. "What the hell do we do?"

"The emergency beacon should be working," Sanderson said. "But I'm not picking up any feedback from the signal."

"Someone must have been playing games," Uzi growled. "Did we pick a shuttle that was due to be scrapped or something?"

"It was listed as being ready to fly," Sanderson snapped back. "And the flight checks we did revealed no problems!"

Uzi cursed, mentally. Sanderson was the most experienced officer in the unit, save for Uzi himself. There were few officers who would have thought to check the emergency beacon was actually working–the units were damn near indestructible, and kept separate from the rest of the shuttle's systems–but Sanderson had thought of it. Losing the main power core might have seemed a stroke of bad luck, aided and abetted by a maintenance tech with wandering hands and low morals; losing the emergency beacon was something else entirely.

"There's no point in snapping at each other now," Uzi said. In some ways, the current situation was ideal. If the Federation won the battle, he could deal with his former comrades and then send a signal, requesting pick-up. But, if the Federation lost, he had an excuse for failing to take Chang Li out of the system. "All we can do is wait and see who wins the coming battle."

"We need to send an emergency signal," Sanderson insisted. "We're not *that* far from the planet."

Uzi shrugged. The shuttle had intended to catch up with Admiral Jalil, then transfer their 'cargo' into his custody. Judging by the look on Chang Li's face before they'd stunned her, it wasn't something he envied the Admiral. But now...they were heading out into space, largely powerless, almost completely undetectable. It wasn't the best of situations, but it definitely had potential.

"That would be risky," he said. "A distress beacon is one thing, but sending out a random signal? One side or the other might mistake the shuttle for a weapon and blow us out of space. No, better to stay where we are."

Sanderson snorted. "And run out of oxygen? The life support system is fucked too."

"There's enough in the tanks to keep us alive for several hours," Uzi assured him. It was true, too. "Once we know who's won the battle, sir, we can make contact with them and arrange pick-up."

"The Federation cannot be allowed to have her," Sanderson said, nodding towards the stunned form of Chang Li. "You know that."

"Then we decide what to do with her if the Federation wins," Uzi said. Sanderson was definitely impressive. It was just a shame he was on the wrong side. "All we can do now is sit here and wait."

ജ ര

"Long range probes are picking up traces of enemy starfighter launches," Lieutenant Thompson reported. "And the enemy superdreadnaughts are altering course again."

"Why am I not surprised?" Roman asked himself. The enemy superdreadnaughts had altered their course several times, trying to make it harder for the Federation to guess when they intended to enter engagement range. Roman hadn't been too impressed, after the first two times they'd tried to confuse him. There would be ample warning of any attack. "Are they trying to coordinate an attack?"

"It looks that way," Thompson said. "I assume the starfighters have extended life support packs."

"They'd need them," Roman said, as the swarm flickered up on the main display. "Pass the word to the CAG. I want our starfighters out there when the enemy ships are ten minutes away."

He frowned as the probes added more detail to the display. It wasn't just starfighters out there, but a wave of gunboats and even small shuttles. Did the Outsiders plan to try to *board* his ships? It didn't seem too likely; they had to know, right now, that his crews were armed and Marines were stationed on every deck. But suicide strikes seemed quite plausible. One could fit a great deal of antimatter on a shuttle...

"And warn him that those shuttles might be suicide runners," he added. "The starfighters should attempt to engage from long distance."

"Aye, sir," Lieutenant Thompson said.

Roman braced himself as a tidal wave of small craft roared down on his fleet. His own starfighters spread out to engage, picking off enemy craft as they approached...

and rapidly proving that he was right and the shuttles *did* intend to ram his vessels. Every time one of them was hit, the antimatter stored in their cargo bays met matter and they vanished in colossal explosions. Three of them made it through the point defense network, despite its best efforts, and slammed into their targets.

"*Bombardment* and *Thunder* have been destroyed," Lieutenant Thompson said. "*Falcon* is intact, but she's taken terrible damage and is falling out of formation. Midshipman Harness has assumed command."

Roman swore. A *midshipman* had taken command? Just how many casualties had the giant superdreadnaught taken? Or, perhaps, the midshipman was the only person in a position to assume command. There was no way to know, not right now.

"Order him to set course for the RV point," Roman said. *Falcon* couldn't keep up with the fleet...leaving her on her own was risky, but there were still few ships in the system that could take on a superdreadnaught, no matter how badly crippled. "And tell him I want a full report once he's put some distance between his ship and the battle."

He gritted his teeth as the starfighters lunged into their targets, then fell back towards the planet, just in time for the enemy superdreadnaughts to open fire. Thankfully, they'd fired at extreme range–the fleet promptly altered course to widen the range still further–but it was still a major headache. The missiles roared towards his ships and just kept coming, no matter how much firepower the point defense weapons spewed out. They were just lucky that the enemy had messed up the timing, if only slightly. It could have been a great deal worse.

Three more ships damaged, he thought, as the last missile slammed into a superdreadnaught and exploded. *It definitely could have been worse.*

"The enemy superdreadnaughts are falling back," Lieutenant Thompson said. "The emperor is altering formation in hopes of driving them off."

"Keep an eye on his progress," Roman said, although he rather doubted the Outsiders would stick around to trade fire with five battle squadrons. They'd done all they could; now, all they could do was fall back and watch helplessly as Nova Athena fell into Federation hands. "And continue our advance towards the planet."

He glanced down at the display. They were only an hour from entering missile range, then the planet's defenses would be at their mercy. They'd already lost a number of starfighters in their attack on the fleet, while Roman had plenty of time to call reinforcements from Task Force 5.2 and reorganize his squadrons. And besides, the fundamental truth about planets was still valid. A planet simply couldn't run. It had to stay where it was and take a beating from the attacking fleet, unless it surrendered.

"Lieutenant," he said. "You are authorized to transmit the surrender demand."

"Aye, sir," Thompson said. "It will be some time before we hear a response."

"Understood," Roman said. There was no point in showing his impatience. No matter what he did, he couldn't avoid the laws of interstellar warfare, not here. There was no StarCom network to use against his enemy. "Send the signal."

ꞩꞨ

Charlie was marginally surprised that his assault force had managed to do as well as it had. Three superdreadnaughts were gone, one had been so badly damaged that it had to retreat and several more were definitely in trouble. But the remainder of the Federation Navy formation, after a brief reorganization, was continuing its advance towards Nova Athena. And he had very little to put in their path before they reached missile range.

"Sir," Commodore Thayne said, "the starfighters are rearming."

"Send them out as soon as they're ready to go," Charlie ordered, although he knew it would be futile. His crews were tired, while the second strike force was nowhere near as strong as the first strike force. He'd expended all of his antimatter-armed shuttles in the first assault, hoping and praying they would do some damage. And they had, just not enough. "Is there any news from Roebuck?"

"No, sir," Commodore Thayne said. He'd expressed his horror, loudly, when Charlie had told him precisely what Captain Roebuck had been ordered to do. In a way, it was hard to blame him for being furious. Charlie had effectively ordered a senior politician kidnapped by military forces. And now she was lost. "Their shuttle took off, sir, and then we lost track of them."

"Fuck," Charlie swore. Had he sent Chang Li to her death? Or had the shuttle crew simply decided to run silent, despite the risk? There was no way to know. "Keep looking for her, all right?"

"Of course," Commodore Thayne said. "But I think there are worse problems inbound."

"I know," Charlie said. He paused. "Is the Shadow Fleet in place?"

"Not yet," Commodore Thayne said. "I don't think it will work..."

"There's no other cards to play," Charlie snapped. "As soon as the fleet is in place, Commodore, send the activation signal."

"Aye, sir," Commodore Thayne said.

"General," a younger officer called. "I'm picking up a message from the enemy fleet."

"Let me hear it," Charlie ordered.

"It's going out on all channels," the officer said. "Everyone will hear it."

Charlie frowned, then forced himself to listen carefully as the message repeated itself.

"*This is Emperor Marius Drake of the Terran Federation,*" a voice said. An analyst window popped up in the display, indicating that the voice patterns matched, although it was still possible it had been faked. "*Your fleets are unable to defeat us and your fortifications are insufficient to prevent us from invading your world. I call upon you to surrender without further delay. If you surrender now, and hand over your fortresses, planetary defenses and remaining starships without crippling them in any way, we will treat you as POWs under the standard conventions.*"

There was a pause. "*If you fail to respond, or refuse to accept these terms, we will advance against the planet and take it by force. Prisoners will be considered illegal combatants and treated accordingly. There will be no further warning. You have one hour to respond."*

Charlie thought rapidly as the message came to an end. He couldn't defend Nova Athena, not now the mobile units had been forced to retreat. But he couldn't let the computer records fall into enemy hands either. That would do more than anything else to bring the war to an end.

Commodore Thayne looked up at him. "Sir?"

"Send the signal to the Shadow Fleet," Charlie ordered. "And let us pray it works."

He gritted his teeth. It wasn't a bad offer, as surrender offers went. But he simply didn't trust the Federation to keep its word, not if they were prepared to demand the surrender of computer databases as well as the defenses themselves. They would have no trouble pressing them back into active service, if nothing else. And they'd be able to go through the databases until they found something they could use to lead them to the hidden bases...

I'm sorry, he thought. *But I don't dare surrender.*

"Send a second signal," he added. If the battle was lost, he still had certain duties to ensure the fallout was as limited as possible. "On my command, every database is to be thoroughly purged, then destroyed."

"There will be nothing left," Commodore Thayne protested. "All our work..."

"Will be seized by the Federation," Charlie said. In a way, he was almost relieved he was stuck on Nova Athena. He doubted he would have survived another Board of Inquiry. "All we can do is make sure it doesn't fall into enemy hands."

ꙮ

"They're launching another flight of starfighters," Lieutenant Thompson reported. "Our starfighters are moving to intercept."

"Get the reserve squadrons out as soon as possible," Roman ordered, grimly. "See how many of the bastards we can kill away from the fortresses."

He watched as the attack developed. The Outsiders didn't seem to have evolved their own starfighter doctrine, as far as he could tell; half of their starfighters stayed and duelled with his starfighters, while the others evaded combat and threw themselves on the capital ships, with desperate fury. Dozens died, picked off by point defense or covering starfighters, but others lived long enough to salvo their missiles into their target's hull. Two more superdreadnaughts shuddered under the attacks, but kept going. Thankfully, the Outsiders hadn't seen fit to add antimatter warheads to the starfighter weapon systems.

That would have been nasty, Roman thought. The Federation had experimented with the idea, once or twice, but it had always ended in disaster. A single mishap could have blown apart an entire carrier. *We would have had real problems if they'd chosen to take the risk.*

He pushed the thought aside as the much-reduced flight of starfighters fell back on the planet, leaving the superdreadnaughts behind. It wouldn't be for long, Roman knew, and then he could start picking apart the planet's defenses. If, of course, the Outsiders didn't see sense and surrender.

"There's still no response, sir," Thompson said.

"Then we do it the hard way," Roman growled. The emperor was not going to be pleased. "Prepare to launch strikes against their fortresses, then target the starfighters against their weak points."

"Aye, sir," Lieutenant Thompson said.

Chapter Forty

The most dangerous moment of any battle is the hour when victory is seemingly within your grasp.
-The Federation Navy in Retrospect, 4199

Nova Athena, 4101
"They didn't send any response to the surrender demand, sir," Commander Lewis said.

Marius leaned forward, outraged. If it hadn't been for Admiral Garibaldi, who had argued there should be an attempt to offer proper treatment to the POWs, he wouldn't have made the offer in the first place. These weren't aliens fighting the Federation, or an independent human power; they were rebels and traitors who'd knifed the Federation in the back when it was weakened by six years of brutal civil war. They deserved nothing, but death by airlock. A bullet in the head was too good for them.

And now he looked weak, because he had made the offer, only to see it thrown back in his face.

"Very well," he said. "Contact Admiral Garibaldi. The battle line is to advance and engage the planetary defenses."

He glowered at the screen. Normally, perhaps, he would have left the defenses to themselves, after blockading the planet. It would have given him time to claim the rest of the system, then wait patiently for the defenders to surrender. But now he needed to make it clear, to the rest of the damned Outsiders, that he would not tolerate them trying to wage war on the Federation. One example, if sufficiently horrific, would convince the wavering planetary governments to rejoin the Federation without delay.

"And pass a message to the CO of the pacification force," he added. "There is to be no mercy."

ᘓᘐ

"There must be something we can do!"

"Like what?" Uzi asked. Privately, he was rather enjoying Sanderson's panic. "Burn up good oxygen by pacing to and fro like a madman?"

"There has to be *something*," Sanderson said. "The Federation is winning the battle!"

"So it would seem," Uzi agreed. "But I think you should remain calm and sit down."

Sanderson whirled around to face him. "How can you be so calm?"

"Because I know better than to panic," Uzi said. He cleared his throat, loudly. "Right now, all we can do is wait to see who comes out ahead. I suggest you sit down, take a breath and *wait*. The outcome will be decided soon enough."

Uzi smiled inwardly as Sanderson reluctantly followed his advice. The Federation definitely seemed to be winning, which meant he would have a chance to hand Chang Li over to their commander as a prize. She would never have a chance to commit suicide, he was sure; either she would have her implants deactivated, if her captors felt it was worth the risk of trying, or she would be interrogated in more subtle ways. There was no shortage of options.

And all he had to do was wait.

"The timing is appalling," Roebuck commented. He'd barely said anything since they'd realized their predicament, merely sat at the flight chair and stared through the porthole into interplanetary space. "What the hell do we do if there's no chance of escape?"

"Blow the shuttle," Uzi said. "The main power core might be offline, but improvising an explosion won't be too hard. Or we could simply force open the airlock and vent the atmosphere into space."

"That would leave bodies behind," Sanderson pointed out. "There would be evidence of her death."

"Then think of something else," Uzi said. "But, whatever you do, don't actually try it until we *know* we're fucked. All right?"

"Yeah," Sanderson said. "But..."

"Relax," Uzi urged. "We're not dead yet."

Sanderson glowered at him. "What happens to a mercenary after he falls into enemy hands?"

"I dare say I'll be executed, now," Uzi said. "Normally, mercenaries serve under the Mercenary Code, which includes bans on taking up arms–directly or indirectly–against the Federation itself. They find me here; they'll probably shoot me in the head or throw me out the nearest airlock. I've crossed the line quite badly since I went to work for you."

Sanderson's eyes narrowed. "So why did you come and work for us?"

"The money was good," Uzi said. He made a show of shrugging, elaborately. "Bad rolls of the dice are inevitable, Peter. You just have to take what you get and run with it."

"Mercenary," Sanderson said. He made the word an insult. "Can we really trust you?"

"I'm loyal to whoever pays me," Uzi said. He smirked to hide his inner alarm. Had Sanderson worked out that Uzi had had ample time to sabotage the shuttle? "Care to join me on the circuit, one day?"

"I believe in the cause," Sanderson said. He looked down at the sleeping woman. "Can you say the same? Do you believe in *anything*?"

"No," Uzi lied. He *did* believe in the Federation, even though very few people knew just what he'd done to keep the Federation's citizens safe and warm in their beds. And if the vast majority *had* known, they would be horrified. "I believe in cold hard cash."

Sanderson snorted, then turned away from him and stared out the porthole.

Uzi eyed the back of Sanderson's neck, considering the blow it would take to break it. It wouldn't be hard, he knew; one blow and Sanderson would be dead. And then Roebuck would be dead too...and he could surrender Chang Li without delay. But he might still need them...

He sighed, then forced himself to wait. There was all the time in the world.

ꕥ

"We will enter firing range in twenty minutes," Lieutenant Thompson said. "The enemy defenses have been targeted."

Roman nodded. Standard procedure when attacking a heavily defended planet was to wipe out the orbital fortresses first, rather than try to land soldiers. The defenders hadn't fixed any of their fortresses in geostationary orbit, ensuring that several of them would have to be destroyed to prevent them bombarding landed troops from orbit. He was irked, but not particularly surprised, that none of the Outsiders had tried to surrender. There were just too many concerns about how willing the Federation would be to honor its own terms.

"Prepare to engage," he ordered. He hoped–prayed–that they wouldn't accidentally hit the planet with an antimatter warhead. Surely, if the Outsiders had any concern for the locals, they would consider surrendering once the missiles started flying. "Order the starfighters to cover the missiles and..."

An alarm sounded. "Sir," Lieutenant Thompson said. "I'm picking up...*my god*!"

Roman switched the display back to the system-wide view. Icons–red icons–had appeared out of nowhere and were heading right towards his ships. The faint fuzz of active ECM shrouded them, but it was clear that they included at least twelve battle squadrons of superdreadnaughts. And the superdreadnaughts that had taken a shot at them earlier were swinging around to link up with the newcomers.

Roman found his voice. "Where...where the hell did *they* come from?"

"Bella, perhaps," Lieutenant Thompson said. She sounded as shaken as Roman felt. "They could have traced our course through the Asimov Chain, then sent for help. Bella has an Asimov Point that leads into the Beyond..."

Roman forced himself to think, hard. The enemy fleet...was it *real*?

It was impossible to be sure. Logic suggested the enemy wouldn't have withheld those ships from Boston, if they'd existed, but they *had* definitely sent enough firepower to take the system given what they *thought* they'd been facing. They'd certainly have refused to surrender Nova Athena if they'd known twelve battle squadrons were rushing to the rescue. And yet...they could have come out of cloak much later, ensuring the Federation Navy ships didn't have a chance to escape. It might have been a blunder, or it might have been a clever trick trying to *pretend* to be a blunder.

In the end, the problem was simple. *If the fleet is real, continuing the offensive is suicide; if the fleet is fake, the offensive can proceed without delay.*

But the only way to test the issue was to attack the enemy fleet...

"Alter course," he ordered. The planet wasn't going anywhere–and besides, they needed time to think and plan. He drew out a course on his console, then forwarded it to the helmsmen. "Take us away from the planet."

ꕤ

For a long moment, the universe seemed to darken, before it snapped back to normal. Marius found himself gasping for breath, even as the red icons moved closer and closer on the display. Twelve battle squadrons! The enemy had known where they were going and laid a trap, baiting it with a target they knew the Federation couldn't ignore. Their tactics, in hindsight, made perfect sense.

"Emperor," Commander Lewis said. "Are you all right?"

"I'm fine," Marius snarled at her. The pain in his chest was fading as anger overwhelmed him. He might have to flee the system, but he was damned if he was allowing the Outsiders to claim victory. They'd recover nothing more than ashes by the time he was finished with their damned world. "Raise Admiral Garibaldi."

Garibaldi's face appeared in the display–and blinked in shock. Marius ignored the astonishment on his protégé's face, even as he struggled to speak. His body was betraying him at the very last. But there was no time to summon the doctor, or do anything other than issue orders. He could rest afterwards.

"Admiral," he said. His voice sounded harsh and broken, even in his own ears. "You are ordered to lock antimatter missiles on Nova Athena and fire."

There was a long pause. "Emperor," Garibaldi said. "Are you ordering me to *bombard* the planet?"

Oddly, being questioned made Marius stronger. "Yes," he said. "You are to fire a full spread of missiles at the planet. Now."

ꕤ

Roman had feared...*something*...from his mentor, although he couldn't have said if he was scared *of* him or scared *for* him. The change in Marius Drake was just too great for him to ignore. But...but he'd never anticipated an order to commit genocide...

...and it *would* be genocide, he knew. A single antimatter warhead striking the planet's surface would be a nightmare. Three or four would be utterly lethal. Anyone who survived the first strikes would die within weeks as the skies darkened, debris fell from high above and radiation oozed over the planet's surface. It would be the end of billions of lives. No one, not even the Federation at its height, could have saved even a tiny percentage of the planet's population.

He couldn't do it. Whatever the cost, he couldn't do it.

"Sir," he said. "That would be an illegal order..."

The emperor's face purpled. "Are you refusing my orders?"

Roman understood, suddenly, just how Blake Raistlin's defense had worked. Was an order, no matter how horrific, actually *illegal* if it came from the wellspring of all authority? And Marius Drake had effectively taken the Grand Senate's place. He *was* the source of authority now...

"Sir," Roman pleaded. He'd killed before, hundreds of crewmen died when even a small destroyer was blown into plasma, but this was on a far greater scale. It was wrong. "You cannot order the deaths of billions of innocent civilians."

"That is an order," Marius snapped. "You will do as I command!"

Roman gathered himself. "It is madness," he said. Professor Kratman had been right, only Roman had been too loyal to see it. "I will not be party to genocide..."

The connection broke.

ƐɔƆɜ

Marius stared at Garibaldi in absolute disbelief, then hit the switch to break the connection before he exploded with rage. How *dare* Garibaldi defy him? Hadn't it been Marius who'd promoted him, forgiven him for keeping Henrietta Beauregard-Justinian's presence a secret and eventually given him command of his own fleet? Roman was almost a *son* to Marius—and he'd betrayed him! How could he?

"Signal the fleet," he ordered, as cold fury overwhelmed judgement. "Lock weapons on *Valiant* and her comrades."

Commander Lewis stared. "Sir...?"

"Do it," Marius thundered. "Or I'll have you relieved and thrown out the airlock!"

Frightened, Commander Lewis turned back to her console.

"Weapons locked, sir," she said. Her voice was shaking. "All batteries are ready to fire."

ƐɔƆɜ

Roman paled as red light washed across the display. Emperor Marius's task force had locked weapons on his formation...*all* of his formation. Urgent messages blinked up in his display, sent by commanders who didn't have the slightest idea what was happening, demanding to know why they were being targeted. Roman barely saw them, because he couldn't believe his eyes. He'd never imagined being at Ground Zero of a civil war...

...And his mentor had gone mad. It was the only logical explanation.

"Stand by point defense," he said. He thought about trying to contact the other commanders of Task Force 5.2, only to dismiss it as futile. The sycophants he'd seen at the dinner wouldn't do anything to dissuade the Emperor, once he'd made up his mind. It was sheer luck that Task Force 5.2 was outside missile range of Nova Athena, or the planet would be radioactive ashes by now. "Open a channel to the other ships..."

Thompson coughed. "Which other ships?"

"All of the Federation ships," Garibaldi said. Maybe he could talk one or two of the Emperor's picked men out of helping him to commit genocide. Maybe, along with his mind, Marius Drake had lost his ability to judge men accurately. "I need to talk to them..."

ƐɔƆɜ

"Admiral Garibaldi is trying to raise the other ships," Commander Lewis said. "Sir..."

"I will not let this rebellion spread," Marius growled. "Fire!"

Commander Lewis didn't hesitate. She keyed her console...and, moments later, *Thunderbird* launched a full spread of missiles towards her targets.

ƐɔƆɜ

Alarms screamed.

"Missile separation," Lieutenant Thompson snapped. "They *fired* on us!"

"Launch scatter missiles and ECM drones, but hold our missiles," Roman snapped. "I say again, do not return fire."

Sweat ran down his back as the display updated. At such range, there was almost no chance of any of the missiles losing power before they entered attack range. Emperor Marius knew that as well as he did, which left Roman with a nightmarish dilemma. He couldn't fire on fellow Federation Navy starships, could he? But they seemed to have no qualms about firing on *him*. Home Fleet's commanders had definitely been picked for loyalty over competence. But then, if Home Fleet had ever been called upon to do its duty, the war would have been on the verge of being lost anyway. The barbarians would have been at the gates.

He clenched his teeth as a second salvo of missiles launched from the Emperor's ships, then the first salvo roared into the teeth of his defenses. Thankfully, Home Fleet's crews were unpractised, or it would have been a great deal worse. As it was, the missiles that made it through the defenses did real damage. He watched, fighting to keep his growing horror and rage under control, as four battlecruisers and a superdreadnaught died in balls of fire.

"*Peterson* is gone," Lieutenant Thompson reported. "*Inflexible* and *Intolerant* have both taken heavy damage..."

"Return fire," Roman ordered.

ꕤ

"They're firing on each other," Commodore Thayne said. "Did you *know* this would happen?"

Charlie shook his head. He'd hoped the Shadow Fleet–nothing more than ECM drones, based on Federation designs but improved by the Outsiders–would convince the Federation ships to flee. It had always been a gamble, particularly if the Federation Navy had decided to fight a long-range missile duel rather than simply run for its life. But he'd never anticipated the Federation Navy ships exchanging fire with each other...

"No," he said. What had happened on those ships? "And all we can do is watch."

ꕤ

"Emperor," Commander Lewis reported. "Task Force 5.1 has opened fire."

"Traitors," Marius growled. Their fire was likely to be heavier–and more effective–than his own. They'd simply had more time to train and test themselves against live enemies, which meant that continuing the fight would be suicide. He hated to run, but there was no choice. "Order all ships to retreat to the gravity limit. We have to get back to Earth."

He clenched his fists so hard they hurt, promising himself bloody revenge. Garibaldi would pay for his treachery, as would the Outsiders themselves. The Federation would survive under his rule, no matter what happened. And God help anyone who got in his way.

ꕥ

"They're retreating, sir," Lieutenant Thompson said. She sounded stunned–and horrified at what she'd seen. It was impossible to blame her. "They're heading for the gravity limit at best possible speed."

She paused. "Should we give chase?"

Roman shook his head. Thanks to the earlier battles, it was unlikely his fleet could catch up with Task Force 5.2 before it crossed the line and vanished into FTL. And there was still that huge Outsider force to consider...

"No," he said, out loud. "Hail the Outsiders. I think it's time we talked."

ꕥ

"Jesus," Sanderson said. "I take it back, Uzi. You were right all along."

Uzi shrugged, confused. The Federation had been winning, then one half of the Federation ships had opened fire on the other half...what the hell had happened? Had someone managed to take over the fire control network or what? And now the remaining half of the Federation formation was actually *talking* to the Outsiders? What the hell was going on?

"Start signalling for help," Roebuck ordered, turning away from the porthole. "Get someone out here to rescue us."

"Yes, sir," Sanderson said.

Uzi kept his face expressionless. Whatever had happened, it had screwed up his plans–both of them. And now, if someone worked his way through the maintenance logs, they might realize there had been nothing wrong with the power core. And then...

But even if no one identified him, he knew, the universe had just changed once again. And he didn't even know *how*.

And, he asked himself silently, *what the hell do I do now*?

End of Book II

The series will conclude in

The Barbarian Bride

Coming Soon!

Afterword

The story of Cincinnatus (Lucius Quinctius Cincinnatus (519–430 BC) is one of those stories that resonate down the ages. Put simply, Cincinnatus was a Roman politician and military leader (the Romans didn't consider the two separate spheres) who was appointed Dictator when the Roman Republic faced a potentially fatal threat from a barbarian tribe. Cincinnatus took command, built an army, defeated the barbarians and returned to his farm, all within fifteen days. As such, he is generally considered a model of civic virtue.

However, his story needs to be placed in context.

The Romans were very suspicious of anyone who sought too much power, to the point where anyone who seemed to be too powerful or too popular would be dragged down by the rest of the politicians. Accordingly, they appointed two Heads of State (the Consuls) who would serve for a year, a system that ensured that the two men would watch each other carefully for signs of undue ambition as well as actually running the government. The system was, in many ways, dangerously unstable. A man who felt himself slighted unfairly by the Senate—like Julius Caesar—might go into open rebellion against the might of Rome.

This was not a system that encouraged single-mindedness. The Romans, recognizing that this was a major problem when the state was under attack, created the office of Dictator. These men were granted absolute power for a fixed period, then expected to shuffle off into the sidelines of history. They were, among other things, spared the threat of criminal prosecution for anything they did while in power. (It is a curious testament to the system that Sulla, who had taken the post by force, was never killed by one of his many enemies after he returned power to the Senate.) The Roman Dictators were never meant to remain in power indefinitely, unlike modern-day dictators.

And yet, so many people have drawn the wrong lesson from the story of Cincinnatus.

There is a curious agreement among thinkers from both the Left and the Right, although both of them would be horrified by the suggestion that they might have something in common. The Far Right does not object to the concept of an absolute dictator, *per se*; they expect only that the dictator be a good and virtuous man. Thus, the concentration of unchecked, unbalanced and fundamentally unaccountable power is only a problem if held by a man they do not consider to be a *good* man. They do not expect the good man to become sullied by the power he holds.

Human history would tend to suggest otherwise. Men of high ideals, good and decent men, have made successful grabs for power, then become corrupted and brought low by their success. Anything larger than a tiny business with a handful of employees cannot be micromanaged by a single person effectively, much less a whole country. Hiccups breed frustration. Dissent and disagreement becomes treachery. All who dare to speak out are crushed mercilessly. Each wave of repression brings on the *next* wave of repression. And then all life is drained out of the system.

The Romans knew the dangers of granting one man absolute power indefinitely. Those who admire the Roman Republic have not learned the lessons of its fall.

But the Far Left, if anything, has a worse problem. This is the concept of government by party. Instead of a single personage, all power is vested in the hands of the ruling body, often the Communist Party. In Russia, they talked of passing all power to the Soviets, then to the Bolsheviks. But when the Bolsheviks took control, the results were, if anything, even worse than the Tsars.

A living dictator can show empathy–or outright sadism. But a bureaucracy, governed by a committee, can be a great deal worse. In the interests of imposing communism, the Bolsheviks starved, slaughtered and crushed independent peasant farmers right across the Soviet Union. They were so intent on imposing their will that they chose to ignore the simple fact that they were crippling their country's ability to produce food, ensuring that Russia would eventually have to buy food from the United States. The committee believed it could determine everything, despite being far more detached from the population than any single dictator, and ruined Russia's ability to create a modern economy.

Both of these examples illustrate the true danger, the willingness to allow power to be concentrated in a single set of hands. Anyone who has done battle with the bureaucracy in just about any country will know how hard it is to get them to admit to a mistake. The people you deal with will either be unable or unwilling to help you. This may not be their fault. A bureaucracy that is trying to run the country will be huge, so huge that the people on the front lines will have no real authority of their own. But the bureaucracy will have no tolerance for its servants who fail to do exactly as they are told. Common sense will take a walk when they are forced to toe the line or get fired. Hence we have problems when a bureaucracy takes a child from his or her parents because that is what the regulations say they have to do, even if common sense says otherwise.

But human nature overshadows both the Dictator and the Committee. They will be tempted–very tempted–to use their absolute power for their own good, not for that of their people. Both will give the best jobs to their relatives, confusing themselves with the state, while milking everything they can from their positions. The Soviet Union was littered with *dachas* that belonged to Party Officials, each one built from public funds, yet denied to the public.

With all of this in mind, why would someone want to give a person–or a committee–absolute power?

About the author

Christopher G. Nuttall is thirty-two years old and has been reading science fiction since he was five when someone introduced him to children's SF. Born in Scotland, Chris attended schools in Edinburgh, Fife and University in Manchester before moving to Malaysia to live with his wife Aisha.

Chris has been involved in the online Alternate History community since 1998; in particular, he was the original founder of Changing The Times, an online alternate history website that brought in submissions from all over the community. Later, Chris took up writing and eventually became a full-time writer.

Current and forthcoming titles published by Twilight Times Books:

The Decline and Fall of the Galactic Empire military SF series
Barbarians at the Gates—book 1
The Shadow of Cincinnatus —book 2
The Barbarian Bride—book 3

The Schooled in Magic YA fantasy series
Schooled in Magic—book 1
Lessons in Etiquette —book 2
A Study in Slaughter —book 3
Work Experience —book 4
The School of Hard Knocks —book 5

Chris has also produced *The Empire's Corps* series, the *Outside Context Problem* series and many others. He is also responsible for two fan-made Posleen novels, both set in John Ringo's famous Posleen universe. They can both be downloaded from his site.

Website: http://www.chrishanger.net/
Blog: http://chrishanger.wordpress.com/
Facebook: https://www.facebook.com/ChristopherGNuttall

If you enjoyed this book, please post a review
at your favorite online bookstore.

Twilight Times Books
P O Box 3340
Kingsport, TN 37664
Phone/Fax: 423-323-0183
www.twilighttimesbooks.com/

CPSIA information can be obtained at www.ICGtesting.com
Printed in the USA
BVOW08s0809240316

441449BV00002B/172/P

9 781606 193204